Fairytale
COME ALIVE

GHOSTS AND REINCARNATION SERIES

KRISTEN

NEW YORK TIMES BESTSELLING AUTHOR

ASHLEY

Fairytale Come Alive
Kristen Ashley
Published by Kristen Ashley

Interior Design & Formatting by:
Christine Borgford, Type A Formatting
www.typeAformatting.com

Cover Art by: Pixel Mischief Design

Copyright © 2016 by Kristen Ashley
ISBN-13: 978-1540500472
ISBN-10: 1540500470

First ebook edition: November 22, 2011
Latest ebook edition: November 2016
First print edition: November, 2016

Discover other titles by
KRISTEN ASIILEY

GHOSTS AND REINCARNATION SERIES
Sommersgate House
Lacybourne Manor
Penmort Castle
Fairytale Come Alive
Lucky Stars

DISCOVER ALL OF KRISTEN'S TITLES ON HER WEBSITE AT:
www.kristenashley.net

PROLOGUE

The Destruction

Prentice

"You're a fisherman," Carver Austin said, his voice filled with derision, even his lip was curled.

Prentice Cameron could not believe this bloke.

His eyes moved from Austin to Elle.

The minute he'd walked into Fergus McFadden's home in answer to Elle's father's summons and laid eyes on Elle, Prentice knew something was wrong.

She wasn't wearing shorts and a T-shirt. Her lustrous, light-brown hair wasn't falling free down her back or pulled to the top of her head in a haphazard knot. Her hazel eyes weren't shining with mischief or humor or happiness.

Instead, her usually thick, wavy hair was smoothed back in a neat ponytail at the nape of her neck and falling in a long sleek column down her back. Not a wild, riotous wave in sight.

Prentice loved her soft, beautiful, unruly hair. He thought it defined her perfectly.

She was also, he had noticed immediately, wearing makeup, which she never did because she didn't need it.

Lastly, she was wearing a sophisticated light-blue dress, which Prentice had to admit looked sweet on her, but he also noted its obvious style and expense.

He knew she was rich but she never acted it, nor did she dress the part.

Never as in *never*.

And Elle was usually chatty and energetic. Unbelievably chatty and energetic. It was difficult to keep her focused and in one place. Even when they were drinking at a pub, she shifted on her stool and chattered away. It was as if she had so much energy, if she didn't fidget and talk to release some of it, she would explode. Prentice was often forced to haul her into his body and pin her to his side or kiss her to shut her up, neither of which he minded in the slightest.

Now, she seemed frozen.

Not as if today's shift from the unusually hot weather they were having to gray and drizzling had caused her to have a chill. It was as if she was frozen from the inside. She'd barely said a word since he'd arrived and she hadn't fidgeted once.

In fact, she'd hardly looked at him at all.

"Elle, are you all right?" Prentice asked and her eyes, which were studying the carpet, flitted to his briefly then slid away.

"Perfectly fine," she replied, her voice strong, cultured, controlled, a voice that he'd never heard before.

Elle was an open, friendly person, everything about her screamed it. The last two summers she spent in the village, she'd charmed every soul there with her nearly pathological sociability. By the end of her first summer, she knew every man, woman and child *and* their pets, and they all adored her (even the pets).

But most especially Prentice.

Now, she sounded like an entirely different person.

Prentice's vague sense of alarm intensified.

"Elle," he repeated, preparing to move toward her. She was seated in an armchair. He was standing, facing off against her father who, from the very beginning of this meeting, made no bones about the fact he didn't like the idea of a lowly Scottish fisherman marrying his wealthy, educated daughter.

Before he could move, however, Austin spoke.

"Isabella has had a change of heart about your proposal."

As Prentice's eyes were still on Elle, he saw her body give a small jolt before he watched her fingers curl into tight fists in her lap.

Prentice's alarm turned to anger.

His gaze moved back to Austin.

"That's surprising," now Prentice's voice was filled with derision, "Elle seemed pretty excited about it when I put the ring on her finger."

This was not a lie. She'd been so excited, she'd tackled him with such force they'd both fallen to the floor, which at first, considering she'd knocked the wind out of him, he thought was disadvantageous. Then, as he got his breath back and realized she was kissing and touching every inch of him she could get her hands and mouth on, *and* they were horizontal, Prentice saw the advantages of the situation.

Austin interrupted Prentice's train of thought. "Isabella and I are leaving today, going back to Chicago. She'll finish her senior year at Northwestern and she won't return."

Prentice glared at him.

No, he could not believe this bloke.

"It's my understanding her plans have changed," Prentice replied.

"I'm quite certain you'll eventually be happy with a woman who has not accomplished a higher education, however, my daughter—" Austin went on.

Prentice cut him off. "No, I'll be quite happy with whatever Elle wants to do. And she's decided she'll finish uni, but after she graduates she'll come back here."

Austin smiled a humorless, condescending smile. "And what, for the sake of curiosity, could she possibly do *here*?"

Prentice's anger escalated.

He'd been born in his village, as had his father and mother and their parents and their parents, for as far back as anyone could remember. It wasn't cosmopolitan by a long shot, but it had charm and it was filled with good people who looked out for each other.

Furthermore, Elle loved it there. He knew that not only because she acted like she loved it but because she'd told him she loved it, about ten thousand times.

Prentice didn't like anything about this discussion and he was beginning to like it even less.

"We're in Scotland, not the wilds of the Serengeti," Prentice returned. "We have trains. We even have cars. She can do whatever she wants."

"It would be quite a commute to any worthwhile employment," Austin retorted disdainfully.

"That depends on your definition of 'worthwhile,'" Prentice shot back.

Austin rocked back on his heels, crossing his arms on his chest.

"It does, indeed," he replied as if he'd made a point.

Prentice was done.

He looked back at Elle.

She was again studying the carpet.

"You want to jump in here, baby?" Prentice asked softly, and he felt Austin's mood shift dangerously at his tone and, likely, his endearment.

Prentice ignored it.

Her eyes lifted to his.

Prentice felt a chill slide through him when her gaze locked on his.

She stood, slowly, lithely, the graceful way she moved was one of the things that first attracted Prentice to her. Even her incessant fidgeting looked like a beautiful dance.

She walked the four feet to where he stood in front of the fireplace and stopped not far but also not close.

She tipped her head back to look at him.

"This was a mistake," she said in that cultured, controlled voice.

Prentice thought she was not wrong.

He'd spent every moment he could with her for two summers. When she was back at home at uni they talked on the phone as often as they could, considering the time difference and the expense (which wasn't often enough for either of them). She wrote him letters and he did the same. She sent him packages filled with cookies she'd baked (at first these had arrived in crumbles and she'd made it her mission to find a way to get them to him with the cookies intact, eventually wrapping each cookie, dozens of them, tightly in cling film) and mad, ridiculous gifts she'd pick up here and there that she told him he "had to have" because they reminded her of him. Prentice had seven Northwestern T-shirts and three sweatshirts and even a pair of sweatpants that had a small Northwestern insignia on the hip.

It was safe to say Elle thought of him often.

They had, essentially, been "together" for fifteen months, unfortunately only six of those being in the same location.

In all that time, she rarely talked about her family, but of course, after he proposed she'd said it was time he meet her father.

She didn't seem excited about this, she seemed worried and Prentice put it down to normal, everyday nerves. Her mother died when she was young and she had no siblings. He assumed she and her father had formed a necessary bond because of this but any father would be cautious about the man to whom he was giving his daughter.

However now he understood her nerves were caused by something entirely different.

"Yes, baby," Prentice took a step toward her, "this was definitely a mistake."

Something flashed in her eyes, something he couldn't read, before they froze again.

Then she lifted her hand and put her fingers to his ring.

It wasn't much, he couldn't afford much. He'd taken three years after school working on his father's fishing boats and saving so he could afford university. Finally, he went, reading to be an architect. His mother told him, since he was a kid he never drew anything but houses and buildings, and when he wasn't drawing he was building with anything he could get his hands on. He built massive structures in the garden, in trees, in the lounge. It drove his mother daft since half the time he was nicking whatever he could, even to the point of dismantling furniture (and their shed), so he'd have building materials.

He went back to the boats in the summers because he needed the money.

The ring he'd given Elle wasn't what he wanted to give her, neither was it what she deserved, it was what he could afford. He'd vowed to himself (although he hadn't told her) that he'd eventually replace it with something that suited her, something bigger, shinier and worth the moon.

He'd been shocked when she'd loved the ring, tears filling her eyes as she examined it after they'd finished their horizontal celebration on the floor.

Her hand close to her face, her eyes glittering with tears, she'd whispered, "It's absolutely *perfect*, Pren. The most beautiful thing I've ever seen in my life."

Now she was sliding it off her finger.

Prentice felt his gut twist as the alarm returned, sharp and vicious.

"Elle."

"This was a mistake. I'm sorry," she said, her voice still strong, controlled. "I got caught up in the whole . . ." she hesitated, and with his ring between her thumb and forefinger she twirled her hand between them in a dismissive way, "Scotland thing."

The gut twist tore upwards, slicing through his innards.

Who was this girl?

"The whole 'Scotland thing?'" Prentice repeated, his eyes narrowing.

"Yes. American girls have a thing for boys with accents," she replied calmly as if her words weren't a verbal knife thrust to his heart.

"You have got to be fucking joking," Prentice hissed.

And if she was, it wasn't fucking funny.

"Mind your language around my daughter," Austin warned, but Prentice didn't even look at him.

His eyes stayed locked on Elle.

"We need to talk," he demanded. "Alone."

"I see no reason to draw this out, Prentice. As I explained, I made a mistake."

He took a step closer. She took a step back.

He stopped.

She'd never retreated from him.

Never.

Even when they were arguing, something that happened often. Elle could be annoyingly if adorably stubborn.

"Don't you see?" Elle asked. "This was a lark. Annie and me—"

Prentice's body jerked. "Don't you fucking tell me Annie and Dougal—"

Her best friend Annie had hooked up with his best friend Dougal the same night he and Elle met. They'd been just as inseparable and had fallen just as deeply in love.

Quickly, she shook her head in a frantic way that was far more Elle than anything he'd encountered that morning, and he watched panic flash through her eyes before she hid it.

"No, no . . . Annie and Dougal are something else," she said swiftly and firmly.

"But you and I are a lark?" Prentice asked, his voice ugly and dangerous in a way it had never sounded before and it surprised even him.

"Well . . . yes," she replied then continued. "I took it too far. Got caught up in it. I'm so sorry, Prentice."

She rarely called him Prentice and he didn't like it, especially not now.

She called him Pren. She was the only one in his life that did so and he liked it when she did.

And furthermore, she didn't look sorry.

She didn't look anything.

She didn't look even a little bit like the girl who tore into town with her crazy antics, her abandoned laughter, her outgoing, fun-loving American cheerfulness, stealing his and everyone's hearts.

She looked like a girl he wouldn't glance at twice.

And she acted like a girl he'd detest.

He couldn't believe he'd been so deceived.

"We need to talk," he repeated.

"There's nothing to talk about," she replied.

He got close and she stood her ground. He tipped his chin down and stared in her eyes.

They were cold.

"Something's happened."

"Yes, my father arrived and gave me a wakeup call," she threw her hands out to her sides. "This isn't my life. I wouldn't be happy here. Honestly, Prentice, the idea is ridiculous. I don't know what I was thinking."

Prentice felt like shaking her.

He also felt like picking her up and carrying her away from Fergus McFadden's posh house and Elle's despicable father and doing everything in his power to bring back his Elle.

He didn't do either.

"I don't know what he said to you—" Prentice started.

She interrupted, "He gave me a few home truths."

"And they were?"

"It doesn't matter."

Prentice lost control of his temper and shouted, "It fucking well does!"

Austin materialized at their side. "Calm down, son."

Prentice turned only his head to Austin. "Don't call me son."

"Prentice, really, don't make a scene," Elle put in sounding, if he could believe his ears, *bored*.

Prentice turned back to Elle. "We weren't a lark."

"Prentice—"

It was his turn to interrupt and his voice held an edge of steel coated with a sheen of deep emotion, which as much as he hated showing the weakness he couldn't quite control. "At least for me it wasn't a lark."

He wasn't sure but he could have sworn Elle flinched.

He decided he was wrong when she calmly held his ring up between them.

Prentice didn't take it.

Instead, he said, "When you're away from him and you realize this is madness, you find me, you call me, you write me, I don't give a fuck what you do." He leaned into her and took her head in both hands feeling her body go solid when he moved an inch away from her face. His voice dipped low when he continued, "I'll be pissed off, baby, and I'll make you work for it. But I love you enough to get over it and take you back. I promise you that."

"Prentice—" she said softly, but he cut her off in the way he always stopped her from chattering.

He touched his mouth to hers.

Without a choice, as usual, Elle went quiet.

Prentice pulled away and looked into her eyes.

"I've had a good life, you know that," he whispered. "Even so, you're the best thing that's been in it."

He watched, up close, as she slowly closed her eyes, emotion washing over her face making her radiant.

That was his Elle.

Whatever this was, he'd made it through.

Thank Christ.

He kissed her forehead, let her go, and without a backward glance at her or her father Prentice walked away.

Chapter
ONE

Romantic Fairytale Come Alive

Isabella

Twenty Years Later . . .

"This is so *exciting*," Mikey cried from beside her in the limousine, practically jumping up and down in his seat.

Isabella looked out the windows thinking that this was absolutely, positively *not* exciting in the *slightest*.

She watched Prentice's village slide by, happy the windows were tinted and no one could see in. The limousine, undoubtedly not a common vehicle to glide down the cobbled streets, was causing quite a stir and everyone was stopping to look.

She recognized more than one face.

Each recognized face caused her heart to contract and her breathing to go erratic.

She curled her fingers into her palms, tight, feeling her nails dig into the flesh painfully.

And familiarly.

The pain, as it often did, calmed her breathing, if not her heart.

"Isn't this *quaint!*" Mikey declared also staring out the window, and Isabella bit back the desire to explain that the British didn't like it overly much when Americans described their homes as "quaint."

She bit back the desire because he was very excited and she loved him.

There were two people she loved on the entire earth, Mikey Bruce and Annie McFadden. Therefore, she'd rather slit her own wrists than do one, single thing that might quell his incalculable glee.

And, for Isabella Austin Evangelista, that was saying something.

"Picnics and dinner parties and log throwing," Mikey kept talking, "I can't *wait!*"

Isabella struggled with her earlier thought because Mikey could be stubborn and so could Annie (to say the least, about *both* of them) and she wanted to try to curb his disappointment and Annie's annoyance because they'd had, Isabella knew, about five hundred conversations about the Highland Games demands Mikey was making on the upcoming festivities.

Therefore, she said softly, "There isn't going to be log throwing, Mikey. Annie explained that."

Mikey turned his gaze to Isabella and waved his hand. "I'll talk her around."

"Please, she has everything planned as she wants it. It isn't like you can throw together an event like that on the spur of the moment."

Mikey's eyes narrowed and Isabella pulled in a breath.

"I'm sorry but this is a romantic fairytale *come alive*. A *Scottish* romantic fairytale *come alive*. When that happens, you can do anything you want! And a *Scottish* romantic fairytale *come alive* means *log throwing!*" Mikey declared.

He was not wrong. Well, he was about the log throwing, but not about the other stuff.

Annie and Dougal getting married, after twenty years and all that had happened in between, was most definitely a romantic fairytale come alive.

Even though she was happy for her friend, very happy, staggeringly happy, Isabella's fingers tensed and the nails embedded deeper into the flesh of her palms.

Mikey looked back out the window and so did Isabella.

————◆————

TWENTY YEARS AGO, as her father had told Prentice, they'd gone back to Chicago the very day Prentice walked out of Fergus's house.

So confident in their love, so confident in *Isabella*, he didn't even look back.

The next week had been the worst in her life (until the week after, of course).

And this was also saying something.

One could say Isabella's life had been filled with "worst weeks."

That was just the worst of them.

Her father had been furious at her "tryst" with "the fisherman" and also about her keeping it from him for over a year. He took every opportunity (and when there weren't opportunities, he made them) to describe to Isabella his extreme displeasure.

And when he did, he did this *at length*.

Sometimes *for hours*.

Isabella had been heartbroken.

So heartbroken, for the first time in her life, her father's verbal tirades barely affected her.

All she could think of was Prentice and that awful, awful, *awful* meeting in Fergus's living room. The way he looked, his anger, his disbelief, his frustration, all of it pouring off him in waves and crashing against her.

And there was not one thing she could do about it.

Not that first thing.

Not that she would have.

She knew better.

And, it must be said, Prentice deserved better.

However, in an unusual moment of courage, three days after their return, she approached her father and told him he'd been wrong. It wasn't a "tryst" and Prentice wasn't just "a fisherman" and even if he *was*, she didn't care. She loved him, she wanted to marry him and she wanted to spend the rest of her life with him in his village and that was that.

Her father had struck her.

Open-handed and brutal.

When her head swung back he did it again.

He had struck her before in her life, not often, seventeen times to be exact (she'd counted, adding those two, it made it nineteen).

But he'd never done it twice in a row.

She'd been stunned and her courage fled as quickly as it came.

She'd been weak. Such a coward.

Always, all her life, a coward.

Just like her mother.

Prentice deserved better than *that*. She knew that to the depths of her very soul.

"I'll not listen to you speak of him again," her father had told her.

She didn't speak of Prentice again.

Never again.

Her father's blows had left a bruise and Isabella had learned her lesson.

And she knew whatever happened in his life, Prentice would have a better one without the likes of her in it.

Two days after that, she got the call that Dougal and Annie had been in a car accident.

By some miracle, Dougal had come away unscathed except for a few cuts and bruises.

Annie had not fared so well.

In fact, for two days it was touch and go if she would survive.

Isabella's father forbade her to return to Scotland to be with her friend.

It nearly killed her to be away from Annie and Prentice and Dougal.

But she didn't disobey her father.

Something happened while Annie fought for her life. Not only did Fergus blame Dougal, and Annie's mother, Clarissa blamed Dougal (Clarissa was divorced from Fergus and still lived in Chicago but she flew to Scotland when Annie was injured), but also Dougal blamed himself.

The minute Annie was stable, Fergus had her moved to a hospital in Edinburgh. The minute Annie was able, Clarissa had her flown home to do her rehabilitation.

Annie did everything she could within her limited power at the time to convince everyone that Dougal wasn't at fault (and she failed).

However, she didn't do anything to try to convince Dougal she still loved him.

Her face had been scarred, quite badly.

And her body . . .

It didn't bear thinking about.

One day when Isabella had taken her to rehab, on the way home Isabella had gently tried to find a way through Annie's disheartening stubbornness.

"Really, Bella, do you think Dougal, *Dougal*, should be saddled with me? Like this?" She pointed to her face then lifted up her weakened arm and jiggled it, before she dropped it and looked out the window. "He's a Scottish *god*. He's the best looking man I've ever laid eyes on. He should marry a supermodel, not a freak show."

"Annie—" Isabella tried, her already broken heart splintering.

"Shut it!" Annie had snapped, her tone nasty, something at that time Isabella was used to. Since the accident, Annie had been nasty, very nasty and very often, to everyone including (and especially) Isabella. "I don't want to talk about it." She paused for emphasis then finished, "Ever."

Being a coward, Isabella didn't bring it up again.

However, two years ago, Annie had had to go back to Scotland. Fergus was ill and he needed his daughter.

Unsurprisingly, Annie had run into Dougal.

She'd had plastic surgeries (three of them) and the scarring had been significantly diminished (but there was still some minor disfigurement). She'd gained back the full use of her arm but, when she grew tired, her gait would weaken and she'd walk with a slight limp.

Miraculously, with a good deal of patience exhibited by Isabella, Mikey, Clarissa and Fergus, Annie had also regained her zest for life and her sense of humor (but unfortunately she'd kept her stubbornness).

Dougal, Annie reported to Isabella, was ravaged by the very sight of her and did anything he could to avoid her and did it spectacularly well, much to Annie's dismay. Although she never said this, Isabella knew it to be true by the sheer amount of time Annie spent talking about it.

In the intervening years, Dougal had been married and divorced.

The divorce, Annie found out (much later), was because the woman he married hadn't been Annie.

Within months, with Isabella's subtle guidance during Annie's many telephone calls that centered mostly on Dougal and the lack of times she'd run into him, which she found increasingly frustrating since she was spending any time away from her father in the attempt to run into Dougal but *telling* herself she was doing errands or the like, Annie had decided to win him back.

This was an effort doomed to fail.

Dougal, evidently, could be stubborn too.

Heartbreak, it was Isabella's *vast* experience, did that to you.

Fortunately for Annie (distressingly for Isabella, though she never said a word, and Annie did her best to be gentle whenever she mentioned it), Annie recruited Prentice and his wife, Fiona.

Four years after Isabella left, Prentice had married Fiona Sawyer.

Isabella knew Fiona and she liked her a great deal. Fiona was pretty and lively and very, very funny. They'd been friends and Fiona often spent time with Annie and Isabella or, with Fiona's boyfriend, Scott, they'd be a threesome going to movies or the pub or to the beach to build a fire and sit in the sand and snog.

Scott and Fiona, obviously, had broken up.

Prentice and Fiona had two children, Jason and Sally. And according to Annie, Fiona had not lost any of her spirited liveliness.

Isabella was glad to hear that, as much as it killed her. Prentice deserved that.

Prentice deserved everything.

With Prentice and Fiona in the mix, Dougal didn't stand a chance.

And the Scottish romantic fairytale came alive, which would, this week, end in happily ever after.

Unfortunately, Prentice and Fiona's romantic fairytale was not to be that long-lasting. After Fiona complained of headaches she'd been diagnosed with a brain tumor and, shockingly to everyone (most especially Prentice, for obvious reasons) she'd been dead within months.

That was a year, one month, three weeks and four days ago.

Fiona didn't live to see her two friends blissfully wed in a week's worth of festivities to celebrate the happy ending it took twenty years to come about.

And Prentice was a widower with two motherless children facing a week's worth of festivities as best man to his best friend whilst the girl-friend who'd heartlessly jilted him was maid of honor.

No, Isabella thought, this was not fun and exciting.

This was agony.

She came out of her upsetting thoughts and realized they were approaching Fergus's stately manor house.

The last time she'd come from America and approached this house, she'd not been in a limousine. She'd been in the back seat of Fergus's Jaguar and she'd been jumping around more than Mikey.

Dougal's beat-up old truck was in the drive.

So was Prentice's beat-up old Harley.

Dougal was sitting on a step.

Prentice was standing at the top, arms crossed on his wide chest, his beautiful eyes on the Jag.

Sometimes, when Isabella was feeling maudlin, she'd take out the photo frame she carried everywhere with her, she'd study Prentice's picture and she'd try to determine the color of his eyes.

When she'd been with him, she'd done it up close.

She could, she thought then (and now) do it for hours.

They were neither green, nor gray, nor brown, nor blue.

They were all of them in an equal mixture.

They were the most beautiful eyes she'd ever seen in her life, before, or since.

Fergus had barely stopped the car when Annie was out the door, flying toward Dougal, who'd stood and was walking with long-legged strides toward her, a huge smile on his handsome face.

Isabella would have done the same, but such was her excitement her fingers were all thumbs and she was having trouble getting her seatbelt unfastened.

At home in Chicago with her father, she was unfailingly sedate, quiet and unassuming, as her father liked her to be.

With Annie in Scotland and at university (where they'd met), she was anything but sedate, quiet and unassuming.

And, with Prentice, she could be anything she wanted to be.

Which meant, with Prentice, she could be free.

Something she'd never been in her whole life.

Prentice had not walked with long-legged strides to her when she'd finally exited the car. His eyes didn't leave her but he didn't smile.

Isabella felt a moment of uncertainty, even though he'd never given her any indication in the months they'd been separated that their summer romance of the year before had cooled.

She felt her step stutter as she walked toward him. He noticed it, his gaze dropping to her feet.

Then he shook his head and grinned.

That was all she needed.

She flew at him so fast he got only one step toward her before she collided with him. His foot went back to brace their bodies, his arms came around her, fierce and tight, and his mouth crushed down on hers.

"Oh for goodness sake, don't they have boys in America?" Fergus interrupted the Snog Fest, his voice filled with amusement.

"Not like they do here, Dad," Annie retorted, her voice happy and teasing.

Isabella didn't reply, she was too busy looking in Prentice's eyes and counting the colors.

"Missed you, baby," he'd whispered and her eyes closed.

She loved it when he called her "baby."

Isabella pressed deeper into him and opened her eyes.

"Not as much as I missed you."

An extraordinary warmth came to his face as he gazed down on her, he grinned again and shook his head.

He had no idea every word she said was utterly true. She was the living dead when he was not with her. His presence, his touch, his kiss, brought her to life.

Like Sleeping Beauty.

Another fairytale come alive.

Or so she thought.

Now, Isabella watched the house get closer and she reckoned she was most likely *not* going to get the same greeting.

Annie had been home to Chicago three times in the last two years, two of those times she'd been back together with Dougal and, one of them, Dougal came with her.

Isabella did not see Dougal.

Although Annie made excuses, Isabella knew Dougal had no interest in seeing Isabella.

In fact, Fergus had cooled toward her after what she did to Prentice, and when she didn't come back after Annie's accident. He'd cooled substantially.

It wasn't until years later, after Fergus had come to Chicago and he and Annie had dinner with Isabella and her father, and Isabella had run into some colleagues from work that Fergus's warmth toward Isabella had come back.

Regardless of the outcome of the evening, Isabella found it supremely humiliating the way her father had behaved.

Her colleagues had been in a good mood, having been out for drinks, and they were loud and happy, asking Isabella to join them some time, *any time*.

They trotted on their merry way and her father stared daggers at them.

Then he'd turned to his daughter.

"You will *not* join those *ridiculous* people for a drink. For God's sake, every last one of them was publicly inebriated. How crass," her father had snapped.

"They're just having fun," Isabella, very unwisely, had stated quietly.

Her father halted, turned, and leaned into her threateningly (and not unusually) and Isabella could actually *feel* Fergus and Annie get tense.

"Are you contradicting me?" Carver Austin asked in a lethal voice that didn't threaten punishment if her answer was incorrect, it *promised* it.

"Of course not," Isabella whispered back immediately, feeling her face getting pale right before she felt the blood rush painfully into it.

"I didn't think so," her father replied, looked at Annie, giving her a head to toe, and then to Fergus. "Firm hand, good man. Doesn't matter how old they are."

With that he'd walked into the restaurant, arrogantly expecting them to follow.

"I think—" Fergus started, his voice sounding weirdly strangled.

Annie cut him off. "Dad, I told you about this."

"It's okay, Mr. McFadden." Isabella had leapt to her father's defense. "Honestly. He's just a little—"

"Don't say another word, Bella," Fergus clipped, and Isabella's mouth snapped shut, mainly because he hadn't called her "Bella" since that last summer (and no one called her "Elle" except Prentice, not in her life, and she loved it when he called her that too). "Not another word." Fergus's eyes went to where they last saw her father, he muttered, "Christ," under his breath and ushered the two women in, his arms protectively held around both of them.

As humiliating as that scene had been, Isabella was glad that Fergus didn't hate her anymore. She'd always liked him a good deal. He was lovely, a wonderful man, a doting father, something, at least from afar, Isabella could definitely appreciate.

She was also glad he'd won his battle over cancer.

And lastly, she would be happy to see him again.

At least there was one thing to look forward to.

"Look at that house!" Mikey cried from beside her, craning his neck and moving around in the back seat, trying to get a look at the house as they rode at a crawl next to it. "It's something out of a movie!"

"Or a modern day fairytale," Isabella teased.

Mikey looked at her and smiled a beautiful, gleaming, happy smile.

She smiled back but it felt funny on her face.

With great exuberance, Mikey vaulted out of his door.

Isabella took a deep breath and, with far less enthusiasm (in fact, none at all), she exited hers.

———•———

Fiona

PRENTICE CAMERON STOOD staring out the window at the sleek limousine, watching as the effeminate man bounded out one side and continuing to watch as the beautiful, elegant woman sedately exited the other.

If Fiona Cameron had breath, she would be holding it.

She stood, ghost-like (because she *was* a ghost) and invisible, behind her husband and watched over his broad shoulder as his first love nodded at the driver regally then looked up at the house, her stunning face blank and cold.

God, Fiona hated her.

Years ago, Prentice had caught Fiona studying a picture of Isabella Austin Evangelista in a glossy magazine.

The picture was amazing.

She'd been wearing a dress that had to cost as much as Fiona's entire wardrobe. She was walking, her gait wide, the slit up the front of her dress exposing thin, shapely legs, and she had on a pair of stylish, strappy, high-heeled shoes.

No one could walk in those dainty, death-defying shoes with grace except fucking Isabella Austin Evangelista. She could probably run in them, dance in them, play netball in them, the bitch.

In the photo, Isabella held a beaded clutch in one hand and the other hand was lifted, holding the thick fall of her (fake, fake, *fake*) streaked honey-and-white-blonde fringe to the side of her temple, her eyes to the ground.

Her cheeks shimmered. Her dark brows were arched perfectly (which had to be the work of what Fiona was certain was a top-notch brow-shaper person at a posh salon). And, lastly, her lips were glossed in a way that it looked like da Vinci himself had held the lip brush.

Fiona was so engrossed in the picture, she hadn't heard Prentice approach and didn't know he was there until she felt his lips at her neck.

"Doesn't hold a candle to you," he whispered in her ear.

Even as she felt a shiver at his words, she laughed and shook the picture in front of him, trying not to be embarrassed at being caught ogling his famous, beautiful ex in a magazine.

"Right."

His eyes had moved to the photo for barely long enough to take it in before they came back to her.

"She's too thin," Prentice had said.

Fiona shook her head and repeated, "Right."

"She wears way too much makeup."

Fiona grinned and repeated again, "Right."

Prentice's face hardened but his eyes got warm as they looked into hers. "She's deceitful, untrustworthy, snobbish, thoughtless and a complete bitch."

That Fiona couldn't contradict.

She knew exactly what Isabella had done to Prentice, *exactly*. He'd told her everything.

And Fiona also knew that Isabella had not deigned to come back when her friend had been fighting for her life in hospital.

Therefore Fiona knew that Isabella Austin Evangelista was all those things.

And more.

And none of them were good.

Before she could say another word, Prentice had kissed her. Then he'd taken her to bed.

She'd never ogled a picture of his ex again.

Ah, she thought, *good times.*

"Prentice?" Dougal called from the doorway and Prentice turned from the window.

Fiona stayed staring out of it.

The man with Isabella rounded the car, staring up at the house with his mouth open and his eyes wide. Isabella gave him a smile that looked like butter wouldn't melt and linked her arm in his.

She was wearing classy, high-heeled black boots, a cranberry-colored wool skirt that hit her at her knees and fit her like a second skin, and a matching jacket that had stylish detailing at the pockets and the lapels. She had on a satin blouse in a color one shade darker than the cranberry suit and it came all the way up to her neck, circling her throat in elegant gathers. Her hair was bunched back in soft but stylish twists that led to a complicated chignon at her nape, the hairstyle so sophisticated there was no way she did it herself. The back of the suit was even nicer than the front, the skirt falling in a row of knife-sharp kick pleats at the back of her knees, the same from the waist of the jacket down to the top of her arse.

Fiona let her ghostly lip curl at the idea that Isabella Evangelista had a stylist do her hair, she wore a fancy, posh suit (of all things) and rode in a limousine to a tiny, Scottish fishing village.

What a daft cow.

"You okay?" Dougal asked, entering the room and closing the door behind him.

"Why wouldn't I be?" Prentice asked.

Dougal's eyes went to the window and Prentice burst out laughing.

"I'm hardly pining for Isabella Austin," Prentice said, laughter still in his voice, and if Fiona had breath, she would have let it out.

"This can't be easy for you, mate," Dougal said softly, and Fiona remembered (as she often did) why she liked Dougal so damned much.

"For God's sake, Dougal, it's been twenty years." Prentice's deep voice still held amusement. "I don't even think of her anymore."

"Maybe no' but you'll have to now," Dougal returned.

"Aye," Prentice agreed readily. "For a week, then she'll be gone back to her life filled with limousines, paparazzi and posh parties and it'll be like she wasn't even here."

Dougal watched his friend.

"It'll be like she wasn't even here," Prentice repeated, his words low and slow and filled with meaning.

Fiona knew he'd been through this before, of course, and he had, with effort, built a life where it was like Isabella Austin had never even been there.

Dougal shifted uncomfortably.

"You should know, Annie has these ideas about Isabella—" Dougal started but Prentice shook his head.

"It'll be fine."

"She says there's reasons—"

"I know she does. She's tried to explain them to me, without making much sense. She's Isabella's friend, she'd try to find some excuse for the way she behaved, no' only to me but no' showing up when Annie nearly died. They're good friends, it's natural and it doesn't mean a thing to me," Prentice stated and when Dougal looked dubious, Prentice approached him and said, "No' a damned thing, mate." Prentice's voice became low again when he continued, "It's been a long time, Dougal, we've all moved on." Fiona watched as her husband grinned his devastating, wicked grin. "Except you, of course."

Dougal relaxed and smiled back. "That's me, stuck in a rut."

"I'll be sure to tell Annie you called her a rut."

Fiona laughed a silent laugh. Annie would *hate* that.

Dougal's laugh (seeing as he was alive) sounded jovially throughout the room.

The door flew open nearly hitting Dougal in the back and Annie was there.

Her hair was wild (it was always wild, a long mixture of thick, dark-blonde frizz and curls, it was manic and gorgeous, just like Annie). On her petite but rounded body she was wearing tight-fitting jeans, a green T-shirt that said, All the other kids are doing it on the front in yellow and blue lettering and a ratty-assed olive-drab cardigan that nearly went down to her knees.

"*Bella and Mikey are here!*" she screeched excitedly, then turned on her Wellington-clad foot and ran from the room.

Dougal and Prentice watched her go.

Dougal sighed before he turned to Prentice. "You know I love her."

"I do," Prentice replied, his fantastic lips twitching.

"You know I love her a lot."

Prentice chuckled. "I do."

"I didn't love her that much, mate, no way in hell I'd walk out of this room and spend a whole fucking week trying to be nice to that bitch."

Prentice shook his head, clapped his hand on his friend's shoulder and they both walked out of the room.

Fiona floated behind them remembering *again* why she really, *really* liked Dougal.

They followed the screeching, Annie's mixed with an unknown, and unusual, masculine-esque shriek.

When they approached the foyer, Annie and the man from the drive were in each other's arms, jumping up and down.

Isabella Austin Evangelista (the daft cow) was standing to the side, eyes on her friends, hugging her elbows in her hands with what looked (shockingly, to Fiona's way of thinking) like an actual *genuine* (but very small) grin on her perfectly lip-glossed lips.

"Bella." They heard, and her eyes moved coolly to the stairs then Fiona watched in dismay as her face melted when she saw Fergus.

Good God, could the bitch be any more beautiful?

Fiona felt Dougal go tense and Prentice stopped moving forward altogether as Isabella's face changed again, the small grin widened, brightened, and the room lit with the radiance of her smile.

Yes, Fiona thought with irritation, the bitch could be more beautiful.

"Fergus," she breathed softly, turned and rushed quickly to the stairs and up four of them to embrace Fergus.

There was nothing cool and disdainful in her embrace for Fergus.

Then again, Fergus was loaded and obviously Isabella didn't have any problem with men who were loaded. It was just lowly fishermen who she had a problem with.

She'd married international playboy Laurent Evangelista and he was so loaded it was unfathomable how loaded he was. Of course, he'd cheated on her very publicly then ditched her even more public-ly, paid her off with an enormous divorce settlement (just as publicly) and was still carrying on with his younger version of Isabella whilst on the Riviera and in Paris and wherever-the-hell-else famous, rich people hung out.

This had, for some bizarre reason Fiona could never figure out when she was alive (nor now, when she was very dead), made Isabella even more celebrated and famous.

She had simply been the fascinating, stylish and beautiful American heiress who had finally landed the equally fascinating, stylish and handsome French-Italian playboy Laurent Evangelista.

For some reason, people took *her* side in the whole messy affair. Then again, no one really knew the true personality of Isabella Austin except those in a tiny fishing village in Scotland.

No one could *believe* Laurent would throw over his lovely, soft-spoken, charity-working, fashion-designer-muse wife for a common (but younger, and it was lost on no one she looked almost exactly like Isabella) strumpet.

There'd even been T-shirts made that you could buy that said, Up with Isabella on the front and Up *Yours* Laurent on the back.

Since then (and it had been years), Isabella became more famous, more hunted by the paparazzi, an object of fascination.

Likely, this was because no one could believe anyone who had all that money, all those good genes, all that fashion sense and a kind soul (*blech*, Fiona thought) could be so humiliated. It made even the common woman feel camaraderie with her, because they knew, if it could even happen to the likes of Isabella Austin Evangelista, it could definitely happen to them.

It also meant they were all waiting with bated breath for Isabella's next catch, hoping he would be devastatingly handsome, romantic and he'd sweep her off her feet and heal all her considerable wounds.

Which meant that every man she even looked at was her latest lover. According to the media, she'd had scores. None of which lasted more than a few months (again according to the media).

Which meant that somehow, fabulous, celebrated, renowned beauty Isabella Austin Evangelista had the every-woman curse of never finding the right bloke.

Which set her up as the Queen of Lonely Hearts and that made the camaraderie extend to every woman in the whole *fucking* world.

If they only knew she'd simply gotten what she deserved, well . . .

"Good to see you," Fergus muttered, his voice thick, his words cutting into Fiona's ethereal thoughts. "Missed you, lass."

Her cheek was pressed to his and her eyes were closed.

"Not as much as I missed you," she whispered in her breathy voice.

With her paranormal senses, Fiona felt Prentice's body turn solid.

She looked at her husband. His face was hard, his mouth tight, his eyes glittering.

Something was wrong.

As quick as it came, his body relaxed and his eyes went blank.

Fiona looked back at Isabella.

Her eyes opened and they focused on Prentice.

The coolness hit her face like an arctic snap and she pulled away from Fergus, her gaze moving to Dougal.

"Dougal," she said softly.

"Isabella," Dougal returned roughly and Fiona could tell he was making an effort to be polite.

She started walking down the steps in her high heels, her head turned to the side, and if Fiona had tried that she would have fallen flat on her face.

Isabella's gaze was on Prentice.

"Prentice." Again, that breathy voice.

What was it with that breathy shite? Fiona thought. She'd never spoken that way when she was there those summers long ago.

"Isabella," Prentice replied.

Fiona stared at her.

Did she flinch?

Flinch?

No, no, Fiona's paranormal senses were heightened but no way would butter-wouldn't-melt Isabella Austin Evangelista *flinch*.

And if she did, why would she, simply upon hearing Prentice say her name?

"This calls for champagne!" Annie screeched, taking Fiona's thoughts from the impossible flinch and rushing forward, tugging the man along with her and linking arms with Isabella.

"I'll get it," Dougal said immediately. "Prentice, a little help?"

"Of course," Prentice murmured but Isabella spoke.

"One moment, please."

Everyone stopped, as they would. Her voice was still soft, slightly breathy but there was something about it that made you pay attention.

God, Fiona hated her.

"Prentice," she held her hand out toward him and Fiona would have sucked in breath (again, if she had any), then Isabella turned to the unknown man, "this is Mikey. A friend of Annie's and mine from—"

"I remember you mentioning Mikey," Prentice interrupted, and before Isabella could say more, Prentice walked forward, hand extended to Mikey.

Isabella dropped her own hand, her gaze moved to Dougal then away as Prentice shook Mikey's hand.

"Pleasure," Prentice muttered but Mikey pumped his arm like their handshake was the last thing he'd do before he died and he never wanted it to end.

"Prentice Cameron," Mikey was staring avidly at Prentice then he turned to Isabella and Annie. "Girls, you were holding out. You said he was delicious but you didn't say he was *dee-lish-us*."

Dougal and Fergus (who had joined them) laughed.

Prentice chuckled and carefully disconnected his hand.

Annie giggled.

Isabella adopted her butter-wouldn't-melt smile, effectively removing herself from the humorous situation entirely as if she was a casual observer, not a participant.

Yes, Fiona hated her.

Before Fiona could let the depths of her hatred settle (which would probably take a million years), the door flew open and Debs, Prentice's sister, flew in.

Everyone turned and then they tensed.

Fiona grinned.

She *loved* Debs.

And Debs *hated* Isabella Evangelista.

This, she thought, was going to be *good*.

Debs, as usual, didn't disappoint.

She slammed the door behind her, took a step forward and opened her mouth.

Then she shouted, "You *fucking* bitch!"

Fiona looked at Isabella, her grin still in place but it faltered when she saw the cool look the heartless cow was directing at Debs who, Fiona knew, adored Isabella like a sister (once).

"Debs—" Prentice said warningly and started forward but Debs was not to be denied (again, as usual).

"I could *not* believe it when I heard you were going to be here." Debs glanced at Annie and snapped, "I'm sorry, Annie, but you know it has to be said."

"Debs—" Prentice repeated, reaching his sister and taking her by the upper arm, which she yanked from his grip while her gaze snapped to his face.

"I know *you're* over it because, luckily, you found a better one and married *her*. But me and everyone else," Debs threw her arm wide to indicate the entire village, "wants her to know she is *not* welcome here." Her eyes went back to Isabella. "So don't think of playing any of your fancy rich girl games with any of our men this time around. Got me?"

"Who *is* this interesting creature?" Mikey muttered to Annie.

"Debs, really, this isn't necessary, nor, might I add, *nice*," Fergus cut in.

"I'm not known for being nice," Debs retorted.

"You can say that again," Mikey told her.

Debs's eyes narrowed on Mikey. "And who are you, her newest victim?"

"No," Mikey replied. "I've been her second best friend for over twenty years and if you don't mind your manners, miss priss, I'll be forced not to mind mine and you won't like that. Do *you* have *me?*"

"*How dare you!*" Debs screeched.

"I dare *easily*, darling," Mikey returned, completely unperturbed.

"Dougal, Prentice, *do something*," Annie beseeched, looking like she was about ready to cry, and Fiona forgot how much she hated Isabella and felt badly for her friend.

Surprisingly, Isabella forged into the breach.

"It's perfectly fine," she said again softly, her voice somehow carry-ing that weird authority and even Debs stopped her tirade and stared at her.

Then, even more surprisingly (and strangely, to Fiona's way of thinking), she murmured, "It's nothing less than I deserve."

"You have *that* right," Debs snapped back.

Isabella leveled her gaze on Debs and, if Fiona could still feel, she would have felt a chill.

"Yes," she said in a strong, cultured, not at all soft or breathy voice, "I do."

And without looking at Prentice, who was staring at her in what Fiona knew exactly was shock, or anyone else, Isabella turned to Annie and said, back to her soft voice, "I need to freshen up. I'll be back for champagne."

She leaned in and kissed her friend, nodded to Mikey and gracefully and slowly walked up the stairs, arse swaying, like she hadn't a care in the world.

Fiona's apprehensive eyes moved to Prentice knowing he was an ass man and that was one fine ass, even as a woman she had to appreciate it. One could safely say Isabella Austin Evangelista had, somehow, since Fiona had died and seen any photos of her, put on a few pounds, but for her they were a few *good* pounds, which Fiona thought was distinctly *unfair*.

But Prentice wasn't checking out Isabella's arse, he was pulling his sister to the door.

"A word," he said in his deep, warning voice that said, quite clearly, Debs was *in trouble* and not a little bit of it.

The door closed behind them and Annie swung around on Dougal.

"Debs is now officially uninvited to the wedding."

"Annie, luv—"

Annie shook her head and lifted her hand. "Nope, nuh-unh, no. Un . . . in . . . vite . . . ed."

After delivering that, she flounced from the room toward the kitchen.

Dougal cast an apologetic glance to Fergus and Mikey and followed her.

"I'm thinking this is going to be an interesting week," Mikey commented blandly.

Fergus looked at his guest. "And I'm thinking you're not wrong, lad."

Fiona couldn't agree with them more.

Then her mind switched to Isabella's (possible but not probable) flinch when Prentice said her name, and again she had to ponder . . . what was *that* all about?

Chapter
TWO

Accommodation Arrangements

Prentice

Prentice opened the front door to his home, trying to unclench his jaw, and turned to Isabella, sweeping his arm wide to indicate she should precede him.

She nodded and did as he indicated, gracefully carrying one of her four suitcases as if it weighed no more than a feather when he knew it did not.

His six-year-old daughter, Sally, followed, not gracefully at all lugging an enormous cosmetics case, not wanting to be left out and having a strange, six-year-old girl fascination with a fancy, huge cosmetics case.

His ten-year-old son, Jason, manfully heaved up the third largest suitcase and entered the house.

Prentice followed with the largest one, dropped it in the vestibule and then moved through the three of them, all of whom stopped and looked at him questioningly.

"Leave the luggage in the hall, kids, I'll see to it later," he ordered, his voice tight, and Jason gave him a look Prentice carefully didn't return as he passed his son and went into Fiona's huge, open-plan great room.

Prentice was going to kill his sister because her behavior had made it impossible to say no when Annie had announced her ridiculously inappropriate plans for the accommodation arrangements of two of her many wedding guests.

Mikey would be staying at Fergus's house.

Isabella would be staying with Prentice, Jason and Sally.

Dougal's eyes nearly popped out of his head when Annie made her announcement. Fergus's eyes had rolled to the ceiling. Mikey's lips had twitched and he looked carefully to the side. Isabella had remained completely cool and took a sip from her champagne.

Then she'd said, "I'd like to stay with you and Fergus, if you don't mind, Annie."

"*I* don't mind but Richard and Robert are going to be here later tonight and *Mikey* might mind." Annie leaned into Mikey and whispered loudly, "They're both *fit* and they're both *gay* and they're both *single*."

Mikey leaned to Annie and whispered back (loudly), "*Really?*"

Annie widened her eyes comically and nodded.

Mikey turned to Isabella. "You're staying with Prentice."

Isabella sighed and replied, "I couldn't impose. I'll get a room in a hotel."

Dougal started nodding and sat forward but Annie got there before him.

"You're in the Scottish Highlands, my lovely, the closest hotel is twenty-five miles away and it's booked with my party guests. Not . . . gonna . . . happen."

Isabella didn't lose even a little of her composure as her eyes moved to Prentice. "Perhaps we should ask Prentice if it's okay if I stay with his family. I'm sure they're very busy with school and work and activities and the like."

She was, to his vague surprise, trying to give him an out.

Or, more likely, covering her own hide as she probably didn't want to sleep under the roof of a man who she'd heartlessly played twenty years ago.

However, twenty minutes after his sister had verbally accosted her in the foyer of her friend's home, he could hardly say no.

Therefore, he'd said, "We have plenty of room." Then he'd lied, "You're more than welcome."

She didn't miss a beat, nodded to him and said, "Well, that's kind of you."

On that she took another sip of her drink and started to study the carpet.

Complete cool.

In fact, ice cold.

How was he once in love with this woman?

An hour later, when he had to pick up the kids, he took her to the school and she stood beside him while Jason had sauntered and Sally had rushed toward the 4x4.

Sally came to a skidding halt and stared at Isabella. Then her wide, glittering, *happy* eyes swung to her father.

"Is she a *movie star*?" Sally breathed.

Isabella startled him by laughing. It was not the uproarious, full-throated laughter he knew from decades ago. This was more controlled but, nevertheless, authentic.

"You're my new best friend," she told Sally.

Prentice mentally braced.

His daughter was all girl, all girl with no mother, and the likes of Isabella was undoubtedly a dream come true.

"I am?" Sally whispered.

"You are," Isabella confirmed on a nod and went on, sealing Prentice's doom, "I like your nail polish."

Sally held up her hands and surveyed them. "It needs changed."

"I'm a pretty dab hand with a manicure," Isabella replied.

Prentice had no doubt of *that*.

"You'd give me a *manicure*?" Sally asked, like this was her most fervent wish when he knew that morning (because she'd told him, twice), her most fervent wish was to have a horse and the morning before it had been to go shopping at Harrods. Not that he knew where she picked up that ludicrous idea and lamented the fact that his daughter had to go to school at all, especially when there were other girls there with imaginations far more vivid than Sally's, which was saying something.

"I'm Bella," Isabella said softly and Sally sighed.

"No, you're Mrs. Evangelista," Prentice stated firmly, and Isabella's head turned to him inquiringly but he ignored her and looked at his daughter. "And she's staying with us for a week. She's Annie's maid of honor."

"And I'm the flower girl!" Sally trilled, rushing up to Isabella and grabbing her hand. "We *are* going to be best friends, even better! Annie's-wedding-friends!"

Prentice sighed. Jason, who had arrived, stared at his sister like she was from another planet.

"This is my son, Jason," Prentice offered.

"Hello," Isabella said softly, studying his son.

Jason moved his stare to her, pink hit his cheeks then he moved to the 4x4 and muttered, "'Lo."

Fiona's death had caused Sally confusion and distress, both of which she worked through with the spirit and zest for life that she'd inherited from her mother.

Fiona's death had caused Jason immense pain, which had not abated in the slightest in over a year.

The drive home had been filled with Sally's chatter which was lucky even as it was annoying.

Now they were home and Prentice had no earthly clue what to do with Isabella Evangelista.

What he did know was that there was only one thing more hateful than having this woman in the home he'd built for Fiona, and that one thing was the fact that Fiona no longer shared that home with him.

Sally, however, knew exactly what to do.

"I'm *starving*," she cried, dancing into the great room, holding Isabella's hand and dragging her along. "Daddy, make us toad in the hole," she demanded.

"I want takeaway," Jason muttered as he slouched through the room, threw the post on the kitchen counter then headed toward the open-backed stairway that led to the second floor.

"We had takeaway last night," Sally whined, "and the night before."
She wasn't wrong.

It had been takeaway the night before that too.

Fiona had done the cooking and the shopping. Since she was no longer there and the only things Prentice could cook that didn't taste crap were cheese on toast, beans on toast and toad in the hole, takeaway was a staple for the Cameron family.

"It's takeaway, lass, I've got things to do," Prentice murmured, hitting the kitchen that opened to the great room, separated by a long, wide, V-shaped counter with stools, and on its other side, floor to cathedral ceiling windows that faced the sea.

He picked up the post.

"I'll cook," Isabella offered and Prentice's head snapped up.

Earlier, he'd been incorrect. It was more hateful having Isabella in Fiona's kitchen cooking than it was simply having Isabella in Fiona's house. Or, more to the point, cooking better than Fiona in Fiona's kitchen.

Fiona was a damn fine cook. However, if memory served, Isabella was an excellent one. Her cooking was a delicious mixture of home-cooking and gourmet. When she'd been there twenty years ago, both summers, she did it often for him, his family, their friends and she'd cooked and served fabulous tasting meals like it was second nature.

Sally's head tilted back excitedly to look at her new idol.

"You cook *and* wear high heels?" she asked as if this was an act akin to negotiating world peace *with* global socialized healthcare thrown in.

"We don't have any food in the house," Prentice cut in and Isabella's eyes moved to him.

"I'll go to the store."

Sally jumped up and down. "Can I go to the store with Bel . . . I mean, Mrs. Evangahlala? Can I, can I, can I?"

"I said takeaway," Prentice replied.

"Daddeeeeeee!" Sally whined.

"Takeaway," Prentice repeated and Sally's face fell.

Fucking, *bloody*, hell.

He gave in.

He couldn't help it. He hated it when Sally's face fell.

However, he needed time to adjust to the idea. He also needed time with Jason to see how his son was faring with movie-star-glamorous Isabella Evangelista in the house.

"Perhaps Mrs. Evangelista will cook for us tomorrow night," he suggested.

Sally jumped up and down, clapping and whirling toward Isabella.

"Will you? Will you, will you, will you?"

Isabella smiled down at his daughter and said softly, "Of course, sweetheart."

Sally stopped jumping and clapping and stared in bright-eyed, happy wonder at Isabella.

At the same time Prentice felt like someone had hit him in the gut with a sledgehammer.

He felt his temper flare.

This woman was not going to turn her considerable charm on his children then walk out of their lives without a second thought.

He started to move around the kitchen counter saying, "Isabella, I'll show you to your room."

"I'll go too!" Sally announced, grasping Isabella's hand.

"No, baby, you go put your books in your room," Prentice ordered.

"Daddy," Sally whined.

"Now, Sally. I need a word with Isabella."

Sally sighed with aggrieved exaggeration and stomped to the stairs.

Prentice headed to the back hall that led to the backstairs that led to the guest suite, which was removed from the family areas. It was a suite he'd designed because Fiona said guests needed privacy, and when she'd been alive, with her many friends and huge family, it had been occupied frequently.

Since her funeral, it had never been occupied.

Isabella followed.

When she walked into the room, she looked around and Prentice closed the door.

She turned to Prentice.

"You have a beautiful home," she said softly.

Prentice ignored the compliment.

"There are sheets in the wardrobe in the bedroom. Towels in the cupboard in the bathroom. This room," he indicated the small but welcoming and cozy (Fiona had made it the latter two) sitting room, "has its own phone line, broadband and television so you can have privacy."

"Thank you."

Prentice decided it was best if he made his wishes very clear and he didn't delay.

"I expect you to be in here as often as possible when you're in my house."

He could swear he saw her body lock.

"Sorry?" she asked, again with that odd, soft voice.

"I think you heard me," he replied.

"Prentice—" she started but stopped when he shook his head.

"I'm sure you're aware that my children lost their mother a year ago. Sally's obviously looking for anyone to fill that feminine gap and it isn't going to be you."

Her face didn't lose any of its composure as her eyes stayed unwavering on his.

"Prentice—" she started again but he kept talking.

"This is a holiday for you but it's their life."

"I wouldn't do—"

Prentice cut her off and his tone was biting. "Wouldn't you?"

She looked to the floor immediately and stated, "I deserved that."

Christ, she was a piece of work.

His temper, already at the surface, boiled over.

"You've said that already but you didn't mean it when you said it to Debs and you don't mean it now."

Her eyes shot back to his and she opened her mouth but he didn't let her speak.

"I don't know what game you're playing this time but I reckon you know I'm no' playing it. What you need to know is, you aren't playing it with my children."

"I'm not playing a game," she returned coolly.

"That's good then," he replied but it was impossible to miss the way he said it meant he didn't believe one word out of her mouth.

And Isabella didn't miss it.

She leaned forward slightly. "I lost my mother when I was young too. I would never *play games* with any children, especially not yours."

"I've no idea what a woman like you does for fun," Prentice shot back. "I just want you to understand whatever fun you intend to have, it will no' involve my family."

She crossed her arms and hugged her elbows, whispering, "I don't deserve *this*."

Prentice was silent.

She held his gaze.

Then, as if unable to stop herself, she asked, "What kind of woman do you think I am?"

She shouldn't have asked it. She knew it and so did he.

He should have let it go.

He didn't let it go.

Instead, he answered, "The kind of woman who'd play with a man's heart without a second thought then leave her best friend in a hospital bed for months without lowering herself for that first god-damned visit."

Prentice watched with detached fascination as her composure slipped for a split second, exposing pain, before she regained it.

Her face softened slightly. "Perhaps I should explain."

"I don't want an explanation," he returned, and he didn't. He was twenty years and a dead wife away from explanations. "I want to know we understand each other."

Isabella was silent for a moment.

Finally she whispered, "Sally likes me."

"Sally likes everyone."

Isabella pressed her lips together for a brief moment and he could swear it was an effort to hide her genuine reaction. This was an effort that worked, she gave not that first thing away.

Then she nodded.

"Of course, Prentice," she gave in quietly. "I'll stay in these rooms."

"Except when you cook Sally dinner tomorrow night. *That's* one promise you're going to keep."

He didn't wait for her to agree.

He left.

And he put her out of his mind while he called for takeaway.

To Sally's dismay and Prentice's relief, Isabella didn't join them for dinner.

———◆———

Fiona

FIONA KNEW SHE should not hang out in the guest suite, but she did mainly because she'd been there when Prentice had told Isabella off and since she couldn't verbally crow, she wanted to ethereally crow.

She shouldn't have.

If she hadn't, she would have missed what Isabella Austin Evangelista did.

See, Prentice brought up her bags and she thanked him graciously while he completely ignored her (this had made Fiona smile).

Then Isabella had taken off her suit jacket and Fiona had been supremely happy she hadn't done it in front of Prentice for the shirt underneath might have had a high neck but it also had no sleeves and it was sexy as all hell.

After that she made the bed and carefully unpacked as if all her precious belongings should be placed in a high security vault, not the lowly (but beautiful) guest suite that Prentice had designed for their home.

She'd placed four leather-bound volumes next to the bed, arranging them amongst her plethora of expensive night creams and eye creams and even (Fiona narrowed her eyes to get a look at the tiny, squirty bottle) *aromatherapy* (for God's sake, *aromatherapy?*).

She'd showered, which Fiona absented herself for and spent some time with her wee ones.

By the time she came back, Isabella had changed into a nightgown that Fiona was really, really, *really* glad Prentice didn't see because he wasn't just an ass man he was very visual and he liked sexy underwear and sexy nighties and that was the sexiest one Fiona had ever seen.

She was writing in her journal but closed it after carefully putting a velvet ribbon in the page and setting it just so on top of the others.

Then she went to the luggage she'd stored tidily in the wardrobe.

She dragged out and opened the biggest bag and got down beside it. Sitting with her legs folded under her, she pulled out the lining and dug in the side, a secret compartment she'd obviously made herself.

And she unveiled a silver double frame that was folded in on itself.

Fiona floated over her while she opened it then floated back several feet when she saw what was in it.

On one side was a photo of Isabella and Prentice together. He was swinging her up in his arms, she had her arms around his neck, her head thrown back, his head was tilted to look down at her and they were both laughing. On the other side was just a photo of Prentice, close up, much younger and, as ever, deliciously handsome.

He was looking at the camera in a way that was familiar to Fiona. It was because his face was soft and warm and infinitely loving.

It was then Isabella Austin Evangelista did the thing Fiona wished she'd never, never, *never* seen her do.

After touching Prentice's face lovingly with just the tip of one finger, she opened the frames, slowly sliding out the photos. Then she tossed the frame back in the bag and replaced the bag in the wardrobe.

She walked to the bathroom.

Standing over the toilet, while Fiona stared in horror, she ripped up the photos in tiny pieces and tossed them in.

But she wasn't done.

Pulling a very thin, delicate, gold chain from her neck, it was freed from the bodice of her nightgown and Fiona saw it held a diamond engagement ring.

Tears falling completely silently down her beautiful face, Isabella Austin Evangelista tossed the engagement ring Prentice gave her twenty years ago in the toilet. A ring Fiona knew, because of the photos and the tears, had been hanging around her neck for every one of those twenty years.

Isabella stared in the toilet for what seemed like forever.

And Fiona stared at Isabella as the tears rolled down Isabella's face, her neck, down her chest, wetting her gown.

So many tears.

God, she didn't think she'd ever seen anyone cry that many tears, especially not silently.

Finally Isabella leaned toward the handle and Fiona found herself trying (and failing) to shout, *Don't do it!*

Isabella flushed.

Then she walked out of the room.

Fiona hovered over the toilet and looked down at it hoping for the first time that Prentice's excellent plumbing would be faulty.

It wasn't.

Fiona floated back into the bedroom. It was dark, Isabella motionless in bed, her eyes closed, but with her super keen, supernatural senses, Fiona saw that her hands were clenched so tightly they were mottled red but white at the joints.

Fiona watched Isabella a long time, not knowing what she was feeling but thinking something pretty colossal had changed in the way she thought about Isabella Austin Evangelista.

She only *knew* it had changed when Isabella finally fell asleep, her hands relaxed to open and Fiona saw the deep grooves that her fingernails had made in her palms.

It wasn't even the new, angry, purple grooves.

It was the overabundance of white, fingernail-shaped scars that surrounded them.

Chapter
THREE

Ginger Snaps

Isabella

Isabella sat next to Prentice the next morning as he drove them toward Fergus's home after they'd dropped the children off at school.

She had carefully missed the pre-school preparations, although she *heard* them because she'd opened her door so she could. Mostly Sally's ceaseless chatter but also Jason's low mumbles and Prentice's deep rumbly commands. It sounded manic but fun.

She'd come down at what she'd hoped was the last minute (and she'd been correct) and did her best to be cool and detached from Sally and failed miserably. She couldn't be cool and detached from the sweet, high-spirited, brown-eyed, brown-haired girl who looked startlingly like Fiona, a fact which had to be both heartbreaking and easing for Prentice.

She'd asked for a ride to Fergus's to which Prentice agreed.

While on their way to school, Sally asked approximately one thousand questions about what "Mrs. Evangahlala" was making for dinner that night, give or take a question or two. Then she'd stood at Isabella's door of Prentice's Range Rover, slapping it and waving madly until Isabella smiled and waved back. Only then did she turn and run toward the school.

Now, Isabella had her hands clenched tightly in fists, feeling the calming pain, her eyes looking out the window.

"This is the last time you'll have to do this. I've a rental car being delivered today," she told him.

"Aye," he replied shortly.

Isabella forged ahead in her attempt to be polite. "I know Annie has a goodly number of guests coming this week but I'll call around to some B&Bs and—"

He cut her off, "I wouldn't do that."

Isabella persevered, "Maybe there's a cancellation or—"

Without taking his eyes from the road, he interrupted her again, "Don't do it, Isabella."

She found this vaguely surprising. He'd made it perfectly clear he didn't want her in his home. He'd made it *infinitely* clear he didn't want her around his children. Why wouldn't he want her to find alternate accommodation?

"It's no bother," she went on. "They have cancellations all the time. I'm sure something will come up.

He glanced swiftly at her then back to the road. "Likely, aye."

"So, I'll make some calls."

"No, you won't."

She turned and looked at him.

Age, she thought, had not been kind to him.

It had been *generous.*

How he could be more beautiful now than when they'd been together when she thought he was the most beautiful man she'd ever seen (because he was) was a cruel twist of fate.

He still wore his thick hair (which she described to her girlfriends at Northwestern as "*exactly* two shades lighter than the darkest, dark brown") a little long. Sun and laughter had given him attractive lines radiating from the sides of his eyes. His jaw had lost none of its sharp angularity, nor had his cheekbones. His eyes were the same unusually beautiful every-color as they'd always been. Even his body had become better. He was bigger, more muscular, more powerfully-built.

She took her thoughts off her latest cruel twist of fate and stated, "I don't understand."

"You're no' unknown around here," Prentice said by way of explanation.

She was not unknown *everywhere* thanks to Laurent and her father and, well, freaking *Laurent* (the jerk).

"I'm used to that," Isabella explained softly.

"Aye, I'm sure you are. Perhaps I should have said you're no' *liked* around here."

Silently, Isabella pulled in breath.

She hadn't expected that.

She should have, especially after what Debs said the day before, not to mention what Prentice had said, both of these instances scoring at her heart.

Luckily, her heart had been lacerated beyond feeling much of anything anymore, so she didn't feel like tossing herself off the nearest cliff, of which there were a fair few around here.

But still, she hadn't anticipated that.

Once upon a time (in other words, twenty years ago), Prentice's village was the only safe haven Isabella had known in her life.

Now, it was a place where she was reviled.

She tightened her fists further and looked out the window, murmuring, "I won't make the calls."

"Aye, smart," he muttered and she got the impression he was barely listening to her.

Which he probably wasn't.

She stayed silent until he stopped in front of Fergus's house. She didn't look at him when she expressed her gratitude for the ride and put her hand to the door.

"Isabella," he called, she stopped and turned to him.

He was holding up a key.

"To the house," he said, dropping it in her palm when she lifted her hand for the key.

His eyes started to move away, but all of a sudden they jerked back, slightly narrowed and focused on her palm.

Instantly, her hand closed over the key.

"I've decided I'll make dinner and then I'll explain to the children that I have a raging headache," she blurted, wanting to divert his attention as his still narrowed gaze followed her closed hand.

His eyes shot to hers, his mouth was tight and he looked *very* angry.

"Why in *the fuck* would you do that?" he bit out, his voice proving she was so very correct about him being so *very* angry.

"Um—" Isabella's mind went blank at his anger.

She remembered a great deal about him (in fact, pretty much everything) but she'd never seen him angry (well, not *this* angry). She didn't know what to say, she didn't even know if she could speak.

Then she remembered what to say.

"So I can leave you to dinner and get to my rooms."

His head gave a small jerk and he looked over her shoulder, probably, she decided, to gain control.

Eventually his gaze met hers.

"Their mother died of a brain tumor," he told her and it sounded like those words were dredged straight out of the depth of some hole inside of him that was too deep to measure.

"I know," Isabella whispered. "Annie told me."

"It started with headaches."

Isabella automatically made a noise as if someone very strong had pressed the breath right out of her lungs.

She was going to cry.

She was going to cry.

Oh no.

No, no, no no, *no!*

She couldn't cry!

Her hands fisted, the key bit into her palm, the pain shot through her and she didn't cry.

Instead, she said, "I'm an idiot."

He turned away, putting one of his hands back to the steering wheel, the other to the clutch.

"I'll come up with something else, I promise," she blathered on.

Only his head turned so he could look at her.

"Food poisoning!" she cried, sounding both stupid and desperate.

"I'm not sure food poisoning is good, Isabella, considering you'll be cooking."

Yes, stupid.

Yes, an idiot.

Yes, desperate.

Triple threat!

"Oh, right," Isabella muttered but he'd already turned back away.

Isabella opened her door, promising again (under her breath this time), "Well, I'll think of *something.*"

She barely got the door closed when he drove away.

She stood in the drive watching his SUV thinking she hated pretty much everything about her life, but the thing she hated most at that particular moment was hearing Prentice address her as "Isabella."

On that thought she turned and walked up to Fergus's house.

—— ◆ ——

Fiona

"FLAPJACKS!" ANNIE SHOUTED from down the grocery aisle, she was holding up a box of flapjacks in each hand and waving them around. "Kids love flapjacks!"

"I'm not stocking their larder, Annie, I'm making them dinner," Isabella called back.

"Nothing wrong with stocking that hot guy's larder, you hear what I'm saying?" Mikey muttered, staring with curiosity at the jam selection.

"Don't go there," Isabella warned softly.

"Time heals all wounds." Mikey was still muttering and his eyes had gone narrow.

Fiona watched closely as Isabella allowed herself an open reaction, considering Mikey was staring at the jams and Annie was tossing flapjacks into the cart Isabella was pushing.

Sorrow.

Unadulterated.

Then she masked it.

No, Fiona thought, time did *not* heal all wounds.

"Where's the grape jelly?" Mikey asked the jam selection.

"They don't have grape jelly here," Annie explained.

"That's un-American!" Mikey shrieked, his head turning to Isabella and Annie.

"Well, yeah, considering we *aren't* in America," Annie drawled.

"Kids love grape jelly," Mikey said with authority.

"American kids like grape jelly. Scottish kids like, I don't know, marmite," Annie replied as Isabella pushed the cart forward.

"Marmite?" Mikey asked then pulled an exaggerated horrified face.

Lime marmalade! Fiona shouted her children's preference.

"Lime marmalade," Isabella said instantly, and Fiona was so shocked she accidentally floated straight through Mikey causing him to shiver.

She hated floating through people and avoided it at all costs. She didn't feel anything physically, just emotionally, but it made her sadder than her normal sad at being dead when the only thing she could make people feel was cold.

"Cat walked over my grave," he whispered, doing another shiver just for effect as Isabella grabbed a jar of lime marmalade. Then she grabbed another one.

"I hate lime marmalade, too sweet," Annie mumbled.

"It's fruit and sugar and fruit *is* sugar so there's no way for it *not* to be sweet," Mikey hilariously explained.

No matter how funny he was being, and Fiona had decided she liked Mikey, Fiona wasn't listening.

She floated close to Isabella and asked, *Can you hear me?*

"So, I'm thinking chicken strips, fries and some kind of vegetable," Isabella, clearly not hearing Fiona's voice from beyond the grave, stated. "What kind of vegetable?"

Peas, Fiona told her.

"Broccoli?" Annie asked.

"I don't *think* so. Forget the veggies, kids hate veggies," Mikey advised, and Fiona forgot she liked him and gave him a dirty look.

For the past year, one month, three weeks and five days (and then some, considering she was super sick before she died but her mum had helped with the cooking then), Prentice hadn't been great on the nutrition front.

Her kids needed their veg.

"How about green beans?" Annie asked.

Peas! Fiona shouted at Isabella.

"Peas," Isabella said, and Fiona stopped floating along with them, her shock and excitement was too profound.

Good God, could the woman hear her?

She was stunned motionless for so long she had to float up and over the shelves to catch them up on the other side.

"What are you making for dessert?" Mikey asked when Fiona arrived.

"No dessert. I don't want Prentice to think I'm trying to make them like me," Isabella answered.

Fiona closed her ghostly eyes.

Yesterday, after her beloved husband told off his hated ex-fiancée, Fiona had wished she could kiss him (not for the first time).

Today, she wished she could kick him (also not for the first time, however, it *had* been the first time since she'd died).

"You make a mean hot fudge sundae," Annie said to Isabella.

Sally would love an American hot fudge sundae, Fiona told her excitedly. *And Jason's favorite food in the world is clotted cream ice cream. Make that!*

"No dessert," Isabella said softly but firmly in her weird authoritative voice.

Annie halted, Mikey halted with her and both of them glared at Isabella, Mikey adding a cross of the arms on his chest that made his glare far more effective.

"Okay, Debs was out of control yesterday. You shouldn't be surprised about that, Debs was *always* out of control," Annie stated. "And Prentice got upset with you but you shouldn't be surprised about that either. First, you dumped him and never explained, which, I will repeat for the five *thousandth* time, you should have. Or you should have let *me* explain it to him and Dougal and Debs and *everybody*. Something, which

I will remind you, you refused to let me do, about . . . oh, I don't know, *five thousand times.* Or you should have let Dad say something which he's been wanting to do *for years.* And last, Prentice lost his wife and he's on edge. He's taking care of two kids, running his own firm, his best friend is blissfully happy and his ex-girlfriend is sleeping under his roof."

"And who arranged *that?*" Isabella returned coolly, and Fiona, floating beside her, nodded in invisible agreement because, especially for Annie, that was underhanded.

Though, Fiona was curious to know what there was to explain and why Isabella wouldn't let Annie or Fergus do it.

Annie had the good manners to blush.

"I want all the people I love to get along," she said quietly and Fiona lost her pique.

So did Isabella.

Even so, Isabella walked around the cart to her friend and grabbed Annie's hand. "First, I think you know why I've never explained or let you explain."

"I know why," Annie returned. "I just don't agree."

"I don't either," Mikey put in.

Fiona floated closer.

"I know you both don't agree," Isabella replied. "But I believe, deeply, it's better this way and I'll ask, again, that you respect my wishes."

Neither Mikey nor Annie looked happy about this but they didn't respond.

Isabella continued, "And, I'm sorry Annie, but Prentice doesn't have to like me. He doesn't even have to get along with me. He has to put up with me for one week. Then, sweetie, I'm gone. Don't put this pressure on him, he's got enough on his plate. Just let me . . ." Isabella stopped, her eyes got big, her usually remote face filled with pleasure, making her beauty radiant as it had been the day before when she'd smiled at Fergus. Then she practically did a small jump in her high-heeled, fancy, posh, brown boots and cried, "I've got it!"

Fiona stared, even Isabella's soft voice had risen with excitement.

"Got what?" Mikey asked, staring at her avidly, a small grin on his lips. The look on his face and the attention he was giving his friend told

Fiona he didn't often see her like this and he was intent on enjoying it on the rare occasions she showed it.

But Isabella had raced back to the handle on the shopping cart and was pushing it with renewed vim and vigor, like she had a new lease on life.

"The food for the kids and Prentice won't be from *me*," she announced, her eyes searching the shelves, her hands reaching for a variety of biscuits and she studied them. "The sundaes won't even be from *me*. I'll tell Prentice that Annie went shopping with me and I'll tell him *Annie* bought it." She stopped studying the biscuits and looked gleefully at the stunned Annie and Mikey. *"He'll never know!"* When she finished, she was almost shouting.

It was so perfect, Fiona nearly laughed.

Instead she shouted as loud (which was silent) as she could, *Chocolate fingers and custard creams!*

"Chocolate fingers and custard creams," Isabella murmured. Fiona just stopped herself from doing a happy, floaty cartwheel that somehow, on some plane, Isabella Austin Evangelista could hear her and Isabella put down the biscuits she had and reached for Jason and Sally's favorites. "And ginger snaps for Prentice," she whispered.

Fiona closed her ghostly eyes.

She remembered Prentice loved ginger snaps.

Fiona wanted to hate her but what woman who carried around pictures of a man she had to love with all her heart in a secret compartment of her luggage and wore his ring hidden around her neck and remembered for twenty years that he liked ginger snaps could be hated?

Not to mention that Fiona had caught her opening her door so she could hear the morning pandemonium in the great room.

Really?

Even his dead ghost wife who seriously *wanted* to think she was a deceitful bitch couldn't hate her.

And anyway, she was finding excuses to put food in the house and giving Fiona's children peas.

Fiona, too, had to put up with Isabella Evangahlala (Fiona cracked up every time Sally called her that) for a week. But if she put good food in her children's bellies and lime marmalade in the cupboard and ginger snaps in the cookie jar, she figured that would be a lot easier to do.

Clotted cream ice cream! Fiona screamed.

Isabella shoved the cart forward, mumbling, "Clotted cream ice cream."

———— • ————

Isabella

ISABELLA WAS IN her rooms in Prentice's house when she heard Prentice and the kids come home.

She'd been there for a few hours, feigning jetlag after they'd dropped off the food and went back into town to do some shopping.

However, shopping in the village became not so fun when Isabella ran into a dozen people she knew and most of them acted like they didn't see her, the others like they didn't know her and one stared at her like she was singlehandedly responsible for famine in Africa.

Even though Annie had set aside that day to spend with her and Mikey before the onslaught of celebrations, both her friends saw the villagers' behavior and they didn't demur when Isabella lied and said she needed to rest.

Being in Prentice's house without Prentice and the children and with time on her hands meant Isabella did something she knew she shouldn't.

But she couldn't help it.

She'd given herself a tour of his house.

Annie had told her that Prentice had left the firm he'd worked for five years ago and started his own. He had five employees and enough work that it was steady, busy and his family was comfortable.

He'd also designed this house.

And it was extraordinary.

The great room with its huge wall of windows, the large, rectangular gleaming dining table at the foot of the stairs, state-of-the-art kitchen with stainless steel appliances and an enormous American refrigerator was, in itself, phenomenal.

The blond wood, open-backed (and sided) wide stairwell, the steps that seemed (because they were) suspended in midair was unusual and amazing.

The upper floor fed off the side into the cliff that rose beside the house, four bedrooms (one which was a playroom-slash-music room) and a full bath with the kids' rooms having their own Jack and Jill bathroom. The master suite (which Isabella very quickly dashed through even though she really, *really* shouldn't have) had a sitting room, bedroom, walk-in closet and bathroom with sunken tub.

Isabella noted that Fiona's clothes and belongings were no longer in the room, and even though that made her heart contract, she was glad that Prentice had moved beyond what she suspected was a very difficult stage of the grieving process.

On her side of the house there was a study (obviously Prentice's), a television room with a big, comfy sectional couch (there was no TV in the great room, or any other room in the house for that matter), a half bath, a large storage area and a mudroom-slash-laundry room.

There were balconies that faced the sea leading from the great room, Prentice's bedroom and even a small private one in her rooms.

The rooms were huge, airy and full of windows. The blond wood floors, timber sashes and skirting boards were gorgeous. The unusual lines of the ceilings and quirky touches were extraordinary.

The entire house was magnificent.

It wasn't decorated to Isabella's taste (obviously). Isabella liked no mess, no clutter, clean lines.

But this was a family home stuffed full with books, picture frames and proudly displayed but poorly crafted children's art. The fridge was covered in bits and pieces. The mudroom was filled with coats and boots and dirty laundry.

Even so, there was a flair to it that reminded Isabella of Fiona. It was comfortably appointed but decorated with a hint of fun and playfulness with bold and bright colors that would only be used by a woman who was confident in herself and her taste.

Exactly the opposite of Isabella who had hired a decorator to decorate her apartment and had very little hand in the choosing of anything, fabrics, colors, draperies, she didn't care. She didn't really even see it.

Her home was the place where she existed just as her life was simply an existence.

Once she'd finished her tour and dinner chores, she'd retreated to her rooms.

Now, to her surprise, she heard scrambling feet coming close and Prentice's voice calling sharply, "Sally!"

The scrambling feet sounded on the stairs and Isabella whirled to the door she hadn't closed.

She'd just finished doing yoga.

She'd asked her doctor to titrate her off the anti-depressants she'd been taking for years. He hadn't wanted to but she didn't want to be zoned out when Annie finally had her dream come true.

In fact, she figured she'd been zoned out long enough.

She'd taken her last pill two days before.

Isabella felt (and convinced her doctor) that she could deal with the dark thoughts and she'd created a variety of mechanisms to help her do it.

She had her journals.

She kept things ordered and tidy around her.

She used aromatherapy to help her sleep and other times besides, like now when she practiced yoga.

Before leaving the village that day, she'd bought four fantastic, homemade candles from Fern Goodacre's cute little shop. One was in the sitting room currently burning a calming scent of lavender, one was in the bedroom and two were in the wardrobe for use by the next guests, a small present for Prentice that he probably wouldn't notice and didn't have to enjoy himself.

She was wearing her roll-top, wide-legged, charcoal-gray yoga pants and a plum-colored, shelf-bra camisole. Her feet were bare and her hair was pulled in a messy knot secured by a ponytail holder on the top of her head.

Isabella was *not* in "company clothes," as her father called them and also demanded that she wear them at all times when "in company" which was, unless she was alone, pretty much all the time.

She had no choice. Before she could move, Sally burst through the door still wearing her school uniform with her pink and purple ruck-sack strapped to her back.

"We're home!" she shouted as if Isabella was at the other side of the house not right in front of her.

Isabella couldn't help herself, she smiled.

"I see that, honey."

Sally took in all that was Isabella and the room including the yoga mat on the floor before she asked, "Whatcha doin'?"

Isabella leaned down to pick up the mat and started rolling it up when she heard adult footsteps on the stairs.

Her heart skipped a beat.

"Yoga," Isabella replied, her hands moving quickly on the mat, un-sure of Prentice's response to Sally's impromptu visit and wanting to be prepared.

Sally lost interest in her answer and danced to the candle.

"What's *this*?" she breathed, getting close and staring at it as if she'd never seen a candle before in her life.

Isabella forgot to concentrate on the sounds of someone approach-ing and took a wide step toward Sally, putting a hand to her shoulder and gently moving her away.

"Careful, sweetheart, that's an open flame."

Sally beamed up at her.

My, but she's a gorgeous child, Isabella thought, her brain erasing of everything else.

She'd wanted children, badly. She could have borne dozens of them. She wanted a wild, happy house filled with photo frames of fam-ily snapshots and poorly crafted children's art projects.

Unfortunately, she'd found she couldn't have them. After years of heartbreaking tests, treatments and procedures she'd learned it was a complete impossibility.

It was also one of the myriad reasons Laurent replaced her, the oth-er mostly had to do with the fact that he was a jerk.

"It smells pretty, like flowers," Sally commented.

"That's what it's supposed to smell like."

"How do they do that?" Sally asked, and Isabella set the mat aside and crouched next to the child.

"They mix special oils with wax when it's hot and liquid, like the top of that one." She used her head to indicate the candle. "Then they pour it in and *voila!*" She threw her hands out and shook her fingers.

Sally giggled and asked, "Are they magical oils?"

Isabella moved the child's long hair off her shoulder and replied, "Well, yes, I guess so, since they're from nature and nature's magical."

Sally wrinkled her nose. "Nature's not magical. It's nature."

Isabella leaned in close. "Then you haven't seen a fabulous sunset or an apple tree in bloom or a Japanese oak in autumn. I'd say all of those are magical."

"To be magic, there has to be pixie dust," Sally declared with authority.

Isabella smiled at her. "I think you got me there."

"Sally," a deep voice said behind them and they both jumped and turned to see Prentice standing inside the door.

"Mrs. Evangahlala has magic candles!" Sally cried.

Prentice's eyes moved to Isabella and she held her breath as she slowly straightened. He watched her do this and then his gaze roamed down her body then up and over her hair.

For some reason, his mouth got tight and his eyes moved back to his daughter.

"Sally, go put away your rucksack."

"Okay," she agreed happily and turned to Isabella. "Are you cooking dinner?"

Isabella kept her attention firm on Sally when she answered, "Yes."

"Can I help?"

Oh dear, what did she do with that?

She just stopped herself from biting her lip before saying, "I don't think so, sweetheart. It mostly involves the stove and oven and that's probably not safe."

Sally's face fell.

Instantly, Isabella felt like a screaming bitch.

"Maybe you can scoop out the ice cream for dessert," she offered.

"*We're having pudding?*" Sally screeched, and her effervescence so surprised and charmed Isabella that she couldn't stop herself from laughing.

"Yes, honey, you're having pudding," Isabella replied and stopped, glanced apprehensively at Prentice then back at Sally. "If it's okay with your dad."

Sally whirled to her father. "Can we have pudding? Can we, can we, can we?"

"Books in your room," Prentice answered. "We'll talk about pudding later."

Sally beamed then leaned toward Isabella and confided in a (very) loud whisper, "Daddy'd have said no right away if we weren't having pudding."

Isabella chuckled and then, all of a sudden, Sally threw her arms around Isabella's legs.

She froze.

It had been a long time since anyone had touched her with spontaneous affection and she didn't know if she'd ever, in her life, been hugged by a child.

It felt good.

Really good.

Lost in Sally, Isabella's hand lifted and she lightly stroked the girl's soft, beautiful hair.

Sally threw her head back and gave Isabella a sunny smile before she dashed from the room.

Isabella watched her then her eyes moved to Prentice.

He looked ready to commit murder.

Oh dear *again*.

Before he could blow, Isabella spoke, "I need a word. Can you close the door?"

Prentice didn't hesitate. By all appearances he needed a word too.

Or maybe several of them.

When the door clicked and he turned, Isabella quickly launched in. "The sundaes are Annie's idea. So is all the food in your kitchen. She went shopping with me and got a little carried away."

Prentice just stared at her but she was pleased to see he didn't look like he wanted to strangle her anymore.

"She's prone to doing that," Isabella went on.

Prentice continued staring at her before he said on a sigh, "Aye, she is."

Isabella couldn't help it, it looked like she was getting away with it and she allowed herself a small smile.

Prentice's eyes narrowed on her mouth.

She stopped smiling.

But she started talking. "I'll make dinner and then come up here. I'll tell the kids I have jetlag or something. The hot fudge is already made, in the covered pot on the stove, you just have to heat it up and pour it over the ice cream. There's whipped cream and cherries and I chopped up some nuts . . ." She hesitated when his face changed in a way she couldn't read but she valiantly forged ahead, mostly in order to get this over with, "If they like that kind of thing." She paused again and he remained silent. "Nuts, that is." More silence. "Kind of the all-American sundae."

"When are you going to eat?" he asked.

"Pardon?"

"You said you'd make dinner and come up here. When are you going to eat?"

"I'll bring something up with me." She wondered if he wouldn't like that, these were nice rooms, clean and tidy, maybe he didn't want food up there. "If that's okay."

That was when he said something completely bizarre.

"So it's the martyr."

She was so stunned, she couldn't control her reaction and she blinked.

"Pardon?" she repeated.

"Your game this time. The martyr."

It felt like he slapped her and reflexively her hands clenched into fists at her sides.

"I'm not playing the martyr," Isabella denied softly.

"You had no dinner last night, no breakfast this morning, unless you had something at Fergus's. You're behaving like you're chained to these rooms."

"You told me you wanted me to spend my time in your house . . ." she lifted her hand and flicked it out, "in here."

"I believe I said 'as often as possible,' not every fucking minute."

"Isn't 'as often as possible' pretty much the same as 'every fucking minute?'" Isabella asked, genuinely perplexed.

"Don't play word games with me, Isabella. I have a university degree. I own a business, a home. I know the fucking English language."

There it was again, the non-physical slap.

There was one thing Isabella Austin Evangelista knew how to do. She knew how to retreat from anger.

Therefore, she whispered, "All right, Prentice."

His brows drew together over angry eyes and he stared at her. She calmly held his stare and her breath.

Then Prentice murmured, "Christ, it's like I've never met you."

She wasn't surprised at his reaction. Twenty years ago their relationship hadn't been totally perfect.

What it had been was passionate.

They'd fought and they'd been good at it.

Back then, she would never have backed down. She knew he wouldn't hurt her with his anger. How she knew this, she didn't understand in the beginning.

Later, she would realize it was love.

Therefore, she felt safe fighting with him.

Isabella wanted to tell him that he *hadn't* ever met her. She wanted to tell him that the girl he knew never really existed.

He'd created her.

Well, Annie did by asking her to spend that first summer in Scotland.

But Prentice had breathed life in her.

This was the real Isabella.

Instead, she remained silent.

They continued to stare at each other.

Suddenly, he looked away, opening the door, muttering, "Eat dinner downstairs, up here, I don't give a fuck."

She watched him walk down the stairs and turn on the landing, out of sight.

Only then did she start breathing again.

Then she wondered if maybe her doctor had been right and she really *shouldn't* have stopped taking her medication.

Finally she turned, picked up her yoga mat and blew out the candle.

Chapter
FOUR

Chicken Bits

Isabella

Isabella waited half an hour (exactly) before she went downstairs.

In that time she decided to keep her hair up in the messy knot because it wasn't that attractive, with bits sticking out everywhere, and it might look like she was trying to be all girlie-perfect in order to cook a simple dinner if she did something with it. She also decided to stay in her yoga clothes because she'd look like an idiot if she changed clothes. She wasn't going to make dinner for the queen, just a family.

She did, however, put on a forest-green tunic that had wide sleeves and a deep slash down the neckline that opened across her collarbone, fell in a hood at the back and exposed her plum camisole.

She kept her feet bare.

In that time she also decided that Prentice had given her permission to be around the children.

Well, not exactly *permission*, as such, but pretty much, or at least she was going to go with that thought.

So Isabella wasn't ever going to be Sally's new best friend and watch her grow into a beautiful young woman whilst Sally shared her secrets about boys she had crushes on, and Isabella imparted crucial wisdom on Sally like how to know when your mascara tube was drying out.

But Isabella at least didn't have to hide from her and break her little girl heart by acting like a cool, remote, American bitch.

Isabella no sooner got out of her room when she heard a discordant plucking of guitar strings.

By the time she made it to the great room, she noticed three things. The first, Prentice was at a drafting board in his study with the double doors that led to that room off the great room open. The second, Sally was sitting on the floor by the huge, square coffee table in front of the big, fluffy royal-blue couch, drawing. The third, Jason was lying on the couch plucking, and not very well, on Fiona's guitar.

Isabella looked at the guitar and she felt tears crawl up her throat.

She'd forgotten about Fiona's guitar.

Fiona didn't take the guitar everywhere but she wasn't often separated from it. She loved it. She'd strum it when they were sitting in a pub and she'd often play it while they were lounging on blankets around a bonfire on the beach.

Isabella was so impressed by (and envious of) Fiona's talent that she'd taken secret lessons when she got home. Her father preferred her playing the piano and violin, both of which he forced lessons on her from the time she was six until she was eighteen.

She'd practiced a lot, sliding the guitar out from under her bed when her father wasn't around, but she'd never been as good as Fiona.

Eventually, she'd quit playing, and when she'd divorced Laurent and moved back to Chicago she'd found her guitar and gave it to a charity to auction.

"Mrs. Evangahlala!" Sally yelled.

Isabella looked at her, swallowed her tears and, with effort, smiled.

"I think I've figured out something you can do to help me with dinner. But we'll need a stepping stool or—" Before Isabella could finish, Sally was up and racing down the hall, rounding the corner on one foot to disappear in the mudroom.

Isabella stared after her not knowing if she should follow when Sally reappeared dragging, with some difficulty, a stepping stool.

"She's mental," Jason muttered from behind Isabella, and Isabella turned her smile on him.

He blushed.

She turned away from Jason, strode forward and helped Sally set up the stool by a counter in the kitchen.

"Get up on the stool, honey, you're going to flour the chicken," Isabella told her.

"I am?" Sally breathed, like flouring chicken was akin to walking down the red carpet at the Academy Awards.

"You are," Isabella confirmed and got out the marinating sliced chicken breasts and the Ziploc bag of seasoned flour she'd prepared earlier. She started to open and close drawers, looking for tea towels. "We just need a few tea towels in case it gets messy."

"Third drawer down, by the sink," Jason mumbled and Isabella's head jerked to the side.

He'd joined them and was slouched in a stool across the counter from Sally. He was feigning disinterest but Isabella wasn't deceived. His eyes (and, incidentally, his eyes were exactly like his father's) were on the Tupperware of chicken. There was a spark of interest in them. Not much, just a spark, but it was something.

Isabella figured boys liked food and not just takeaway.

She was pleased he'd joined them. She didn't show this, however.

She wrapped a tea towel around Sally's waist and one, bib style, around her neck and showed her what to do.

"Now, if you've got the buttermilk marinade on your fingers, don't get it near your eyes. It's got salt and Tabasco in it and it'll burn," Isabella warned.

"Okay," Sally said, carefully pulling out a chicken slice and making a face at the squishy feel of it.

"If you don't want to do it—" Isabella started.

Sally interrupted her by shouting, "I wanna do it!"

"All right, sweetheart," Isabella murmured on a grin. "Have at it."

Sally stuck her little tongue out the side of her mouth while she concentrated on wiping off the marinade before she tossed the chicken slices in the flour mixture, and Jason watched her doing it.

Isabella moved away and started preparations for the rest of dinner.

For some crazed reason that was beyond her to understand, she asked, "Is that your mum's guitar?"

Instantly she wished she could take the words back.

What was she thinking?

Why'd she ask that?

Why?

"How'd you know that?" Jason's voice was gruff.

"It just looks like the one she used to lug around all the time," Isabella mumbled, her mind tripping over itself to find another topic of conversation.

"You knew my mum?" Jason queried, sounding surprised.

Oh Lord, now what had she done?

Of course they didn't know about *her*, the awful American who screwed over their father before he met and fell in love with their mother.

That likely wasn't bedtime story material.

Oh well, she started it, she'd have to go with it.

She turned from filling a pot with water at the sink to look at Jason. "Yes. A long time ago we used to be friends."

"Did you ever hear her play?" Jason asked, and Isabella couldn't help her reminiscent smile.

She turned off the water and took the pot to the stove. "Yes, I've heard her play. She used to do it all the time. I was jealous of her. She was very talented."

"*You* were jealous of *mum*?" Jason sounded incredulous and Isabella, surprised at his reaction, looked over her shoulder at him.

He looked as incredulous as he sounded.

She turned and walked up behind Sally, doing what she'd wanted to do since the moment she laid eyes on the girl. She pulled Sally's long, soft hair back in both of her palms and then ran its length down Sally's back through her hands.

While she did this (and repeated it then repeated it again), she said with utter truthfulness, "Yes, Jason. Your mum was hilariously funny and incredibly sweet and very, very talented. There was a good deal to be jealous of." Isabella's voice went quiet when she said, "She was also lovely. You and Sally got the best of her. I can see it all over you." She paused before she finished on a smile, "But you have your father's eyes."

"Daddy says I have Mummy's eyes," Sally announced, and Isabella gave her a teasing tug of her hair as her heart lurched.

"Yes, you do, sweetheart. You're the spitting image of her," Isabella told Sally, starting to look down at the child when she saw movement to her side.

She looked to her right, saw Prentice arrive, resting a hip against the counter, crossing his arms on his chest and giving her a look filled with thunder.

Before the breath could entirely evacuate her lungs at that look pinned on her, Jason shouted, "Sally, you're supposed to—!"

Too late.

When Isabella looked down, she saw that Sally had started to shake the chicken in the Ziploc bag but hadn't locked it shut. There were flour and chicken bits all over the counter, down the cabinets, all over the floor and also, top to toe, all over Sally.

Isabella stepped to the side as Sally slowly turned toward her, the mostly empty Ziploc bag still in her hands.

Sally was covered in white.

Isabella stared down at her and Sally, head tipped back, stared back.

Suddenly, Isabella couldn't help it, the girl looked too adorable for words and the situation merited it, she threw back her head and burst out laughing.

She heard Sally's giggles and Jason's muttering of, "Totally mental."

His words made her mirth boil over again, and with eyes nearly shut with laughter she leaned down, put her hands on either side of Sally's head and dipped her face to the child's.

"You look like a snow angel," she told her.

"I do?" Sally asked.

Isabella nodded, still giggling, then reached out and picked a chicken strip off Sally's shoulder and showed it to her. "A snow angel with chicken bits."

Sally giggled harder and so did Isabella.

"I take it we're not having chicken anymore," Jason asked dryly.

Isabella looked toward Jason and burst into renewed laughter, catching his tentative grin before she took a step back and wrapped her arms around her aching sides.

She hadn't laughed this hard since . . .

Since . . .

"Sally, come here, baby, let's get you cleaned up." Prentice had walked forward two steps and was holding his hand out to his daughter.

He was smiling warmly at his daughter but he wasn't amused. How Isabella knew this, she didn't know.

But she did.

Isabella's laughter died away.

Sally dropped the bag on the counter, hopped down, still giggling and trailing flour, and took her father's hand.

Isabella watched them turn the corner to walk down the hall to bathroom.

She decided she couldn't worry about Prentice.

So he thought she was playing a game. He would think that, of course.

But she wasn't and that was the truth.

She'd just ignore him and focus on the children.

And Prentice would just have to . . .

Well . . .

Deal.

Isabella looked at Jason, tipped her head to the counter and suggested, "Let's see what we can do about this chicken, shall we?"

Without further coaxing, Jason jumped off the stool to help.

———— • ————

Fiona

FIONA FLOATED CROSSED legged above the floor next to Isabella's bed while Isabella slept.

She poked and poked again, and again, her finger going through each time, at the leather-bound book on the top of the pile on the nightstand.

She'd gone back to hating Isabella Austin Evangahlala.

Not because Isabella had said she'd been jealous of Fiona, and sounded like she meant it.

Not because she said all those nice things about her, and sounded like she meant those too.

Not because she looked good in yoga pants, that arse would look good in anything, even a muumuu, and those shoulders . . . and *her arms*! Bitch.

No, because she'd filled Fiona's house with laughter, she'd made Jason grin and she'd also not only miraculously rescued dinner, the children had loved it and even Prentice, who looked like he wanted to rip Isabella's head off all night, though he was careful not to show it in front of the children, cleaned his plate (twice).

Fiona wanted her family to have a decent meal and she wanted them to start laughing and smiling again.

Of course she did.

But she also didn't.

Not with Isabella or any other woman for that matter, except her sister, Morag, or Prentice's sister, Debs, but *especially* not Isabella.

Throughout dinner (*and* pudding), Sally had chattered, a far more relaxed, almost but not quite like Bella of old Isabella had encouraged it, and even Jason had entered the conversation whenever there was a lull in Sally's prattle, which wasn't often.

Her family had eaten the food like they'd never get another meal, the sundaes had been a huge hit, and Isabella, who surprised Fiona, she wouldn't have expected fancy, American heiress Isabella Austin Evangahlala capable of it, left the kitchen spotless clean.

With all her anger at being dead (which was a *lot*) and all her anger at Isabella Evangahlala being alive (which was also a *lot*), Fiona poked at the book.

It moved.

She stared at it.

She'd been poking at things, pushing things, trying to blow on things now for over a year and she'd never made even one of Sally's drawings on the refrigerator so much as sway.

But that book was half an inch off-kilter from the rest of them and that was *not* how Little Miss Tidy and Perfect Isabella Evangahlala left it.

In that instant she heard it and her ghostly head snapped to the side.

Jason.

She dematerialized and materialized in his room.

She should have known when he got out the guitar. It happened every time he brought out her guitar. It hadn't happened in a while, so long, Fiona thought it was over.

He was screaming.

Nightmares.

He'd had them since before she died. So, when she was just sick in bed and too weak to get to him, she'd heard that screaming with her true ears and she'd detested it but detested it more that she was the cause of it.

She still detested it.

Prentice was in the room in a flash and he knew the drill.

Hands on Jason's shoulders, he sat on the side of the bed, his naturally deeper than deep burr rumbling with sleep and emotion. "Jason, mate, it's a dream. Just a dream."

"*It's not a dream!*" Jason shouted. "She's gone, isn't she? *Gone!*"

And so it began, the battle, loud and agonizing.

Jason would often get physical and tonight was one of those nights.

Fiona hovered and watched for a while then she floated through her bairns' bathroom to Sally.

Sometimes she slept through it.

Tonight, unfortunately, wasn't one of those nights.

Sally was sitting up in bed, her head turned in the direction of the noise, her little face pale.

All of a sudden she threw back the covers and Fiona knew where she was going.

She always went to Prentice's bed, got in, pulled the covers over her head and waited until it was over and Prentice was back. Then she'd cuddle close, his arms would wrap around her, and she'd sleep with her daddy.

When this happened, Fiona would stay with them for a while and then she'd spend the rest of the night hovering next to Jason.

Sally jumped out of bed and Fiona floated with her.

But Sally didn't go to Prentice's room.

She ran to the stairs. Then she ran down them. And she ran through the great room, down the hall and turned to the stairs to the guest suite.

Fiona's ghostly bottom half kept floating forward even as her ghostly torso locked in place and she stared with ghostly eyes at what she saw.

Sitting on the stairs, leaned nearly double, her elbows at her knees, her forehead resting in the palms of her hands in a pose that screamed anguish, was Isabella Evangahlala.

As Fiona's legs settled back, Isabella's head came up and her eyes locked on Sally.

She opened her arms and legs, and Sally, who had halted, raced into the woman's arms.

Those arms closed around Fiona's daughter.

And they closed tight.

They held on to each other while the muted sounds of Jason's shouts drifted toward them.

Finally, Sally's head tilted back.

"Can I sleep with you?" she asked in a timid, sad voice that tore at her mother's ghostly heart.

"Of course, sweetheart," Isabella answered softly.

And, even though Fiona knew Sally had to weigh a ton, Isabella picked her up and carried her to bed.

Fiona floated next to the bed as Isabella tucked Sally's back to her front, cuddling her close cradled in her arms, and she started singing Springsteen's "Thunder Road" softly into the back of Sally's hair.

Sally fell asleep.

Isabella curled her neck so her face was in the top of Sally's hair.

Then Isabella fell asleep.

And Fiona decided that yes, she was back to hating Isabella.

Because now, *Fiona* was jealous of Isabella Austin Evangahlala.

And Fiona had a lot more to be jealous of.

————— ♦ —————

Prentice

PRENTICE WAS SURPRISED to go back to his room and see his bed empty.

He thought after that episode with Jason (likely made worse by Isabella foolishly, and unkindly, talking about his dead mother), Sally would have woken and climbed in his bed.

In case she was awake and upset in her own bed, Prentice went to her room. She wasn't there either.

He felt fear slice through him and he moved out of her room, checked the playroom and then went swiftly down the stairs.

She wasn't on the couch in the great room or the one in the television room. He looked in his study and then stood in the hall wondering where the hell his daughter was.

Slowly, his head turned to look down the hall.

Sally would go there. No doubt about it.

The door to the guest suite was open but Sally wasn't on the couch.

The door to the bedroom of the suite was open as well and Prentice stood in it seeing Sally's dark hair and Isabella's blonde against the pillows.

He walked to the side of the bed and looked down at them in a room bathed in moonlight.

His daughter was nestled snug in the curve of Isabella's body, her arms tight around the girl. Isabella's hair was blended with Sally's, dark and light. The sheet was down at Isabella's waist and he could see she had some lacy nightgown on.

Prentice's first demented thought was to climb in bed with them.

He had no idea where that thought came from and he cast it aside instantly.

His second thought was to rip his daughter from that bitch's arms and take her far away.

Instead, he strode from the room, went to his study, poured himself two fingers of whisky, walked to his bedroom, put on a sweatshirt and walked onto the balcony.

Dinner had been interesting.

The woman he'd fallen in love with twenty years ago had come back, though not completely.

There was no fidgeting energy and mile-a-minute conversation, not that Isabella could get a word in edgewise.

But she had her long, thick hair (and it pissed him off but he had to admit that he liked the blonde, it looked too fucking good on her) tied up in one of those haphazard knots that made her look effortlessly beautiful (which she, unfortunately, was) rather than coolly beautiful.

She wasn't dressed in some ludicrously expensive designer outfit that made her look untouchable but track pants and a tunic that made her look real as well as sexy as all hell.

She laughed uproariously and uncontrollably when Sally had her incident with the flour, and he further hated to admit it but Isabella's face in abandoned laughter was, just as he remembered it, stunning.

And she hadn't made his daughter feel a fool for her childish mistake.

She'd smiled often at both Sally and Jason during dinner, engaging with Sally in her jabbering and carefully drawing out Jason like she was a qualified grief counselor.

And she cooked like a fucking dream.

But she completely ignored Prentice like he didn't exist.

Completely.

Prentice found this annoyed him.

Then he found the fact that this annoyed him annoyed him even more.

Now he found the fact that he was thinking about it at all annoyed him even more.

He sipped from his drink.

Isabella seemed determined to insinuate herself in his children's hearts.

And she was, as ever, fucking good at it.

Sally was already half in love with her and Jason hadn't talked about his mother with anyone but Prentice since she'd died.

Prentice took another sip from his drink.

He had two choices. Kick her out or let her do her worst with his children and pick up the pieces when she left them behind.

Kicking her out meant breaking Annie's heart, and Annie had enough heartbreak in her life, she didn't need any more.

And his children had been left behind by a far better woman than Isabella Evangelista and they were surviving.

And, even though Isabella was a part of it, Prentice liked hearing laughter in his kitchen and seeing his son grin. Jason hadn't grinned for months.

He took another sip of the whisky.

He had no choice really and he found that annoyed him most of all.

"Fucking hell," he muttered to the sea.

———————— ◆ ————————

Fiona

YOU CAN SAY *that again*, Fiona's silent words were lost on her husband.

She floated with him as he finished his drink, his beautiful eyes never leaving the sea.

He'd found that piece of land for them, paid a fortune for it and carved a house out of a cleft in the cliff.

Fiona hadn't wanted to be out of the village even though it was only a ten-minute drive away. But Prentice wanted privacy and space for his family.

And he *needed* the sea.

So she had no choice, really.

He put the glass on the railing which irritated her.

He always did that when he was out on the balcony brooding, which wasn't often but it happened.

Prentice could be moody, mostly about work stuff and lately about having-a-dead-wife stuff.

She'd find his whisky glasses, sometimes days or even weeks later and they'd be filled with rainwater and mucky. It was ridiculous. Why couldn't the man carry his glass inside?

He walked into the room, pulled off his sweatshirt and got into bed.

She knew the minute he fell asleep which was a long time after he lay down.

Then she hovered by his alarm clock poking the "off" button again and again, her finger going through each time.

It was late. He'd had the episode with Jason, he'd found his daughter had not gone to his bed for safe haven but she'd been cuddled with his ex and he'd brooded, and brooding had to take a lot out of him since he did it so damned well.

The kids were out of school the next day so they could attend Annie and Dougal's picnic. He didn't have to get up early.

And he needed his sleep.

Fiona poked and poked and poked and then, when she lost her temper and gave it one final *poke*, the button depressed, the light indicating that the alarm was on went out and Fiona smiled a gleeful, triumphant smile.

Then she laughed a gleeful, triumphant (but silent) laugh.

She laid a ghostly kiss on her husband's cheek that caused him to turn with agitation in bed, which was what he always did which was so very *not* what he'd do when she'd kissed him while he was sleeping when she was alive, so she wondered why he did it while she was dead.

And finally she went to her son's room and hovered beside him while he slept.

Chapter
FIVE

The Picnic

Prentice

Prentice opened his eyes to see the late September sun shining through the windows that made up one wall of his bedroom.

He stared through the windows.

Then his eyes cut to the alarm clock.

He leaned toward the clock, saw the alarm, which was never turned off, had somehow been turned off.

He'd slept in.

"Shit," he muttered, throwing back the covers and knifing out of bed.

He needed to get the children up, fed, showered, dressed, and he needed to get some work done before the picnic.

Not to mention he needed to do laundry or the children wouldn't have any clothes to wear to the picnic.

He walked out the door to his rooms and stopped dead.

He heard Sally's chatter then he heard Jason's low mumble and he also heard Isabella's laughter, not wild and uninhibited but softer, more controlled and also clearly genuine.

He felt something settle in his gut at hearing those sounds in his home and that something, to his surprise, was not unpleasant.

Regardless, this annoyed him.

He strode to the stairs and surveyed the scene in the great room as he walked down.

Sally and Jason, both still in pajamas, were sitting at stools at the counter, their backs to him, and they appeared to be eating.

Isabella was at the stove, and as Prentice made his way down the stairs she turned, skillet in one hand, spatula in the other.

She caught his movement and did a little stutter step, stopped dead and stared up at him with her lips parted.

From the depths of his memory, he recalled that stutter step. She was grace personified but when she'd get surprised, become uncertain or was overwhelmed by her own enthusiasm, she could be clumsy.

Back then, Prentice found it adorable.

It was no less adorable now.

Fucking hell, he thought.

"Daddy!" Sally shouted, obviously following Isabella's gaze. "Mrs. Evangahlala made us nanola pancakes!"

"*Gra*-nola," Jason corrected, looking and sounding not surly and exhausted as he usually did the morning after an episode but instead rested and more like his normal self than he'd been in well over a year.

Sally looked at her brother and repeated, "*Na*-nola."

"*Gra*-nola," Jason reiterated.

"That's what I said," Sally retorted impatiently. "*Na*-nola."

Jason's gaze slid to Isabella and he muttered, "See? Mental."

Isabella smiled a dazzling smile at Jason. A smile that, upon seeing it, Prentice also felt in his gut and that wasn't unpleasant either which further annoyed him. Then she slid what appeared to be an enormous, perfect, golden pancake out of the skillet and onto Jason's plate.

Prentice stopped at the side of the counter and studied the pancake. Jason was wasting no time buttering and pouring golden syrup on it. And Prentice was right, the pancake looked perfect.

Prentice turned his study to Isabella.

Her hair was up in another messy knot but one long, thick tendril had fallen out of the knot and was curling along her neck, down past her collarbone to rest against the skin of her chest.

She was wearing a satin dressing gown much the same color as the track pants she wore yesterday. It was cut in a man's style but came down only to the tops of her thighs. It was tied at the waist but the front had come open, wide and gaping, to expose a black lace nightie.

The nightie fit her like a glove, with lace scallops tantalizingly edging the swells of her breasts. Her cleavage itself, although there wasn't much exposed, was even more tantalizing.

He couldn't see the hem of the nightie under the dressing gown which meant it had to be shorter than the gown.

A mental picture formed of what Isabella's nightie looked like without the dressing gown and his body had another physical reaction, not in his gut, it was elsewhere, and it too was far from unpleasant.

And it was intense.

"I want another one!" Sally shouted, luckily erasing Prentice's mental picture of Isabella in a short, tight, black lace nightie.

"You've already had two, sweetheart," Isabella responded.

Sally grinned. "I know but they're yummy and I want another one."

"Why don't you let Mrs. Evang*elista* have one," Jason emphasized the proper pronunciation of Isabella's name and then went on, "And, maybe Dad might want one too."

Prentice watched his daughter give his son a hilarious, wrinkled-nose "go to hell" look.

Prentice watched his son roll his eyes at Sally's hilarious, wrinkled-nose "go to hell" look.

Prentice nearly laughed at their interplay, something he had done very rarely in the last year because they'd very rarely done anything to laugh about or, more accurately, Jason hadn't.

"Give it time and let those settle in your belly, Sally," Isabella advised softly as she turned back to the stove. "You don't want to be over-full for the picnic."

"Okay," Sally agreed readily which was also surprisingly.

Prentice watched Isabella walk to the stove, his eyes captivated by her ass swaying beneath the satin then captivated by her long, tan legs moving gracefully through his kitchen.

She turned when she'd made it to the stove and her hands came up to pull her robe tightly closed. "Would you like pancakes, Prentice?"

His gaze snapped to her face.

It was not open and engaging as she looked at his children. It was cool and remote.

"Please," he replied and walked to the coffee.

The pot was mostly full.

Fiona always made the coffee and his wife made great coffee. Prentice's coffee, as was his cooking, was crap.

When Fiona was sick and after she was gone, nearly every morning Prentice had to make the coffee except for the mornings his mother, Fiona's mother, Debs or Morag were there which, at his request, in order to try and get the children back to a different kind of normalcy once Fiona died, his family hadn't been coming around to help for months.

It had been a long time. He hadn't woken to a pot of coffee since . . .

Prentice didn't finish his thought as that feeling intensified in his gut.

Fucking hell, he thought again.

He poured himself a cup while Isabella slid butter into the hot skillet, which melted immediately. He watched while she poured batter on the butter and saw her coffee cup was sitting by the stove, the cup mostly full as the pot had been.

She'd been so busy feeding his children, she hadn't had time for a cup of coffee.

Fucking hell, he thought yet again.

Sally chattered. Jason ate. Isabella concentrated on his pancake and Sally's blather. And Prentice felt, like last night, that she'd forgotten he was even there.

For reasons unknown to Prentice but likely because he found her new game immensely irritating and he decided instantly he too could play a game, he walked to the side of the stove, close to where Isabella was working. Turning his back to the counter, he rested his hips against it and sipped his coffee.

The coffee was fucking heavenly.

Christ.

"Will you give me a manicure before the picnic?" Sally asked Isabella.

Prentice turned to look at her and saw, to his surprise, that Isabella was fidgeting. Moving the handle of the skillet this way and that, she was twirling the spatula in her other hand in an absentminded way. Her eyes, however, were not on the skillet. They were on the counter behind Prentice.

"I can't, Sally," she answered the counter. "After breakfast, I've got to get to Annie's to help with the picnic."

"Can I go?" Sally yelled. "Can I, can I, can I?"

Isabella didn't respond.

She stepped around him then halted in a jerky way. She tipped her head to the side, surveyed the counter, sighed, tilted it back and looked at him.

Her face a mask of good manners, she said softly, "I'm sorry, Prentice, do you mind? You're standing in front of the granola."

He examined her makeup-free face, and even with that detached expression he thought, since she'd been back, she'd never looked lovelier.

Feeling the need to be perverse, instead of moving out of her way, as she clearly wanted him to do, he twisted, grabbed the bowl of granola he was blocking, twisted back and handed it to her.

She took it.

"Thank you," she said quietly and politely.

She moved to the stove and used a graceful hand to sprinkle granola on the pancake before she set the bowl aside, in the opposite direction to Prentice, and flipped it expertly.

Prentice watched her do this like it was fascinating which, bizarrely, it was.

"*Well?*" Sally shouted.

Prentice stopped watching Isabella's hand and looked at his daughter.

"Can I go too?" Jason asked quietly, his attention on the tiled floor of the kitchen.

Prentice froze at this request from his son who hadn't been willing to participate in much of anything since his mother died.

Strangely, he felt Isabella freeze at his side too. Slowly, she turned and looked at Jason. Her profile was not polite and detached. It was soft and warm and unbelievably striking.

Again, Prentice felt that weight hit his gut.

Her head twisted, her features rearranged swiftly back to aloof and she looked up at Prentice inquiringly.

"Sorry kids, you need clean clothes and I need to do laundry," Prentice answered.

"No you don't," Sally proclaimed. "Mrs. Evangahlala and I've been doing laundry all morning."

Prentice's body turned to stone.

All except his eyes which narrowed and sliced to Isabella.

Instantly, Isabella whirled to the stove and started to fidget with the skillet on the burner.

"We've done two loads!" Sally announced triumphantly.

"You've been very busy," Prentice murmured and he watched Isabella's body get stiff, her hands fisted tightly and she moved to a cupboard.

Unfisting her hands with visible effort, which Prentice found peculiar and vaguely disturbing, she pulled down a plate, got cutlery, slid the pancake on the plate and handed it all to Prentice.

"The butter and syrup are on the counter," she informed him softly, tipped her head to the counter and then immediately dismissed him and moved away.

Prentice put his coffee cup down next to Isabella's, walked to the other counter, and while he prepared his golden, fluffy, delicious-looking pancake, he said to his children, "We'll all go."

Sally threw her hands up so fast she nearly teetered off the stool as she shouted, "Hurrah!"

Prentice smiled at his daughter.

He'd hoped that Annie and Dougal's wedding would bring some happiness to his family, cutting through the undercurrent of despair

Jason was always emanating that Prentice, for the life of him, had no idea how to chase away, likely because he couldn't cut through his own.

It appeared this was working, even for Jason.

Regrettably, Isabella was the catalyst for it.

But Prentice would take what he could get.

Including her doing the laundry which was a chore he detested, something else Fiona did.

And her brewing fucking heavenly coffee.

Prentice decided if Isabella wanted to play house and that came with good food and clean clothes, he'd fucking well let her.

Once he'd finished with the butter and syrup, he walked back across the kitchen and resumed his position next to Isabella while she cooked another pancake.

He thought, but wasn't sure, he heard her suck in an exasperated breath.

This pleased him.

Then he tasted his pancake. It was superb.

He trained his eyes on his children. "If you're done, dishes in the sink, beds made, showers, let's go."

Jason slouched off the stool and slunk to the sink, carrying his plate. Sally followed him doing the same but with much more enthusiasm.

Jason headed up the stairs.

Isabella gracefully strolled across the kitchen and took Sally's plate from her.

"When are you going to give me a manicure?" Sally asked as Isabella turned to the sink and deposited Sally's plate in it.

"We'll find some time, honey."

"Can we do it before the picnic?" Sally pushed.

"Sally," Prentice warned but Isabella's hand had lifted and she grabbed a thick hank of Sally's hair and started twisting it gently around her finger.

She leaned down and smiled at his daughter, getting close to her face. This, unfortunately, gave Prentice an indication of just how short her nightie was as her dressing gown rode up and he saw more of her shapely thigh but he still didn't catch a glimpse of the nightie.

Isabella spoke softly, taking his mind off her thigh (and ass *and* nightie).

"We'll see, Sally. Do as your father said now. Okay?"

Prentice's daughter knew that no's came swiftly and maybes usually meant yes. Therefore she beamed at Isabella, nodded, turned and raced up the stairs.

Prentice finished his pancake while Isabella cooked the next one, alternately tidying the kitchen.

When it was done, she wordlessly slid it on his plate as if he was a statue holding a platter to display her glorious pancake. She switched the stove off and slid the skillet to another burner.

"Aren't you having one?" he asked as he walked back to the counter for the butter and syrup.

"No," she replied distractedly, and he turned from his task to see her taking the bowl in which she'd mixed the batter to the sink.

It was empty.

"Isabella, have this one," he offered.

She slowly turned and stared, aghast, at his plate. Then she carefully arranged her features, shook her head and turned again to the sink.

"No, thank you. I'll have some toast."

His annoyance returned.

He walked to her and demanded, "Isabella, take it."

She didn't look at him, busy rinsing dishes. "I'm fine, Prentice."

His annoyance flared to anger.

"Christ, just eat it."

She twisted her head to look at him and said in a flat, calm voice, "I said I'm fine."

"Aye," he returned, "as am I. I don't need a second one. You can have it."

Something lit in her eyes swiftly and, Prentice thought, intoxicatingly, as it also lit her entire face.

Then she snapped (but softly), "For someone who knows the English language you don't seem to comprehend it very well. I said, *I'm fine.*"

Prentice felt an odd sense of satisfaction at her irate response no matter if it was *quietly* irate, and his anger fled instantly.

He smiled at her and replied casually, "All right. I'll eat it."

Her eyes fastened on his mouth, her face seeming dazed for a moment before they lifted to his and she gave him a look that indicated she thought *he* was mental.

He nearly laughed.

And he thought perhaps this time, considering he knew the rules and the score, her game might be fun.

She busied herself tidying the kitchen and making herself toast.

Prentice ate and watched her knowing this irritated her and enjoying that knowledge.

"You're good with the kids," he remarked and she didn't reply.

She was back to ignoring him.

He instinctively knew somehow, this morning he'd gained some advantage in their game.

Therefore, he pressed, "Why didn't you have any?"

Her body stilled, her hands fisted then he could have sworn she actually forced herself to relax before she answered.

"I can't."

"Sorry?" he queried.

The toast popped up, she snatched it, put it on a plate and walked to the counter. "I can't have children."

Prentice stared at her back.

She had millions of pounds. Millions of her own, inherited from her mother and to be inherited from her father when the bastard thankfully left this earth, and millions in the divorce settlement given to her by her bastard ex-husband.

She could easily afford to pay top-notch fertility specialists, the best in the world.

Regardless of the fact that it was absolutely none of his business, he asked, "Have you seen a specialist?"

He watched her head move, slowly, gracefully, her ear dipping down toward her shoulder then her neck twisting to the side.

There was something poignant about this movement. Poignant and distressing.

Prentice braced.

She turned to him, lifted her eyes and locked them with his.

"Ten," she said shortly.

"Ten?" he replied, stunned by her earlier movement and therefore not comprehending her answer.

"Ten specialists in four different countries. Five years of tests. Five years of fertility medication and two rounds of IVF. All of which failed." Prentice watched her talk, her expression carved from stone, a weight settled in his gut and this one *was* unpleasant. "I can't conceive," she finished.

And, obviously, she'd tried.

Everything she could.

Christ.

"Isabella," Prentice murmured, getting the distinct feeling he'd not only lost his advantage but he'd been an incredible ass.

Before he could say more, she snatched up her plate of toast, sauntered to her cold cup of coffee, hooked it with a finger and started to walk out of the room, saying softly, "I need a shower. I'll see you at Fergus's."

With that she rounded the corner and she was gone.

He watched the entrance to a hall for a good, long while.

Then he muttered out loud to himself, "Fucking hell."

———— ◆ ————

Isabella

ISABELLA SAT ON the couch in the great room facing Sally, one of her legs bent and pulled up on the seat, Sally's hand flat on her thigh. As she had been during the whole polishing portion of the shaping, buffing, varnishing manicure, Sally was calm and docile while Isabella put the last coat of clear varnish over the hot pink she'd already brushed on the girl's final fingernail.

"All right, Sally honey, you're done but you've got to sit there for a good ten minutes to give it time to dry."

Sally surveyed her fingernails with a rapt expression on her face as Isabella caught movement out of the side of her eye and saw Prentice exit his study.

He stopped and leveled his gaze on them.

"They've never looked this pretty," Sally breathed as if Isabella didn't give her a manicure but instead painted her portrait displaying more talent than Gainsborough.

Isabella hesitated, fighting an urge that was nearly overwhelming because Prentice was standing right there.

Then she thought, *Screw it.*

Sally was just too danged cute.

Again, Prentice would just have to *deal.*

And anyway, it was all his and Fiona's fault for having an endearing daughter.

She leaned forward, kissed the top of Sally's head then got up, repeating, "Ten minutes, sweetheart."

"Ten minutes!" Sally chirped and then sat statue still on the couch.

Grinning to herself, Isabella went to the mudroom to get the laundry, walking by Prentice without looking at him but *feeling* his eyes on her as she went.

The tumble dryer had buzzed five minutes ago and she hustled in to fold the clothes before they became wrinkled.

She had no earthly clue why she woke up with Prentice's family's laundry on her mind but she did. That was her first thought, as if someone had shouted at her in her sleep to get up and do the laundry.

Which she did and it needed to get done.

Even though it felt strange and intimate handling Prentice's clothes, there was a mountain of laundry. She'd done four loads now and there were at least two more to go (probably three). So much, she'd even run down between doing her makeup and hair to switch out the washer and dryer.

She'd just finished folding and was setting aside the pieces that needed to be ironed when Jason rounded the corner into the room.

"Dad says he's ready to go," Jason announced, and Isabella thought that was a strange way to voice such an announcement, considering they were driving separate vehicles and they could go when they wanted.

She'd phoned Annie and let her know she'd be a little late as it was a moral imperative to give Sally a manicure. Annie had laughed and agreed that manicures for six-year-old motherless girls were, indeed, a moral imperative.

One example of millions as to why Isabella loved Annie.

"Could you do me a big favor?" Isabella asked, shaking out one of Prentice's shirts and throwing it on a pile of other shirts to be ironed. "When you have a minute, can you take these latest piles upstairs?"

Jason had been delivering the stacks of folded clothes to their respective rooms all morning. Isabella had arranged it at breakfast, pre-Prentice showing up, and her mind moved to Prentice and that morning.

He had shown up bare-chested, barefoot, hair tousled, looking unfairly, even, one could say, *criminally* attractive . . .

Oh, and when he'd offered his pancake to her, *on his plate*. The very thought of her doing something as intimate as eating off his plate was not to be *borne* . . .

Oh, and when he'd smiled at her, the first smile he'd sent her way since she'd been back. Well, she thought for a second that she was going to pass out, literally fall in a dead faint on the floor.

"I'll do it now," Jason mumbled, picking up a pile of Prentice's clothes and fortunately taking Isabella away from her thoughts.

"Thanks," Isabella whispered, wanting to touch him, tousle his hair, anything to show the boy a little affection after what she heard last night.

But she didn't.

She had four more days with this family, an unwelcome guest, and when she was gone, she would be *gone*.

What she had to give was pancakes, laundress service and manicures.

And that was what she was going to give.

She wasn't going to be able to wring miracles, take the tightness away from Prentice's mouth (no way in hell) or cure Jason of his nightmares.

But she could sure as heck make pancakes.

And good ones.

She'd taken the clothes from the washer, put them in the dryer and was shoving another load in the washer when Prentice's tall frame filled the door.

She twisted her head and visions of him in only pajama bottoms filled her brain.

She'd seen him shirtless twenty years ago, of course, and memories of his body, the defined muscles, the hair that matted his chest (not too much, *just enough*) had been fodder for many a fantasy when they were apart and the twenty ensuing years besides.

Now, the defined muscle had more bulk, more power. Even the way he held himself that, back in the day, was confident to the point of almost swaggering, was now *more* confident but without the swagger.

He knew who he was, had settled into his physique and the result was enthralling.

Still, he *could* have absented himself that morning and put on a shirt. It was the polite thing to do. She knew it was his house and she was a guest he'd rather not have but, really. To wander around the kitchen half-naked, standing close to her (probably so he could keep an eye on her and wrestle her out of the room if she did anything too friendly with his children), it was too much!

"Yes?" she prompted when he seemed fascinated with watching her measure soap into the load.

Prentice's gaze cut to her face and took in her hair then her body before coming back to her eyes.

"We're leaving."

"I'll see you there," she turned away, dropping the lid on the washer, turning the dial and hitting the button.

He was still standing in the door when she made to leave the room.

"You're coming with us."

Isabella halted. Then she stared at him.

"I'll drive myself," she said.

"That's unnecessary considering we're both going to the same place."

"I'd prefer to drive myself."

"Why?"

Why, indeed.

Her hands clenched into fists.

Because being with you is killing me, especially since you obviously hate me and I've never fallen out of love with you.

Because realizing there are more reasons why it was for your own good that I broke your heart hurts like hell. No Sally, no Jason, even with Fiona dead you had more in those years from her than you'd ever get from me.

Because I need a moment away from all that is you and your beautiful children to get my head together so I can deal with the day.

All of this Isabella thought but did not say.

"I just would," she said instead.

"You're coming with us," he repeated.

"Prentice—"

"Sally wants you with us."

Isabella snapped her mouth shut.

Well then, who could argue with that?

"I'll get my purse," she muttered, and to her dismay he barely shifted to the side so she had to squeeze by him, sucking in her belly and breath to get around him, and her breasts *still* brushed his chest when she went by.

A heady thrill jolted through her body at that slight touch. A thrill he'd given her before, many a time. A thrill that she remembered like the last one she'd had was only yesterday.

Her fists tightened, her nails bit into her palms and she hurried to her room.

———— ◆ ————

Fiona

FIONA FLOATED WITH her family (and Isabella) to the front door.

Prentice was furious. Jason seemed confused. Sally was simply tired.

Isabella was wearing a brave face but the hideousness of the day had taken its toll. She was pale and there was a tightness about her eyes that was heartbreaking.

And her hands were clenched into permanent fists.

Fiona had been born in her village and she'd been proud of being a member of its community her whole life.

Until that day.

She knew, because she felt it herself, that everyone had felt duped by Isabella, not just Prentice. They all loved her, including Fiona. It got worse when she never returned even after the terrible accident that tore Annie and Dougal apart. That feeling had intensified further as she'd publicly moved on, living the high life of international fame and celebrity.

But, even if only for Annie's sake, they could at least attempt to be polite.

Instead of vicious.

At Annie's request, the minute Isabella hit Fergus's house, she ran to the kitchen to start making dozens and dozens of Annie's favorite cookies. The picnic was catered, including a luncheon and then an American-style bonfire that night, roasting hot dogs on sticks and making s'mores, which Fiona had never had but thought they looked delicious.

Isabella let Sally help but the making of cookies put Prentice in a bad mood which drove him to broody, something that Isabella ignored. In fact, she seemed to be doing her best to ignore Prentice as much as she could which, in turn (strangely, Fiona thought) was something Prentice seemed to be working at not allowing.

Fiona knew why the cookies made Prentice broody.

Isabella used to send him cookies from America, not to mention make them weekly for him when she was in Scotland. He'd told Fiona that when he told her about Isabella.

What Fiona didn't understand was, if Prentice had "moved on" as he'd told Dougal he had, why the cookies would make him broody at all?

That day Isabella didn't make them for Prentice, however. She made them for Annie and Dougal's guests.

And the minute those guests (at least the villagers, Sally and Jason ate around a million of them and Prentice wasn't far behind) found out she'd made them, they avoided them.

Pointedly.

Not only that, one villager, Hattie Fennick, actually made a point to take a bite then *spit it out* right when Isabella was watching her.

Hattie had always been a cow, especially around Fiona, who Hattie made no bones about not liking. Then again, she didn't like pretty much everyone including Prentice, who Fiona had known for years Hattie had a raging crush on even after she hooked up with her husband Nigel. But Prentice had never shown an interest or shown that he knew she existed at all unless he was vaguely irritated by something she'd done, which made her act even *more* of a cow.

And that wasn't all.

They made nasty comments, some of them loud, most of them when Isabella was in earshot.

They at least shielded Annie from it. She didn't hear a word, for which Fiona was grateful. They'd also been careful around Jason and Sally (Sally was oblivious as usual, Jason had overheard a few things, which pissed Fiona off). The rest of the time they ignored her, cast her dirty looks or walked away when she approached.

Although they shielded Annie, they hadn't any qualms about doing their worst in front of Fergus, Mikey, Dougal or Prentice.

Which made all four men livid, even Dougal, probably on Annie's behalf.

The picnic had started at two o'clock. It was now ten.

Eight hours of torture for Isabella.

At first, Fiona had been shocked at how she coped. She acted for all the world as if she didn't give one whit and spent her time talking with Fergus, Mikey, Annie, Sally and Old Lady Kilbride who wasn't capable of hating anyone and had always stuck up for Isabella, unpopularly saying, "We don't know. There are *always* two sides to every story."

Isabella even spent time with Jason, which was surprising since Hattie also commented loudly within Isabella's (and Prentice's) earshot, "God, the nerve of the woman. Fiona's *children*. *Jason*. Who's been *devastated*. The absolute *nerve*."

But as the hours slid by, it had begun to wear, her façade slipped, as anyone's would, and Fergus, Mikey, Dougal, Jason and, most especially Prentice, noticed.

Fiona was back to not hating her. In fact, she felt sorry for her. She had no idea what she would do if she'd been alive at the picnic rather than dead and haunting it, but she hoped she wouldn't have done *that*.

Of course, she did realize that, as a ghost, she had access to information that the villagers couldn't know, but *still*.

They hit the great room and Isabella turned immediately toward the hall.

"I'm going to call it a night," she said softly, her hands still fists.

Prentice opened his mouth to speak but Sally got there before him.

"Will you read me a story?" Sally asked, her voice tired.

"Sally—" Prentice began but Isabella talked over him.

Without hesitation, she switched directions, unfisted a hand and held it out to Sally, saying, "Of course, honey."

Sally took Isabella's hand and they walked up the stairs. Prentice's eyes followed them, his face tight.

"Dad—" Jason began when the two females disappeared.

Prentice looked at his son. "Not now, mate."

Jason wasn't to be denied. "I heard some things—"

"It's late, go to bed," Prentice ordered.

Jason stared at him, defiance written in every line of his body.

Fiona felt worry tear through her. How was Prentice going to handle this?

Her husband sighed and turned to his son. "All right Jace. As you know from last night, a long time ago, Mrs. Evangelista used to holiday here."

"Aye," Jason prompted when Prentice stopped speaking.

"She did a couple of things that angered a few people. They haven't gotten over it."

"What'd she do?"

"It doesn't matter now."

"What'd she do?"

"She hurt some people's feelings."

"So?" Jason asked. "People get their feelings hurt all the time. Worse stuff happens."

Prentice's face changed, anguish tore through it because both her husband and son had learned that lesson.

And Jason was right. Worse stuff happens, that was the God's honest truth. Fiona was beyond-the-veil-existence proof of it.

And now Fiona knew that something did not quite fit together with Isabella Austin Evangahlala.

There were, indeed, two sides to every story and no one knew Isabella's.

Except perhaps Annie, Mikey and Fergus, and they were all intensely loyal to her, something Fiona never understood about Annie or Fergus and didn't think much about.

Until now.

Fiona felt another bolt of worry tear through her.

"Aye, Jason, worse stuff happens," Prentice agreed.

"You should have said something," Jason accused, and Fiona was surprised at the heat behind his words.

He was defending Isabella. Fiona didn't know what to feel about that but she had to admit the first thing it *felt* like she felt was pride.

Then again, Jason had always been a good lad.

"Jason—" Prentice started.

"You know she's no' a bad lass. You ate her pancakes."

"Jace—" Prentice tried again.

"And she liked Mum," Jason kept at it.

"Jason, it's complicated," Prentice finally got out.

"I don't know what's complicated about it. She's nice and she painted Sally's fingernails. And people like *you*. You've been living here all your life. They'd listen to you."

Fiona watched as Prentice approached his son, reaching him and putting his hand on Jason's tense shoulder.

"You're right, I should have said something."

"Next time, you hafta say something."

Prentice nodded. "Aye, I will."

Jason stared at him and Prentice held his stare. Then Jason nodded back and mumbled he was going to bed. Prentice went to his study and Fiona hovered with him until they heard Isabella come down the stairs. The minute he heard it, Prentice got up and walked into the great room, Fiona floating after him.

Isabella didn't hesitate or look at him, she went straight toward the hall.

"Goodnight, Prentice," she whispered, intent on (nearly) ignoring him.

Prentice had other ideas.

He took two long strides and his hand wrapped around her upper arm, halting her.

Fiona watched Isabella's hands ball into fists and she bit her ghostly lip.

She was beginning to hate it when Isabella did that.

Which was *a lot.*

Isabella's head tilted back and she looked at Prentice. "Is there something you want?"

"Aye," Prentice answered. "I want to know if Sally's asleep."

Isabella nodded. "Pj's on. I even got her to brush her teeth before getting into bed. I didn't get halfway through the book before she was out."

Prentice didn't move nor did he take his hand from Isabella's arm. She shrugged her shoulder, bringing his attention to his hand. He still didn't remove it.

"Prentice, I'm tired," she said and she *sounded* tired.

She sounded shattered.

"Today—" Prentice started.

"*No!*" Isabella's tone was sharp and it so surprised Prentice (and Fiona) that they both jerked (even Fiona).

Isabella twisted her arm but Prentice didn't let her go.

"Isabella—" Prentice began again.

She stopped twisting her arm and glared at him. "Let me go."

"I'll have a word with—"

Isabella turned to face him, her expression grew cold and her brows went up. "What word will you have, Prentice? And with who? And *why*? In four days I'm gone."

"But you still have four days."

She laughed.

It was an ugly sound.

Fiona felt something pierce her non-existent heart and she saw Prentice's body go completely still.

"Trust me, Prentice, in my life four days of this is nothing. Four days is a walk in the park."

Fiona saw Prentice's hand tighten just as his brows drew together.

"Maybe I'll take that offer you made a few days ago and you can explain," Prentice said quietly.

She twisted her arm and she did it viciously, winning freedom from Prentice's hand.

But she didn't move away.

"Too late," Isabella replied, her voice back to soft. "In four days, I'll be gone and you'll forget about me." She threw out her arm, a movement that signified the villagers. "They'll forget about me." She pointed up the stairs and her voice changed, it grew rough as if coated with unshed tears. "And *they'll* forget about me."

Prentice got closer. Isabella stepped back.

When Prentice spoke again, his voice had grown soft and rough with emotion too.

"You're not easy to forget."

Isabella's head tilted to the side as if genuinely perplexed.

"Really?" she asked quietly. "You could have fooled me."

With that successful parting shot, she turned on her booted foot and walked away.

Prentice watched her go. Then he watched the empty hall. Finally, as Fiona knew he'd do, he went to the study, got himself a whisky and went to the upstairs balcony to study the sea.

After some time, he went back to his study, refilled the glass and resumed his position on the balcony.

He left *that* glass on the railing beside the other one.

Chapter
SIX

Knight in Shining Armor

Isabella

Isabella sat in the car beside Mikey as he drove them back to Prentice's house after they'd had the formal tea with Annie's bridal party, select close, female friends and Mikey, Robert and Richard.

Today had not been as bad as yesterday mainly because there were very few villagers there (especially Hattie Fennick, who Isabella always thought kind of disliked her but then again, Hattie seemed to kind of dislike *everyone*) and Clarissa, Annie's Mom, had finally arrived and she was another one of the few people on the planet who liked Isabella.

Also making the day not so bad was the fact that Isabella only saw Prentice for a very brief period of time.

She'd woken early, done the ironing, had the coffee brewed and was pouring herself a second cup by the time Prentice came downstairs wearing, by the by, a shirt that was very handsome on him but *really* needed to be ironed.

His beautiful eyes never left her as he moved directly to the coffeepot, saying, "Morning, Isabella."

"I'm making the children breakfast," she blurted in reply, rather impolitely, and her voice didn't sound soft and foggy like it did when she was on the anti-depressants but almost, to her own ears, *defiant*.

His attention turned away from the cupboard from which he was pulling a mug to her and his brows were up.

His face changed, she didn't know how but it did.

"You are?" he asked quietly.

She instantly had second thoughts about defying Prentice Cameron. If yesterday was anything to go by, he could be moody, and if the days before were anything to go by, he could be *mean*.

She didn't reply, just held his stare.

"What are you making us?" he queried.

He said "us."

That word out of his mouth gave her a shiver up her spine.

Earlier, while she was ironing and psyching herself up to approach him about breakfast, she hadn't thought forward to what she was actually going to make, just that she was going to demand the right to make it.

She made a quick decision and announced, "A fry up."

He burst out laughing.

Isabella stared.

God, she forgot how handsome he was when he laughed. She thought she remembered but she sure as heck *didn't*.

Or, maybe it was that he looked better now.

She hid her reaction to his laughter and calmly waited until he got over his bizarre hilarity.

He turned his attention to the coffee, saying, "You feed my kids a fry up before school, they'll be asleep within fifteen minutes of hitting their desks."

"Children," Isabella retorted, her voice cold and authoritative, "I've read, need a good breakfast before school. Brain food."

Prentice turned to her, leaned a hip to the counter and sipped his coffee, his eyes never leaving her.

Then he replied, "Porridge is brain food. Make them porridge.

There's instant—"

She cut him off by declaring evenly, "I'm *not* making instant oatmeal."

He studied her for a long moment before he grinned and gave in, saying, "Suit yourself."

With relief, she tore her gaze from his sexy, grinning face and walked away, murmuring, "I will."

She didn't go the way of the fry up (it wouldn't be good if the kids fell asleep in school, that would be yet *another* thing the villagers could hold against her).

But she did make scrambled eggs with cheddar cheese, bacon and toast coated in butter and lime marmalade.

And she made it for all of them.

Including Prentice.

While the kids were leaving the kitchen and Prentice (she thought) was in his study, Isabella caught Jason and said, "I've done the ironing, including your father's shirts. Can you take them upstairs and put them away before school?"

"Can't I do it tonight?" Jason asked.

She leaned in conspiratorially and asked in a teasing tone, "Honey, have you seen his shirt?" She shook her head. "No, you can't do it tonight. You might forget and I don't know when I'll be back. It must be done," her voice lowered jokingly to indicate the gravity of the situation, "and it must be done *now*."

Jason grinned at her dramatic delivery then his eyes slid to the side, caught on something and he let out a little snicker.

Isabella felt the hairs on the back of her neck stand up. She slowly turned and saw Prentice there, arms crossed on his chest, eyes on her, facial expression indicating that, perhaps, he heard every word she said.

"Is there something wrong with my shirt?" he asked in a low tone.

Yes, he heard.

Oh dear. What did she do now?

Well, she might as well be honest.

Her eyes dropped to his chest then went back to his face.

"It's a lovely shirt. It just needs ironing."

His hands went to the buttons while he inquired, "Should I do that now?"

"No!" she (nearly) cried, taking a swift step forward and putting a hand up, *not* wanting to see his chest again, ever, until the day she died.

He went on, "I wouldn't want to embarrass the Cameron name."

He couldn't do that even if his shirt was in tatters.

And his pants.

He looked over her shoulder and winked at his son.

Isabella relaxed.

Prentice was teasing, not *her*, but Jason.

She could deal with that.

"I'll get you another shirt," she offered on a whisper, not looking at him and moving toward the mudroom.

"I'd be obliged," he murmured as she rounded him and felt his eyes on her.

There were, luckily, no more incidents but Sally demanded Isabella stand on the front steps and wave them away "until we're out of sight."

Which she did.

"How are things with Mr. Broody-Hot?" Mikey asked, taking Isabella out of her thoughts.

Mr. Broody-Hot. Where did Mikey come up with this stuff?

"If you mean Prentice," Isabella answered, "they're nearly one day closer to me being out of here."

"That bad?" Mikey asked quietly.

Isabella looked at her friend's profile. "Next time you love a man for twenty years, return to him and he thinks you jilted and made a fool of him and you have to sleep under his roof for a week, slowly falling in love with his two children then you can tell me how bad it is."

"I'd say that's bad," Mikey returned.

Isabella didn't reply because she didn't need to.

"You're falling in love with his children?" Mikey asked, voice still quiet.

Mikey knew *all* about her quest to get pregnant. He'd lived through it with her, though he'd been in Chicago and she'd been, well, globe-trotting with Laurent.

"There's a good deal to love."

Mikey sighed. "I noticed they're good kids."

Isabella was again silent.

"They like you," Mikey said.

Isabella looked out the window. "More fool them."

She felt Mikey squeeze her thigh. "There's a good deal to like, girlie-girl."

Hardly, she thought but she kept her silence.

Mikey slid to a halt outside Prentice's house and ogled it through her window as he had that morning when he came to pick her up.

"I've got to say, Bella darling, this house is *something else.*"

She couldn't agree more.

She stared at the house, sprawling and imposing on its cliff, somehow looking like it erupted from the cleft where it was situated and belonged there.

She hadn't seen any of his other work but if this was anything to go by, Prentice was very talented.

Not for the first time she thought her father was an idiot. Even Carver Austin, who could find fault in anything, wouldn't have been able to find fault with this house.

She pulled her eyes from the house and turned back to Mikey while saying, "Thanks for the ride."

But she said it to no one. Mikey was out of the door and closing it.

She didn't have a good feeling about this.

Isabella got out her side and slammed the door, calling, "Mikey, what're you doing?"

"Bumming a meal off Mr. Broody-Hot," Mikey scarily answered. "I'm famished."

Isabella, mind scrambled near to panic at the very idea of Mikey sharing a meal with Prentice and his family without a variety of other distractions available to Prentice, Sally, Jason *and* Mikey, opened the back door and grabbed one of the bags of groceries she'd bought (it was early enough for her to intervene in takeaway and she fully intended to do it).

"You'd be bumming a meal off *me*," she told Mikey. "I bought the food and I'm saying no, you can't stay."

Mikey reached in, grabbed the other bag then threw the door to. "You can't say no, it isn't your house."

"You can't stay," Isabella retorted, standing out in the crisp, chill air and perfectly willing to stand out there until Christmas if it took that long to talk him out of staying for dinner.

"Why on earth not?" Mikey inquired.

Mikey loved her unreservedly. Isabella had no problems being honest with Mikey.

"Because you can be unpredictable," she answered.

Mikey mixed with Prentice mixed with *Sally*, for God's sake. That was a recipe for *disaster*.

He grinned at her. "Life's a lot more fun that way."

Life was never fun at all in Isabella's estimation.

He started marching to the door, Isabella's panic escalated, she opened her mouth to protest but the door opened and Sally shot out of it, screeching, *"You're home!"*

Oh dear.

Sally entered the mix.

Sally came to a skidding halt and stared at Isabella.

"I *love* your outfit!" she shrieked.

"And I *love* this child," Mikey muttered.

Isabella gave him an "I told you so" look. Mikey smiled.

Sally started her dash again, collided with Isabella and threw her arms around Isabella's thighs.

Isabella steadied her body and allowed herself to let the sweet feeling of Sally's hug wash over her.

"She can hardly make you dinner if you hold her captive on the front walk, darling," Mikey drawled, but the smile was still on his face and his eyes were on Sally.

He said this just as Prentice hit the door.

Wonderful.

Prentice was now in the mix.

Sally threw her head back and yelled, "You're making dinner? *Again!* Hurrah!"

"Only if you haven't had something," Isabella answered, ignoring Prentice.

Sally disengaged but caught Isabella's hand, explaining, "Daddy was just going to order takeaway." She saw her father and shouted, "Daddy! Mrs. Evangahlala's home in time to make dinner!"

"I heard," Prentice replied dryly. "The village heard and we live five miles away."

They'd come abreast of Mikey and Sally leaned toward him and whispered loudly, "Daddy thinks I can be loud sometimes."

"Only way to be heard," Mikey replied blandly.

Sally grinned.

"Mikey," Isabella said in a warning tone.

"What?" Mikey asked, poorly feigning an innocent look.

Isabella gave him a glare then controlled her expression and transferred her gaze to Prentice who was blocking the door.

She stopped in front of him. "Mikey would like to stay for dinner, if that's all right with you."

"No," Mikey said, coming up behind her. "I *am* staying for dinner," he announced, eyes on Prentice. "I've made myself Bella's designated bodyguard."

Prentice's mouth got hard and Isabella held her breath.

"Why does Mrs. Evangahlala need a bodyguard? Is she famous?" Sally asked in a breathy voice and Mikey looked down at her.

"Mrs. Evangahlala is quite famous, cutie pie, but she doesn't normally need one. It's just here, where—"

"Well!" Isabella cried (also loudly), interrupting Mikey. "I better get a move on with dinner or it'll be the children's bedtime."

She lifted her brows at Prentice who still looked angry but he stepped forward and took her bag from her. She started to tighten her hold on it but realized it would be silly to wrestle over a grocery bag so she let go.

He moved to the side, motioning with a wide sweep of his arm that she should precede him and she quickly did so, dragging the lagging Sally, who still had hold of her hand, with her.

She and Sally hit the great room, Mikey and Prentice following and she saw Jason was on the couch, his feet flung over the back, a book in his hands.

His eyes came to her.

"Hey, Mrs. Evangelista."

"Hello, Jason."

"What *is* this Mrs. Evangelista business?" Mikey asked, going directly to the kitchen counter and dumping his bag. "She's feeding you. You should call her Bella."

"Mikey," Isabella said, again in a warning tone, and Sally danced to the kitchen, climbing up on a stool and rooting through the bag.

"What? Seriously, you've twice now bought them a boatload of food," Mikey returned.

Prentice was also depositing his bag in the kitchen and his head came around, his eyes pinning Isabella.

Well, one could say that Mikey didn't waste any time with creating havoc.

Then again, he never did.

"I thought Annie bought the food," Prentice said in a voice that was deeper, thus obviously not so happy.

Isabella opened her mouth to speak but Mikey, unfortunately, beat her to it.

"You didn't buy *that* did you?"

Prentice's eyes narrowed and Isabella wondered if Prentice would find it untoward if, in front of his children, she took off her pump and threw it at Mikey.

She figured he would.

Therefore, Isabella decided to ignore any of this was happening and focus on dinner.

And nothing but dinner.

Except maybe Sally.

And, of course, Jason.

"I'm going to get changed before I cook," Isabella announced and turned to her friend. "Mikey, come with me to see the pretty guest suite that—"

"No, darling, I'm going to stay here. Unpack groceries. Examine

Sally's fabulous manicure. Tour this spectacular house." He grinned at Isabella. "Take your time."

Well, maybe she couldn't ignore everything and focus on dinner because she sure as heck couldn't leave Mikey *alone* with Prentice and his family.

"Really, Mikey, you need to see the guest suite. It's lovely," she pressed.

"Really, darling, I *need* a cocktail." He turned to Prentice. "What do you have to drink around here?"

"Whisky," Prentice replied shortly, having come to the edge of the counter that led to the great room and leaned a hip against it, arms crossed, face closed, now so, *very* (and obviously) not so happy.

Mikey stared at him and waited for his list of other alcoholic beverages on the premises that were available to be consumed to continue.

Prentice didn't say another word.

"Whisky it is then," Mikey muttered.

Prentice walked to the study.

Isabella made a split second decision and followed.

At the double doors, she grabbed one doorknob then reached for the other, leveled her eyes on Mikey and mouthed, "Stay and be good."

She closed the doors and turned to Prentice.

His side was to her but his neck was twisted so he could face her. He still didn't look happy.

She couldn't stop herself from licking her lips. Prentice's eyes dropped to her mouth.

She caught her breath, crossed her arms on her middle and hugged her elbows.

Then she launched in, "I'm sorry about Mikey. He can be a bit overwhelming."

Without a word Prentice turned toward a cabinet, opened it and pulled out two glasses and a very good bottle of whisky that was also mostly empty.

"He can be overprotective," she went on as Prentice poured the whisky but he still didn't speak.

Isabella continued, "And he doesn't fancy Robert or Richard and

I think he's kind of bored at Fergus's house, considering Annie spends most of her time with Dougal . . . when she's not wedding planning, that is."

Prentice put away the whisky but he did so silently.

Once he was done, he turned to face her.

"It'll be okay eventually. He'll calm down. You just can't," she hesitated, "*listen* to anything he says." She paused again. "Or take him seriously." She drew in breath before she finished, "At all."

Prentice remained silent and simply regarded her.

"I'll buy you more whisky," she told him.

Prentice finally spoke. "I think you've bought enough, don't you?"

Oh dear.

He wasn't happy about the groceries.

But he wasn't done.

His eyes swept her from top to toe and then they settled on her face, "Go get changed, Isabella. You're in a family home in the wilds of Scotland, not about to step out with the glitterati."

There it was again. The non-physical slap.

She barely held back a flinch but she managed it.

"Of course," she muttered, starting to turn to the door.

"It makes me wonder," Prentice started conversationally, she turned back and saw his gaze was speculative.

"What makes you wonder?" she asked when he didn't continue.

"This," he replied nonsensically.

"What?"

"This desperate warning not to pay attention to your best friend. It makes me wonder what secrets you're keeping."

"I'm not keeping any secrets," she replied softly and it wasn't exactly a lie.

It was just that he lost the privilege to know her secrets twenty years ago when he walked out of Fergus's living room and didn't look back.

Prentice went on, "If you don't mind, I think I'll pay close attention to *everything* he says."

As a matter of fact, she *did* mind.

Mikey could be considered certifiably insane on entire continents. No one knew what was going to come out of his mouth. That was why he was still single.

Furthermore, why would Prentice *care*?

"If you'll open the doors, Isabella, I'd like to serve my guest his drink."

With nothing else for it, she opened the doors and walked out beside Prentice.

"Thank *God*! My cocktail," Mikey exclaimed.

Isabella gave him a look that would turn marble into sand but it bounced off Mikey. She smiled weakly at Sally and Jason. She ignored Prentice completely. Then she turned on her spike-heeled pump and used everything she had to force herself to walk calmly down the hall and to the guest suite.

Once there, she dashed around like a crazed demon, yanking off her (very pretty, she thought, still it *was* expensive but then practically everything she owned was expensive, she was rich, for God's sake!) sapphire-blue dress. She tugged off her matching sapphire-blue suede pumps and pulled on a pair of jeans and a sage-green, tunic-style sweater. It had a boat neck and bell sleeves and was hand-knit from the finest wool by what could only be considered a craftsman. It was one of a kind and cost a mint.

It would have to do.

She snatched the bobby pins out of the complicated chignon she'd fashioned at her nape (she'd always been good with hair, it was one of her few true talents, even her father begrudgingly admitted that) and shook out her hair. Once she'd done that, she piled it up on her head in a messy knot and fastened it loosely with a ponytail holder.

She allowed herself a split second to look in the mirror to see if she was fit for spending the evening in "a family home in the wilds of Scotland."

She decided she wasn't but she took off out the door anyway.

When she hit the kitchen, Sally and Mikey were in it, Jason was seated at the counter and a quick glance showed that Prentice was on the phone in his study.

Maybe her luck had changed.

"We've decided to call you Miss Bella!" Sally shrieked from her place on the stool at the counter, tea towels already wrapped around her.

"Have you, now?" Isabella muttered, entering the kitchen to see the groceries unpacked, the peas were at the boil and the water for the noodles was already at a flame on the stove.

At least Mikey had some uses.

"Mister Mikey says I can help," Sally announced.

Isabella gave her a smile and started to get busy. "That you can, sweetheart. Your choice, you can do the crunchy bit or the smushy bit."

"Can I do both?" Sally asked.

Isabella set a bowl in front of her, leaned in to kiss the top of her head and murmured there, "Why not?"

Sally threw both her hands up, nearly hitting Isabella in the jaw and shouted, "Hurrah!"

"Mental," Jason mumbled.

Isabella looked at him and chuckled.

"I wish I found making tuna casserole so exciting," Mikey re-marked, carrying his whisky around the counter to sit beside Jason.

"You're too cynical," Isabella told him, opening cans of mushroom soup. "Making tuna casserole *is* exciting."

And it was when one was making it for Prentice, his family and one's best friend.

"*She's* mental," Mikey stage-whispered to Jason, and Jason grinned as Prentice joined them from the other room.

Well, that reprieve didn't last long.

Sally didn't waste any time getting Prentice up to speed.

"Mister Mikey says we can call Mrs. Evangahlala, Miss Bella and I'm doing the crunchy *and* smushy bits for dinner."

"Crunchy and smushy," Prentice murmured, his eyes warm on his daughter. "Sounds like dinner is going to be interesting."

"Tuna casserola!" Sally shouted and Prentice looked at Isabella.

Isabella busied herself with draining the tuna.

"Have you had her tuna casserole?" Prentice asked.

She looked over her shoulder and saw he was talking to Mikey. The palms of his hands were at the edge of the counter and he pushed up to sit on it.

"I've sampled Bella's entire culinary arsenal," Mikey replied. "It must be said, the woman can cook."

"We know. She made us chicken fingers, homemade, the other night. They were brilliant," Jason put in.

Isabella ducked her head and bit her lip at the compliment while she went to stand behind Sally and set the cans around the bowl.

"All right, honey, we need to dump all this into the bowl and then smush it together. Yes?" she told the girl softly and Sally nodded exuberantly.

She handed Sally a spoon and Sally went straight for the mushroom soup as Isabella, her arms around Sally, her eyes looking over the girl's shoulder, used a fork to flake out the tuna.

Isabella was attempting to ignore *everything* and focus on the food and Sally.

This was difficult.

It became more difficult.

"Isabella doesn't seem the type of woman to have tuna casserole in her culinary arsenal," Prentice commented and Isabella felt her shoulders get tight.

Didn't he remember she cooked for him all the time twenty years ago?

Didn't he remember *what* she'd cook for him?

She'd never made him tuna casserole, of course, that was winter food and she was only there in the summers.

But, still . . .

Mikey laughed, loud and with great hilarity.

When he was done, still chuckling, he replied, "Bella's the Queen of Comfort Food. She used to cook all the time when she, Annie and I shared an apartment at Northwestern. Annie and I both gained fifteen pounds, *each year*."

That wasn't true. Mikey had gained twenty pounds.

"Did you meet her at uni?" Prentice asked.

"Sure did," Mikey replied. "I saw her walking on campus our freshman year and I said to myself, 'Who *is* that *gorgeous* girl with those *sad* eyes? She needs a little bit of Mikey in her life.'"

Isabella's hands stilled but only for a moment.

Then she whispered in Sally's ear, "I have to get the peas. Keep scooping."

"Sad eyes?" Prentice asked, his voice had grown quiet.

"Yep," Mikey answered shortly and also quietly.

"Why were you sad, Miss Bella?" Jason called.

Isabella dumped the peas in a colander, put them under a cold tap and turned to Jason.

"If memory serves, I stubbed my toe," she lied. Jason's head tilted to the side, Isabella felt Prentice's eyes on her as well as Mikey's and she ignored that too. "Badly. And everyone knows it hurts to stub your toe."

"I hate stubbing my toe," Sally declared, smushing the tuna and soup together. "It *does* hurt. That would make *me* sad."

Thank goodness for Sally.

"You shared an apartment?" Prentice asked, unfortunately deciding this once to ignore his daughter.

And he asked even though he knew the answer. Or, maybe, he didn't remember.

Isabella shook the water off the peas as Mikey answered, "Yep, sophomore and junior year."

"Not your last year?" Prentice sounded surprised and she knew why.

Because he remembered.

And suddenly Isabella found it *most* irritating that Prentice had a good memory.

She knew that he knew, because she told him, that she shared an apartment with Annie and Mikey and that they'd be going back to it their senior year.

Except they didn't.

Well, Mikey did, but Annie and Isabella didn't.

Annie was in hospital then in rehab. Isabella was on house arrest after her father found out about her "tryst" with Prentice.

However, she was allowed to go to class and also to help Annie.

"Nope," Mikey answered.

"Why not?" Prentice queried.

Isabella turned from draining the peas, placed a tea towel under them and walked back to Sally, sending Mikey a pleading look.

Mikey ignored her altogether and kept right on talking.

"Because Bella was closer to Annie at home." He waved his whisky glass around and went on, "Would take forever for her to drive from Northwestern to Clarissa's every day." Mikey looked at Jason and announced, "Florence Nightingale is making you tuna casserole, bucko. Count yourself lucky."

"Who's Florence Nightingale?" Sally asked.

"She's an angel from heaven," Mikey answered.

"*Really?*" Sally breathed.

Isabella disregarded this, poured the peas into the bowl Sally was mixing and, attempting to shift the conversation, advised, "Be careful now, stir it gently. You don't want to smush up the peas too much."

Prentice decided against going with Isabella's lame attempt at changing the topic of conversation.

"Florence Nightingale wasn't an angel from heaven, Sally. She was a nurse," Prentice informed his daughter.

"As was Bella when Annie was sick," Mikey put in.

"You're a nurse?" Jason asked Isabella.

"No," Isabella answered. Having put the colander in the sink, she was opening the bag of pasta.

"I don't get it," Jason muttered.

"Neither do I," Prentice added.

"Jason," Mikey started and Isabella turned to him and shook her head but he took no notice of her, "a long time ago, Annie was in a terrible car crash. Did you know that?"

Sally had stopped smushing and Isabella couldn't see her face but she could see Jason's.

"Mikey," Isabella said softly.

"Well, she's all right now. Everyone can see that," Mikey defended.

Isabella tightened her fists and let her glance slide to Prentice who was silently watching Mikey, obviously not going to intervene.

She turned to the boiling water on the stove and poured in the noodles.

"I know about it. Mum told me that's why she limps sometimes and has that scar on her face," Jason said quietly.

"Yes, well, back then," Mikey continued, "she was really sick. And she was really sad. And she didn't want to get better."

"Why wouldn't she want to get better?" Jason asked.

"Because she was sad and being sad makes you do silly things," Mikey answered. "She wouldn't listen to anyone. Wouldn't go to the hospital so they could make her better. So, Bella *made* her go to the hospital. Three times a week she showed up at Annie's house and took her there herself. Every other day, she went to Annie's house and made her do her exercises so she could get strong and fit. Annie was sad and upset and she didn't like this and she could be mean to Bella. But Bella didn't care. She took every mean thing Annie had to dish out, and there was a lot, bucko, let me tell you. But it didn't penetrate our girl here. She took every mean thing Annie threw at her and she helped her friend get better. Like a nurse. Like an angel from heaven."

When Mikey got close to the end of his story, he was whispering. When he stopped talking, the room was silent. Isabella ignored it, her back to the room and she stirred the noodles.

After several long moments, Mikey called, "Bella?"

"Can we stop talking about Annie's accident?" Isabella softly asked the noodles.

More silence.

Then, also speaking softly, Prentice ordered, "Jason, set the table, mate."

"Okay, Dad," Jason replied quickly.

Isabella would have given Prentice a grateful look if he existed in her world at that moment.

Since he didn't and only the noodles did, she continued to stir them.

"Are we having pudding?" Sally asked her back.

Isabella took in a deep breath, turned down the noodles, allowed the family home in the wilds of Scotland and its inhabitants to penetrate her mental health fortress and turned to smile at the girl.

"Apple crumble and custard," she answered.

"Hurrah!" Sally cheered.

Carefully avoiding Prentice's eyes, she set about getting the ingredients for the topping so that Sally could make the crunchy part.

And she silently prayed the night wouldn't get any worse.

She should have prayed harder.

———— ◆ ————

DINNER WASN'T *THAT* bad.

Though it wasn't *good* either.

Actually, Isabella could just say it didn't kill her.

Though it left her wanting to kill someone, namely Mikey.

The best part of the evening was that Prentice unearthed a bottle of wine.

The rest didn't go so well.

The peas in the tuna casserole were smushed to mush but it didn't taste bad, mainly because Isabella added tons of cheese and cheese makes anything taste better, not to mention Sally's crunchy bit concoction for the topping (with Isabella's helping hand) was first-rate.

Mikey had decided the sad story part of the evening was over and regaled them with tales of Annie, Isabella and himself doing crazy things while at college.

Neither of these were the reasons why the dinner was murder plot worthy.

It went bad when Prentice queried, "When did you three find time to study?"

"We *two* got by on a wing and a prayer," Mikey returned. "Bella burned the candle at both ends and graduated summa cum laude. She even made deals with her professors when she had to miss classes to be with Annie."

Prentice's eyes cut to her and Isabella's eyes cut to her empty plate.

"That's impressive," Prentice said it like he meant it.

"That's Bella," Mikey remarked and then finished in a tone filled with acid, "No way she was going to take home anything but top marks to that father of hers."

At that, Isabella's head shot up and she actually *felt* her face grow pale. Then, quick as a flash, she threw her napkin on the table and stood up.

"Seconds for anyone?" she asked the table at large.

Jason and Sally both looked startled. As did Mikey.

Prentice's eyes were locked on her and his brows had knitted.

"My first portion was fit for an elephant, so, no, I don't want seconds," Mikey replied.

"I want pudding!" Sally cried.

"I could take seconds," Jason answered and Isabella could have kissed him.

"I'll get the casserole," she declared, bent to Sally and whispered, "Pudding in a second, sweetheart." Then she walked as calmly as she could to the kitchen.

"You know her father, of course," Prentice said as she moved away and his voice had a tinge of acid as well.

Isabella's fingers curled into her palms tightly and briefly, the flash of pain not near enough to get her through *this*.

"The Wicked Warlock of Chicago?" Mikey drawled. "Wish I didn't but I do."

Bella wished at that moment for the first time in her life that she didn't know Mikey.

"The wicked what of what?" Jason asked, his voice tinged with humor.

"You know Annie and Dougal are a Scottish fairytale *come alive?*" Mikey asked Jason as Isabella returned with the casserole dish and scooped a heavy spoonful onto Jason's plate.

"What?" Jason asked, voice now tinged with confusion but also still with humor.

And who could blame him.

Where was Mikey going with *this*?

It was only seconds later Isabella found out she didn't want to know.

Mikey waved his hand around. "Separated for decades by tragedy, reunited, getting married, the whole fairytale come alive. That's Annie and Dougal. Well, Bella's fairytale includes a wicked warlock of a father and an evil duke who stole her away and was a cad and a bounder. But she finally escaped him and now she's waiting for her knight in shining armor," Mikey explained.

Isabella stood, holding the mostly empty casserole dish, staring at Mikey in horror.

Jason and Sally were both staring at Mikey with rapt faces. Then their eyes moved to Isabella.

That whole time, Prentice was simply staring at Isabella.

"You were married to a duke?" Jason asked.

"No, she was married to a—" Mikey started.

Isabella swiftly interrupted him by asking, "Prentice, do you want seconds?"

His eyes still locked on her, Prentice shook his head.

She walked directly to the kitchen wishing she could ignore this but she damn well couldn't.

Sally turned to her father and asked, "Daddy, what's a bounder?"

"Aye, and what's a cad?" Jason asked right after Sally.

Isabella wondered how long it would take for Mikey's body to wash ashore after she threw him over a cliff.

And, also, would they consider foul play if it was just a push?

"Both are names for not very nice men," Prentice answered his children.

"I don't like Miss Bella being with a not very nice man," Sally said quietly.

Well, maybe Isabella would stab Mikey before pushing him.

Or, at least, conk him on the head.

"I don't either," Jason mumbled.

No, she decided she'd go with stabbing.

"How'd you get away from the evil duke?" Sally yelled as Isabella slid the apple crumble out of the oven and put it on a hot pad.

"She divorced him," Mikey answered for her. "And took a boatload of his money with her when she did, thank God."

Isabella rolled her eyes heavenward. She rolled them back and switched off the oven.

"Is she rich?" Jason asked, now amazement was tingeing his voice.

"Filthy," Mikey answered.

"Miss Bella's not filthy," Sally stated crossly.

"Filthy *rich*, cutie pie," Mikey amended.

Sally looked to her father as Isabella reluctantly resumed her seat next to the girl. "What's that mean?"

"It means Miss Bella has a lot of money, baby," Prentice answered, eyes on his daughter.

"Then *Miss Bella* can buy me a horse!" Sally shouted, turning bright eyes to Isabella.

Isabella turned irate eyes to Mikey.

Mikey grinned.

"She's not going to buy you a horse," Prentice stated.

"But—" Sally began.

"No," Prentice's tone was firm and unyielding.

Sally's face drooped into a pout, and Isabella decided she'd conk Mikey on the head *before* stabbing him and *then* she'd push him over a cliff.

But before that, she had to make it through the night.

She turned to Sally. "I can't buy you a horse, honey, but you can help me make the custard."

"I like custard but I like horses better," Sally retorted through her pout.

Isabella wrinkled her nose and replied, "Horses smell funny and they eat a lot. Custard smells yummy and *you* get to eat it."

"Do *you* have a horse?" Sally asked and Isabella shook her head. "A dog?" she went on and Isabella kept shaking her head. "A cat?" Sally continued and Isabella grinned but kept shaking her head.

"I had a fish once," she told the girl.

"You can't pet a fish," Sally returned.

"This is true," Isabella murmured.

"And you can't ride it, unless it was a dolphin. Was it a dolphin?" Sally asked.

"It was a goldfish and you couldn't ride it. But it had a frilly tail and I named it Goldie."

Sally gave herself a moment to consider this information.

Then she concluded, "A horse is better than a fish."

Isabella's grin widened to a smile and she leaned into Sally. "You got me there. A horse is definitely better than a fish. But horses are still smelly and eat too much. Now, do you want to help with the custard or not?"

Sally gave herself a moment to consider this as well, the pout disappeared, her eyes lit up and she awarded Isabella with a small grin.

"I wanna help with the custard," Sally answered.

"Good girl," Isabella whispered then looked at the table.

Jason was watching them with a goofy grin on his face.

Mikey was watching Prentice with a satisfied grin on his face.

Prentice was watching Isabella with an unreadable expression on his face.

Isabella decided to ignore it all and wait for Jason to finish his second helping.

"Do you want me to warm that up?" she asked Jason with a polite nod of her head to his plate.

Jason took the hint and started eating.

Mikey chuckled.

Prentice took a sip from his wine without taking his eyes off Isabella.

Sally asked, "Do we have to wait for Jace to finish to make the custard?"

"Yes," Isabella replied at the exact same time Prentice answered, "Aye."

At that, Mikey, for some barking mad reason, burst out laughing.

———— ◆ ————

IT TOOK TWO and a half books to get Sally to sleep that night likely because she was wound up over dinner and guests and tales of knights in shining armor who had not yet arrived.

After tucking her in tightly and turning out the light, Isabella hustled out of her room.

Mikey had been downstairs alone with Prentice for two and a half books. No telling what antics he'd get up to.

She quickly walked down the dark hall and was closing on the stairs when she heard the end of something Prentice was saying.

" . . . Jason and Sally."

To which Mikey immediately replied, "Of course she would. She lost her mother when she was eight. It isn't the same, considering her mother slit her wrists, but she still lost her."

Isabella's body rocked to a halt and she stood, statue still, out of sight at the top of the stairs.

She'd never told Prentice about how her mother had died. She wanted to, she'd even rehearsed what to say, but she never found the right time.

And, if she was honest with herself, she didn't want him to think bad things about her mother or *her* and what her mother's act might make him think about Isabella.

There were bad vibes rolling up the stairs and pounding against Isabella but her mind was blank with panic and her body was numb with fear.

"I'm sorry?" Prentice asked softly.

"You didn't know?" Mikey replied, then after a long, pregnant moment, he muttered, "Oh my God, you didn't know."

There was more silence, more bad vibes rolling and Isabella didn't move a muscle.

Mikey decided he hadn't yet finished sharing. "She found her, Prentice. Eight years old and Bella found her mother in a bathtub filled with blood."

Isabella's mind shut out the rest of the words and she took a step back then another one, automatically seeking retreat.

She ran into something.

She whirled and stared at Jason who was standing behind her in the dark but she could see his face was white as a sheet.

He'd heard.

"Jason," she whispered, horror saturating her.

"Your mum died when you were eight?" Jason whispered back.

"Jason," Isabella repeated, her mind unfocused, unable to think of anything else to say.

"*You found her?*"

It was a shout, a shout filled with sheer agony, and it felt like it tore apart her ears and her heart.

She instantly dropped to a knee and grabbed Jason's hands as she heard quick footfalls on the stairs.

"Jason, listen to me, it was a long time ago," she whispered urgently.

"You found her," Jason repeated, and Isabella felt Prentice with them but her eyes were riveted on his son.

"A long time ago, Jason."

"Your mum's dead, like mine."

She scooted closer, squeezing his hands, and whispered, "Honey."

He shook his hands free but he didn't run away.

He threw his body into hers, nearly taking her off-balance, and his arms closed around her so tight it hurt.

It didn't hurt her body. It hurt her heart.

Isabella gathered him close.

"You know how it feels," he mumbled into her neck, his voice thick with unshed tears.

She melted into his ten-year-old grieving boy's arms.

"I know how it feels, sweetheart," she whispered, her hands moving on his back.

"You know how it feels," he repeated.

"Yes, sweetheart."

"Jace, come here, mate," Prentice said gently from close, and Isabella could feel a soft tug pulling Jason's body from her arms but Jason stayed fix and the tugging stopped.

"Does it still hurt?" Jason asked, and Isabella closed her eyes, stopped stroking his back and held on to the boy even tighter.

What she didn't do was answer.

Jason pulled a little bit away and looked in her eyes.

After what felt like an eternity, he muttered, "It still hurts."

She should lie. It would make it easier at that moment for both of them.

But he'd eventually know she lied and she didn't want Jason Cameron to think she was a liar.

Ever.

So she didn't lie.

Instead, Isabella put her hands to either side of his head, leaned in close and said quietly, "I'm sorry, Jason, but yes, it still hurts."

He swallowed.

Then he nodded.

And with that he pulled away, turned and walked to his room.

Isabella didn't look at Prentice as she straightened but when she was upright she saw his broad-shouldered back turning into his son's room.

Slowly, she walked down the stairs. Mikey was standing, face pale as a ghost, in front of the couch.

Isabella wished she felt fury. Instead, she felt nothing but heartache.

When she got close, Mikey asked in a low voice, "Girlie-girl, why didn't you tell him?"

She shook her head, too weak even to speak.

And besides, what little strength she had she was using to stop herself from weeping.

"Tonight . . . all my stories . . . he didn't . . ." Mikey stopped and his eyes grew narrow with confusion and sadness. "When you were with him, did you tell him *anything*?"

She shook her head but this time, she explained.

"When I was here, I wasn't that girl with sad eyes," Isabella whispered in a voice that could barely be heard. "When I was with him, I could be free."

"Oh darling," Mikey muttered, pulling her in for a close hug and he hugged her for a long time. Finally he murmured in her ear, "Walk me to the door, darling."

She did as she was told.

He hugged her again at the door and then looked her in the eyes.

"You should tell him, you know. Everything."

It's too late, way too late, she thought.

But she said nothing.

Mikey gave her a look before he sighed, kissed her temple and walked out the door.

Isabella went back into the great room and stood motionless, waiting for Prentice to return. It felt like years but was more likely five minutes when she saw him walk down the stairs.

He stopped four feet away from her, his beautiful, every-colored eyes locked on her, his face closed.

"I'm sorry," she whispered.

"It wasn't your fault," he replied.

"I'm still sorry," she pushed.

He gave a jerk of his chin but said nothing else.

"Is he okay?" Isabella asked.

"He will be," Prentice answered.

Isabella slowly closed her eyes.

She opened them and repeated, "I'm so sorry."

Prentice didn't reply.

Isabella squared her shoulders and licked her lips, waiting for him to say something.

He said nothing. In fact, he looked like he was waiting for *her* to say something.

She pulled in a deep breath. She let it go.

Then she said something.

"I'll just . . . head to bed," she told him.

He didn't say a word.

She turned to the hall.

"Fifteen months," Prentice said.

She turned back to Prentice.

"Pardon?" she asked.

"Fifteen months we were together and you didn't say a fucking word. We spent every minute we could together when you were here and when you weren't we spent every minute we could talking and you didn't say a fucking *word*." Isabella felt her heart start beating faster but Prentice wasn't finished. "Did you give a fuck about me at all?"

Bile started climbing up her throat, she ignored it, clenched her hands in fists and simply replied, "Prentice."

"No." He shook his head. "You didn't. If you did, you would have fucking shared your life with me. At least part of it. You didn't share fuck all. I was in love with you, I asked you to *marry* me, for fuck's sake, and I didn't even know you."

Her heart stopped beating faster and started slamming against her chest, her nails tore fiercely into her palms and her eyes flew to the stairs.

"Prentice, the children," she warned.

"Tell me now," he demanded.

Her eyes jerked to him and her heart stopped.

"What?" she breathed.

"All of it, Isabella. Tell me now."

"But . . . why?" she stammered.

He leaned forward at the waist and clipped, "God damn it, tell me *now.*"

Isabella could take no more.

"Why?" she snapped, throwing her unclenched hand through the air. "What does it matter now?"

But he wasn't paying attention to her. His eyes had followed her hand.

"Jesus," he muttered, anger out of his voice, gaze still on her hand. "You're bleeding."

She quickly looked at her palm, saw he was right and closed her hand into a fist.

As she did this, he advanced so he was close.

Very close.

She tipped her head back to look at him and declared, "It's nothing."

His head was bent toward her hand, his fingers closed on her wrist and he said, "Elle, you're bleeding. Let me look."

Isabella blinked, feeling the name only he used wash over her like she hadn't had a bath in decades and that name was warm, clean water.

"Open your hand," he ordered. His thumb insistently pressing on her fingers, he looked distractedly over his shoulder to the kitchen and asked, "Did you break a glass washing up?"

"It's nothing," she repeated.

His head came back around and he lifted her hand between them, thumb unrelenting, trying to open her closed fist.

"Let me see," he murmured coaxingly.

Panic stricken, she jerked her wrist and he lost hold. When he did, his gaze snapped to hers.

"I said, it's nothing," she whispered.

Prentice stared at her.

Isabella took a step back, holding her wrist where his hand was, feeling his warm strength still there. Memorizing it, she pressed her hand against her chest.

His eyes dropped to her hand. Then they went back to hers.

And they were cold. So cold, she shivered.

"Secrets," he said softly, his voice awful. "Which is the same as lies. Secrets and fucking lies."

She held his gaze, it cost her but she held it and didn't breathe a word.

After long moments, Prentice looked to the floor and shook his head.

He turned away and asked, "Turn the lights out, will you?"

Then he walked up the stairs and disappeared from sight.

Chapter
SEVEN

Elle

Prentice

Prentice stood on the terrace of the pub, whisky in hand, eyes on the sea.

Two days it had been since he'd discovered Isabella had *not* abandoned her best friend in her hour of need but, against the odds (and Annie could be stubborn so Prentice knew the odds were most assuredly against Isabella), she'd nursed Annie back to her old self.

Two days it had been since he'd discovered she'd endured only the beginning but most definitely not the end of a fairytale.

And two days since he'd discovered that, at eight years old, she'd found her dead mother in a pool of her own blood.

His hand tightened on the glass as his jaw tensed.

He hadn't handled that *last* very well. In fact, he'd been a complete, selfish jackass.

It had been two days and those two days had not been uneventful.

To say the least.

The first morning after dinner with Mikey, Prentice had woken up to find his closet full of ironed shirts.

When he went downstairs, he found the coffeepot full.

Isabella was not there, however, and didn't make an appearance until the children came downstairs.

Then she arrived wearing jeans and a thin, mostly see-through, skintight, scoop-necked, cream T-shirt with a camisole under it. Her feet were bare but her wild, tangle of hair had been sleeked and pulled into sophisticated ponytail at the back of her head and she'd made up her face.

She also had a band of white gauze wrapped around her hand.

She'd arrived to make breakfast, chat with the children and ignore Prentice.

Sally was unaware of the drama the night before though she was highly curious as to the white gauze which Isabella airily informed his daughter was "nothing."

After what occurred the night before, Jason, it appeared, had formed some kind of motherless-child bond with Isabella and decided to cast himself as her protector. He was watching her carefully as if she was made of fragile crystal and he was going to be there to catch her before she fell and shattered on the floor.

Isabella quickly realized this and just as quickly (and skillfully) teamed up with Sally, using his daughter's constant good cheer and Isabella's own charm to tease and joke with Jason until he was smiling and even laughing.

It was quite a feat but she mastered it effortlessly.

When the children disappeared to get their books, without a word, Isabella headed to the hall.

"Isabella," he called.

She stopped and turned polite eyes to him in inquiry.

He looked at her and realized they were, indeed, playing a game.

It was the game of life. His life and his children's life.

And also Isabella's.

Too much had passed, he'd moved on and so had she, neither, it seemed, to things that ended well.

But this game didn't have to end ugly and his children needed every friend in their life they could get.

And Prentice thought Isabella would make a good one.

With a new strategy in mind, Prentice walked directly to her and got close.

She stiffened but didn't retreat, simply tipped her head back and looked at him, eyebrows raised.

"We need to talk," he told her.

"There's nothing to say," she replied, her tone cultured, controlled, remote.

"You're wrong," he returned.

Her face remained polite but expressionless. "Well then, there's no time. You have to take the kids to school and I'm going to Annie's and I won't be home tonight. It's her hen night tonight, it'll go late and I'll probably crash on the couch at Fergus's."

"We'll talk tomorrow."

She shook her head. "Tomorrow is the day before the wedding. I'll be tied up all day helping Annie and tomorrow night is Dougal's stag night."

He got closer and her body went solid as a rock.

This he took as a good sign.

He dipped his face close to hers, willing for some flash of *something* to light in her eyes, but he got nothing.

"You don't have to explain the schedule to me, Isabella, I know it," he said quietly.

"Then you know there's no time to talk."

"We'll make time."

She remained silent and remote.

He decided to change subjects and asked, "How's your hand?"

Then it came.

Her eyes flashed and her gaze moved over his shoulder.

"It's fine."

"That's good," he replied softly.

Her gaze shot back to his.

She opened her mouth to speak but he got there before her. "I have to admit, you look nice, Elle, but you look better when your hair's a mess and you aren't wearing that mask."

And it came again.

Her eyes grew slightly wider and her lips parted softly.

He took in her open expression of astonishment and finished by muttering, "Beautiful."

Then he walked away.

———— • ————

THAT DAY, ON a visit to one of his building sites, Prentice approached Nigel Fennick, who was a laborer on the site.

Nigel gave him a chin's up and said on a grin, "Dougal's stag night still on for Friday?"

"Aye," Prentice replied. "Annie's hen night is tonight."

Nigel's grin widened. "Annie can be a wild one."

Prentice knew that, hell, everyone knew that. Even so, he didn't return Nigel's grin.

"I want to talk to you about Hattie," Prentice said and Nigel's grin faded.

"Had calls from Fergus. Dougal too," Nigel surprised him by saying. "They gave me an earful, mate, but you know Hattie."

Prentice did. He'd known her all his life and he never really liked her. He liked her less after her behavior at the picnic.

"She going on Annie's hen night?" Prentice asked.

"Aye," Nigel nodded.

"She'll be nice to Isabella," Prentice stated.

It wasn't a request, it was a demand.

Nigel gave him a look. "Never was able to control Hattie."

He was right. Nigel and Hattie had been married for nearly two decades and she wasn't nice to her husband either.

"You'll have a word." Another demand.

"Already did, after Fergus and after Dougal. She's got it in her head—"

Prentice cut him off by repeating, "You'll have a word."

"Prentice—"

"Nigel, have a word with her."

Nigel's look turned probing. "Mate," he said softly, "things have got to be rough with Fiona gone but you're not . . . not again."

Prentice got closer. "This isn't about me and Isabella. This is just about Isabella. She's here for her friend and she's been good to the children. If you won't have a word, I'll have a word." Prentice pulled his mobile from his back pocket. "Give me her number."

Nigel's look turned incredulous and, Prentice noted with surprise, slightly fearful. "Now?"

Prentice's look was already hard. "Aye. Now."

Nigel hesitated before he sighed, "I'll have a word."

Prentice nodded. "It doesn't work, Nigel, and I hear Elle didn't have a good night then *I'll* have a word with Hattie."

The threat hung in the air for a moment before Nigel dipped his chin in acknowledgement.

Prentice was a man known not to make idle threats.

"See you Friday," Prentice said by way of farewell.

"Aye, Friday."

Prentice turned and walked away.

————◆————

THE CHILDREN HAD not had to endure takeaway that night.

This was because, when Prentice and the kids came home, Jason found a note on the counter from Isabella informing them there was a shepherd's pie in the fridge, explaining how to heat it up and telling them that the vegetables were already cut up and ready for boiling.

Jason may have found the note but Sally honed right in on the homemade chocolate cake that was sitting on the counter.

"PS," Jason read as Sally was screeching about the cake, "tell Sally I've made cake for pudding but she has to eat all her broccoli. There's ice cream in the freezer."

When he was finished reading, Jason's eyes moved to Prentice.

Sally danced around the kitchen chanting how much she *loved* chocolate cake.

Prentice smiled at his son.

His son smiled back.

———◆———

MIKEY WAS RIGHT.

Isabella could cook comfort food.

The shepherd's pie was delicious.

And the cake was fucking exquisite.

But Prentice overcooked the vegetables.

———◆———

IT WAS PITCH dark when Prentice jerked from a deep sleep, body alert after hearing the crash.

Tense, he listened to the sounds of his house for a moment and he could have sworn he heard a loud, drunken giggle.

He threw back the covers, knifed out of bed, exited his room and flipped the light switch on at the top of the stairs.

The lamp by the couch was on the floor, its ceramic base in pieces.

He was walking down the stairs when he saw movement in the hall. It was Isabella walking into the room wielding a broom.

Or, more accurately, Isabella *weaving* into the hall wielding a broom.

When she saw him, she stopped dead but her body swayed.

Then she smiled a huge, radiant smile that started at her hazel eyes and lit her entire face.

At the sight of her smile, Prentice felt the warmth of that satisfying weight hit his gut.

"Hi!" she cried happily as if it was the height of pleasure to see him.

"Isabella."

She stared at him a moment or, more to the point, she stared at his *mouth* a moment. Then she looked at the broom in her hand as if she'd never seen one before and had no idea why she was carrying it.

Light dawned, her face fell and she looked back at Prentice, admitting, "I broke your lamp."

He started to come into the room. "I can see. I could also *hear*."

"I'll buy you another one," she told him immediately.

He shook his head. "You don't have to buy another one."

Her face lit again and she declared gleefully, "I'll buy you three!"

He barely stopped himself from laughing. "You definitely don't have to buy me three."

"Lamps are good to have around," she informed him authoritatively. "Even if you don't use them all, you can keep them in storage as backups."

This time, he couldn't contain his chuckle.

She was rat-arsed. Completely drunk.

"It isn't a common occurrence that we break lamps, Elle. We don't need backups."

This seemed to confuse her as if she broke lamps with great regularity and had a ready supply to act as replacements.

"Just in case," she muttered then her eyes narrowed on him and her face became severe. "Don't take another step."

He'd neared her and didn't stop moving while he said, "Sorry?"

He barely got out the word when she suddenly, for some drunken reason, swung the broom at him. He had to jerk his torso back to miss being hit.

This movement sent her off-balance, so much so, she collided with the chair. Twisting to right herself, she dropped the broom and Prentice swiftly moved forward and caught her at her waist, yanking her upright and into his body.

He watched her profile as she glared at the chair.

"Who put that there?" she snapped, continuing to scowl at the chair like she was willing it to disintegrate from the heat of her gaze.

"It's always been there."

She twisted her neck to look at him and announced, "It has *not*."

He was finding it very difficult not to burst out laughing but somehow he succeeded in this task.

"It has," he said.

"It hasn't," she retorted.

"It has."

"It. Has. *Not*."

He chuckled as he said, "Elle, it *has*."

"Well!" she snapped. "That's a silly place to put a chair. It's dangerous, especially with the children around." She caught his eye and advised stoutly, "You should move it."

He put his hands to her hips and started to push her to the hall murmuring, "I'll consider it."

She suddenly stood stock still and cried, "You're barefoot!" She whirled to face him and announced, "Not another step, Prentice Cameron, you might cut yourself. I'm going to clean up the lamp."

"I'll clean it up after we get you to bed."

"I broke it, I'll clean it up. And anyway, you're barefoot," she returned.

"I'll put on shoes. You're in no state to clean up the lamp."

She tilted her head, her face a wild range of expressions as she considered this.

Prentice watched her face, explicitly reading every thought that passed through her mind and enjoying the show.

Eventually she nodded. "Okay, you can clean it up but you have to promise to get every . . . single . . . *piece* so Sally doesn't accidentally hurt herself."

Her concern for his daughter also settled in his gut, it also was a warm, satisfying feeling, and Prentice gently turned her around and pushed her again toward the hall while saying gruffly, "I promise."

"All right then," she gave in.

With difficulty he guided her through the hall. She couldn't walk a straight line if paid a bigger fortune than she already had to do it.

"I thought you were staying at Fergus's," he remarked.

"I thought so too but Annie said *no*. No, no, no, no, *no*. No friend of *hers* was sleeping on a *couch*. We were all in the taxi and she made them all come right *here*. First! Even though Fergus's is closer to the village," she finished this story and slipped on the stairs, nearly going down, her hand thrown out to catch her fall but Prentice was close and hooked an arm around her waist again.

His arm tightened and he lifted her, carrying her the last two steps to the landing. He put her down and moved her around the corner, keeping his hands on her waist as he guided her up the last flight of steps.

When they hit her rooms, he let her go, flipped on the switch and she meandered in a random zigzag pattern to the bedroom.

All the while she meandered, she chattered.

"I love your children. They're *the best*. But I especially love Sally." She stopped, swayed, righted herself, twisted to look at him and said, "No, Jason. I especially love Jason." Her eyes went unfocused and she bit her lip before saying, "No, Sally." Her face filled with confusion before it cleared and she finished, "Oh hell, they're both *great*."

With that she swayed back around and zigzagged into the bedroom toward the lamp.

He quickly followed her as she got close to the lamp, deciding it best at that juncture that he operate the household electronics. He gently moved her and turned on the lamp.

She plunked down on the side of the bed and bent double, her hands going to her shoes. Prentice prepared to leave her to it.

But he didn't when she spoke. "We had so much *fun*." Her head tilted back sharply, her ponytail flying and she smiled radiantly at him. "People were even *nice* to me."

The different, unpleasant weight settled in his gut.

She turned her attention back to her shoe. "I know it was for Annie's sake but still, I could pretend."

Looking at the back of her head, Prentice had the odd but very strong desire to wrap that sleek, shining ponytail around his fist, pull her head back and kiss her.

Before he could process this disturbing thought, she lifted her torso up jerkily and twisted her leg at an impossible angle so her knee was wrenched, her calf was on the mattress at her side and her hand went back to her ankle.

"What is *with* these straps?" she muttered in frustration, yanking at the strap of her sexy, high-heeled sandal.

Prentice crouched in front of her and moved her hands away. "I'll do it."

She pushed at his hands, declaring, "I'll do it."

He pushed at her hands. "I'll do it."

"I can do it!"

He caught her eyes and said low, "Elle."

She stared at him then huffed out a sigh, "All right, you do it."

Then she whipped her leg out, he reared back to miss being hit by her flying foot, and she held it out for him to take off her sandal.

He straightened and took the back of her heel in one hand, the fingers of his other working the strap.

But his eyes were on her.

He should have focused on her shoe.

He watched as she yanked out her ponytail holder and tossed it on the nightstand amongst a tidy display of pumps and jars and a stack of leather-bound journals.

Then she mussed her hair, the heavy, blonde locks flying everywhere.

It was an extraordinary show and Prentice felt his body instantly and pleasurably tighten in response.

Christ, he had to get out of there.

He unfastened the strap and slid her shoe off, dropping it to the floor.

She immediately lifted her other foot to him while using both hands to lift her hair up at the nape of her neck before she plopped back onto the bed, throwing her arms wide. Her long hair splayed on the bed around her and his mind took that opportunity to consider what Isabella, and her hair, would look like, and feel like, if she was underneath him.

Naked underneath him.

His mind moved swiftly away from that delightful mental image, his gaze moved away from the equally delightful vision of Isabella on her back on the bed, his hand curved around her heel and he went for the other strap.

"Annie's so happy," she whispered wistfully, and at her words Prentice's eyes sliced back to her. Her gaze was as wistful as her tone and it was on him. "All these years. I never thought I'd see it, Pren."

This time, his gut tightened.

No one called him Pren but Elle. His mother hadn't allowed his name to be shortened when he was a lad and Prentice just stuck.

But he (and his mother) let Isabella call him Pren.

And she hadn't called him Pren since their last night together.

In a flash, the memory came from somewhere deep and it was as clear as if it happened only yesterday.

They were in his car when he brought her back to Fergus's after dinner and drinks. It was late, it was dark, she was across the seat, her back to his thighs, her arms around his neck, his hands in her shirt and they were kissing.

He'd never made love to her. They'd done almost everything else but she'd been a virgin and he'd decided, if she'd lasted twenty years, she could last until he had a ring on her finger.

She hadn't decided that. Isabella made it clear she was ready to give herself to him when he was ready to take her.

But Prentice had thought at the time that he could wait until he gave her his name as his gift to bear the rest of her life and only then would she give him her virginity as hers.

The next day she was going to the airport to get her father and spending the day with him. The night after that, she was going to make dinner for Prentice and her father.

They never made it that far. Prentice had received the summons from Carver Austin to appear at Fergus's the morning after he arrived.

He had no idea that would be the last time he would hold her in his arms. If he had, at the time, he wouldn't have taken her back to Fergus's.

He would have driven her to the ends of the earth.

He'd stopped kissing her before it got too heavy (or, to the point of no return as it already was heavy) and muttered, "You have to go."

She looked adorably disappointed before she sighed, "I have to go."

Prentice grinned at her, put his forehead to hers and whispered, "Love you, baby."

She closed her eyes, her hand coming to his neck.

She squeezed, opened her eyes and said, "Love you too, Pren."

Then she'd touched her mouth to his and exited the car, blowing a kiss at him through the window before running gracefully up the steps. There she stopped, turned to him, waved wildly and blew him another kiss.

He'd waited until the door closed behind her.

That was the last time anyone had called him Pren.

Until now.

And that was the last time he saw his Elle.

Until now.

Yes, he definitely needed to get the fuck out of there.

He freed the strap, slipped the shoe off her foot and dropped it to the floor.

Before he could move, she was up, moving lithely, standing in front of him and she slapped her hands on his chest so hard, it stung.

This surprised him.

It surprised him enough that he didn't move.

What she did next would surprise him more.

She leaned in, her bodyweight resting against his, her hands sliding up so her fingers could curl on his shoulders and the sting disappeared instantly and another feeling altogether stole through him.

Face tipped to his, she breathed, "Can you believe? Annie and Dougal. Mikey's *so* right. It *is* a fairytale come true."

Prentice noticed at once that she smelled of fruit.

Any other drunken person smelled unpleasantly drunk. Only Elle could smell like fruit when she was smashed.

And the smell was intoxicating.

"What have you been drinking?" he asked, his hands going to her hips for the sake of comfort and finding far more than comfort when his fingers curled into her soft flesh.

"Lemon, lime cordial and vodka," she answered. "Annie introduced me to them and they're great. They taste like candy."

"Aye, but candy can't get you pissed."

She squeezed his shoulders and exclaimed, "You've got that right!" Then she giggled.

Before he could process his more than pleasant reaction to her giggling while pressed against him, her hands slid from his shoulders to around his neck, she went up on tiptoe and pressed her soft body to his, giving him a tight hug.

"Two days, Pren," she whispered in his ear. "Two days and Annie and Dougal are finally going to be married." Her arms tightened, her head turned and he could feel her lips against his neck and he liked it, too much. "Twenty years, and finally they're happy."

She held on to him and his arms slid around her, holding her close.

This was the woman he fell in love with.

Twenty years and he again had her in his arms.

Fucking hell.

His chest got tight and his arms got tighter even though he didn't will them to do so, and in turn she gave him a squeeze.

"Elle—" he started, having no fucking clue what he intended to say but all of a sudden she tore out of his arms.

He stared as she whipped her T-shirt off, exposing the camisole underneath.

She threw it over his shoulder and smiled at him brightly. "I'm so *happy!*"

Before he could say a word, she twirled around and crawled into bed on all fours, her ass in those tight jeans on dazzling display in front of him for a moment before she collapsed on her side, back to him.

She curled her knees into her belly, burrowed her head in the pillow and whispered, "I won't have any trouble sleeping tonight."

He should have left.

He really should have left.

He didn't leave.

He sat on the edge of the bed, pulling the soft, heavy hair away from her neck before he curled his fingers there.

"Do you normally have trouble sleeping?" he muttered, unable to use a stronger voice as her head had tilted and her shoulder flexed to hold his hand captive.

He found this gesture so appealing it didn't feel like a weight in his gut.

Instead it sent a sweet warmth throughout his system.

Her body relaxed, releasing his hand and she mumbled, "Mm."

"Elle," he prompted.

She nestled her body deeper into the bed before she murmured into her pillow, "Every night. Sleep and I are *not* friends."

Prentice did not like her answer.

His fingers tensed.

She sighed.

Then she whispered, "'Night, Pren."

He ran his thumb along the curve of her jaw before he murmured, "Goodnight, Elle."

She snuggled into her pillow.

He watched her a moment that slid into two then became three before he forced himself to stand, pull the covers out from under her sleep-heavy body and over her.

He turned out the lamp, walked into the sitting room and switched off the light, went to the great room and cleaned up every, single piece of the lamp.

———— • ————

THE NEXT MORNING he was making coffee when Elle came downstairs.

He had spent most of the night trying to forget about the episode they'd shared.

Then he spent most of the early morning realizing he couldn't and trying to figure out what the fuck he meant to do about it.

All of this flew from his mind when she turned the corner and he saw her.

She was wearing another pair of those loose-fitting, knit trousers that, regardless if they fit loose, they still clung to certain parts of her (the alluring parts), drawing attention.

This pair was black and she wore them with a matching zip-up hoodie with gathers at the pockets. He could see a dusty blue camisole peeking over the zip at her cleavage.

Her hair was in a wild mess on top of her head, spikes poking from it and long tendrils falling down her neck.

Her face was makeup free.

It was also pale.

She looked sicker than a dog but still somehow beautiful.

He took this all in in an instant and then let out a bark of laughter.

She flinched at the noise and at her flinch he bit back his laughter but kept chuckling.

"How're you feeling?" he asked.

She walked into the kitchen, got close to him (but not too close) and leaned heavily against the counter.

"I'm never drinking again."

He grinned at her. "Everyone says that."

Her eyes locked on his. "No. Seriously. I. Am. Never. Drinking. Again."

The way she enunciated every word with complete and hilariously adorable seriousness gave him the sudden and intense urge to kiss her.

He also needed, very badly, to laugh.

He did the latter.

She glared at him which made his laughter deepen.

Then she scowled, her eyes moved to the filled coffee filter in his hand, her scowl disappeared and her eyes grew wide.

"What are you doing?" she asked.

He looked down at the coffee filter in his hand, thinking it was readily apparent what he was doing.

He then looked at her and stated the obvious, "Making coffee."

"How much coffee?" she asked, eyes still on the filter.

"A pot."

Her gaze slid to his face. "Prentice, that's enough coffee to make an *urn* and when I say *urn* I mean those industrial-sized urns they have in cafeterias that serve a hundred. How strong do you like your coffee?" The last came out high-pitched and incredulous.

So *that* was what he was doing wrong.

She didn't wait for him to answer, she moved into his space, shuffling him out of the way at the same time deftly confiscating the overfilled coffee filter.

"I'll make the coffee," she muttered, dumping half the grounds back into the canister. She then reached into the spice drawer, pulled out cinnamon and sprinkled it on the top. She put the filter in the machine, slapped it to and flipped the switch.

Cinnamon.

That was why her coffee was so heavenly.

That and the fact that there wasn't far too much coffee in the filter.

She took down mugs and he settled in watching her. She settled back to ignoring him.

This made him smile.

"What are you making the kids for breakfast today?" he asked.

She blanched visibly at the mention of food and then swallowed.

"Don't know," she muttered to the coffeepot, which she was watching with avid but feigned fascination.

He decided to torture her. "A fry up?"

She curled her fingers around the counter and swallowed yet again before whispering, "I don't think so."

He bit back his laughter.

Then he called, "Elle," and watched, with some surprise, as her body grew tight.

She turned only her head to him.

"I'll make you toast and I'll make the kids breakfast," he told her.

"I can cook."

"Aye, you can, very well. This morning, however, you aren't."

She turned her body to him and repeated, "I can cook."

"Aye, but this morning you aren't."

Her shoulders went straight. "I am."

"You aren't."

"I *am*," she snapped and then winced at her own intensity.

He grinned, walked the stride it took him to get to her, put his hands to her waist and lifted her. She let out a startled cry and her fingers curled on his shoulders before her ass hit the counter. He placed both of his hands on the counter on either side of her hips, leaned his face to hers and spoke.

"You aren't. Sit. Stay."

Her eyes flashed with anger, her mouth opened to speak, he felt another, deeper, desire to kiss her and then her gaze darted over his shoulder.

Her pale face grew paler and her hands shot from his shoulders as if his skin burned.

Prentice straightened, looked over his shoulder and saw Sally and

Jason both standing there, both their eyes locked on Prentice and Elle.

How had they missed the children arriving?

Sally looked like Sally, happy and carefree (though silent).

Jason looked astounded.

Prentice moved to Isabella's side, a comfortable distance away and he held his son's gaze.

From there he watched as Jason's lips twitched to the side and his eyes grew bright before they dropped to the floor, but Prentice could have sworn he saw a smirk before they did.

"What's for breakfast, Miss Bella?" Sally asked, skipping into the kitchen.

"Elle's sitting this one out. I'm making porridge," Prentice answered, reaching for the bread to make Elle's toast.

Jason's head shot up and the smirk was gone. "Elle?"

"Aye," Prentice replied immediately.

That was who she was no matter who she wanted him to think she was.

Prentice kept his attention locked on his son and watched as Jason's gaze slid to Elle and the smirk returned before he went to the fridge to get the milk.

"Can we call her Elle?" Sally asked.

"No," Prentice answered.

"Can we sit on the counter like Miss Bella's doing while we eat our porridge?" Sally asked.

"No," Prentice repeated.

"Can we have chocolate cake instead of porridge?" Sally went on.

"No," both Prentice and Elle answered.

"But there's a lot of cake left!" Sally cried. "If we don't have it for breakfast, we're never going to eat it all!"

"Sally, stool. Sit. Now," Prentice ordered.

His daughter pouted and flounced to a stool.

Prentice went back to preparing the toast but his eyes caught on Elle and he saw she was watching Sally with a soft, warm, amused expression on her pale face.

And it hit him she wasn't drunkenly declaring her love for his children last night. She was honestly doing it.

Prentice, luckily, had no idea the depth of longing of a motherless child who had no ability to have children of their own.

Or, he had no idea until he saw that look on Elle's face and realized that, within days, she'd fallen in love with his children.

Fucking hell, he thought.

They really needed to talk.

He made the toast. He made porridge. They ate and the kids scrambled up the stairs to get their bags.

Elle hopped off the counter and started clearing the dishes.

"Dougal's stag night is tonight and the kids—" Prentice started while watching her move through his kitchen.

He didn't finish.

Her head whipped toward him and she said quickly, "I'll watch them."

That warm weight settled in his gut again.

And it felt good again.

He walked close to her, put his hand to her neck and he felt her still under his fingers.

"I've already arranged for Debs to pick them up from school. They're spending the night with her," Prentice said.

He saw disappointment. It was fleeting but he saw it.

His fingers curled into her neck.

When he spoke, he did it softly, "I'll come home tonight before I go out with Dougal, take you out to an early dinner and we'll talk."

"I think I'll be busy with Annie," she replied, pulling her neck away and starting to move but he caught her hips.

She stopped, stiffened and looked at him, face again paler.

"You just said you'd watch the kids," he reminded her.

"I forgot about Annie," she lied.

"Elle—" he began.

She cut him off. "I'm here for Annie."

"We need to talk." His voice was firm.

That was when he lost her. Her face went cold.

"No, Prentice, *we* don't need to do anything. *I* need to get through two more days of this. Then I'm gone."

His fingers flexed at her hips as his good humor slipped at her words. "You're not."

"I am."

"No, you're not."

"Yes, Prentice, I *am*."

He got closer and his burgeoning anger strengthened. "Isabella, you're not leaving my children behind like you left me behind."

He watched her head jerk and she flinched.

Then she recovered.

"It's for the best."

Yes, he was getting angry.

"How do you figure that?" he returned.

"Trust me," she shot back.

He said it even though he wasn't certain he meant it.

Not anymore.

"Not likely."

She pulled her hips from his hands and gazed up at him, her face remote. "You just proved my point," she replied softly. "Like I said, it's for the best."

Before he could say more or figure out how in *the* fuck their situation degenerated so quickly, she turned on her bare foot and disappeared.

"THIS IS THE worst stag night in history with the best man standing out in the freaking cold drinking alone."

Dougal's words made Prentice's body jolt as his mind was torn from Elle.

Prentice looked at his friend.

Dougal was smiling but his smile faded when he saw Prentice's face. When Prentice saw the humor die out of Dougal's expression, he decided that tonight was not going to be about Prentice or Elle or Jason or his dead wife Fiona.

It had been about all that shit for far too long.

It was going to be about Dougal.

"Sorry, mate. Have a lot on my mind," Prentice murmured, stepping away from the railing.

"I can tell," Dougal replied softly.

Prentice came abreast of his friend and he smiled.

"Let's get you drunk," he said.

Dougal watched him closely.

Then Dougal grinned.

And they went inside and got drunk.

Chapter
EIGHT

Aromatherapy

Prentice

The taxi slid to a halt and Prentice paid Harry, the driver, a man he'd known his whole life.

He exited the car and walked up to his house, seeing most of the windows were dark but the outside light was on and he saw soft light shining from the windows in the vestibule.

Elle had lit his way.

Seeing that, the decision he'd made at the pub cemented in his brain.

He and Elle were going to talk.

And they were going to do it *now*.

Prentice was drunk. Not rat-arsed but he certainly was *not* sober.

And he didn't give a fuck.

He opened the door, switched off the outside light, flipped the switch on the light in the vestibule and walked into the great room.

A soft light was burning from a brand-new lamp by the couch.

She'd replaced the lamp.

He surveyed the room noting something was different and it wasn't just the fucking lamp that he *told* her not to replace and he instantly remembered that Elle could be just as stubborn as Annie when she got something in that head of hers. Hell, she could be *more* stubborn which was fucking saying something.

He narrowed his eyes and saw, to his shock, she'd also swept the wood floors. And there were fresh vacuum marks on the rugs where she'd hoovered. *And* she'd tidied away the bits and pieces the children had left lying around.

Fucking hell.

Yes, they were fucking well going to talk.

And they were fucking well going to do it *now*.

He pulled off his coat, threw it on the armchair Elle drunkenly advised him to move and walked directly down the hall and up the stairs to the guest suite.

The door was closed.

Since she'd stayed with them, he'd not come up the stairs to see the door closed. Of course now the kids were out of the house. It was just Prentice and Elle.

Which meant she closed the door.

His jaw grew tighter and his resolve grew firmer.

He didn't bother to knock, just opened the door to the darkened room.

The door to the bedroom wasn't closed and he walked straight to it, seeing her clearly in the moonlight lying in bed.

She was on her stomach, her head facing him, her hand on the pillow in front of her face. The covers were down to her waist and the nightgown she was wearing was satin or silk. He couldn't distinguish the color but he could tell it was one or the other from its sheen.

"Elle," he called loudly.

She didn't move.

He sat heavily on the bed by her hip and put a hand to the small of her back, repeating her name.

Her body jerked, her head twisted to look at him and she jerked again.

She came up on an elbow and whispered sleepily (and disbelievingly), "Prentice?"

"Get up, we need to talk," he replied, his voice curt.

She didn't move.

"Up. Now," he ordered, speaking to her like he spoke to his children when they resisted his commands.

"What?" she breathed.

He stood. "Elle, *up*."

Having delivered his demand, Prentice walked out of the room.

He meant to turn on a light but before he could he glanced her way and saw she was out of bed reaching for her dressing gown, which was thrown over the armchair in the corner.

He also saw the nightgown was a light color and it was edged in lace at the bottom, the lace a far darker color.

It was also very short and, with Elle bent to reach for her dressing gown, it had ridden up, exposing her thighs all the way up to the very edge of her ass.

Prentice felt his body respond to that very alluring sight.

He gritted his teeth.

She walked in, shrugging on the dressing gown.

When she hit the room, she pulled her hair out of her face, keeping her hand at the top back of her head, her hair bunched in her fist.

Her eyes were on him in the moonlit room.

"Are you drunk?" she asked softly, dropping her hand and the heavy fall of her hair settled around her face, on her brow and even in her eye.

He watched this.

He liked it.

And when he responded, he didn't lie.

"Aye."

She regarded him silently for a moment.

"Maybe you should go to bed," she suggested, her voice still soft.

"I don't want to go to bed. I want to talk and we're fucking well going to talk."

"We'll talk in the morning."

"No, you'll make excuses in the morning. You'll avoid me or ignore me and that'll piss me off. Then we'll have words which will piss me off more. So, we're no' talking in the fucking morning. We're talking *now*."

"I think—" Elle began as she started to move.

He had no idea where she was going just that it was away from him.

And he was not having that.

He caught her upper arm in a firm grip, pulled her in front of him and shuffled her back, his intent to get her attention and negate any attempt at retreat.

He succeeded when her back hit the wall.

He closed in, pinning her.

She made a noise that he couldn't decipher, fear or anger, he had no idea.

He also didn't care.

Because it was then he smelled her.

Her scent was extraordinary and it was strong. He'd never smelled anything like it. It wasn't her perfume that was enticing but it was also delicate.

This was something else.

Something he had to have more of.

Immediately.

His resolve to talk flew from his mind as he dipped his face to her neck, running his nose along its length, breathing in deeply.

God, she smelled good.

Elle went solid.

"Prentice?" Her voice was hesitant.

Nose behind her ear, he asked, "What *is* that?"

Her body jerked and she inquired, "What's what?"

"That fucking smell."

"I . . . um . . . what?" she stammered, her hands coming to rest on his waist, putting gentle pressure there to move him away.

He resisted.

She gave up.

His head came up and he stared at her face in the moonlight.

Christ, she was beautiful.

"That smell," he said. "What is it?"

He watched her blink.

Then she answered, "Aromatherapy."

He didn't reply. This word meant nothing to him. He just continued to stare, feeling her hands on him, her touch light.

She went on and now she sounded nervous, "I use it to sleep. The scent relaxes me. I rub it behind my ears, on my temples, at the nape of my—"

She stopped speaking because Prentice felt it necessary to experience this phenomenon and his nose went to her temple, his lips brushing her cheekbone.

He heard her take in a breath.

Then his hands slid along the silk at her waist, curving around her back. Her rigid body hit his as the fingers of one hand curled in at her waist, holding her captive against him. The other hand went up, encountering her soft, thick hair. He gathered it in a fist and used it to push her head down and twist it to the side so he could bend his neck and smell that scent at her nape.

Christ, she felt good.

And she smelled good.

And, he decided, since his mouth was right there, he might as well see if she tasted good.

Which he did, sliding his tongue around her neck where it met her shoulder and pulling her head back at the same time.

She shivered.

Yes, she tasted good.

"Prentice—" she whispered, but he realized where his hand was and he also decided to see how that fucking ass of hers felt in his hand.

He released her waist and his hand drifted over the silk and down her ass, cupping it gently and pulling her into his hard thighs.

That didn't feel good.

That felt fucking *great*.

"Prentice, step away," she whispered, her voice not soft but throaty.

Now she *sounded* good.

Fucking hell.

He didn't respond verbally.

But his stiffening cock went rock hard.

His lips trailed her jaw.

Her hands came up to his shoulders and she gave a weak push.

"Prentice, step away. We can't—"

His mouth went to hers but he didn't kiss her.

He looked her in the eyes and remembered, instantly, what she liked. He remembered how he could make her wild. He remembered that once he'd made her come simply by manipulating her nipples while she rubbed her crotch urgently against his thigh.

They hadn't even disrobed.

And he remembered her face when she came.

And he wanted that *now*.

His hand moved away from her ass, trailing up her side, his fingers curving around her breast and his thumb slid across her already tight nipple as he slid his thigh between her legs.

Her lips parted, she audibly sucked in breath and her hips automatically ground down on his thigh.

Holy fucking *Christ* but she was magnificent.

"That's it, baby," he encouraged as he closed a finger and thumb on her nipple and rolled.

She gasped, her eyes drifted closed, her head tilted back, her hips bucked against his thigh and then she moaned, soft and sweet.

Hearing that, feeling her, seeing her, her scent all around them, Prentice lost control.

And he determined that she was going to lose hers too.

And, like he used to do, loving her beautiful, animated face when he got her excited, he was going to watch.

With his fist in her hair, keeping her head positioned so he could see her, he pulled down the lace of her nightgown and his fingers went back to her nipple. Relentlessly, he manipulated it and she didn't disappoint. She rocked against his thigh, grinding down harder, harder, until her breaths were sharp and her movements were urgent.

Her hands yanked his shirt free of his jeans, fingers roaming his back, nails digging in.

She fought his hand in her hair, seeking his mouth with her lips.

He didn't allow it. No way in hell.

He was enjoying the show.

When her movements became frantic and he knew she was close, his fingers stopped, his hand curled around her warm, soft breast and she gasped in protest.

"Do you want me?" he asked, his voice a low growl.

"Yes," she whispered immediately, her hips still moving insistently on his thigh.

"Say it," he demanded.

Again, she didn't hesitate. "I want you."

He was ruthless, for some reason needing it, he pushed, "Say it with my name."

She kept grinding against his thigh, arching her back to press her breast into his hand, seeking his mouth with her lips. "I want you, Prentice."

"Call me Pren," he ordered.

She tugged her hair free enough to get her mouth on him but he avoided it and her lips hit his neck, her nails scraped along his back and his cock jerked in response.

He knew he couldn't take much more of this. It had been a long fucking time and she was magnificent.

She didn't make him wait.

"I want you, Pren," she whispered against his neck then he felt her tongue there.

His finger and thumb closed on her nipple. She moaned with pleasure, the sound rent right through him and her teeth nipped his neck. His hand left her hair and slid down her back, around her waist to her belly and down to cup her over her underwear.

He felt her wetness.

She was drenched.

She couldn't force that. That wasn't a game.

That was all Elle.

His Elle.

He made her that wet.

Yes, she fucking wanted him.

The feel of her arousal nearly made him come.

Then she pressed herself into his hand and he was done.

Hooking her underwear with his thumbs, he tore it down her legs. She stepped out of it while he held her to the wall with a hand on her belly and his other hand went to his zip. He freed his swollen, aching cock and then he grasped her hips.

She helped. Giving a soft hop, she jumped up, opening her legs for him as he positioned between them, her sweet, soft ass and the weight of her settling into his hands.

Fucking magnificent.

He drove into her.

Wet, slick and tight.

And unbelievably beautiful.

She cried out, her legs wrapping around his hips and her arms holding tight around his shoulders as he thrust into her, hard, deep, violent and not in his control.

She tilted her hips and met his thrusts, her mouth back to seeking his, one of her hands in his hair trying to guide his head to hers.

He resisted, watching her efforts, getting off on her need for that connection, the pleasure he could see, even in the moonlight, making her beautiful face stunning.

He was going to come, he was ready, and they'd barely started.

He was never going to last until she climaxed.

"It's never . . . not ever," she moaned, her voice rough but it still sounded like silk. "Pren, it's never been this good."

Then her neck arched and her body bucked uncontrollably in his hands so forcefully he nearly lost hold. Prentice watched her come, her sex clenching and releasing, rippling wildly against his driving cock.

The glorious sight and incredible feel of it sent him over the edge. He slammed into her one last time and joined her.

She was right.

It had never been this good.

Not ever.

Phenomenal.

When he finished, his face buried in her neck, his breath heavy against her skin, he flexed his fingers into the soft flesh of her ass and ground his hips into hers.

In response, her arm around his shoulders tensed, the fingers in his hair drifted and she trembled.

The feel of her body wrapped around him, her ass in his hands, her still gently convulsing wetness tight around his cock, the scent of her, her lips against his neck, Prentice regretted the fact that the kids were only gone for one night. He disliked the fact he was best man to Dougal and she was maid of honor to Annie at a wedding to be held the next day.

Instead, he wanted what they just had, again and again, until he'd had his fill.

Which would take weeks.

Maybe months.

Probably a lifetime.

He felt her body grow tight against his and her mouth came away from his neck.

"Prentice, put me down," she demanded, her voice suddenly cold.

At the sound, his head came up and he looked at her.

Her face was as cold as her voice.

Oh fuck. What could possibly be going through that head of hers now?

"Put me down," she repeated.

"Elle—" he began.

Her hands shoved at his shoulders angrily.

"Don't call me that," she hissed. "Put me down. Now."

He was confused. He was also on guard.

What on earth could make her upset after *that?*

"Are you angry?" he asked.

She opened her mouth, closed it then opened it again to speak. "Are you *serious?"*

"Elle—"

"I said, *don't call me that!"* She shoved again.

His guard came down and his temper started rising. "What the fuck's the matter?"

"What the . . . what . . . what's the matter?" she stuttered, giving him another shove.

"Aye, what's the matter?" he repeated, pressing her into the wall and not letting go.

Her eyes leveled on his and she said in a voice that dripped icicles, "You just fucked me against the wall like a common whore."

No, his temper wasn't rising.

It had exploded.

Even so, his voice was low, even and rumbling when he asked, "How in *the* fuck do you figure that?"

Her body jerked, she glared at him then he watched something dawn on her, her face going slack before she winced.

"This is punishment," she whispered.

He was back to confused.

But he was also still furious.

"Punishment?"

"I don't deserve this," she said softly.

He was losing patience, not that there was much to lose.

"Elle," he clipped, "explain."

She went back to her earlier theme. "Put me down."

"No."

"Put me down!" she cried.

"No!" he shouted.

"I can't believe this of you. Not you," she snapped then her voice dipped quiet, even hoarse, as if she was fighting tears. "Not you."

Something was happening and the situation, out of his control and degenerating quickly (as . . . fucking . . . *usual* with Elle), was hitting the danger zone.

"Explain, Elle."

She shook her head and pressed against his shoulders.

He pressed her deeper into the wall. So much deeper, he heard the breath escape her lungs.

"Now, Elle. Explain how the fuck you can twist what just happened into something bad."

She stared at him and he could swear he saw wetness trembling at the bottoms of her eyes.

"You treated me like a whore, to punish me for what I did. I can't believe you'd do that," she whispered.

Christ, what was the matter with her? Was she mad?

"I *didn't* do it," he bit out.

"Yes you did."

"How could you think that?" he clipped.

He could barely hear her when she finally explained, "You didn't kiss me."

But he heard her.

And his body went solid.

For a second.

Then he relaxed, buried his face in her neck and burst out laughing.

He felt her stiffen again in his arms.

"This isn't funny," she whispered.

He lifted his head then he pulled her away from the wall. He walked with her in his arms to the bed.

"Prentice—"

His mouth went to hers. "Baby, I didn't kiss you because I wanted to watch you come and I can't do that when I'm kissing you."

He heard her sharp inhalation of breath and her fingers curled into his shoulders.

They reached the bed and without hesitation he took them down, him on top.

His hand went to the side of her head, his thumb brushing along her cheekbone as he looked into her eyes in the moonlight.

"This time, you can come while I'm kissing you."

"Prentice—"

"But you'll be naked," he went on.

"Prentice—"

"And so will I."

"Pren—"

She didn't finish his name because he kissed her quiet. And he remembered he used to do that all the time too. And he remembered how much she liked it when he kissed her.

Because now, immediately, as she had done twenty years ago, the minute his tongue touched hers, her soft body melted into his.

And he kissed her a lot. And he did it everywhere.

And, much, *much* later, when they were both naked, he was rocking deep inside her tight, wet silkiness, he knew exactly what she looked like with her hair spread across the bed and her body underneath him, Prentice made her come while he was kissing her.

And that, too, was phenomenal.

———— ♦ ————

Fiona

FIONA WAS BACK in the place she went to when she died.

She hadn't been there in ages.

It was nice enough.

Well, actually, it was lovely. With a gently rolling stream, trees in fragrant bloom, abundant wildflowers, the grass so green it nearly hurt her eyes and it was so thick, you could sleep on it.

There was a big tent there, made of silk, next to an apple tree, its blossoms carpeting the roof of the tent and all around. The flaps of the tent were opened wide and inside there were soft rugs, a comfy armchair with ottoman next to which there was a ready supply of the grisly crime novels Fiona liked to read. There was also a lovely guitar she could play and a big bed with a downy mattress, stacks of pillows and a fluffy duvet.

Fiona was real there. She walked with her feet on the ground, she didn't float. Her body was solid, not see-through. She could feel things and move things without concentrating.

And there was night and day and she slept there.

She went there directly after she died and she thought, at first, it was heaven.

It was heavenly enough but she was alone and she didn't think heaven would be eternal solitude. That would stink, and heaven, in her mind, didn't stink.

But she'd been tired back then, tired from fighting the pain and tired from knowing what her body's weakness was doing to her family.

So, when she first arrived, she slept a lot. And she slept well. And she got used to no pain and tiredness (but not to being dead).

Then one day she was walking along the stream and trying to figure out the different scents of the trees (because what the bloody else was there to do?) and *zip*, all of a sudden she was a ghost in her great room watching Prentice and Jason, both looking handsome but haggard, in dark suits, and Sally, looking confused and exhausted, in a pretty little black dress, coming through the front door.

At first, she didn't know she was a ghost and thought she'd been granted a reprieve.

She was back, she was in her home, she had no pain and there was her family.

It didn't take long to realize they couldn't see her because, looking down, she could barely see herself and that she was dead, dead, *dead* because they'd just arrived back from her funeral.

It *did* take a while for her to get used to this cruel twist of fate, but she did and she'd been with them ever since. She spent her time haunting them (of course), being pissed off (of course) and learning how to materialize and dematerialize, not only in her house, but anywhere in the village.

She tried to go somewhere else, like Los Angeles, where she'd always wanted to go, but she couldn't leave the village even in the company of, say, Prentice or her sister Morag when they left town. Any time she'd try, she'd automatically dematerialize and end up back at the house (which also pissed her off).

She hadn't been able to be seen or heard, not that she tried too hard because she'd involuntarily damaged her family psychologically enough without them hearing her ghostly voice or seeing her ghostly body.

Now, with Bella around, she'd been so excited about her new abilities, she'd spent the last two days testing them.

And she'd spent that time watching Prentice and Bella play their crazy game.

The abilities part was good. She was getting stronger, understanding the focus she needed to manipulate things, happy that her anger, frustration and grief at being dead had *some* use. She got so good at it, she couldn't only move things, she could even pick things up and hold them.

She was also able to talk to Bella. Bella *definitely* heard her. That was why the laundry got done, the ironing got done, the vacuuming and sweeping got done (her house was going to be taken over by dust mites if Bella didn't do something about it, and she did, without hesitation, after Fiona screamed at her that it had to get done) and Sally got a chocolate cake (her favorite) but *only* after she ate her broccoli.

Of course, Bella did these things for other reasons too. Fiona knew that. After all she saw and heard these last days, she knew Bella wasn't what she'd thought Bella was for all those years.

Instead, Fiona knew Bella's soft heart and unique understanding meant Bella would have taken care with Fiona's children, even if, perhaps, she wouldn't have ironed Prentice's shirts while she was doing it.

And Fiona had to admit, she was grimly fascinated by Prentice and Bella's game.

They bickered a lot.

And Prentice obviously enjoyed it.

In the time Fiona and Prentice were courting before they married and a few years after, Fiona had worried she'd never live up to all that was Bella.

Prentice and Bella had an obviously passionate relationship. Everyone knew it because they saw it and they were amused by it because, even all that fighting and bickering was somehow sweet, especially considering, when they weren't fighting and bickering, they were clearly deeply in love.

It was something he and Fiona didn't have.

Prentice and Fiona had a comfortable, easy life filled with laughter.

They had great sex, a lot of closeness and Prentice was affectionate, but Fiona wasn't nearly as passionate as he was so that part stayed only in the bedroom.

It didn't spill out to life.

It spilled out *everywhere* with Prentice and Bella.

Bella and Prentice, when they were together, fought and they bickered.

And Bella challenged Prentice in a way Fiona knew she never could.

Bella was well-educated, read a great deal and she'd traveled. Prentice, too, got top marks, got into a top university, read any book he could get his hands on and had spent three summers abroad, backpacking on the cheap and with a relentless schedule to see as much of the architecture in Europe as he could.

Fiona liked it in her village and rarely left, though she wanted to see Los Angeles, not enough actually to go when Prentice offered it as a family holiday. Fiona said they'd go when Sally was older so Sally could go to Disneyland (what a fool she was). She read her crime novels but she didn't read anything high-brow and she didn't read many of her crime novels either.

She was happy with the simple life and, after a while, Prentice convinced her he was happy with it too.

But the longer Bella remained in the house, the more alive he seemed.

And if she wasn't already dead, watching that would have killed her.

She was back to hating Bella when, the night of the stag party, even though she knew it wasn't right, she started to read Bella's journals.

She floated, cross-legged above the floor by Bella's bed while Bella slept and Fiona read.

And she couldn't believe what she read.

One day, years ago, Fiona was in the fruit and veg shop when Hattie had made some vicious comment about some famous pop star who'd gone off the rails and Old Lady Kilbride, who was also there, heard her.

"You don't know the demons she carries, Hattie Fennick," Mrs. Kilbride said sharply. "You don't know. Her life may seem charmed and glamorous to you but everyone has demons. Everyone."

Old Lady Kilbride was right.

And Isabella Austin Evangahlala had demons and her demons were doozies.

She seemed like she had it all. She was beautiful, rich, well-educated, jet-set, stylish, classy.

But she had an abusive father who used to verbally berate and alternately beat her mentally unstable mother.

This, Bella had witnessed.

He also verbally berated and sometimes slapped Bella.

She had a best friend who'd lost her joy for life and Bella worked for years trying to help her find it again and luckily succeeded. Fiona learned through the journals that while she and Prentice were encouraging Dougal from close by, from a distance, Bella was also encouraging Annie.

Bella also had a husband who played around on her constantly, even once she'd walked in on him and another woman.

He'd also taunted her with her inability to give him children, something Bella yearned for to the point of despair.

And he'd not allowed them to settle down even though she wanted a home. They owned several properties but they never stayed in one long. They traveled around like nomads from party to party, yacht to yacht, ski resort to ski resort, event to event, incessantly.

Bella missed her mother who she adored and she had vivid, excruciating dreams, even after all these years, of finding her dead in the tub.

And last, but not least, Bella loved Prentice in a fierce, beautiful way that Fiona had to admit that even *she* hadn't loved him.

And that love never, *never* died.

Ghostly tears were falling from her ghostly eyes at all Bella had endured (and it was never-ending, no wonder the woman clenched her fists, all that pain had to be unleashed *somewhere*) when Fiona sensed Prentice's presence nearing the house.

She flipped shut the third journal (her ghostly abilities extended to super-fast reading which had been a boon) and carefully arranged them in the tidy pile in which Bella liked them.

Then Fiona dematerialized and materialized in the living room.

Prentice was standing stock still staring at the rug.

He looked angry.

Oh for goodness sakes. What was he pissed off about now?

Then he took off his coat, flung it on the chair and stalked to the hallway.

Fiona followed him, worrying so much she was wringing her hands and shouting at him to leave Bella be. She needed her sleep. She had to get some rest for the wedding tomorrow. She didn't sleep well and she was sleeping soundly now.

But, of course, he didn't hear her. In fact, when he encountered Bella's closed door, instead of knocking or, better yet, turning away, he walked right in.

Fiona followed, and as she would have floated over the threshold, she disappeared and reappeared in her whatever-it-was place.

And there she remained, all night.

She'd tried to dematerialize and go back but she couldn't. Her efforts exhausted her and, finally, she slept.

Opening her eyes, she saw the light coming through the silk tent.

She threw off the covers wondering again why she was bloody well there, hoping she wouldn't be there long and terrified she'd be there for eternity.

She had to warn Bella that Prentice was angry.

She walked out of the flaps of the tent and instantly vaporized, returning to her home.

Returning to the guest suite in her home.

To be precise, the bedroom of the guest suite in her home.

She floated back, reeling at what she saw and nearly floated through the wall of the room (she tried not to float through walls, it gave her a spooked feeling, seeing insulation and floating through supports, it was creepy).

She drifted and stared at the bed.

Prentice and Bella were in it sleeping, the sunlight shining through windows on their bodies.

They were naked, the covers down to their waists though Fiona couldn't see much of anything considering Prentice had Bella tucked tight to him, his arm around her, his biceps shielding Bella's breast from view. His arm was cocked, as was hers under his, their fingers laced, hands resting on the mattress in front of her face which was tilted forward on the pillow. Prentice's head was tilted too, his face in the hair at the back of her head.

Fiona felt her ghostly chest tighten at the sight of them.

Prentice cuddled Fiona *only* after they'd made love and *sometimes* when they went to bed together (he usually worked late or read and came to bed after her).

And he usually did this only for a while, eventually rolling away from her.

Never sleeping with her cradled in his arms. *Never* holding her all night like she was a precious possession he was keeping safe.

Fiona knew why whatever powers that be sent her from her home last night.

And she was thankful for that.

But she was in agony over what she was witnessing right now.

She wanted to scream. She wanted to rail. She wanted to tear her hair out or, better yet, Isabella Austin Evangahlala's long, thick, golden tresses.

But before she could do any of this, Bella's eyes opened.

For a second she looked sated, satisfied . . .

Happy.

Nearly instantly, that look disappeared and utter fear filled her expression.

Fiona forgot her wrath and stared.

What on earth?

Taking great care, Bella uncurled her fingers from Prentice's and, gently, with agonizing slowness, she exited the bed.

Prentice didn't move.

Once he was in a deep sleep, Prentice could sleep through almost anything. Fiona had been lucky he didn't snore, he would never wake if she had to shove him or kick him, that's how deeply he slept (which meant, when they were babies, Jason and Sally never woke Prentice with their middle-of-the-night cries and Fiona practically had to push him out of bed when it was his turn to feed them which drove Fiona up the blooming *wall*).

Therefore, Prentice slept through Bella leaving him in bed.

And he slept through Bella, on silent feet with silent but trembling hands and completely silent tears, packing every single possession that was hers in the guest suite.

She did this quickly but tidily, leaving behind only the scented candles she bought.

Then she dressed in jeans, a sweater and high-heeled boots that she'd set aside. She carried her cosmetics case and her heaviest suitcase out to her rental car.

Fiona floated in the bedroom while all this happened, not sure what to do.

Fiona Cameron, Prentice Cameron's wife, wanted the woman gone.

But Fiona Cameron, the dead woman who loved her husband and children, had conflicting thoughts.

She looked at Prentice, unaware and asleep.

He was a handsome, fit, forty-five-year-old widower who deserved more out of life than grief, a heavy workload, an anguished son and a constant mountain of laundry he hated to do.

He deserved to bicker.

He deserved to be challenged.

He deserved to laugh.

He deserved to have a beautiful, rich, well-educated, jet-set, stylish, classy woman in his life (and, also, one who was corporeal and breathing).

A woman who had loved him for twenty years.

A woman who had carried around his photo in a silver frame and wore his ring on a chain around her neck for twenty *fucking* years.

As much as Fiona hated it, she knew he deserved it.

And her son deserved to live with a woman who understood the depths of his pain.

And his daughter deserved chocolate cake and she needed someone to teach her how to make them and, Lord knew, Prentice couldn't do that.

And Bella . . .

Well, Bella wasn't the only one with a soft heart and Fiona knew that Bella deserved all of them.

When Bella came back to get the last two cases, Fiona's decision made, she dashed to her and started shouting.

What are you doing? Don't leave, don't leave, don't leave!

Bella shook her head as if clearing her thoughts and Fiona knew she could hear her.

Don't do it, Bella. Don't. He needs you and you need him! You need all of them!

Fiona heard Bella's breath hitch as she held back a sob but she exited the front door and threw her cases in the boot of her car.

Think of Annie! Fiona cried.

"I'll not let Annie down," Bella murmured and Fiona would have gasped (but, obviously she didn't as she couldn't) when Bella spoke directly to her.

Good, then go back!

"I can't go back."

Fiona closed her ghostly eyes and shouted her frustration.

Then she panicked.

For, she knew, Prentice was a two strikes kind of man.

He'd forgive you anything.

Once.

Twice, he'd never forgive.

Wrong him twice and you were dead to him. If Bella left him twice he'd never forgive her.

Ever.

Fiona thought fast as Bella slammed the boot of the car.

Then it came to her.

Go back, write him a note. You don't have to explain. Just say goodbye.

Bella shook her head again, moving toward the driver's side door.

Just goodbye. That's it. Don't leave without saying goodbye.

Bella opened the door.

Fiona wrapped her hands around Bella's arm and pleaded, *Please, tell him goodbye. He deserves that!*

Bella shivered and looked down at her arm.

Please, Bella, just tell Prentice goodbye.

Bella hesitated, shook her arm and, Fiona saw with great relief, headed back to the house.

Fiona's eyes rolled skyward and she said a hearty thank you.

Then she darted after Bella.

Floating horizontally over her head, Fiona watched Bella write the note.

I'm sorry, Prentice. This can't work. No good will come of it. I'm so sorry. Goodbye, Isabella

Fiona would have written different words like, *I've loved you for twenty years,* and, *You're the best thing that ever happened to me,* and, *Don't be a jackass and let me go this time.* But she didn't have a say (well she did, she shouted her opinion, Bella just didn't listen to her).

Fiona watched Bella turn to the door but she hesitated, did a stutter step, stopped and turned back.

She made coffee, all but switching on the pot, including sprinkling the ground coffee with cinnamon.

She went back to the note and added a PS and propped it against the coffee machine.

Then she took in a deep breath, looked around the house, a single tear slid down her cheek and she gracefully walked out the door.

Fiona floated to the note and read the postscript.

PS: The coffee's made, just flip the switch and there's Danish in the breadbox.

Reading it, Fiona burst into silent, ghostly laughter.

———◆———

FIONA WAITED (IMPATIENTLY) watching while her husband slept the morning away.

Then she watched as he woke, instantly reaching out to an empty bed.

He came up on an elbow, his eyes narrowing on the bed. He sat up and looked to the bathroom.

The door was open.

His eyes fell on the nightstand. Bella's things were gone. Fiona saw that he noted that immediately.

He got out of bed and stalked naked to the wardrobe.

Empty.

He strode angrily to the bathroom, pulling the chord for the light, yanking back the glass door to the tub (even though he could see through the glass, for goodness sake).

He went back to the bedroom, tugged on his jeans and stopped, gazing around, jaw tight, fury pounding off of him.

His gaze caught on the scented candle Bella left behind on the nightstand. Fiona watched him pick it up. He studied it for a moment. Then he pulled off the stoppered top and smelled it before he calmly put the top back on.

He stood silent and still as he continued to examine the candle.

Suddenly, with a twist of his torso and a brutal underarm throw, he hurled the candle across the room.

The glass broke and the sheetrock dented as it hit the wall and fell with a clunk to the floor.

Fiona floated behind him as he grabbed his clothes and stalked angrily out of the room.

He tossed his shirt and socks into the clean, tidy and dirty-clothes-less laundry room, making to move by it but he thought better of it. He stopped, walked back a step and glared into the room, his face a ferocious scowl.

He continued into the great room, Fiona drifting after him. He dumped his boots on the floor and started up the steps. He got halfway up before he pivoted and walked right back down. Still scowling, furious and looking like he was ready to commit murder, he walked right up to the coffee canister.

Wrenching it open, he moved to the pot.

He saw the note and stilled.

He set the canister aside, seized the note and read it, his jaw tightening so much, a muscle ticked there.

Unexpectedly his jaw went slack and his lips parted.

Fiona watched his eyes scan the note again.

Then she watched as he threw back his head and burst out laughing.

Still chuckling, he flipped the switch to on, and still holding the note he moved to the stairs and bounded up them, two at a time.

Chapter
NINE

Tiny Dancer

Isabella

"I don't get to keep the petals?" Sally asked from beside Isabella in the back seat of the Rolls Royce.

Sally was carrying her basket of velvety red rose petals, still wrapped in film.

"No, sweetheart, you have to throw them on the ground so Annie can walk on them," Isabella answered, fidgeting in her seat.

She'd managed to remain calm and act joyful during the entire morning of getting ready at Fergus's house. But now, with the church getting closer and closer (thus, seeing Prentice after last night getting closer and closer), she was losing it.

Mikey, Isabella worried, saw through her artificial calm, considering he spent a lot of time giving her questioning looks, which she ignored.

But Isabella remained focused. Annie was beside herself with nerves, terrified some hideous event was going to happen to stop the day's festivities.

"Tidal wave!" she'd shouted at one point even though the sun was shining and the nip in the air had disappeared and it was an unseasonably warm day.

"Annie, there's not going to be a tidal wave," Isabella replied sedately, watching from her place lounging fully dressed and completely done up on her friend's bed as the stylists fashioned Annie's hair.

"What's a tidal wave?" Sally whispered loudly, lounging beside her.

Isabella looked at Prentice's daughter.

From the minute Debs had deposited Sally at Fergus's that morning (which caused Isabella more anxiety but Debs had only looked at her inquisitively then she'd shocked Isabella by giving her a tentative smile and she'd transferred Sally's small hand directly to Isabella's and left without uttering a single word), Sally had barely been away from Isabella's side.

"I'll explain later. Miss Annie is having a crisis of the mad mind," Isabella whispered back, also loudly.

"I'm not mad," Annie snapped, sounding mad.

Sally stared in astonishment at the usually good-humored Annie.

Then she whispered, again loudly, "What's a crisis of the mad mind?"

Isabella laughed and gave the girl a hug, promising into Sally's hair (which, at Sally's insistence, Isabella herself had done), "I'll explain that later too."

The stylists had managed to tame Annie's mad hair. The makeup artist had managed to make up her face through Annie alternately ranting and squirming. And Isabella and Annie's other two bridesmaids had managed to get her dressed.

And she looked stunning.

Surveying her, Isabella remarked, "I think the only thing you have to worry about is knocking Dougal dead when he sees how beautiful you are."

At her words, Annie jumped forward, covered Isabella's mouth and shouted, "Don't tempt the fates!"

Isabella laughed under Annie's hand. This she did before she hugged her. Then she gave her the sapphire and diamond bracelet that was to be her friend's something new and part of her something blue. After that she gave Annie her mother's sapphire and diamond earrings that were to be her something old. Finally she gave Annie her own sapphire and diamond pendant that was to be her something borrowed.

When she was done, Annie burst into tears and the makeup artists had to do a touch up.

Now, they were on their way, Isabella and Sally with Annie's two other bridesmaids, Patty and Hannah, sharing one Rolls. Annie following with Fergus in the other. Neither bridesmaid was a villager (thankfully). Patty was an old friend from Northwestern who Isabella had long since lost touch with and Hannah had been a trainee physical therapist Annie met during her rehabilitation.

Patty and Hannah were both wearing lovely, but differently styled, sapphire-blue dresses.

That day, Isabella discovered that *they* were allowed to choose their style dress.

Isabella's was Annie's choice. A strapless sheath, it fit her like a glove and had no ornamentation.

Until just above her knees.

There, it burst in a wide slit, the hem and slit sporting two, layered, opulent ruffles that trailed down and back in a short train (neither Patty nor Hannah's dresses were anything near as lavish).

Annie had also chosen her shoes, ultra-sexy, very-high, spike-heeled, delicate strappy sandals that were even a challenge for Isabella to wear and she wore high heels all the time.

The dress was gorgeous, as were the shoes. But both were sexy, managing to be sophisticated as well as daring.

She looked like a cosmopolitan flamenco dancer.

It was too bold and too chic for a church wedding attended by villagers who hated its wearer.

Fortunately (or *unfortunately* as the case definitely was), Isabella had bigger things to worry about.

Things as big as a handsome, tall, powerfully-built architect who was likely not going to be happy he woke up alone.

She had *no idea* what came over her last night. She'd barely even *tried* to push Prentice away.

No, she knew what came over her. Prentice had always had a unique talent with being able, quickly, to excite her.

Laurent, her only other lover, had called her frigid on more than one occasion (in other words, regularly).

For twenty years, she'd lamented the fact that she and Prentice had never made love. She'd fantasized about it again and again, when she was with him and after they were over.

And last night, she had it.

And, to her shock, it was better than any of her fantasies.

Far better.

Way far better.

And because of that, she'd been weak. A coward. And selfish, selfish, *selfish*.

She hadn't protected him. She'd taken what he gave and then got greedy.

She didn't know what he was thinking and couldn't let her mind go there. She just knew that her life was not filled with lucky happenstance. Where she went, tragedy and despair followed.

And Prentice, Jason and Sally had enough of that.

Too much.

Therefore, she was sticking to her plan regardless that things seemed to change last night and change a great deal.

She was leaving directly after the reception.

She'd even talked Fergus into following her to the estate where they were holding the reception so she could drop her fully packed rental there and make a fast getaway.

In the car on the way back to his house, Fergus had offered, "With Annie gone tonight, if things aren't working at Prentice's, you can sleep in her room."

"Thank you, Fergus, but I need to get going."

"Your flight doesn't leave until tomorrow," he reminded her.

"I know and things are fine at Prentice's. Really. It's just too much, for all of us." She turned from her study of the landscape to look at his handsome profile and asked softly, "You understand, don't you?"

"Haven't had any time with you myself, lass."

Her heart lurched. He was right, and she remembered again just how much she liked Fergus.

She did her best to ignore her heart and her best, as ever, wasn't good enough.

"Come to Chicago next year with Annie and Dougal. I'll spend loads of time with you there. I'll even take you to a Cubs game," she suggested.

He glanced at her out of the corner of his eye and shook his head.

Then he said, "Never understood American baseball."

"That's fine. I've never understood English football," she returned teasingly.

"Football's football, the world over, except in America, where its soccer. Always have to buck tradition, you Americans."

She laughed, Fergus chuckled and she relaxed.

For about two seconds.

Then her mind filled with Prentice again and she started fidgeting.

"They're too pretty to be walked on!" Sally exclaimed, taking Isabella from her thoughts.

"What are, honey?" Isabella murmured distractedly.

"The petals!" Sally cried.

Isabella turned to focus on the girl, kissed the top of her head then put her hands to both sides of her beautiful face.

She examined it at the same time she memorized every feature.

Then she whispered, "It's tradition. A magical tradition. Every heroine at the end of a fairytale gets to walk to her hero on a bed of rose petals. And you get to create that magic. Don't you want to do that for Annie?"

Sally's face had gone from near to pout to spellbound.

"I didn't know it was *magic*," Sally breathed.

Isabella heard Hannah chuckle.

"Well it is," Isabella told Sally.

Sally nodded enthusiastically. "I wanna create magic."

"We all do," Patty commented. "But this time, it's all yours, precious."

Sally, eyes wide, sat back and sighed in happy contentment.

Isabella looked out the window and her heart leapt to her throat in terror.

They were arriving at the church and Prentice, wearing a dark suit (not a tux or morning suit, Dougal had put his foot down) that not only fit him beautifully but he was wearing unbelievably well, was standing outside.

Oh dear.

The Rolls Royce barely halted before Prentice was there, hand to the door handle, pulling it open.

He leaned in, his every-colored eyes pinning Isabella to the spot before he grasped her hand and pulled her from the car.

"What on earth?" Hannah whispered.

"Daddy!" Sally shrieked.

The minute her feet hit the pavement, Isabella didn't get the chance to say a word, Prentice started walking, dragging her behind him.

Annie was out of her Rolls, her face white as a sheet.

"Is something wrong?" she asked as Prentice and Isabella came up to her.

Prentice halted and when he did so, he yanked Isabella against his side and his arm clamped firm around her waist.

Annie's eyes dropped to his arm. Fergus had also alighted and his eyes did the same.

"Everything's fine," Prentice announced but his voice was tight. "The groom is waiting and he's a fucking wreck, wanting you to beam here using space-age technology from a television show rather than ride here in a car. Clarissa called and she and Jennifer's car had problems but everything is fine now and they're five minutes away. We'll start when the mother-of-the-bride and the mother-of-the-groom finally arrive."

Annie breathed an audible sigh of relief.

Prentice's eyes sliced to Fergus.

"Keep Sally here. Elle and I have to talk," he ordered.

At his words, Annie started, her eyes getting wide.

Fergus's gaze moved to Sally, who had joined them and was looking from one adult to another appearing happy but confused.

Light apparently dawning (what light, Isabella didn't know), Fergus grinned. He curled firm fingers on Sally's shoulder, pulling her to his legs and he nodded to Prentice.

Prentice didn't hesitate further. Dropping his arm from her waist, he took her hand again and dragged her around the side of the church.

"Prentice," she snapped, tugging at her hand unsuccessfully, her heart tripping over itself. "Stop! What are you doing?"

He didn't answer. He dragged her around the side of the church to the back where he stopped.

"What on earth?" she asked irately, deciding to go with anger because fear was not an option.

She could *be* weak she just couldn't *show* weakness. That was a lesson her father drilled into her using a variety of different methods.

Prentice tugged her toward him, she collided with his hard body then he stepped forward, taking her with him.

She hit the stone wall of the church, tipped her head back, mouth open to give him what for, for scaring Annie and dragging Isabella around, but she didn't get out a sound.

He kissed her.

Hard, demanding, wet, deep and thorough.

It was a great kiss.

Of their own volition (not that she had the will to stop them) her hands slid up his shoulders, around his neck and she melted in his arms.

After he was done and she was putty in his hands, he lifted his head and his eyes bored into hers.

"*That's* what I would have done if you'd have woken up in my arms," he told her.

Her breath caught and her body trembled.

"Or part of it," he finished.

"Prentice—" she started.

"I've changed my mind," he cut her off. "I don't want to talk. I don't want any explanations. I don't give a fuck. I just want you."

Her heart turned over and her belly clenched.

She tried to pull away.

He yanked her back.

"No, you don't," he warned, his voice low, his meaning crystal clear.

"Prentice, you don't . . . you can't . . ." She couldn't think then she blurted, "Fiona."

"Aye, we'll talk about Fiona when the time is right."

"But—"

His face dipped close to hers, his eyes went gentle and his voice went soft. "I told you, baby, when you came back to me, I'd make you work for it but I'd take you back. You may not want to be back but I don't give a fuck. I'm keeping you this time."

He remembered.

He remembered what he said.

She remembered it too. Every single word.

She felt tears sting the backs of her eyes.

"I—"

He touched his mouth to hers and she went silent.

Then he rested his forehead against hers and for some insane reason he was grinning.

"Don't cry, Elle. Save it for when Dougal and Annie say, 'I do.'"

"Pren—"

He kissed her silent again, this time with more than a brush on her lips.

When his mouth released hers, he didn't give her the chance to speak. He took her hand and dragged her around to the front.

Dazed and panicked now for a different reason, Isabella noted that Clarissa and Dougal's Mum, Jennifer, had arrived.

Everyone turned to them when Prentice dragged Isabella to the group and then fixed her to his side again with a strong arm at her waist.

"Are we ready?" he asked.

"Daddy, are you wearing lipstick?" Sally asked in return, her voice high and disbelieving, her face agog.

Fergus coughed into his hand.

Annie started giggling.

Clarissa beamed.

Jennifer stared.

Patty and Hannah started shuffling, ducking their grinning faces.

Isabella closed her eyes tight.

When she opened them, Prentice was casually wiping her lipstick from his mouth with a handkerchief.

When he'd completed this task, he tilted his head down to look at her and grinned before he whispered, "You might want to fix your lips, baby."

Then he bent low, touched his lips to hers in front of *everybody* (including Sally!), left her swaying and entered the church.

————— ◆ —————

Fiona

FIONA REALLY WISHED she could get drunk.

Sure, it was lovely watching Annie and Dougal say, "I do."

Bella had cried. Clarissa had cried. Old Lady Kilbride had cried. Hell, there was barely a dry eye in the house even amongst the men. Even Sally had burst into tears, just for the sake of not being left out, at which Bella had handed her and Annie's bouquets to the next bridesmaid in line and picked Sally up, right in front of the congregation, cuddling her close as Sally sobbed baffled tears.

Fiona had also cried.

Hell, if you *didn't* cry, you'd have to have a heart of stone.

Then they all went to the reception and in front of all and sundry, Prentice had pulled Isabella away while she was in the act of gracefully entering the Rolls.

With everyone watching in stunned, avid silence, he whirled her around and manhandled her into his Range Rover with Sally alternately skipping and dancing behind them, swinging her empty flower girl basket. Jason had followed slowly, a knowing but happy smirk on his face.

At the reception, Prentice glued Bella to his side. If she even considered making a run for it, Fiona would have sworn he'd have tackled her and wrestled her to his 4x4 and driven off into the sunset (after he'd ordered Jason and Sally into the car, of course).

He didn't only glue her to his side, he made a public statement (but Fiona reckoned this statement was mostly directed at Bella) by being openly affectionate toward her in a way that could in *no* way be misread.

Annie looked delighted. It was the wedding gift she wanted above all, that was plain to see.

Dougal, at first, looked concerned. Then, as Prentice glared at the villagers, practically *daring* them to be mean to Bella so he could take them out (he'd even raised his brows at Hattie Fennick when she was approaching them, a nasty look on her face, but she read Prentice's challenge, visibly paled and switched directions at the last minute) Dougal started to become amused. Finally he approached his friend, clapped him on the back and gave a surprised Bella a genuine, hearty hug.

Fergus and Clarissa were both obviously gleeful. As was Old Lady Kilbride.

And Mikey was practically crowing.

Some of the villagers seemed wary but most of them went with the flow.

It was only Bella who seemed to swing between puzzled and alarmed. The only time she seemed sure of herself was when she was with Jason or Sally (which went a long way at helping the villagers to decide to go with the flow).

And Fiona didn't get it.

Clearly, she had a purpose for being on earth with her family. To make certain that everything was going to be all right. Now she figured that purpose was gone and her still being there was just plain mean. Or, perhaps, whatever powers that be were busy and she was low on the priority list.

Sure, she *supposed* she was happy that her family was healing and moving on.

But did she have to have her nose rubbed in it?

She understood when the dancing started.

The first dance was for Dougal and Annie and, again, there wasn't a dry eye in the house.

Then Annie danced with Fergus and Dougal danced with Jennifer.

As they were taking their seats, Annie grinning for some reason nervously, Fiona materialized behind her. She was seating herself beside Bella and as the DJ asked the best man and maid of honor to take the dance floor, Annie quickly turned to her friend.

"I'm sorry, Bella. I arranged this a long time ago and—"

She didn't get to finish, Prentice, never far from Bella, claimed her.

Wordlessly pulling her out of her seat, he guided her to the dance floor and then he took her in his arms.

And they danced alone on the dance floor, everyone watching, to Elton John's "Tiny Dancer."

For those who didn't get it, watching Prentice and Bella sway barely moving, they would get it.

Even Fiona had to admit they fit perfectly. Prentice's handsome dark head bent, his cheek pressed to hers, his lips at her ear. Bella's beautiful white-blonde head tipped back, her cheek against his, her eyes carrying a sheen of tears, her lips trembling. Prentice's arm was around her waist, noticeably tight. Her arm was around his shoulders, holding on as if that hold was the only thing keeping her standing.

His fingers, laced in hers, were lifted and pressed with Bella's hand twisted and resting against his heart.

The room had melted from existence and everyone in it knew they were superfluous to what was happening on the dance floor to the sweet words of a sad, sad song.

It was a Scottish fairytale come alive, right before their eyes.

And Fiona could take no more.

She had a soft heart but this was ridiculous.

But, on the closing notes to the song, a cold, imperious, *loud* voice sounded across the room.

"I should have known."

Bella went still as a statue, almost like she was made of marble.

Prentice's head shot up.

Fiona drifted so she could stare toward the edge of the dance floor.

An older man with impossibly good posture stood there wearing a suit and a venomous expression on his face.

Fiona had never seen him in her life and she still didn't like him.

Bella slowly unlaced her hand from Prentice's and turned around.

"Dad," she whispered in a horrified voice, "what are you *doing* here?"

Oh God.

That was Bella's father?

He took a step forward and raked scathing eyes down Bella's body.

"Dressed as a whore, acting like a whore. *Again*," Carver Austin said.

This time, Prentice's body turned to marble.

Gasps were heard around the room.

But he had yet to do his worst.

Bella came unstuck and walked swiftly to him.

"Dad, let's just go outside and—"

She didn't finish.

When she got close enough, Fiona and everyone else was shocked to see, his hand came back and he slapped her, sadistically. The fierce crack of his palm hitting her cheek sounded revoltingly throughout the room.

She was wearing hopelessly high heels and lost balance, falling to all fours at his feet.

The air in the room turned static and nobody moved.

Except Prentice who was there in a flash. Bending low, his arm around Bella's waist, he pulled her gently up in front of him and took five steps back, his face a mask of rage.

"Get out," Prentice growled, voice rumbling with fury, and Fiona feared he'd do harm to the older man, not that the old tosser didn't deserve it, just that it wouldn't have been a fair fight.

Bella's father barely glanced at Prentice, his voice went high and mocking when he taunted, *"Dad, I love him. He's not just a fisherman but even if he was, I wouldn't care. I love him. I want to marry him. I want to spend the rest of my life in that village with him."*

When he was done, everyone in the room, including Fiona, knew Mr. Austin was taunting Bella with her own, heartbreaking, long-ago-uttered words.

Most especially Prentice, whose face had gone white and whose arm around Bella had tightened.

But Carver Austin wasn't done.

"And here you are, first chance you get, throwing yourself at him like a common tart. What is the *matter* with you?"

"Carver, I think you should leave." Fergus was close, Dougal and Annie at his back.

Carver glared at Fergus then his eyes scraped over Dougal. "*You* should know better," he said scornfully, speaking to Fergus but referring to Dougal.

"Carver, leave," Fergus demanded.

"I'll go and I'm taking Isabella with me. I should have *never* let her spend time with your daughter."

Prentice opened his mouth to speak but Jason was suddenly standing in front of Carver Austin, *close* in front of him.

"You're not taking Miss Bella anywhere!" he shouted and Carver didn't hesitate. He shoved Fiona's son aside, striding toward his daughter.

Fiona prepared to launch a ghostly attack but she didn't get her chance.

Bella wrenched free of Prentice's arm and she took two angry steps toward her father, switched directions and caught Jason with an arm around his chest. Pulling him roughly so his back was against her front, she backed up, dragging Jason with her.

Her hold and actions fiercely protective, her words, spoken in a tone so harsh, it was scratching and hard to hear, seconded her actions.

"Don't you *dare* touch him. Don't you *dare*. Hit me, humiliate me, criticize me, but don't you *dare* touch Jason."

She backed into Prentice and stopped. His arm slid around her waist instantly. Sally, face full of fear, ran through the crowd and threw her arms around Bella's thighs. Burying her face in her own arm, Sally held on to Bella as she trembled.

Bella's hand not around Jason went to the nape of Sally's neck.

Carver took this all in, not missing a thing, especially not the fact that Jason shared his father's unusual eye color.

"Well done, Isabella. Ready-made family. You claimed your fisherman and now you can finally play house like you've always wanted."

The cruelty of his words sent Fiona reeling back several inches.

Was this man actually Bella's *father*?

Prentice had a different reaction.

Again in a growl, this one as frightening as it was threatening, he demanded, "Fergus, I swear to Christ, get him *the fuck* out of here."

It was Dougal that strode forward stating, "You're done, mate."

Carver glared at him. "Don't lay a hand on me."

"Allow *me* to lay a hand on you," Mikey said from behind Carver then he bunched Carver's suit jacket in his fist, turned and hustled the older man inelegantly out the door.

Fergus and Dougal's father, Hamish, followed.

Bella and Fiona's family stood still on the dance floor, the eyes of everyone in the room were on them.

Bella moved first. Pulling free of Prentice's arm and gently disengaging from Sally and Jason only long enough to crouch down, she brought Sally in close with her arm, and with her other hand she cupped Jason's jaw and looked in his face.

"Are you okay, Jason?" she asked softly.

"Is that your dad?" Jason asked in reply.

Tears threatening to roll down her cheeks, Bella didn't answer. She just nodded.

"He's a wanker," Jason announced.

Fiona thought her son was *not* wrong.

Bella gave him a trembling smile.

Then she stood. Letting go of the children, face pale, tears now rolling silently down her cheeks, she took in the assemblage gazing at her with varying degrees of sadness and compassion.

Her eyes caught on Annie.

"I'm so sorry," she whispered.

"Oh Bella," Annie whispered back and started to walk toward her but Bella's hand shot up.

"No," she said, taking in a breath. "It's me. That dark cloud follows me. I shouldn't have come."

Fiona's heart squeezed.

Bella wrote *a lot* about her "dark cloud" in her journals.

A lot, a lot.

"Bella," Annie breathed, obviously knowing about the dark cloud.

But Bella looked away.

She laid a hand on Jason's head. Sliding it down to rest on his cheek, she allowed herself that minute touch and then her hand dropped away.

She turned to Sally. Cupping Fiona's daughter's cheek in her trembling hand, her fingers curled and she stroked that cheek with her knuckles before she turned to Prentice.

"Elle," he murmured, his hand moving to her waist but she scurried away.

"I shouldn't have come."

"Baby."

That was something else Fiona could do without. Prentice called Sally "baby" and Fiona had heard, a long time ago, him calling Bella that same endearment.

He'd never called her anything but "Fiona" or, when he was feeling affectionate, which she had to admit was often, he called her "Fee."

She could do without hearing her husband's deep brogue calling Bella "baby" in the same way he held her in bed that morning. Like she was precious.

"I shouldn't have come," Bella repeated.

Then she turned on her hopelessly high heel and she gracefully ran.

Fiona always *knew* she could run gracefully in those heels.

Prentice didn't hesitate, he went after her.

"Watch the children," he ordered Debs when he passed his ashen sister.

Fiona sped behind them.

He caught her at her rental car.

Hands to her hips, he pulled her from the open door, slammed it, twirled her around, took a step into her and pinned her against the car.

"You didn't leave me," he declared, his voice hoarse.

She shook her head, those silent tears sliding down her cheeks.

"What did he do to you?"

She shook her head, refusing to answer.

Prentice's hands went to either side of her neck and gave her a gentle squeeze.

"Did he hit you?"

She stared up at him, mutely crying.

Prentice dipped his face to hers and his voice got soft, "Baby, did he hit you?"

She bit her lip and her eyes slid away.

Prentice's head came up.

"*Christ!*" he swore so viciously, Fiona was surprised the windows on the cars didn't shatter.

Bella winced.

"He kept you from Annie, didn't he? When she got hurt. Because she was here. He kept you from her to keep you from me."

She closed her eyes slowly.

She opened them and nodded.

"I can't fucking *believe* this," Prentice growled.

Bella finally spoke, her voice timid and soft. A voice Fiona had never heard. A voice *Prentice* (by the looks of him) never heard.

Nor did he like.

"It was for the best."

"It was for the best?" he repeated, sounding appalled.

"I'm . . . you . . ." she stammered. "You wouldn't have Jason. You wouldn't have Sally." It was Prentice who closed his eyes then and Bella went on, her voice getting stronger, "You wouldn't have had Fiona." Prentice's eyes opened and pain was there, Bella saw it and she swallowed. Her hand lifted and she touched the laugh lines at the sides of his eyes with her forefinger. "You wouldn't have those, Prentice, because you wouldn't have had the laughter I know Fiona gave you."

Fiona felt her throat close as she watched Prentice bend his neck and rest his forehead against Bella's.

"I have to go," she whispered and his head shot right back up.

"Sorry?" he asked in a dangerous tone.

"I have to go," she repeated.

Fiona watched Prentice's eyes narrow. "What the fuck are you on about?"

"I have to go," she said yet again.

Fiona got close and shouted, *Don't. Don't Bella. This isn't you. You aren't the dark cloud. That was all your father. Don't do this. Don't go.*

"You aren't going," Prentice declared.

"I am. I have to," she told him.

"You aren't and you can't," he shot back.

"Don't you see?"

"No, I fucking well do not."

Her body jolted. "Annie and Dougal's wedding, perfect, except for me."

"You didn't ruin their wedding."

"No? Who did? Me being here brought my father here and—"

"This is insane, Elle. You aren't—"

"Insane? Like my mother?" Fiona watched Prentice's head jerk but Bella wasn't done. "She was insane, Prentice. People in their right minds don't kill themselves."

"People in their right minds find reasons to kill themselves every day," he returned.

"You don't know."

"You don't either."

"I know my mother wasn't in her right mind. I know that for certain."

"Elle—"

"And you don't need *that* in your life *or* in your children's lives."

Prentice's face grew stunned. "Are you saying—?"

"I'm saying I'm a product of *her* and *him* and *that* is what you'll have around your children if we carry on with this madness."

"You may be a product of them, Elle, but you're *you*."

"And who's that, then? You said yourself you don't even know me!"

"Yes, I do. You're the girl I fell in love with twenty years ago. That girl came home drunk two nights ago. Last night, she let me make love to her, telling me it's never been that good, and later, she slept in my arms."

"That girl isn't *me*."

Prentice glared at her.

Bella glared back.

All of a sudden he tore his hand through his hair, and at that gesture

Fiona knew he was losing patience because she'd seen him do it many times before.

"This is ridiculous," he clipped.

Yes, losing patience.

"I agree, just let me go."

His eyes narrowed. "I told you, this time I'm keeping you."

She put her hands to his chest and gave a hearty shove. Prentice's torso rocked back but then came in closer.

"You can't *keep me*," she snapped. "I don't want to be *kept*."

He put his face close to hers. "Bollocks."

She pulled in breath through her nose and looked at the heavens.

When she looked back at him, she asked, "Prentice, don't you *see?*"

Fiona shouted, *No! No, he doesn't see! You have to tell him. You have to tell him so he can sort you out. He has no idea. You HAVE GOT to TELL him.*

Bella shook her head to clear Fiona's words.

And then she said, "It's for the best. It was twenty years ago, and you can't deny that." His mouth got tight at that and Bella went on, this time quietly, "It will be again. You'll find happiness, Prentice. It's just never something you'd find with me."

Prentices eyes got hard. "Elle, you get in that car and drive away, that's it. You leave me *and* the children this time, if you get second thoughts and you come back, I'll no' make you work for it. There'll be *nothing* to work for."

To Fiona's shock, disappointment, anger and sadness, although Bella's face paled and her throat convulsed, her head nodded.

Prentice felt those same four emotions and he didn't hide them.

His voice was gruff when he stated, "The last time, even though I didn't know it, you were taken from me. This time, if you leave, it's all you."

Fiona saw Bella's eyes flash with indecision.

"Prentice," she whispered.

Don't get in that car, Bella, Fiona shouted, *Don't do it.*

Then, seeing Bella make her decision (the *wrong* one) and shift toward the door, Fiona tried yelling at Prentice.

Don't let her go. She needs you to save her. She needs her knight in shining armor, not a man who'd let her go. This is twice, Prentice, and you don't even know this is all on you. Twenty years, and it's all YOU. You should have gone to save her the last time and you let her go. This is the same. She isn't leaving you, she has this idea that she's saving you. This is NOT her LEAVING. This is YOU LETTING HER GO!

As usual, Prentice didn't hear a word Fiona said.

And by the time she was done yelling, Bella was in the car and she didn't even look at Prentice's angry, tight face as she reversed the rental out of the spot and she didn't look back as she drove away.

Chapter
TEN

Isabella's Return

Isabella

The next three weeks went by in a fog for Isabella.

Well, not all of it.

She remembered texting Annie and Mikey repeatedly to let them know she was okay and not about to drive her car over a cliff.

And she remembered Fergus showing up at the hotel she'd checked herself into after her mad flight from the wedding reception. She remembered him having a drink with her in the bar, guiding her to her room, holding her while she cried and tucking her into bed when she was exhausted from her tears. She also remembered him taking her to breakfast the next morning and to the airport that afternoon.

She also remembered her heretofore unknown fury likely induced by her not sleeping (even a little bit) and her mind playing and replaying the night before and day of Annie and Dougal's wedding, second by second, in a constant loop, boiling up and rolling over.

This gave her the equally heretofore unknown courage to confront her father days after her return.

She walked right into her childhood home and asked him why *on earth* he'd shown up and ruined Annie and Dougal's Scottish Fairytale Come True Wedding and she'd used those exact words. And she asked him why *on earth* he'd come tearing to Scotland when he'd heard she was there and then treated her like a fifteen-year-old he'd caught heavy petting with her boyfriend in a car instead of a forty-year-old divorcée dancing with a man at a wedding.

And she remembered his answer.

"Isabella," he'd started on that disappointed sigh she knew *way* too well, "after this last stunt, I've given up on you. No matter what I've done, how hard I've worked, you've turned out *just* like your mother. Therefore, in a way, I'm glad you came because you should know and it's saved me the trouble of seeking you out. You're disinherited. My will has already been changed. I'm giving my legacy to the Art Institute of Chicago. We're in discussions for them to name a wing after me."

Isabella stood in front of him, stunned at his answer which, incidentally, was *not* an answer at all but simply a mean, nasty statement.

And she stood in front of him stunned that he showed not one smidgeon of regret or embarrassment for striking her in front of an audience to the point she fell to her knees.

Then she surprised herself by replying coolly, completely in control and without a shred of fear (something Carver Austin taught her well, just not how to do it with him), "Well, when you're dead, and they've named that wing after you, I'll be sure *not* to visit. Until that time, *you* be sure *not* to contact or come near me again."

And with that she'd turned on her hideously expensive, high-heeled pump, which regardless of her losing her father's legacy she still could afford since her mother was loaded too and *she* willed every penny to Isabella.

She also remembered making the harebrained, insane decision that she might never be going back to that village and she might never see Prentice or Jason or Sally again but that didn't mean she couldn't send Sally a box of American candy.

So she did.

She bought every kind of candy and chocolate you could get in America that you couldn't get in Scotland (and some that you could, just so Sally could make a taste-testing comparison) and she Fed Exed it to Sally.

After she'd done that she worried that giving Sally a box of candy would make Jason feel left out, so she Fed Exed him a book on how to teach yourself to play guitar.

Days later, she walked by a store where in the window she saw a little girl's magic wand that had all sorts of glittery ribbons trailing from it and a big, puffy, lilac satin star at the tip. She walked in and found the store had all sorts of magic-oriented little girl stuff that Sally would love. So she filled another box and Fed Exed it.

To even things out, she bought Jason a Bears jersey and a Cubs baseball hat and Fed Exed that.

Further, she remembered spending a lot of time remembering every minute she spent with Sally and Jason.

And every minute she spent falling right back in love with Prentice (not that she ever fell out of love with him).

And she remembered a lot about that.

She remembered Prentice winking at his son.

She remembered the warm looks he gave his daughter.

She remembered him offering her the pancake on his very own plate.

She remembered when he told her she was not easy to forget.

She remembered how he guided her to bed, took off her shoes and held her drunken body, giving her a tight squeeze when they shared a moment of happiness for Annie and Dougal.

She remembered him laughing at her but taking care of her when she was hungover.

She remembered his hands on her, his mouth on her and the incredibly beautiful feel of him inside her.

She remembered how sweet it was when he called her "baby."

She remembered him telling her, "I just want you."

She remembered that *he* remembered the words he said to her, twenty years ago, the same words that were seared into her brain.

She remembered how much she loved it when he called her "Elle" because the Elle he knew was who she had always wanted to be.

She remembered swaying in his arms to a sad song and letting herself believe, if only for three minutes, that she might get her fairytale too.

And, lastly, she remembered the look on his face in her rearview mirror when she drove away.

But other than that, she was in a fog, mostly because she was trying *not* to remember.

———————•———————

IT WAS THE dead of night and Isabella was dozing, still unable to sleep, when she heard the phone ring.

She reached for it, put it to her ear and said, "Hello."

"Bella?"

Isabella came up to an elbow and her heart thumped painfully in her chest when she heard Annie's tone.

"Annie? What is it? Are you back from Greece? Is everything okay?" Isabella's questions came out in a rush and her mind was racing.

God, she hoped Dougal was all right, they'd only just come back from their honeymoon.

And Fergus, he beat cancer, but Isabella heard that comes back all the time.

And Clarissa, she could be crazy, just like her daughter. Anything could happen when you were always doing crazy things!

And Prentice . . . but Isabella didn't go there.

Those questions were greeted with silence.

Isabella waited.

"Annie?" she prompted.

"Yes, Dougal and I are back from Greece."

Annie stopped talking.

Isabella waited.

Then she pressed, "And?"

Another pause then, "It's Sally," Annie answered softly, and Isabella's thumping heart stopped dead. "She's been knocked over by a car."

Isabella lay still in her bed, her eyes unfocused, her mind filled with images of Sally.

Isabella hadn't thought to worry about Sally. In her mind, Sally was invincible, protected by her youth and her shield of impenetrable cheerfulness.

Nothing could happen to Sally.

Especially not something so horrific as being hit by a car.

"Bella? Are you there?"

Isabella's voice was a croak when she asked, "Is she okay?"

"Broken bones and—" Annie stopped.

"And what?" Isabella pushed.

"They've induced a coma because of the head injuries."

Isabella threw the covers off the bed and jumped out.

"Bella, I know something went wrong with Prentice." Annie was talking as Isabella ran from her room, down the hall to where she stowed her luggage. "He's not talking to Dougal, and Dad told me to leave you alone, you needed time and then you'd call me. I know you probably don't want to come all the way back here but—"

Isabella cut her off. "I'll be on the next flight."

A moment of silence then, "What?"

"I'll be on the next flight," Isabella repeated as she lugged out one of her bags and carried it down the hall.

"You're . . . coming?" Annie sounded astounded.

"I'll call you back when I have details."

"You'll . . . call?" Annie *still* sounded astounded.

Isabella didn't have time for Annie's astonishment.

"Annie," Isabella said evenly, using everything she had to calm her breathing, her heart and her mind and not scream with fear, anger and impatience, "I need to get off the phone and call the airlines. I'll ring you when I know when I'm arriving."

Another moment of silence then, "Okay."

Isabella nodded and was about to take the phone from her ear and hit the off button when Annie spoke again.

"Bella, honey, it's going to be all right."

Isabella was no nurse (no matter what Mikey told the children) but she knew inducing comas because of head injuries made the chances of everything being "all right" pretty dismal.

And Isabella had learned, over and over, that very little ended up "all right."

But she couldn't think of that now.

She had a plane to catch.

She didn't know which one yet or when it left but whatever or whenever, she was going to catch it.

———— · ————

Prentice

PRENTICE STOOD LOOKING out the window of his daughter's hospital room thinking that there was only one thing worse than watching your always full of life and laughter wife wasting away in a matter of months.

That was seeing your always full of life and laughter six-year-old daughter lying in a coma in a hospital room.

These were his thoughts when the door opened and Annie walked in.

Prentice began to smile a tired smile. The accident was two days ago and Annie had barely left the hospital. Debs and his mother had fallen to pieces but Annie had been a rock.

The smile died when Annie, who was setting down suitcases, was followed by Elle.

For the first time in forty-eight hours, Prentice forgot about his daughter and he stared at Elle in shock.

In his memory, both recent and past, he never remembered Elle looking bad.

Decades ago, she was always bright-eyed, pink-cheeked and cheery, a healthy glow emanating from her. She wore even her casual clothes with a grace that made them stylish.

More recently, she was cool and refined, classically beautiful, her poise alluring. She wore her sophisticated clothes with a grace and assurance that made them striking.

Three weeks she'd been gone and now she looked gaunt and

fatigued. She'd lost weight. Her pallor was startling. There were soft, blue shadows under her eyes. Her hair was tied up in a mess on top of her head and her blouse and jacket were wrinkled as if she'd slept in them.

Her tired eyes skittered across him and went direct to the bed.

Prentice watched as she lifted her hand, held on to the edge of the door with white-knuckled fingers and her eyes closed slowly.

He wanted to be furious at her unbelievable cheek.

He couldn't be.

He didn't have the energy and he didn't have the capacity when her face filled with the worry he'd experienced gnawing at his gut constantly for two days.

He watched as she opened her eyes, let go of the door and strode into the room to Sally's bed.

Then he watched as she reached out and touched the cast on Sally's arm with her fingertips.

Finally he watched her head turn from Sally to him.

"I'm sorry, Prentice."

Christ. Even her voice sounded exhausted.

"Aye. I am too."

Her head tilted slightly. "Do you mind if I stay awhile?"

Prentice shook his head. "No, she'd like that."

And she would. If Sally was awake, she'd be in fits of glee.

Elle's departure had left Jason moody and confused. This had only shifted (slightly) when Elle's boxes started to arrive.

Sally, on the other hand, chose to think Elle had gone on an enchanted holiday meeting dukes and princes and talking birds, and she chatted about all these magical fairytale possibilities and Elle incessantly. Her blind adoration of Elle only intensified when the boxes started to arrive.

Elle grabbed a chair and dragged it to the side of the bed. She dumped her purse on the floor, sat down and got close. Leaning forward, she crossed her arms on the bed and put her chin on them.

Then, with her head turned toward Sally, she started whispering to his daughter.

Annie moved to Prentice.

"I had to call her," Annie said softly.

Prentice tore his gaze from the bed to look at his friend.

"Aye."

"She came straight away," Annie informed him.

If you told him four days ago his daughter would be knocked over by a car and Elle would come straight away, he wouldn't have believed it. Two months ago, something happened to Annie or Fergus, if you told him Elle would come straight away, he wouldn't have believed it.

Looking at her, he knew without a shred of doubt she came straight away.

Prentice didn't know what to do with that so he didn't do anything with it.

"Aye," he repeated.

"I know this is going to sound, erm . . . mad . . ." Prentice thought most everything Annie came up with was mad but he watched her mutely and she went on, "But, do you mind taking Bella to Dad's place later? I promised Mrs. Kilbride I'd take her to the shops today. If I don't go round, she won't have tea."

Oh, he minded. A great deal.

And it *was* mad.

As mad as it was when Annie finagled his last reunion with Elle, which incidentally ended very badly.

At that moment, Prentice wanted to spend time with Elle only slightly less than he wanted his daughter to be in a coma.

Annie leaned in. "Please, Prentice. I wouldn't ask if—"

Unfortunately, he was too tired to fight it.

"Aye, I'll take her to Fergus's before I go get Jason."

Annie squeezed his biceps and walked to Elle. She leaned into her friend, Elle's head turned from Sally to listen and Annie whispered in her ear.

Prentice watched as Elle's wan face grew ashen and her eyes flew to Prentice.

She tore her gaze from Prentice, looked at Annie and he watched her lips form the word, "Annie—"

"It's only a ride." He heard Annie reply before she squeezed Elle's shoulder.

Without hesitation, Annie hurried out the door not giving Elle time to protest or Prentice time to change his mind.

Yes, Prentice decided, Annie was mad.

"I'm sorry," Elle said again and his eyes went from the closing door to her.

He didn't reply to her words.

Instead he said, "I'm getting coffee. Do you want one?"

She shook her head.

Prentice left.

When he returned, her head was back to her arm on the bed but this time it was her temple not her chin resting on them. And this time one arm was slightly extended, the fingers of her hand curled lightly around Sally's cast.

Prentice walked up behind her and was about to speak when he saw her eyes were closed.

She was asleep.

He studied her tired face for a long moment and then went back to the window. Looking out, he sipped his coffee, wishing it was whisky.

He stood there a long time.

Too long.

It came to the point where he needed to pick his son up from school.

But, God help him, he didn't have the fucking heart to wake Elle.

———— ◆ ————

Isabella

THE RIDE FROM the hospital to the school was silent.

They were late.

Isabella was horrified she'd fallen asleep.

Now they were late picking up Jason so Prentice couldn't drop her off at Fergus's first. And Jason would be waiting for Prentice and likely worried. And Isabella hadn't given herself time to think about what she would do or say when she saw Prentice again (or Jason).

Even though it took ages to get there, all her thoughts had been centered on getting to Sally. She hadn't let herself think of Prentice or, she knew, she would have lost what little courage she had and she would never have come.

And more, she was sleep-deprived, jetlagged, her short nap had exacerbated that and she felt muddled.

Not muddled enough not to want to push Annie off the nearest cliff for getting Isabella stuck in a car with a weary, unhappy Prentice who hated her again though.

On this thought, the school came in sight.

Jason was outside with some boys, unenthusiastically kicking around a soccer ball.

One of his friends saw Prentice's Range Rover and jerked his chin to Jason.

Jason's head turned, he caught sight of his father's car, started to wave to his friends and then his eyes locked on Isabella.

His arm dropped and he started running to the car.

Oh dear.

She didn't know what to expect.

Whatever it was, she had no choice but to tough it out and she had Annie to thank for that too.

When Prentice stopped the car, Isabella got out.

Jason skidded to a halt in front of her and shouted, "You came back!"

This was an interesting greeting, one, in her muddled state, she couldn't quite decipher.

"Jason," she said softly.

He dashed forward and threw his arms around her, giving her a fierce hug right in front of his friends.

This was a far better greeting.

Isabella relaxed, let his hug warm away some of the coldness that had imprisoned her heart since she drove away from Jason's father three weeks ago, put a hand to the back of his neck and closed her eyes.

She opened them when he pulled away and proclaimed, "I knew you'd come back. I knew it when you sent me that book."

"Jason," she repeated, wanting to say something. She had no earthly clue *what* but she knew she should say something.

Jason interrupted her by jerking his head to the side and announcing, "Dad, she's back!"

"I know, Jace," Prentice's deep voice answered, and Isabella looked toward the sound to see he'd joined them.

The happiness in Jason's face faded and he looked back at Isabella.

"Do you know about Sally?"

She nodded. "Yes, honey, we've just been at the hospital."

"Did you come to see her?" Jason asked.

Isabella nodded.

"She'll be happy to see you when she wakes up," Jason declared, and Isabella swallowed and forced herself not to look at Prentice.

"I hope so," Isabella replied.

"Get in the car, Jace. We've got to take Elle to Fergus's before we get tea."

Prentice started to move back around the car and Isabella began to turn to get in but both of them noticed that Jason didn't move.

They both turned to Jason.

"Jace, mate, in the car," Prentice reiterated.

"Why's Miss Bella going to Fergus's?" Jason asked, looking confused and, for some reason, borderline angry.

"She's staying there," Prentice answered.

"Why?" Jason asked, now borderline belligerent.

"Because the last time I was here I didn't get to spend any time with him," Isabella explained.

"But . . . you stay with us," he replied as if she'd been a frequent visitor since the time of his infancy and regularly was their guest.

Isabella's heart started racing.

"Pardon?" she asked.

"When you're here," he answered. "You stay with us when you're here."

"Jace—" Prentice began.

Jason was not to be denied.

Definitely belligerent he asked Isabella, "Are you here to see Fergus or are you here to see Sally and Dad and me?"

"Jason—" she began.

He cut her off by demanding, "Well?"

"Mate, she's staying at Fergus's," Prentice said firmly.

"No, she's not. She stays with us. She's here because Sally's hurt. She's here to take care of us. She can't take care of us at *Fergus's*."

Isabella took a step forward, saying, "Yes, I can. I'll rent a car and—"

Jason took a step back, locked his ten-year-old boy's body and shouted, *"You're staying with us!"*

Isabella stopped moving.

Then she drew in a breath.

She chanced a glance at Prentice.

His jaw was tight and she saw a muscle tick there. She'd never seen Prentice's jaw do that but she figured it was probably not good.

Prentice's eyes sliced to her and he shocked her to her core when he jerked his chin and ordered, "Call Fergus."

"I don't—" Isabella started but stopped when Prentice's head slanted sharply to the side and his face went hard.

Now, she decided, staring into his hard face, was *not* the time to defy Prentice Cameron.

Therefore she whispered, "I'll call Fergus."

———— • ————

Fiona

FIONA WAS PLUCKING at her guitar in the children's playroom when she sensed their return.

Quick as a flash, she dematerialized and materialized in the great room.

The hospital was outside the village limits.

Fiona couldn't get there, no matter how hard she tried (and she'd tried *hard*).

She wanted news of Sally.

She watched the door open and stared at Prentice holding four carrier bags of groceries, two in each hand.

Fiona continued to stare.

Groceries?

Prentice had been to the grocery store once since Bella left mainly because it took that long to eat through the abundant provisions Bella had purchased when she'd been there.

Fiona watched as he stopped, jerked his head at something behind him and then her ghostly mouth dropped open when Bella walked through the door, carrying a bag in each hand.

Fiona would have been surprised that Bella was even there but she was too busy being *more* surprised that Bella looked like hell.

Bella always looked good.

Once, way back in the day, Bella got a summer cold that took her out of commission for a few days. When Fiona and her ex-boyfriend Scott had come round to Prentice's mum's place to see her, Bella had been lounging on the couch, nestled in Prentice's arms. She'd been, reportedly, sick as a dog, but she'd looked fabulous.

Now she didn't look good. She didn't even look bad. She looked *awful*.

Such was Fiona's shock, she just floated in the great room while Bella and Prentice walked in, Jason following (also carrying three carrier bags). All of them were silent as they dumped the bags on the kitchen counter.

Bella and Jason got busy unpacking the groceries while Prentice walked away.

Bella saw him going.

She started toward him, saying, "Prentice, please don't. I'll get my bags."

She stopped talking when Prentice sent her a look that would turn a gaily running creek into an ice rink in a blink.

Prentice turned away and walked back out of the house.

Bella bit her lip and walked back into the kitchen.

"Dad's been in kind of a bad mood for a few weeks," Jason muttered.

Bella sighed and Fiona laughed for the first time since Bella left (except for when the kids got their boxes from Bella, firstly she laughed then because the children had been so happy and secondly because

Prentice had looked so cross and then he'd brooded (more) for entire *days*, and Fiona, for some reason, found that hilarious).

"It's okay, sweetheart. Why don't you take your books upstairs and I'll deal with this?" Bella replied.

"I'll help." Jason was still muttering, and he was also putting groceries away with a determination that, both Fiona and Bella noted when they glanced at Jason, no one could undermine.

Intelligently, Bella didn't try.

Fiona watched (again with surprise) as Prentice brought in Bella's two suitcases and carried them down the hall to the guest suite while Jason and Bella unpacked groceries.

What in bloody hell was going on?

She could have shouted it but, of course, no one would answer.

She'd just have to watch and see.

Prentice returned and disappeared in his study.

Bella immediately began making tea once the groceries were unpacked and Jason ran his book bag upstairs.

Fiona took her opportunity and zoomed close to Bella.

How's Sally? she shouted.

All right, so Bella was there out of the blue after the whole fiasco at the wedding. She looked like death warmed over and she was staying with Prentice and Jason.

But . . . priorities.

Bella could hear her, even once spoke directly to her and Fiona needed news of her daughter.

Bella didn't answer. She didn't flinch. She didn't even twitch.

Bella! How's Sally? Please tell me, Fiona shouted again, this time louder (but still silent, of course).

Fiona waited.

Bella kept rubbing butter into the skin of the chicken, giving no indication she heard one single word Fiona said.

Fiona groaned in frustration.

Before she could ask again, Jason returned and Fiona was astounded to see her son immediately began to help Bella with tea (something he *never* did for his mother unless threatened with certain death). All the while they worked Bella quietly gave Jason directions that he followed to the letter.

Bella had the chicken in the oven (stuffed with delicious-looking stuffing), Jason had cleaned and carefully chopped the broccoli and carrots under Bella's relentlessly vigilant eye at Jason wielding a knife and was cutting up the potatoes that Bella had peeled when Prentice walked into the kitchen.

He stopped and stood for a while, watching this activity, a muscle ticking in his jaw.

And Fiona knew what he saw that made him so annoyed.

Firstly, Jason was helping with dinner. That was worth putting in your journal (if you had one, which Prentice did not). But, more to the point, he was helping *Bella* with dinner.

Secondly, Bella looked ready to drop. You could actually *see* that the woman had no energy. How she was remaining upright and cooking was a mystery.

Prentice, Fiona knew, was also tired. He hadn't slept in two days. He hadn't slept well in three weeks.

But, as tired as Prentice had to be, Bella was more tired it was plain to see.

And it wasn't only from worry over Sally being knocked over.

Life, Fiona knew, was finally wearing Isabella Austin Evangahlala down.

Just what Fiona needed, something *else* to worry about.

Who said you could rest when you were dead? Whoever it was, they *lied*.

"Jace, give me a minute. I want to talk to Elle," Prentice said to his son.

Fiona watched Bella's shoulders get tight as Jason turned to give his father an assessing look.

Prentice held his son's gaze and Fiona would have laughed if she wasn't holding her non-existent ghost breath.

They were having a showdown.

The last time Jason was with Bella, her father walked into the wedding reception and struck her so forcefully she went down to her hands and knees. After that hideous event she'd disappeared for three weeks coming back looking like the walking dead.

Now, it was plain to see Jason wasn't leaving Bella's side even at his father's command, not if he thought something would harm her even if that something was his father.

Fiona had only nine years to raise her son right and she was pretty pleased with herself that she'd accomplished this feat (with Prentice's help, of course, but, at that moment, Fiona decided to take all the credit).

"I'll finish the potatoes, Jason. Do as your dad says, okay?" Bella said quietly, and Fiona looked to her to see she was watching the show-down and it had alarmed her.

Prentice's eyes cut to Bella and his mouth got tight as Jason turned his assessing look to her.

Then Jason nodded and loped up the stairs.

Bella went back to the potatoes and started cutting.

Prentice moved in close (as did Fiona) and Fiona watched as he took the knife right out of her hand. Her body jolted, her surprised eyes turned to Prentice and she opened her mouth to speak.

Prentice got there first. "I don't need your help making Jason mind."

Well, Fiona thought, *that wasn't a good start.*

Bella's mouth stayed open not because she wanted to say something but because she was shocked.

"Go to bed," Prentice ordered.

Bella's eyes got wide.

She closed her mouth then opened it to ask, "What?"

"Go to bed. I'll finish this."

Bella glanced with bewilderment at the potatoes then back at Prentice and, even Fiona had to admit, regardless of how drawn she looked she was still adorable.

"But I'm cooking," she replied, clearly confused.

"You're about to pass out."

Light dawned on her exhausted mind.

She looked away and started to turn from Prentice, saying, "I'm fine."

Prentice stopped her by curling his fingers on her upper arm. Her head tilted back to look at him.

"Elle, I said, go to bed."

Her cheeks flushed with anger as she returned, "And *I* said, I'm *fine.*"

Prentice moved closer to her at the same time he brought Bella closer to him with his hand on her arm.

Fiona watched Bella stiffen.

"Go to bed," he repeated.

"I'm finishing tea."

"Go to bed."

"No!" she snapped.

His face dipped close to hers as he made his threat, and since Fiona knew Prentice didn't make threats, it was more a promise.

"You can go to bed or I'll carry you there."

Bella's mouth dropped open and so did Fiona's.

He wasn't joking.

"I'm very serious," Prentice warned, sounding very, *very* serious.

There it was, he wasn't joking.

"Prentice, I don't see why—"

Prentice interrupted her, his voice harsh. "I have enough to worry about, and so does my son, without either of us having to worry about you."

Well, Fiona had to admit, that was true enough.

The color went out of Bella's cheeks again and Fiona reckoned Bella agreed.

"Go to bed," Prentice repeated.

Bella looked to the oven, her shoulders fell then she looked back at Prentice.

"The chicken has another hour to cook. It needs to be basted every fifteen minutes. The vegetables—" she began.

"Aye, I'll do it."

"The chicken has to be cooked through, if it isn't—"

He cut her off by saying, low and rumbly, "Elle."

She snapped her mouth shut.

Then she nodded.

Prentice let go of her arm, she started to walk away, stopped and turned back.

"Are you going back to Sally after tea?" she asked.

"Aye," he answered shortly.

She hesitated and crossed her arms on her middle, fingers curled around her elbows. She licked her lips, stared at the floor a second then took a deep breath and inquired in a voice so soft, even Fiona with extra-sensory abilities due to her ghost-dom could almost not hear, "If I'm awake, can I come with you?"

Prentice glared at her.

Bella withstood the glare but Fiona saw her swallow nervously.

Then he grunted, "Aye."

Her lips turned up in an almost smile.

With that she left the room.

Prentice stared after her for a long time.

Finally he tore his hand through his hair as he bent his head to stare at his boots.

Then he ruined tea.

————•◆•————

ISABELLA WAS AWAKE when the food was ready.

She just laid there, eyes open, face sad, and Fiona shouted at her to get up, get up, *get up*.

Fiona didn't know if it was her shouting or the sounds that came from the kitchen through the opened doors to the guest suite but Isabella finally heaved a big sigh, got up, wandered down and ate with them.

The chicken looked heavenly.

The vegetables were way overdone.

Neither Isabella nor Jason uttered a word mainly because Prentice's brooding glower did not invite this.

The three of them went to the hospital after tea.

When they came back a lot later, Fiona didn't have to shout her questions to Isabella in hopes of finding out how Sally was.

The worry etched into their faces told the tale.

Chapter
ELEVEN

Celebrity Gossip Magazine

Isabella

"Can I have Miss Bella's chocolate cake for breakfast while I'm recupralating?" Sally asked from her place, buckled safely in the back of Prentice's Range Rover.

Isabella looked over at the child as Jason twisted around from the front and corrected, "Recuperating."

"That's what I said, *recupralating*," Sally shot back.

Isabella smiled.

From behind the wheel, Prentice replied, "No."

Sally's face turned obstinate then it brightened as a new idea came to her. "Since I got knocked over by a car, can I have a horse?"

"No," Prentice answered.

"A puppy?" Sally tried.

"No," Prentice repeated.

"A kitty?" Sally pushed.

"No, Sally," Prentice returned.

"A *fish?*" Sally cried in desperation.

Prentice chuckled before he replied, "We'll see about a fish."

Sally smiled cheerfully at Isabella, and Isabella smiled back.

A miracle had happened.

When the doctors woke Sally after her brain swelling had gone down, she was groggy, in pain and confused, but mostly she was Sally.

They did tests and found no memory loss, her concentration and recall were excellent, in fact all functions were a go.

The doctors were stunned.

Prentice, Jason, Debs, Annie, Dougal, Fergus and Prentice and Fiona's families (not to mention Isabella) were relieved.

A miracle.

Isabella had never witnessed a miracle. In all her life, the only kind of miracle she'd experienced was Dougal and Annie finding their way back to each other.

Isabella was used to tragedy and disaster. She didn't know what to do with a miracle.

She found she didn't have a great deal of trouble coping.

The last week had gone by in a blur.

If she wasn't at the hospital with Sally, she was at the market (there always seemed to be something they needed in the house that wasn't *in* the house—they ran out of salt, they ran out of laundry detergent, they ran out of furniture polish, it was never-ending).

If she wasn't at the market, she was mopping, sweeping, vacuuming, doing laundry, ironing, stripping beds, making beds or dusting. Prentice, it was obvious, had done very little (if any) housework since she'd left.

If she wasn't doing that, she was (at Prentice's surprising request) running Jason to school, from school or to football practice in her rental car when Prentice couldn't do it because he was at work or had to be at the hospital for one of Sally's tests.

If she wasn't doing that, she was spending time with Sally or Fergus and Annie.

Another, smaller miracle had occurred that week too.

For, when she was in town or waiting with the mothers and fathers for football practice to end, the villagers didn't avoid her or give her nasty looks. People she knew way back when (and some she didn't know), smiled at her when they caught her eye. Some said hello. A few even engaged her in conversation, asking about Sally, Jason and Prentice and even how she, Isabella, was bearing up under the strain (and offering help!).

Isabella figured this about face had a good deal to do with the fact that her father humiliated her in front of the entire village.

Which, in itself, was refreshed humiliation.

However, Isabella was too exhausted to focus on that. Instead, she focused on their kindness which was a great deal easier to deal with.

Even though her days were mentally and physically strenuous, her nights were spent tossing and turning. She rarely slept and most of the time forgot to eat (probably due to the fact that she wasn't hungry).

Isabella was running on empty. She knew this but had no clue what to do about it or any time to come up with a solution.

Except when she was tossing and turning but most of *that* time was spent thinking about Prentice sleeping in his own bed under the same roof not far away and how much she'd like to crawl out of her bed and into his and what she'd like to do with him there. She thought both about the semi appropriate things, like giving him the affection he surely needed, and the very inappropriate things, like putting her hands and mouth on him.

Likely, this didn't help her sleeplessness.

She decided not to think about that either.

"Miss Bella," Sally called, taking Isabella from her thoughts. "When we get home, are you going to teach me how to be ambidextry?"

Isabella started to answer but Jason turned (again) and corrected (again), "Ambidext*rous*."

Sally glared at him, losing patience, "Jace! That's what I said! Am-bee-dex-*try*!"

Isabella leaned toward the girl, wrapped her hand behind her head, gently pulled her close and kissed her shining hair.

Then she answered, "I'll do my best."

And she would, in the few days she was going to remain there.

Sally was gaining strength. She'd broken her right forearm, which was in a cast thus Isabella had told her she'd need to learn to be ambidextrous while her arm healed. She'd also had a couple of ribs broken that they'd been told would heal quickly. She'd had a number of deep contusions that were fading.

Other than that, shockingly (and thankfully), she was fine.

Therefore, Isabella reckoned, she'd get Sally settled. This, she decided, would take a day or two (or three). And then she'd get out of Prentice's hair.

It must be said she didn't want to *be* out of Prentice's thick, dark hair.

In fact, Isabella spent way too much time thinking how much she wanted to run her fingers through it.

Nevertheless, although Prentice had been polite and even grateful for her help, he was just that. Nothing more. His politeness and gratitude were of the distant variety and not, Isabella guessed, just because he had a lot weighing on his mind.

Which meant it was time for her to go.

At least, she thought (with not a small amount of sadness), this time it wouldn't be ugly.

Things were settled between her and Prentice, in a way. It was over. They were acquaintances, ex-lovers of both varieties. There was so much water under the bridge, it was a wonder the bridge wasn't flooded.

Even in the short expanse of time after the drama of their mini-reunion, they'd moved on.

Or, at least, it was clear Prentice had.

Isabella was just pretending. Then again, she was good at it as she should be, she'd had enough practice.

But the good thing was that meant that this time she could stay in touch with the kids from afar and not worry that Prentice was going to blow his stack.

Prentice rolled to a stop in the drive of his house and Isabella watched him as he looked around at the cars parked everywhere.

She bit her lip.

She probably should have told him about the party.

It wasn't her idea. It was Annie and Debs's idea.

She'd just cleaned the house and baked the chocolate cake and, maybe, bought all the decorations, blew up the balloons and hid them in her rooms.

He turned in his seat and locked eyes on Isabella, who was sitting behind Jason.

Isabella sucked in breath.

When she returned a week ago, he seemed somewhat angry and definitely impatient.

This had gone away.

She could easily read annoyance and impatience in his eyes now.

Annie and Debs had talked Isabella into the party, insisting it was a *fabulous* idea. The latter who, during their planning session the day before, had shown absolutely no ill-will to Isabella and was again treating her like the sister she always wanted but never had, a change in attitude that Isabella was also too exhausted to process.

Looking at Prentice, Isabella felt maybe they were wrong.

"Um . . ." she started hesitantly and he shook his head.

Then he turned away and got out of the SUV.

Isabella scrambled out and saw that Jason was looking around, eyeing the cars, a smirk on his mouth. Prentice unbuckled Sally and carried her in his arms as Jason hurried forward to open the door. Isabella, ever the coward, trailed behind.

So far behind, she heard the congregation inside shouting, "Surprise!" but she didn't see it. It took her a couple of seconds before she entered behind Prentice and his family.

In the great room were Annie and Dougal, Fergus, Dougal's parents, Prentice's parents, Fiona's parents, Debs, her husband and two kids, Morag, her husband and two kids and Mrs. Kilbride. The great room was festooned with pink and white streamers, bunches of pink and white balloons were fastened here and there and there was a big banner hanging on the stairs that read, "Welcome home Sally!"

There were trays groaning with food all over the bar-slash-counter that delineated the kitchen from the great room. The *pièce de résistance*,

Isabella's chocolate cake on a high cake stand Isabella had unearthed, the chocolate frosting decorated with swirls of pink and white icing, sat right smack in the middle of the culinary extravaganza.

But it was worse.

Annie was holding a little, adorable, squirming black kitty with a pink and white bow around its neck.

Isabella stopped next to Prentice, spied the cat and mumbled, "Oh dear."

Sally's eyes honed right in on the feline.

"*Kitty!*" she shrieked with pure joy.

"Oh dear," Isabella repeated.

Prentice put Sally on her feet as Annie came forward with the cat. Then his gaze cut to Isabella.

At the look in his eyes, Isabella went directly on the defensive. "I didn't know anything about the cat. I swear."

He straightened and turned to her. "The party?"

Isabella bit her lip but decided it best not to answer.

"The cake?" he went on.

Isabella hugged her middle and cupped her elbows with her hands. She'd snuck down to the kitchen in the wee hours of the night to make the cake on the sly.

She didn't explain this. Instead, again, she decided not to answer.

"Christ," he muttered under his breath.

Sally was on her knees, Annie in a crouch in front of her. The kitty was jumping excitedly around Sally as Sally tried to stroke it with her good hand, and Annie was doing her best to keep the cat from overwhelming the just-knocked-over-by-a-car little girl.

Sally tilted her head back to Prentice and requested loudly, "Can I keep her, Daddy? Can I, can I, can I?"

"Sorry, mate," Dougal murmured, and Isabella saw that he'd sidled close to Prentice's side, "you know Annie."

Annie grinned up at Prentice, completely unrepentant.

"I vote we push her off a cliff," Isabella said in a soft whisper and then felt the blood drain out of her face because she meant to *think* it not to *say* it.

Dougal and Prentice's heads turned to Isabella.

Isabella's hands released her elbows and clenched into fists.

Dougal burst out laughing.

Prentice didn't laugh but his face changed. He stared at her as if he'd never seen her before. Then his eyes dropped to her hands and she forced her fists to uncurl.

He quickly guarded his expression and looked down at his daughter. "You can keep her, baby."

"Hurrah!" Sally shouted.

Prentice bent down and picked up Sally, carrying her to the couch. "But you've got to rest. You're just out of hospital."

"Can I have cake?" Sally asked.

"In a minute," Prentice answered.

"Hurrah!" Sally repeated.

The partygoers closed in on Prentice and Sally. Jason and his cousins claimed the attention of the cat. Annie got close to Isabella.

"I need to talk to you," Annie said out of the corner of her mouth, being cloak and dagger.

Isabella looked at her friend, knowing Annie's cloak and dagger was never a good thing but she had other, more pressing things on her mind.

"And I need to talk to you." Her look turned severe. "Annie, a *cat*?"

Annie gave Isabella a "What?" look and Isabella gave her a "You know!" look in return.

Then Annie grabbed Isabella's hand and dragged her down the hall, up the stairs and to the guest suite.

"Annie, what on earth?" Isabella asked when Annie stopped them in the sitting room.

On the couch were coats and bags. Annie dug through them, pulled out her big, suede, satchel purse and yanked out a magazine.

"I'm sorry, Bella, something's happened," Annie said and handed the magazine to Isabella.

Isabella took it, saw it was one of the way too many celebrity gossip magazines and she stared at the cover.

Confused, she looked at Annie and asked, "You dragged me up here because you're upset Bianca Preston is adopting another child from Africa?"

Annie's eyes bugged out and her hand shot forward. She ripped the magazine out of Isabella's hold and opened it to a page that Isabella saw had been marked by Annie turning down the corner. She flipped it in half and handed it back to Isabella.

Isabella instantly understood.

She saw a full page photo of Prentice, Jason and herself walking from the Range Rover toward the hospital. It had been taken several days before.

Prentice was close to Isabella, guiding her with a hand at the small of her back. Jason was walking close to Isabella's side. Isabella and Jason had their heads bent, eyes to the ground as they walked. Prentice was gazing straight ahead.

They all looked pale, tired and worn.

Isabella's eyes flew to the caption.

Socialite Isabella Evangelista, with her new beau, handsome, award-winning architect Prentice Cameron and his son, Jason, visiting the hospital after a tragic accident involving Cameron's daughter.

Isabella's eyes flew to Annie and she said the first idiot thing that came to mind.

"Prentice has won awards?"

Annie's eyes bugged out further before she snatched the magazine from Isabella's hands and snapped, "That's not the point. Prentice is going to *freak*."

She wasn't wrong.

Prentice was going to more than freak.

He'd always wanted a quiet life, a simple life and that was what he'd given his family. He'd moved them to their private house on the cliff close to the sea. He (obviously) excelled at his work (awards!) and she knew he enjoyed travel (or, he did twenty years ago, she had no idea about now).

But he wasn't the kind of man who wanted his photo in celebrity gossip magazines.

And he wasn't the kind of man who wanted his *children's* photos in celebrity gossip magazines.

And he certainly didn't want to be referred to as Isabella's "new beau."

"This isn't good," Isabella whispered.

"No, it isn't," Annie returned.

Always, for Isabella, it was something.

Something dark.

Something bad.

Even in the middle of a miracle.

Isabella gazed at her friend. "What am I going to do?"

Annie got close. "Show him the picture. Talk to him for once. Explain how this is for you and how you deal with it."

Isabella sighed and nodded but added, "And I need to go. They're going to be all over the village—"

Annie grabbed Isabella's hand. "No, you don't need to *go*. You need to *stay*. You're experienced with this. They aren't."

Isabella stared at her friend. "If I go, the photographers will lose interest."

Annie snorted and shook the photo in front of Isabella's face. "Hardly. Prentice is hot. Look at him. Incredibly photogenic. And Jason is a good-looking lad. You've all obviously been run through the mill and you *still* look amazing together. And it looks like you're definitely *together*. They're going to eat this up. They always do when it's about you. Bella, they're going to descend on them like flies on doo-doo."

Isabella looked to the photo.

Prentice did look great. Even though his face was tired and his mouth was tight, he'd never looked so handsome.

And Jason *was* a good-looking lad, with his father's eyes and his mother's hair. Pre-teens the world over were going to be in throes of ecstasy.

Isabella closed her eyes.

Then she muttered, "Damn it."

"Talk to him," Annie encouraged.

Isabella opened her eyes. She had no choice.

"I'll talk to him."

Annie squeezed her hand.

Isabella took the magazine, shoved it in her nightstand and they went back to the party.

It was a smash hit, especially the kitty and the cake.

Everyone was nice to her, more than nice, even so far as being warm and friendly, like she was welcome.

Like she belonged.

It was a nice day and Isabella had to admit that Annie and Debs were right. A party after a tragedy that ended in a miracle rather than further despair was just the thing.

Isabella did her best to keep Sally from tiring herself out too much, the exuberant kitty from causing Sally further injury and she consistently cleared away party debris so clean up later wouldn't be overwhelming.

The only weird thing that happened was when she was standing, talking to Debs and Fergus, Prentice brought her a plate piled high with food.

Without a word, he handed it to her and walked away.

Fergus, Debs and Isabella stared at the plate. Isabella with surprise, Debs and Fergus with knowing looks.

Not hungry, Isabella nibbled from the plate then put it aside.

Not long after, she was gathering discarded plates for the bin when fingers curled firmly around her upper arm.

She looked at the strong hand at her arm and then at Prentice, who the hand belonged to when he pulled the rubbish out of her hands, dragged her to the bin, dumped it in then dragged her to the counter. He prepared another plate for her, setting it on the counter and piling the food on it while he kept her imprisoned next to him, his hand still on her arm.

When he was done, he turned to her, plate in hand, and demanded, "Eat."

"But—" she began, so shocked she didn't know what to say.

He interrupted her. "Eat."

"I had some. It was lovely but I'm full. I couldn't eat more," she explained.

"You had barely any. It *is* lovely. There isn't any way in hell you're full. And you're going to eat more." He paused then said, "Now."

She stared at him stunned before she replied, "Prentice, really, I'm full."

His eyes narrowed, he (and the plate) got close, his face dipped to hers and he asked in a low, quiet, dangerous voice, "Do I have to feed you?"

Her mind filled with images of Prentice feeding her finger food. Her body reacted pleasantly to these mental images.

She swallowed, shook her head and took the plate. He dropped her arm.

Isabella ate while Prentice stood watching her. This was a difficult task. Firstly, she was confused as to why he was practically force-feeding her. Secondly, his eyes on her did crazy things to her heart, her belly and her head.

When she cleaned the plate, she asked, maybe a little snotty (but really, he was force-feeding her!), "Happy?"

"Not really," he returned. "But it's a start."

And with that he walked away.

Isabella glared at him and then felt eyes on her. Prentice's mum was looking at her as was his sister, Jason and Mrs. Kilbride.

They were all grinning.

"You're getting too thin," Mrs. Kilbride called out then she advised helpfully, "Now you should have some of your delicious cake!"

At that, Prentice pivoted on his boot, went directly to the cake, cut an enormous piece, slapped it on a plate and handed it to her.

Dougal burst out laughing.

Prentice tipped his head to the cake.

Isabella glared at him.

Prentice calmly accepted her glare.

His every-colored eyes on her did funny things to her heart rate.

She ate the cake.

Seriously, she needed to get out of there.

As soon as she could.

―――――◆―――――

Prentice

THE LAST PARTYGOER was gone, and except for the decorations which Sally didn't want them to take down yet, everything was clean and tidy and his children were in bed.

Even Sally's new cat, christened Blackie, was curled asleep at Sally's feet.

Prentice needed a whisky.

In case he received a middle of the night phone call with bad news that would necessitate him being alert, he'd refrained since Sally had her accident.

With Sally home recovering, still in possession of all her important faculties, now asleep in bed *and* with Elle knocking herself out to care for him, his offspring and his home, including throwing a welcome home party for his injured daughter as well as sleeping in a bed not far away from him, he needed a fucking whisky.

He was considering what to do about Elle as he poured it.

This was a departure since for the past week when he wasn't worried about Sally, Jason and getting the work done on a deadline that was fast approaching, he normally spent his time considering all the things he'd like to do *to* Elle.

Regardless of the fact that she still looked exhausted and was losing weight mainly because the woman kept so busy she didn't fucking *eat*, not to mention the fact that she'd left him and his family four weeks ago without looking back and for reasons only known in that crazy fucking head of hers, he couldn't deny that he was attracted to her.

He didn't want to be attracted. He wanted to be over it and move on, as she clearly was.

But he was attracted to her.

Very attracted.

In fact, he thought about this so often and there were so many different options, his mind had automatically started cataloguing the things he wanted to do to her. Where he wanted to put his mouth, his hands, his fingers, the different positions he wanted to try, the various rooms and furniture available.

Christ, it consumed him.

He'd never experienced anything like it, not even twenty years ago.

Then again, he hadn't had her twenty years ago.

He was replacing the bottle when he heard, "Prentice?"

His eyes cut to the door of his study.

Elle stood there wearing jeans that fit her too well (even if she had lost weight) and a stylish but see-through purple blouse with tiny pleats down the front and a camisole he could see underneath. Her feet were bare, her hair was in a messy bunch that had slid to the back of her head and she'd taken off her jewelry but still wore her makeup.

She looked like she could be photographed for a magazine.

Instead, she was casually standing in the doorway of *his* study in *his* home gazing at *him* with soft, weary eyes and, if he took six steps, she could be in his arms.

On that tempting thought and to take his mind from it, his eyes fell to her hands, something he didn't realize he habitually did, and he saw she was not clenching them in fists (something he *did* realize *she* habitually did) but she was carrying a magazine.

"Is something on your mind?" he asked, his gaze going back to her tired face.

"Um . . ." she started but she stopped.

This annoyed him.

The first time she came back she seemed cool and in control except, of course, when they were bickering, but even then she'd seemed in control.

This time she seemed less sure of herself, more hesitant and it irritated him because it made her warmer, more approachable and unbelievably appealing.

He watched as she looked to the ceiling then asked, "Is Sally okay?"

"Aye."

Her gaze came to him and her head tipped to the side. "Jason?"

"Aye."

"Are *you* okay, um . . . after all of this?"

He liked it that she asked. Especially since she asked in a way that indicated she cared.

That familiar heavy, warm feeling hit his gut.

He ignored it and repeated, "Aye."

She stopped speaking and took in a breath.

With little patience, wanting to be out of her presence, wanting to be outside with his whisky, Prentice asked, "Elle, what's on your mind?"

She swallowed and then ran the tip of her tongue along her upper lip. His body responded strongly to the sight of her tongue.

More of his low volume of patience ebbed away.

"Elle, I'm tired. I want to wind down after—"

"I have something to show you," she said quickly, taking two steps into the room before she halted. He watched as she visibly lost courage, looked at his whisky and asked, "Can I have one of those?"

Careful to shield his still ebbing patience, he poured her a whisky. They walked toward each other, closing the distance between them and he handed it to her.

She took it and belted back a healthy swig.

Too healthy.

After she swallowed, her mouth dropped open, she sucked in breath as if it burned and tears sprang to her eyes.

"It's meant to be sipped," Prentice advised, but as he was talking she took *another* healthy swig.

He stared in surprise.

This was something the crazy Elle who was friends with the mad Annie would do twenty years ago.

They'd get up to anything.

Much like her comment earlier about voting to push Annie off the cliff.

Elle and Annie, twenty years ago, would say practically anything as well (Annie still would), most of it hilarious.

She finished the whisky on a third swig, shut her eyes tight and winced.

When she opened her eyes to look at him, she breathed, "Good stuff."

God, she was cute when she behaved like this.

He didn't need cute Elle sleeping under his roof either.

No, he *especially* didn't need that.

"Elle—" His patience was running out.

"I have to show you something," she blurted, interrupting him.

"All right."

"You're going to be angry."

His eyes went to the magazine. Then they returned to hers.

He didn't speak.

"Likely very angry," she went on.

He still didn't speak.

"Probably very, *very* angry."

"For Christ's sake—" he clipped but didn't finish as she flipped open the magazine and showed him a page.

He couldn't believe his eyes. On it was a photo of Elle, Jason and him walking into hospital days before.

Jason, he noted with pride, held his body with surprising confidence for a boy his age, and even though he looked worried he was still a handsome lad.

Elle, he noted with annoyance, held her body with unsurprising poise, and even though she looked worried she was still a beautiful woman.

He didn't bother studying himself.

Prentice pulled the magazine from her hand and read the caption.

Then he exploded, "*Fucking hell!*"

"I *knew* you'd be angry," Elle replied swiftly.

He narrowed his eyes on her and snapped dryly, "Oh, you knew that, did you?" Flipping to the front of the magazine and seeing it was a celebrity gossip rag, published undoubtedly on a variety of continents he exploded again, "*Christ!*"

"Annie says I should talk to you. Explain how I deal with this kind of thing," Elle said quickly.

He looked at her and his tone was biting when he asked, "Aye? You have sage advice on how I should deal with the fact that *my son*, without my knowledge and against my wishes, has his photograph in a trashy magazine? You have experience with that, do you?"

He watched her face pale.

Fuck.

His anger and impatience, this fucking situation, the last fucking week, hell, the last fucking *month*, had pushed him over the edge. He hadn't thought about his words and he'd gone too far.

Way too far.

"Elle—" he started, instantly filled of regret.

"No," she cut him off, cute Elle gone, warm, appealing Elle

vanished, cool and aloof Isabella in her place.

He wouldn't have said it two minutes ago but he wanted the other two back.

"As you know, I do not," she went on. "However, I know what it's like having *my* photo in trashy magazines without my knowledge and against my wishes. Nonetheless, I'm not a parent so you're correct, I don't have any sage advice for this."

She bent to put her glass on the table and he knew she intended to leave.

He should have let her go.

But Prentice was fucking tired of letting her go.

Therefore, he didn't let her go.

He slammed his glass beside hers, caught her upper arm in his grip and was surprised at her reaction.

It was violent.

She twisted her arm in a way that he had to release her or he'd hurt her. Which meant to keep her from leaving he had to find other purchase.

So he did.

He put both hands to her hips and yanked her toward him.

Her body slammed into his.

It felt fucking great.

Before he could react to this, she tipped her head back, he saw her eyes flash and she demanded in a voice that was not cold at all. It was heated.

And loud.

Loud enough for the children to hear.

"Take your hands off me, Prentice Cameron!"

Damn, but she looked fucking gorgeous when she was angry.

He didn't do as she asked.

He shuffled her back toward the open doors. Sliding an arm tight around her waist, he held her front against his side as he reached out, grabbed one door then the other and pulled them to.

That done, he pinned her in front of him against the doors.

She was breathing heavily, her breasts pressing against his chest with each breath.

Through gritted teeth, he said, "Now, if you'll give me a fucking second before you run away, *again*, I'll apologize for being a thoughtless bastard."

"Fine. Apology accepted. Now step away," she snapped, giving him a push with her hands at his waist.

He resisted the push by leaning further into her which pressed them together from hips to chests.

Her hands stilled and she tilted her head back further to look at him. He could see from the healthy pink in her cheeks that he had her attention.

"No," he belatedly replied to her demand. "Now, you'll explain how I deal with seeing my children and myself in those magazines when we're with you."

"You won't," she returned, her voice still hostile but now also breathy.

"You can promise that?"

"Yes, I can since you won't be with me."

Her words felt like a knife twisting in his gut.

She continued before he could react to that as well, "They'll probably bother you for a while after I'm gone. Then they'll lose interest. You just have to learn to ignore it. It gets worse if you react. Trust me."

He wasn't listening. His mind was stuck on her telling him he wouldn't be with her.

And stuck on her telling him she'd be gone.

"You're leaving?" he asked.

"Of course," she said shortly, her tone still that mixture of antagonistic and out of breath.

"When?"

"In a few days."

"Why?"

Her lips parted and Prentice's gaze riveted on them.

Therefore he watched them form the words, "Prentice step back."

His eyes went back to hers. "Elle, answer me."

She seemed puzzled for a moment then shook her head as if to clear it.

"Because . . ." She stopped and her gaze slid to the side.

He pushed closer. Her gaze snapped back.

"Sally's fine," she answered. "She's going to be okay. And this isn't my home, this isn't my life. I have a home and a life in Chicago. I need to get back."

He stared at her.

When she spoke again, it was softer and the hostility was gone. "They shouldn't get used to me."

"Too late," Prentice returned, watched as her eyes closed and felt his already heightened anger rising even further. "So this is it?" he asked. "This is what you're going to do now?"

Her eyes opened again and he saw confusion.

"Pardon?"

"Slide into their lives, light up their worlds, slide out, leave me to deal with their disappointment while you send boxes filled with expensive presents from wherever you are, making certain they'll be thinking of you even though they'll never be certain they can have you?"

Her face filled with shock and her mouth opened to speak but she didn't when his anger boiled over.

He let her go and took a step away.

"All right, Elle, if I can guide them through losing their mother, I can guide them through losing you, *repeatedly*. At least I have practice with *that*."

He regretted his words again when her face assumed an expression like she'd just been struck.

But he was angry enough that he didn't take them back. Furthermore, they were the fucking truth.

He watched as she rearranged her features but she couldn't quite hide the hurt.

"What do you want me to do?" she whispered.

"Don't leave," he replied instantly.

Her eyes grew wide.

"You want me to . . . to . . . to *move* here?"

Christ, how had *this* come about?

But he knew. This came about because this was Elle and every situation with Elle deteriorated to something out of his control.

He glared at her for a long moment before he answered, "No. I don't want you to move here. But I want you to stay until Sally's fit again. Until there's a good time to explain the situation so they know what you are to them and what they can expect."

"What am I to them?" she asked him, now *sounding* confused.

He simply stared at her.

She definitely was mad.

When she continued to gaze at him in that baffled way, he inquired with disbelief, "You're serious?"

"I—"

He tried to gentle his tone when he said, "Think about it, Elle. You lose your mother and, a year later, a glamorous woman who understands your loss floats in the front door baking cakes and telling stories about your mum and varnishing your fingernails. You lost your mum, Elle. If you had a woman like that come into your life, what would she be to you?"

Her eyes skittered to the floor. She examined it for a while before she sighed.

"I really messed this up, didn't I?" she murmured in a voice so soft, he barely heard her.

For some reason her words disturbed him so much his anger immediately evaporated. They were uttered in a way that made it seem she took sole responsibility for everything that befell her, Prentice and his children when practically none of it (but her leaving him the second time) had been in her control.

Before he could stop himself, his hand came to cup her jaw and his thumb stroked her cheek.

At his touch, her gaze went back to him.

"You didn't mess anything up, Elle," he replied quietly. "This is bloody life. Life is always messy. Now we just need to sort it out."

She nodded, the soft skin of her face moving against his hand, her eyes still confused and tired but they'd grown warm.

Before he did what very much he wanted to do, slide his thumb along her lower lip then put his lips where his thumb had been, he dropped his hand.

"Go to bed and get some sleep. We'll talk when you're less tired."

She nodded, pulled in a breath and with a heavy tone, she whispered, "Prentice, I'm so sorry about the magazine."

There was more weight to those words than was required. She hadn't sold the fucking photo to the magazine.

"It isn't your fault," he pointed out the obvious.

"I'm the reason—"

His hand came back to her jaw and she stopped speaking.

"It isn't your fault, Elle," Prentice repeated firmly.

"Okay," she replied quickly but not very convincingly, and before he could say another word, she said, "Goodnight."

He watched her whirl, open the door and then disappear.

Prentice stared at the door, feeling a vague sense of unease about that entire scene and *not* for the obvious reasons one would be uneasy about that scene.

His eyes on the door, he tried to call up what troubled him.

When he failed, he strode back to his glass, grabbed it, went to the cupboard, tagged the bottle of whisky by the neck and took the whole fucking bottle up to his balcony.

———— ◦ ————

Fiona

YOU SHOULD READ *her journals,* Fiona told her husband as she floated with her arse close to the railing of the balcony where he was standing.

She was floating as if she was sitting there, her ghostly elbows to her ghostly knees, her ghostly eyes on his brooding face.

He didn't respond because he didn't hear her.

Nevertheless, she kept talking.

You'd understand if you read her journals.

Prentice kept his eyes to the sea as he took a sip from his glass (the third glass, Fiona was counting).

She sighed a ghostly sigh.

Then she said, *I don't know why the powers that be did this to me and I hate it. But I love you enough to want you to have the world and she's been your world for twenty years. If I wasn't already dead, that would kill me. But even I can see that you two were meant to be. Why can't YOU see? Why don't you FIGHT for her?*

Prentice continued to stare at the sea.

You don't want her to leave, Fiona told him.

He didn't respond.

Quietly, with all the feeling a dead woman could feel for the live woman who made the words true, Fiona stated, *She'd lay down her life for our children.*

"Aye," Prentice said softly to the sea.

Fiona melted through the railing.

Swiftly, she bolted back.

Did you hear me?

No response.

Prentice! Fiona shouted, *Did you hear me?*

He threw back the remainder of his whisky but didn't give any indication he heard her.

Fiona didn't give up.

Read her journals! Look at her palms! TRY to understand her, Prentice! she shouted. *Don't let her go again. She needs you to fight for her! Fight for your happiness, for her happiness, for our children's happiness! Fight so Bella can be free. Fight for ME to be free!*

Prentice set his glass next to the three that were sitting on the railing.

Naturally, he took the bottle inside and put it on the bureau before he changed and went to bed.

Fiona glared at her husband as he lay in bed for a long time, arms crossed behind his head, head on his hands, eyes to the ceiling, sleep eluding him.

You're an idiot! she snapped.

"Aye," he murmured, rolled to his side and fell asleep.

Fiona considered throwing something at him which she could do.

Instead she dematerialized and materialized in Bella's room.

Bella was lying on her back, arms crossed on her belly, eyes to the ceiling, sleep eluding her (again!).

You two are doing my head in! I wish you'd found some other dead woman's husband to fall in love with! Fiona shouted.

"I do too," Bella whispered, rolled to her side and fell asleep.

Fiona glared at her.

Then she spent the rest of the night with Sally.

Chapter
TWELVE

You Can Call Her Elle

Isabella

It was the blood.

It was always the blood.

It wasn't her nudity, her open, lifeless eyes, her blue, bloodless skin.

It was the glaring red against the clean, stark white of the tub.

All she saw was *all that blood*.

Isabella screamed.

"*Elle!*"

When she heard her name, she jolted awake.

Prentice was crouched before her beside the couch, his hand on her arm shaking her, his face a mask of alarm.

She jumped to her feet, nearly knocking Prentice off his.

She wasn't thinking. Her mind was in turmoil as it always was after those dreams.

He surged up and caught her on the run. His arm curving around her waist, he pulled her in front of him, his arms locking tight around her.

She struggled violently.

His arms grew tighter.

"Jesus, Elle, what the fuck?"

Suddenly, she felt his warmth, his strength, his arms holding her captive against his solid, strong body.

Feeling all that was Prentice, Isabella collapsed in his hold.

Grabbing fistfuls of his shirt, she buried her face in his chest and burst into body-wracking, silent sobs.

She felt one arm leave her waist then the ponytail holder was pulled gently from her hair. Her hair tumbled into his hand and he ran his fingers through its length.

"Baby," he said softly.

At his sweet endearment, she could take no more.

She'd been holding it in for years, the grief. Holding it in so her father wouldn't see. Keeping it secret. Keeping it silent. Keeping it inside so her father wouldn't judge, wouldn't get angry.

She *had* to get it out.

"I hate it! I *hate* it when I have those dreams! *Hate* it!" she cried into his chest through her sobs. She tilted her head back to look at him and continued, "Dad hated it too. Said I was weak. Said I should *get over it*. He didn't find her! He didn't find her dead in . . . *that* . . . *fucking* . . . *tub!*"

Vaguely, she felt Prentice's body go solid against hers but she was too far gone to process it.

She buried her face in his chest again and sobbed, "I'm so tired of those dreams, Pren. So tired. So damn tired." She tipped her head back and cried fiercely, "Why can't I stop having those dreams?"

His hand cupped the back of her head, carefully twisting it so he could press her cheek to his chest as he replied gently, "I don't know, baby."

"I'm . . ." She hiccoughed through her tears. "I'm so tired." She clutched his shirt tighter. "So, so tired."

His thumb was drawing soothing circles against her temple, his fingers curled into her hair. She held on to him, arms wrapped around him tight, weeping.

He felt so good. Tall and solid and strong. Warm. Safe. His arms so tight.

He felt so . . . very . . . good.

He pulled her head from his chest and dipped his chin to look at her.

She looked back.

His handsome face was full of concern.

And he *was* handsome.

So . . . very . . . handsome.

It made her heart skip.

His thumb rubbed along her cheek, trailing through the tears but his beautiful every-colored eyes never left hers.

"We need to get you to bed," he murmured. "You need sleep."

It came to her in a flash.

Isabella didn't need sleep. She was tired but she didn't need sleep. She needed *him*.

Before her turbulent mind settled enough to stop her insane actions, she took her hands from his shirt and curled them at his neck.

She put pressure there, coming up on her toes.

His body grew solid again. "Elle—"

It was good he said her name because his mouth was open when she kissed him.

Since she wasn't thinking, she didn't think forward to what he would do when she kissed him.

He could have rejected her.

If she *had* been thinking, that would have been her guess.

He didn't reject her.

His head slanted, his tongue tangled with hers and then overpowered it when he took over the kiss.

It was beautiful.

She melted into him and her fingers, which had itched to do it for over a week, slid into his hair.

The kiss was hard and it was wild and it left Isabella wild.

Mouth still engaged with Prentice's, she tugged his shirt from his jeans, her fingers shoving in, up, encountering the sleek skin and muscle of his back.

That was beautiful too.

She dug her fingernails in.

He groaned into her mouth.

His groan slashed through her, blazing a heady trail straight between her legs.

She pulled her hands out of his shirt and her fingers went direct to his buttons.

At that, he tore his mouth from hers and Isabella made a mew of protest, but he didn't move away. She watched as he lifted both arms. Hands grasping between his shoulder blades, he pulled his shirt over his head, ripping it down his arms, the buttons of the cuffs popping as he yanked it off and tossed it away.

His chest was right there.

Right before her eyes.

And he had a beautiful chest.

She didn't waste the opportunity he afforded her.

Her mouth went to him. Lips, tongue, she tasted him, her hands roaming, fevered, desperate, wanting to memorize every inch.

Down she went, down, until she was on her knees in front of him. She tugged back his belt, opened his jeans . . .

"Elle." His voice came at her as his hands settled at her jaw, putting pressure there to pull her up.

She resisted.

She'd found him.

She wanted him.

And she was going to have what she wanted.

For once.

She pulled him free, took his thick shaft in her hand then slid it in her mouth.

His fingers left her jaw and glided in her hair as he groaned, *"Baby."*

It was all the encouragement she needed.

He tasted beautiful. He felt beautiful. He *looked* beautiful.

She couldn't get enough and he couldn't give her enough, bucking against her mouth as she held on to his hips.

God, she was going to come just from the beauty of it.

His hips jerked back, pulling free.

Before she could protest, his hands were under her armpits and he yanked her up.

"Pren—"

"Quiet."

He shifted them around and sat on the couch, positioning her standing in front of him. His hands curling into the waistband of her yoga pants, he tugged them down, taking her underwear with them.

With a forceful pull at her hips, he yanked her forward. She fell into him. Her feet kicking off her clothing, her legs opening, her knees came up and she straddled him.

He fell to the side, taking her with him, dropping to his back.

Her hand went between them, she found him, wrapped him tight, guided him inside, lifted her torso up and he filled her.

"*Heaven*," she breathed.

Her back arched, her hips ground into him, tilting, grinding further, reveling in Prentice's hardness buried deep.

Connected.

Intimate.

Isabella and Prentice.

She thought it was the most beautiful thing in the world.

She felt his hand cup her breast at the same time his fingers touched her *right there* between her legs.

Her head tilted down to gaze at his beautiful face as his thumb stroked her nipple.

"Pren," she whispered as her eyes locked on his.

Then she came, her body bucking, her sex rippling.

It was shattering.

It was magnificent.

It was *beautiful*.

Dimly, she felt his hands leave her as one slid into her hair, cupping her head, pulling her torso to his. He switched positions, moving her to her back, coming over her and then slamming deep inside.

She wrapped her legs around his hips, her arms around his shoulders and held on.

She watched him move over her, her eyes barely open, glorying in the feel of Prentice driving deep inside her.

His hand went to the side of her face.

"Christ," he bit out, his breath coming fast, his strokes coming faster, pounding harder, thrusting deeper, "You're so *fucking* beautiful."

She gazed at him for a mere moment, feeling all the magnificence that was Prentice wrapped in her limbs, pressing her to the couch, slamming deep inside her, before his head came down and he kissed her.

She accepted his groan in her mouth as he reared one last time, plunging so deep it felt like he pierced her heart.

His lips slid from her mouth, down her cheek and he buried his face in her neck.

He pressed his hips into hers. Her limbs tensed, holding him tighter.

She loved every inch of him.

At that thought, her turbulent mind settled and reason intruded.

She stiffened.

The instant she did, he felt it.

His face came out of her neck as she whispered, "Pren—"

She didn't finish his name. He kissed her.

Her mind descended back into beautiful chaos.

His mouth released hers and he pulled out, lifted up, tugging her up with him until they were on their feet.

He'd unzipped her knit jacket and pulled it down her arms and had his hands in her camisole when her thoughts yet again cleared.

"Prentice, we shouldn't—"

He whipped off her camisole, and before her arms settled down to her sides and his swift actions settled through her brain, she was in his arms and his mouth was on hers again.

He kept her mind jumbled with his kisses as he disrobed, turned out the light in the sitting room and then carried her to the bed.

When he had her on her back, the covers pulled over them, his heavy warmth pressed down the length of her side, his elbow in the pillow, head in his hand, other hand resting at her neck, eyes resting on her face . . . only then did he speak.

"Now you can talk."

"I—" she began to tell him that she was sorry, she shouldn't have started this, this was *wrong, wrong, wrong.*

And selfish.

And stupid.

And a million other things.

But he interrupted her, "Tell me about the dream."

Her mouth snapped shut.

His hand tightened on her neck but his voice was gentle when he demanded, "Elle, tell me."

"What . . ." she stammered, unsure of the state of affairs and equally unsure she wanted to explore said state of affairs. She'd rather talk about her dream which was saying something since she *hated* those dreams. "What do you want to know?" she asked.

"You've had it since it happened?"

She nodded but said, "Not so much anymore. Just occasionally. Only when I'm stressed or anxious."

"You had them when you were with me?"

She pulled in breath. Obviously, she'd never told him about the dreams.

"Yes," she whispered, terrified about his response.

It wasn't the insulted betrayal she expected. The betrayal he'd felt and angrily shared with her when he found out about her mother. Instead, his head tilted toward her, he touched their foreheads together a moment and he sighed.

This tender reaction made Isabella relax.

No, she didn't relax.

She *relaxed*—her body, her mind, her heart, even her *soul* felt like it relaxed.

He drew away and said, "You need to talk to someone about it."

"I have," she explained softly. "They couldn't help."

His fingers flexed then eased.

His voice dipped lower when he asked, "Your father said you were weak?"

She couldn't decipher if he was angry or disturbed by this.

She also didn't answer verbally.

She just nodded.

This was met by silence.

Then in a voice that was lower, rougher and definitely angry, Prentice bit out, "He's a fucking piece of work."

"He's out of my life," she assured him quickly.

"He didn't seem out of your life when he waltzed into a fucking wedding reception and right in front of everyone, including me and *my children*, literally brought you to your knees."

All right.

Well.

Since his voice was even lower, rougher and now *rumbling*, Isabella thought it was safe to say he was now *seriously* angry.

"Prentice," she murmured placatingly.

"Tell me how he's out of your life," Prentice demanded, not sounding placated even a little bit.

"We had words. He's disinherited me."

There was silence for a moment then Prentice's head went back and he laughed. Regardless, he didn't sound amused.

This alarmed her at the same time it confused her.

"Prentice?" she called.

His laughter died away and his head tipped back to look at her.

"*He* disinherited *you*. That's rich. I love that. What an unbelievable ass."

He wasn't wrong about that. And he didn't love it at all. He was angry on her behalf.

Oh dear.

She was beginning to think she was in trouble.

Prentice fell silent.

Isabella couldn't cope with silence.

"I told him I never wanted him to come near me again," Isabella informed him.

Prentice's thumb stroked her jaw and his voice lost its edge when he muttered his warning, "Don't expect him to adhere to your wishes,

Elle. That man will do whatever he damn well wants to do."

She suspected Prentice was right.

However, it was time for another topic.

"What were you doing in my rooms?"

He dropped to his side but his arms came around her and rolled her to hers, facing him. One of his hands drifted up her back into her hair and he pressed her cheek to his chest.

"I came home, saw a light coming down the hall, heard the television on. I came up to talk to you and saw you were asleep. I turned off the telly and you started to move, like shudders, like you were cold. They got worse. Then you were making these noises, like you were terrified. That's when I woke you."

Well, that made sense. It was horrifying he saw that but it made sense.

"I'm sorry you saw that," she whispered.

He was silent.

She took in a breath and screwed up her courage.

The latter bit took a while.

Finally, she said, "We should talk about—"

She didn't finish.

His hand twisted in her hair, gripping it. He pulled her head back and his own came down, his lips finding hers and he kissed her.

His hands started roaming.

Then his lips started roaming.

Then his tongue started roaming.

A long time later, after he made her come with his mouth between her legs and she helped him come by opening those legs for him and taking him inside, he tucked her back into his front and held her close.

"Pren—"

"Quiet."

"But—"

"Sleep."

"We should—"

His hand came up, fingers curling around her breast, thumb gliding across her nipple.

She fell silent and a delicious tremble slid through her body.

"Elle. Sleep," he ordered, pressing deeper into her.

She supposed they could talk tomorrow.

Or maybe she'd write him another note.

After she packed her bags, of course.

On that sad thought, she said, "Okay."

His fingers tensed at her breast.

She let out a sigh.

Surprisingly, within minutes, she fell dead asleep.

No bad dreams. No turbulent thoughts. No tossing. No turning.

Just blissful, healing, beautiful sleep.

———— ◆ ————

Prentice

PRENTICE WOKE BEFORE Elle and carefully disengaged from the dead weight of her sleeping body.

He pulled on his jeans, walked to the travel alarm on her nightstand, studied it, discovered how to turn it off and did so.

He put the clock back in its place, stood beside the bed and for long moments he watched her sleep.

Then he looked around the room.

Nothing untidy, nothing out of place, her jars and bottles arranged just so on the nightstand. Four journals perfectly stacked, precisely positioned.

He looked back at her, her face relaxed in sleep and he realized for twenty years he hadn't seen her face looking like that.

Relaxed.

At ease.

Determinedly, he set aside the thoughts that wanted to intrude in his brain.

Thoughts of Elle standing removed from the Annie and Mikey reunion when he'd first seen her after she came back.

Thoughts of Elle staring into the pasta as she stirred it when Mikey explained how she'd taken Annie's abuse and patiently forced her friend to heal.

Thoughts of Elle clenching her fists tightly when she became anxious.

Thoughts of Elle on her hands and knees after her father struck her.

Thoughts of Elle lying on the couch last night, her body trembling violently, the terrified noises she made scoring his heart.

Thoughts he'd refused to let himself think, not now, not yesterday, not five days ago and not in the weeks after she got in her rental car and drove away from him without looking back.

Instead, he focused on something else.

He pulled on the rest of his clothes and found her handbag. Digging through it, he located her passport in a travel purse, pulled it out, shoved the travel purse back into her bag and slid the passport in the back pocket of his jeans.

That accomplished, Prentice walked to the wardrobe and found her two pieces of empty luggage neatly stowed. He grabbed them both and took them out to his Range Rover, tossing them in the back.

He went back inside and made coffee.

He went to his rooms and took a shower, dressed and woke the children with a word of warning that Elle was still sleeping and they needed to be quiet so as not to wake her.

Even Sally complied with his command.

As he made his children porridge, he thought of the three days since they had their scene in his study.

He'd seen her frequently. At breakfast. During dinner. In the evenings.

He'd spoken to her infrequently.

Their picture in a gossip magazine had whetted the villagers' appetites. The house was treated to the constant comings and goings of friends and acquaintances who said they wanted to see how Sally was doing (and they likely did).

Mostly, however, they wanted to see what was going on with Prentice and Isabella after their very quick, very public and very short reconciliation ended in an unexplained three-week absence that put Prentice (and Jason) in very bad moods.

They were disappointed. Elle was a gracious hostess but her focus was the children, Sally's health, Jason's studies, their dinner, their scheduled bedtimes.

So focused was she, she had no time to focus on Prentice.

As for Prentice, he had a deadline to make and the doorbell going every fifteen minutes didn't help.

Yesterday, he'd called Isabella and left a voicemail on her mobile telling her that he needed to work late.

She'd called him back but he'd missed the call. When he checked his voicemail, he heard her voice.

Something about hearing her voice leaving a message made him lose concentration. He didn't hear a fucking word she said.

He just listened to the sound of her voice leaving him a voicemail like she did it every day.

That warmth hit his gut and this time it was far stronger, nearly enough to knock him to his knees.

After he got over acting like a fifteen-year-old boy with a fucking crush, he replayed the message and listened to her speak.

"Prentice? It's Isabella. I got your message. Listen, I'm sorry but there was a photographer in the village today. He took photos of me and Sally. I got away as quickly as I could. I . . ." She hesitated then rushed on, "I just thought you'd want to know. See you later."

Unfortunately, if he wanted to feed his children that "later" needed to be much later for, as much as he wanted to be home and not only eat her food but see her in his kitchen cooking it, he had to work.

He'd come home to a light outside, a light in the vestibule and a lamp lit in the great room, all indicating that Elle had again illuminated his way.

When he had them all off and the house secured for the night (something he never did, until he saw his son's photograph in a gossip magazine, they lived remote at the end of a winding one lane road you'd have to really want to drive up), he'd seen the dim light and heard the hushed sounds of the television in Elle's rooms.

He thought she was awake, watching television.

And he knew he shouldn't go to her.

He was fucking overjoyed he went.

"Why's Miss Bella asleep?" Sally asked on a loud whisper as Prentice put her bowl of porridge in front of her.

"Because she's tired?" Jason replied to his sister sarcastically.

"Jason," Prentice warned.

"But she's always awake," Sally countered, ignoring Prentice and unaffected as ever by her brother's sarcasm.

"She needs her sleep, baby," Prentice said. "She's been very busy and she's very tired."

"Tired like spending the day at the beach tired?" Sally asked.

"Even more," Prentice answered.

Sally's eyes got big and she breathed, "That's *tired*."

He smiled at his daughter before he said, "This morning you're coming to work with me. We'll let Elle sleep in. I'll bring you back later."

Sally tucked into her porridge and replied brightly, "Okay."

Prentice watched his daughter and wished his life was that simple.

Unfortunately, it was *not*.

Jason made a noise and Prentice's eyes moved to his son. When they did, he noted immediately that Jason had something weighty on his mind.

Uncharacteristically, Jason didn't delay in sharing what was weighing on his mind.

"How long is Miss Bella staying this time?" Jason asked his porridge.

Clear evidence that his life was not simple.

Prentice made a decision.

"You can call her Elle," he told Jason, and Jason's head shot up.

"Hurrah!" Sally cheered.

"Be quiet, baby," Prentice gently admonished his daughter.

"Hurrah," Sally whispered, grinning huge.

Prentice looked at his son. His head was bent to his porridge.

But he was also grinning.

Looking at his son, Prentice changed his mind.

Maybe life *was* that simple.

Chapter
THIRTEEN

All of It I Carry Safe

Fiona

Fiona floated behind Bella as Bella paced the great room.

And as Fiona floated, she giggled.

Bella was cross.

Very cross.

Fiona thought it was hilarious.

After Prentice came home last night and headed to the guest suite, Fiona followed him.

The minute he crossed the threshold to the room and Fiona would have floated after him, she'd popped right back to her tent by the stream.

She knew what *that* meant.

At the current stage in Prentice and Bella's game, Fiona found this surprising (and heartbreaking, but only for Fiona, still, she didn't go there).

Nevertheless, after she had a good night's sleep, the next morning she was wandering down to the stream when she popped back into the bedroom of the guest suite.

It was morning. Bella was sleeping in bed.

Prentice was standing beside it, wearing just his jeans, watching her.

Then Fiona watched Prentice get dressed, go to Bella's handbag, pocket her passport, then go to her wardrobe and grab her luggage. She floated after him as he carried it out to the Range Rover. After tossing it in, he walked back into the house.

Fiona stayed outside, staring at Bella's empty luggage in the back of Prentice's 4x4. After a while she burst out laughing.

Prentice got the kids ready and out of the house and Fiona went to Bella's room, wiling the morning away reading the rest of her journals.

By the time she was done, she was shedding ghostly tears again.

Seriously, Bella's father was a tosser.

And that ex-husband of hers? There were no words to describe what *he* was.

She was still holding the journal when Bella moved.

Quickly putting the journal back and arranging it in Bella's exacting way, she looked to the bed.

Bella was sitting up in bed covers held to her naked chest, head turned away from Fiona, staring in horror at the clock saying it was twelve after eleven.

Abruptly she was a flurry of motion.

She threw back the covers, catapulted out of bed, snatched up her discarded clothes from the night before and threw them on.

She went directly to the wardrobe. Tugging the doors open, she even leaned in to grab her suitcases before she realized they weren't there.

She stared at the empty space.

Fiona giggled at Bella.

She couldn't help it, Bella's face was just *too* funny.

"What on—?" Bella started to say, stopped then searched the room.

Then she searched the house.

Thoroughly.

Finally, she saw Prentice's note propped up against the coffeemaker.

Fiona stood behind her, reading over her shoulder as Bella read it.

E,

S is with me so you can sleep in. Call me when you wake up and I'll bring her home.

P

PS: The coffee's made, just add cinnamon and flip the switch.

Fiona floated to Bella's side and saw her face was the picture of shock, her eyes wide, her mouth had dropped open.

Fiona started giggling again.

Really, she was hilarious.

Fiona glided behind her as Bella ran to the guest suite.

Grabbing her bag, she started digging. She pulled out an elegant, rich leather, designer travel purse, snapped it open and stared inside. Her brows drew together and her fingers sifted through its contents. Not locating her passport, her face grew pale and she started to shake the travel purse as if shaking it would make her passport magically float to the surface.

She gave up, dropped the travel purse and started digging in her bag. Eventually she started *frantically* digging through her bag. Finally she dumped the contents of her bag on the couch and pawed through them.

Then she stood, face still pale, staring at the contents of her handbag scattered on the couch. Contents that no longer included her passport.

Her hands were clenched and Fiona bit her ghostly lip.

Fiona watched the expressions cross Bella's face and Fiona knew Bella made the decision not to be anxious but instead to be angry when Bella unclenched her fists and her eyes flashed.

Fiona stopped biting her lip and grinned.

This was going to be good.

Bella snatched up her phone and dialed Prentice.

Fiona got as close to her as possible without getting into shivering distance.

With super-ghost hearing, she listened to their conversation.

"Elle," Prentice said in greeting.

"Pren—" Bella started.

"You're awake," Prentice cut her off.

"Yes," Bella said curtly. "Prentice, I can't—"

He interrupted her again, "I'll bring Sally home. We'll leave in fifteen minutes. Be home soon."

"Prentice, I—" Bella began but Prentice had rung off.

Bella took her phone from her ear and stared at it with that wide-eyed, mouth-open look.

Fiona started giggling again.

Then she watched Bella dial again.

Fiona got close. Bella got voicemail.

Fiona started giggling (yes, again!).

Bella pressed a button with her thumb angrily and she threw her mobile on the couch.

She took a shower, got dressed and was in the great room, hair wet, face murderous, feet pacing when Prentice and Sally walked in.

"*Elle!*" Sally screeched the minute she saw her.

Fiona's daughter ran direct to Bella, throwing her arms around Bella's legs as if she hadn't seen her in years rather than hours.

The anger in Bella's face instantly melted away and it got that soft look it got every time Sally hugged her.

Fiona watched as Bella placed a hand to Sally's hair.

Fiona really liked it when Bella touched Sally's hair for, she suspected, Sally really liked it too.

Bella's eyes drifted to Prentice as he got close and the soft look vanished.

She opened her mouth to speak but his hand shot out. Fingers curling around the back of her head, he leaned into her over Sally, pulling her to him at the same time.

He kissed her, hard but fast.

Fiona could have done without seeing *that*.

Luckily, it was short.

With his hand still in her hair, faces close, he murmured, "Can you pick Jason up from school?"

Mutely, eyes glazed, lips parted, Bella nodded.

His hand slid to her jaw, his thumb stroking her cheekbone, his gaze roving her face, Fiona registered that he was pleased with what he saw.

"I'll see you tonight," he finished.

With that he let her go and he was gone.

Bella stared at the door.

Sally stared up from her place in front of Bella, her little arms still wrapped around Bella's legs.

"Daddy just kissed you," Sally breathed.

Bella's head jerked down.

It was clear she had no idea how to deal with this. None whatsoever. Clueless.

Fiona giggled again.

"Yes," Bella croaked, her voice scratchy. She coughed to clear her throat.

"I think he *likes* you," Sally whispered.

"I . . . uh . . . erm . . ." Bella stammered.

Suddenly, Sally let her go and skipped away, happy as a clam and onto a new topic, asking, "Can we have pancakes for lunch?"

Fiona watched Bella's shoulders droop, why, Fiona didn't know. Relief that she'd been saved from the Sally situation by Sally's short attention span. Admitting defeat about the Prentice situation.

Whatever.

Thankfully, Bella didn't make Sally pancakes. She made her grilled cheese with carrot sticks on the side.

It looked delicious.

Later, Bella picked up Jason and got the kids sorted. She was making dinner when Prentice called.

Fiona was floating with her arse over the stool next to the one her son was sitting on when the phone rang. She dematerialized and materialized close to Bella and listened in.

"Hello?" Bella greeted.

"Elle," Prentice said, but he didn't wait for a response, "I'll no' be home for dinner."

Bella's head twitched when she heard his voice and with a darted glance at Jason at the counter and one to Sally laying on her back on the couch (playing, with difficulty but determination, one-handed with her new kitty), Bella started down the hall.

Fiona followed.

"Prentice—"

Prentice cut her off. "What are you making?"

Fiona watched Bella's head jerk as she stopped outside the laundry room before she asked, sounding flummoxed, "Pardon?"

"For dinner. What are you making?"

"Gammon and egg with chips and peas," she answered, then went on quickly, "Prentice—"

He interrupted again, "Pudding?"

"What?"

"What are you making Sally for pudding?"

Bella tilted her head back and looked at the ceiling, visibly seeking patience.

Fiona giggled yet again.

"Treacle sponge with custard," she replied, her eyes moving away from the ceiling. "Now, Prentice, listen to me—"

He didn't let her continue. "Is it homemade?"

"What?"

"The sponge. Is it homemade?"

Bella sighed. Heavily.

"Yes. But Pren—"

"Save me some sponge."

"Prentice—"

"I'll be home as soon as I can."

Talking so swiftly her words ran together, Bella declared, "Prentice, we have to talk."

His voice was soft when he responded, "Aye, but I have a deadline, baby. We'll talk when I get home."

Bella made no response and Fiona saw her eyes were glazed again. And Fiona knew why.

Prentice had an attractive voice but when it got soft and he talked to you with love in his tone, well, *that* would make *anyone's* eyes glaze over.

Fiona floated listlessly as she heard Prentice repeat, "I'll be home as soon as I can."

He then disconnected.

Bella gazed dazedly at the phone for several long seconds before she pressed the button to turn it off.

Fiona decided she hated her again.

Prentice might not have called Fiona "baby." And he might not have cuddled her in bed all night long.

But he *had* spoken to her with love in his tone.

She hadn't heard that in well over a year.

She missed it.

Terribly.

Bella went back to making and serving dinner. While they ate it, Fiona thought about leaving them and going somewhere else to haunt for a while. She was going over her options when Jason made a statement that piqued her interest.

"Kids at school say I'm in a magazine."

Bella was rinsing the dirty dishes.

She glanced over her shoulder from her place at the sink, her gaze hesitant and she said gently, "Yes, sweetheart."

He grinned his cheeky grin.

All grin. All cheek. All Jason. No sadness in his eyes. Nothing held back.

Fiona hadn't seen that in well over a year either.

She missed that too.

"Do I look good?" Jason asked.

Bella smiled.

All of a sudden looking strangely indecisive, she stilled.

Finally, making her decision, she walked to Jason and put her hand on top of his head. Leaning in, her hand slid down to his cheek.

Her face got close. "With your father's eyes and your mother's hair, it's impossible for you *not* to look good."

Jason stared at her, probably because her voice shook with emotion.

Bella's fingers slid through his hair as she watched her hand, the look on her beautiful face a mixture nostalgic and heartbroken.

She caught his eyes and whispered, "You know, she's with you every minute. Here." She tugged his hair gently. "Here." She let his hair go and tapped his head with her finger. "And here." She put her hand over his heart. "I learned that a long time ago," Bella whispered. "My mom left me but she left a lot *with* me and all of it I carry safe, every moment, *right here.*" She pressed her hand on his chest for emphasis and Jason closed his eyes.

Ghostly tears slid down Fiona's cheeks and she decided she didn't hate Bella anymore.

Fiona watched as Bella leaned in and kissed the top of his head and then she went back to tidying the kitchen as if that touching moment hadn't happened.

Eyes never leaving Bella, Jason made a noise in the back of his throat then gulped in an effort to control his emotion.

Bella, astutely, ignored it.

He slid off his stool, went to get Fiona's guitar and the book Bella gave him to teach himself how to play it and he brought them downstairs.

Seeing him with her guitar and Bella's book, Fiona finally got it.

And she looked to the woman who was teaching her daughter how to dangle the new cat toy she'd bought Blackie when she was with Sally in the village and Fiona fell in love.

This world was meant to have Jason and Sally in it.

So, as ugly as it was, Bella and Prentice could not be.

And Fiona and Prentice were meant to be.

But, as ugly as it was, Fiona was not meant to inhabit that world for very long.

So, when she was gone, someone had to take care of her family.

And there was no better person to do it than the beautiful woman gamely ignoring her son plucking discordantly at guitar strings while she laughed and played with Sally and her kitten.

Now, Fiona realized, was the time Bella and Prentice were meant to be.

Fiona hovered, shaken by this new knowledge, as Bella put Sally to bed and came back down to Jason.

Then she surprised Fiona further as she gently took the guitar away from him. Expertly tuning it (she had a good ear), she explained what she was doing as Jason looked on with a rapt expression.

After she tuned, she played.

Fiona was stunned. Bella hadn't played twenty years ago. She wasn't talented but she knew what she was doing and it sounded lovely.

When she stopped, Bella surprised Fiona even *further* when she explained to Jason, "I was so impressed with your mum's playing, when I went home I took lessons." Her face and tone grew wistful when she said, "I haven't played in years. I forgot how much I like doing it." She gained control and grinned at Jason. "But it makes your fingers hurt."

Jason grinned back.

Bella handed Jason Fiona's guitar and finished, her face soft, "That's what your mum gave to me, my love of the guitar. And a lot of happy memories filled with laughter. Those things are what I carry in *my* heart, gifts from Fiona."

Jason's grin died and he gulped again.

Fiona gulped too but she didn't succeed in holding back her tears like her son did.

Quickly, Bella moved past the moment and with great patience she gave Jason a few pointers. After a while, his discordant plucking became something else altogether. Finally, she sent him off to bed with the guitar.

She went to her rooms. She opened the nightstand and pulled out a new journal. Opening it to the first page and picking up her expensive pen, she wrote about Fiona's children while Fiona hovered over her and her book, unashamedly reading while Bella wrote.

And Fiona knew those words were some of very few good ones in any of those books.

It was then Fiona decided Sally and Jason were meant to exist in part to heal Bella.

And, as crazy as it sounded, Fiona was proud to have had a hand in that.

When Bella finished, she left her rooms to shut down the house.

All except the light outside, the light in the vestibule and a lamp in the great room.

Then she paced while Fiona trailed behind her. The longer she paced, the more cross she became.

And the more hilarious Fiona found it.

Fiona felt Prentice's presence first.

She dashed in front of Bella so she could watch her face when she realized he was home.

Bella heard the 4x4. She stopped pacing and glared at the door.

Fiona couldn't wait to see what happened next.

The door opened.

Bella tensed.

Fiona popped back into her tent by the ever-blossoming apple tree.

"Bloody hell!" she shouted at its silk walls.

———— • ————

Isabella

ISABELLA DIDN'T THINK she'd ever been that angry.

He'd taken her suitcases. *And* her passport.

It had to be him. Who else could it be? They hadn't disappeared into thin air!

And *why?* Why had he taken them?

It was mad. Utterly insane.

She had to go, for his own good, even for the children's!

Especially after last night.

No, she couldn't think about last night. She just couldn't let last night happen again.

Ever.

She just had to get . . . out . . . of . . . *there!*

Not for herself, but for him.

Her father, who was a jerk, who both she and Prentice knew would always be doing jerky things that would drive Prentice up the wall.

And Jason and Sally would witness it. Heck, they already had! They could even be caught up in it (her father didn't hesitate with his venom, no matter what your age, that Isabella knew all too well). And this was something which didn't bear thinking about.

And the photographers, who were annoying, who both she and Prentice knew would always be hounding her and now him and the children. And Prentice would hate that then begin to hate *her* for bringing that in their lives.

And she was . . .

She was . . .

Weak.

Not like Fiona, who was good and talented and funny and loving and strong and confident enough to use bold colors while decorating her house.

Isabella was weak.

And, whatever was in his mind now (and something was definitely in his mind, Isabella just didn't understand it), Prentice would begin to hate that too.

She had to get out of there. For his own good.

Didn't he *see* that? Why couldn't he see? Why was he keeping her there? Why was he doing this? Why wouldn't he just *let her go*?

It was exceedingly *exasperating*.

She heard the SUV and her eyes turned to the door.

She was going to let him have it the moment he walked in.

She'd practiced her whole speech. Heaven knew she had enough time waiting for him.

And her speech was *perfect*.

The door opened, Prentice entered and every practiced word flew from her mind.

He walked into his home casually because he did it every day (so of course it would be casually).

But there was something about watching him coming home after work that hit Isabella in a strange way. It wasn't unpleasant, not in the slightest.

And he looked good.

Wearing a tan-colored, all-weather canvas jacket that was worn in enough to look good and fit him well, but not worn out, a deep-blue button-up shirt, a pair of jeans that were also worn enough to fit (too well) but not worn out and boots.

He was the kind of man who made any clothing look good (too good) and Isabella noted this fact with inappropriate fascination at that juncture, since she should have been giving him what for.

She also noted that his hair was slightly disheveled, probably from the wind outside.

That looked good on him too (too good).

She watched mutely as he secured the door and turned out the lights.

Then she noticed as he walked through the vestibule and into the great room that his eyes were on her.

Her mind kicked into gear.

"Prentice, we have to talk," she announced as he got close.

Too close.

Toe to toe with her, right in her space.

She decided to hold her ground so as not to appear weak.

This was the wrong decision.

Ignoring her announcement, his head started to come toward hers, his eyes on her mouth.

She contradicted her earlier decision and decided it was time to re-treat. She leaned away and started to take a step back but, quick as a flash, he had a hand at her hip and his other was cupping the back of her head. He held her steady while his mouth descended to hers and he kissed her.

Hard, thorough, deep but not long.

He lifted his head and looked in her eyes.

The kiss was nice. Too nice.

"Did you save me some sponge?" he asked softly.

Her mind was adrift, still reeling from his kiss.

Sponge? What was he talking about?

"Wh-what?" she stammered, her focus on getting her heart to stop beating so fast not to mention uncurling her toes.

"Sponge. Did you save me some?"

"In the kitchen," she answered in a breathy voice.

His hands dropped and he moved away. Shrugging off his jacket, he threw it on an armchair and headed to the kitchen.

Stupidly, Isabella watched him.

Then her eyes moved to his jacket.

Really, she should ignore his jacket. It wasn't harming anything, lying there on the armchair. There were other, more important things to do.

But she couldn't ignore it. It wasn't where it was supposed to be.

She hurried forward, grabbed his jacket and took it into the vestibule. She hung it on the hooks with the other jackets and then used all of her willpower not to run to the kitchen.

She had to be cool, calm, and collected.

She had to concentrate.

She had to get this done.

Now.

Prentice was pressing buttons on the microwave when she arrived in the kitchen.

"Pren—" she started.

"Just a minute," he cut her off. Turning, he walked with long strides to the stairs and up them.

Isabella stood in the kitchen, listening to the microwave whirring, staring blankly at the stairs.

She did this for a while. She did it until Prentice walked back down at the exact same time the microwave dinged.

He went directly to the refrigerator.

"Pren—" she began again.

He interrupted her by asking the inside of the refrigerator, "I see the kids are asleep. Were they okay tonight?"

"Yes," Isabella answered quickly. "Now—"

His head came out of the fridge and she saw he had the bowl of leftover custard in his hand.

"Sally?" he inquired.

"Fine," Isabella replied, and because she knew he'd want to know went on to explain, "She tires out easily but she had a nap this afternoon before we went to get Jason and I put her to bed earlier than normal.

She was wiped out. Even so, it was like the accident never happened. She's adjusting to the cast unbelievably well."

Prentice nodded while he walked to the microwave.

She took a deep breath and launched in, "Prentice, we need to talk about—"

She stopped speaking when she saw him take what was the remainder of the sponge out of the microwave (and it was huge) and he poured the remainder of the custard over it (and there was a lot).

She gaped as the custard covered the piece of sponge.

Completely.

And she continued to gape as Prentice grabbed a spoon and commenced eating.

"That's . . ." Isabella began in a strangled voice, her eyes on the mammoth portion in his bowl. She paused then continued, "Prentice, that's enough to feed a professional wrestler."

Or two. Or, probably, three.

"Aye," he replied. "Missed dinner."

Her gaze flew to his face. "You . . . missed dinner?"

His eyes on Isabella, he swallowed a mouthful.

Then he repeated, "Aye."

That would *not* do.

She started to move away, mumbling, "I'll fix you something. A sandwich."

She didn't get very far.

His arm curled around her waist and he shuffled her so she was against the counter and he closed in, standing in front of her, imprisoning her.

He took his arm from her waist and calmly continued eating.

She blinked up at him before she informed him, "You can't eat sponge for dinner."

His mouth twitched before he asked, "Why not?"

Was he mad?

"Because it's *sponge*," she explained unnecessarily.

His twitching mouth spread into a handsome smile. She blinked again as his smile hit her, affecting various parts of her body.

Specific parts.

And the effect was staggering.

"Aye. It's sponge," he said, thankfully taking her mind off the specific parts of her body that were, at that moment, tingling. "It's good sponge. And it's *your* sponge."

After telling her this, he went back to eating.

Isabella watched him. She found this fascinating too.

She endeavored to concentrate on the matter at hand.

"You need something substantial," she declared.

"This is pretty substantial," he returned.

He wasn't wrong about that. Steamed sponge was *very* substantial, dense, rich, heavy.

It was just . . .

Well . . .

Sponge!

"You won't let Sally have cake for breakfast. You can't have dessert for dinner," she told him severely.

He was still smiling when he replied, "Sally's six. I'm forty-five. Sally does what I let her do. I do what the fuck I want."

Isabella couldn't argue with that. And why were they talking about this at all?

"Prentice—"

But he'd finished his sponge and moved away from her. Having grabbed the empty custard bowl, he walked to the sink.

Isabella squared her shoulders.

"Where are my suitcases?" she asked his back as he put the bowls in the sink and ran water in them. "And where's my passport?"

"They're at my office," he answered immediately.

Her mouth dropped open.

She didn't know what response she'd get to those questions considering it was insane that he'd stolen her passport and suitcases in the first place. But she hadn't expected *that* or his immediate honesty nor did she know what to do with it.

"Why?" she inquired, her voice pitched higher.

He put the bowls and spoon in the dishwasher, closed the door and walked to her saying, "So you wouldn't pack them, write some mad note and disappear halfway around the world."

She opened her mouth to speak but couldn't form a response. She couldn't even think of one.

She'd *practiced* this. Why was she messing it up?

She had no time to figure it out, he'd taken her hand and was pulling her behind him as he walked to the light switch in the kitchen and flipped it off.

He was tugging her down the hallway toward the guest suite, her hand still firm in his when she declared, "You can't *steal* my passport and luggage."

"That's funny, since I did," he returned.

He was unbelievable!

What was going on in that head of his?

No, she didn't want to know. She just wanted *to go*.

She tried to yank her hand from his. This endeavor failed.

Instead, Prentice suddenly halted, turned and yanked *her* hand.

He was stronger and she flew to him. He dropped her hand but caught her hips and pushed her up against the wall.

His body got close, so close she could feel his warmth *everywhere*.

Her mind scrambled.

"Why do you want your things?" he asked softly.

She blinked up at him, finding her attention wandering considering his proximity and that soft, deep voice he was using.

With effort, she explained the obvious, "They're mine."

"Aye, but why do you want them?"

"Because they're *mine*."

In the darkened hall, she saw his white teeth flash in a smile.

Her heart skipped as her temper flared.

"We've established that," he replied. "Now, *why* do you want them?"

"I just do," she shot back.

His hand lifted, coming up to cup her jaw and he tipped her head further back as he got even closer.

"All right, you can have them back," he murmured.

Suddenly, she didn't want them back.

With more effort, she remained focused.

"Thank you." It was meant to come out condescendingly but it came out breathily.

"When I'm ready to give them back," he finished.

She opened her mouth to protest, which was a fool thing to do as his head had slanted and it was coming closer.

"Pren—" she got out before he kissed her.

This time it was hard, thorough, deep *and* long with the addition of being wet, hot and tasting deliciously of custard and sponge.

As she always did, always, always, always, she melted into him. Her hands glided into his soft hair and she held his head to hers as her body ignited.

He stopped kissing her but didn't take his lips from hers.

"Let's go to bed," he whispered.

Lost and no longer thinking about her suitcases, her passport, getting away, saving him and his children from the misfortune that seemed to plague her or the fact that he had an enormous piece of sponge for dinner, she pressed into him and nodded.

———— ◆ ————

Prentice

ELLE SPOONED IN front of him, the fingers of one of Prentice's hands between her legs, the others curled around her breast, her sweet ass nestled in his groin, his cock still imbedded inside her, her sex rippling against it in the aftermath of her orgasm, Prentice buried his face in her fragrant hair and tried to even his breathing as he listened to Elle doing the same.

Christ, she was magnificent when he fucked her.

Testing this theory, he pressed his still-swollen cock deeper, his thumb and forefinger rolling her taut nipple, his other fingers putting pressure between her legs. She emitted a sexy, lusty sigh and nuzzled her ass into his lap.

Welcoming his attention.

Inviting it.

Getting off on it.

Yes, he was correct.

Magnificent.

He could enthusiastically say that night and the one before, Prentice had sampled a variety of items in the catalogue of things he wanted to do to Elle and he was not disappointed.

When he wasn't close to her, touching her, kissing her, fucking her and she wasn't around his children, she was hesitant and unsure, aloof and cool or unapproachable and distant.

When she was with his children and when he was close to her, touching her, kissing her, fucking her, she was not hesitant, not remote, not unapproachable.

She was completely his.

His Elle.

The one he'd fallen in love with twenty years ago.

He just had to work on the rest of the time.

During those times, when she was with his kids or he was close, he had her back. Not exactly the same, not with her rabid energy and joy of life but instinctively he knew that would happen.

Or, more to the point, he intended to *make* it happen.

And to do it, he had to keep her off-balance or stay close or be touching her, kissing her or fucking her.

He looked forward to this challenge.

And Prentice Cameron hadn't looked forward to anything for a very long time.

Gently, he pulled his hand from between her legs and wrapped his arm around her middle as he cupped her breast and slid his cock out of her, craving their connection instantly after it was lost.

Her breathing had steadied and her bodyweight settled into his arms.

She'd slept late that morning but she'd been worn out. He wouldn't be surprised, after what they'd done (and they'd sampled four positions in his catalogue, all of which they both enjoyed to the fullest), if she fell asleep.

His head came up and he shifted her hair off her neck with his chin before he asked softly in her ear, "You asleep, baby?"

He was surprised when she whispered, "No."

He kissed her neck then absorbed her shiver, something which made him smile.

"Do you want to talk?" he asked her neck.

She was still whispering when she replied, "No."

That was perfectly fine with him.

He settled in behind her, tightening his arms.

She didn't fight it. She cuddled closer even though there was no closer to get, still, she sought it.

This pleased him.

Perhaps he was getting somewhere.

His face went back to her hair and his arm left her waist. His hand traveled down her arm and found her hand.

Realizing vaguely he was relieved to find her hand open and relaxed, he threaded his fingers in hers.

Her fingers closed tight.

Yes, he was getting somewhere.

"Sleep," he encouraged.

"Okay," she whispered.

He stayed awake until he knew she slept.

And he stayed awake longer, unconsciously waiting for her to have that dream.

When time slid by and she didn't but instead laid peaceful in his arms, Prentice finally fell asleep.

Chapter
FOURTEEN
Miracle Worker

Isabella

In the moments before fully waking, Isabella felt that sweet, long-lost sense of contentment she'd only experienced once in her life for fifteen months twenty years ago.

Then her travel alarm sounded.

Her eyes opened.

The warm solid weight at her back shifted, the fingers laced in hers released, and Prentice pressed into her back as she saw his arm reach out, his hand tagging the clock.

The bed moved as she felt him get up on an elbow and she stared at her clock held before her in his hand.

"Christ, how do you turn this fucking thing off?" he growled, his voice gruff with sleep.

Evidently, Prentice was *not* a morning person.

She took it from him and pressed the off button. Without delay, he pulled it from her hand and put it back to the nightstand.

She tried to get her thoughts together but they were randomly and determinedly skipping from one to another, all of them centered around how *very much* she liked waking up next to Prentice (even grouchy Prentice).

His body was warm, it was big, it was strong, it was pressed up against hers and the bed felt cozy and safe with him in it.

His face went into her neck and she felt his lips there.

She liked that too.

His hand glided up her belly to between her breasts as he said, "We have to be quick, baby. Need to get the kids up and fed."

Those breasts his palm rested between started tingling.

"Quick?" she asked, her mind muddled, nothing he said made sense.

And, anyway, she didn't want him to make sense. She wanted to nestle into him and go back to the dreamless, restful sleep she only seemed to have when he was with her.

She realized what he meant when his palm moved from between her breasts to cup one of them and his teeth nipped her earlobe.

She trembled.

"Quick," he replied.

Before she could catch a thought his face went away from her neck, he pressed her to her back, rolled over her, his mouth captured hers in a heady kiss and then Prentice deliciously guided them through "quick."

It wasn't until they were naked in the shower and the water was sluicing into her hair and down her body that Isabella's thoughts semi-focused.

They focused first on the fact that she was naked with Prentice in the shower and she wasn't certain she was entirely comfortable with that.

Then they focused on the fact that Prentice was naked with her in the shower and she was very certain she was comfortable with that because he had a fantastic body.

Finally they focused on the fact they were all of a sudden *in* the shower even though she'd barely had time to recover from the climax he'd just given her. He hadn't even let her get her breathing regulated or her heart rate slowed before he pulled her out of bed and hustled her into the bathroom.

He definitely didn't let her get her thoughts sorted.

She tipped her head back, blinking against the spray and looked up at him.

"Pren—"

She, yet again, didn't finish his name.

"Jesus, Elle, with all this shit, do you have any shampoo?"

Her blinking eyes saw he had two of her bottles in his hands and he was studying them.

"That's body wash," she informed him inanely, pointing to the bottle in his right hand. "And that's body scrub," she went on, pointing to the bottle in his left.

He put them down and grabbed another one.

"That's conditioner," she said quickly.

He looked at her, put the conditioner down and grabbed another one.

"That's shave lotion."

With her shave lotion still in one hand, he straightened and hauled her to him with his other arm as he burst out laughing.

Before she could process their scenario, standing naked in the shower Prentice holding her and laughing about showering products, he pulled away.

He reached for the last remaining bottle, muttering with obvious amusement, "Process of elimination."

He turned her to face away from him and she stared at the tile wall, her mind snapping into focus.

"Pren—"

She interrupted herself this time as his fingers slid pleasantly strong through her hair and against her scalp.

He was washing her hair.

She supposed at some point her mother washed her hair when she was younger. But she didn't remember.

And, of course, when she was at the stylists, they washed her hair and gave her a head massage and she always enjoyed that.

However, *this* was something else.

This felt marvelous.

Her mind erased, her head bent forward and her body automatically relaxed back into Prentice's. He took her weight as his hands worked in her hair.

When he was done, he gently moved her forward under the spray. Supporting her weight against his body with an arm at her waist, he used his other hand to rinse the soap from her hair.

He repeated this delightful sequence of actions.

Then he progressed the shower by using his hands, soapy with her body wash, to cleanse her from neck to feet.

Thoroughly cleansing her.

That felt marvelous too.

So marvelous she didn't protest and was still dazed when he carefully maneuvered her out from under the spray and positioned himself in it.

She was still dazed when he said, "We need to hurry, baby. Help me out."

She looked up at him, blank, as he squirted her shampoo in his palm.

"Help you?" she asked stupidly.

He set the shampoo aside and gave her the body wash. She stared at it, her mind freezing as she understood what he meant.

She stared at him.

And said the first thing that popped into her head.

"If I use this, you're going to smell like lilies of the valley."

He grinned as his hand shot up, curving around her neck and he pulled her face to his.

"Means I'll smell you all day," he said against her lips before he touched his there and finished in that soft tone that did funny things to her entire system, "Works for me."

He released her and went back to shampooing.

Isabella stared at the body wash in her hand. Then she stared at his body. Her mind fogged, but that was fine considering her hands didn't need her mind to work to do what they wanted to do.

She was thoroughly enjoying running her soapy hands along the slick, wet, soapy skin and hard muscle of Prentice's body, *very* thoroughly enjoying it, when Prentice's fingers curled around her wrists. He pulled her up against his body by wrapping her arms around his waist.

The water cascaded down both of them but his head shielded her face, which was tipped to look up at his.

His every-colored eyes were so warm they were burning and her breath caught.

His voice was a husky rumble as he murmured, "I think you got it."

"Okay," she whispered, vaguely embarrassed because she was over-enthusiastic with the body wash.

Mostly, she was lost in counting the occurrence of each color in his irises and comparing the numbers.

She distractedly noticed something changed in those eyes, and her mind only fully processed the change when his hand came to her jaw.

She blinked and focused on the look in his face and her belly dropped.

"What?" she whispered.

His thumb slid along her bottom lip.

His voice was again a husky rumble, this one softer and definitely sweeter when he whispered, "You haven't looked at me like that in twenty years."

Isabella's throat closed and her body went solid.

For half a second.

Then his fingers slid into her hair, cupping the back of her head, his arm sliced around her waist, pulling her deeper into his body and he kissed her.

Hard, long, and beautiful with the warm water sliding down their bodies and lilies of the valley fragrancing everything around them.

Heaven.

When she was putty in his hands, he released her but kissed her forehead and stepped out of the shower before she could think another thought.

She watched mutely through the glass door as he toweled off then wrapped the towel around his hips and turned to her.

"I'll get the kids," he said before he strode from the room.

She stared at the empty room a moment before her body jolted.

This wasn't right.

Well, it *was* right, in a perfect-world type of way.

But Isabella existed in a world that was far from perfect.

And she needed to shield Prentice and his children from that world.

She turned off the water, jumped from the shower, toweled off and ran into the bedroom. Dragging on underwear and a bra, she opened the wardrobe doors and stilled, staring at her clothes.

She'd packed in a panic, not thinking of much except making certain she had the bare necessities. She never dreamed she'd be there for over a week. Everything she had in the wardrobe, Prentice had already seen.

It was too early to start recycling outfits.

And she needed a good outfit.

They'd had great sex last night and woke up together for the first time *ever*. That alone meant she needed a good outfit.

But they'd also just had great sex that morning and showered together for the first time *ever*.

That meant she needed a *great* outfit.

One part of her mind stopped the ridiculous rampaging thoughts of the other.

What was she thinking? She wasn't trying to impress him with her style and flair.

She grabbed a pair of jeans and ran to the bureau and snatched a long-sleeved, dusty pink, thin, fitted T-shirt. She tugged these on and started to run from the room when she realized the towel was still wrapped around her hair.

She ran back, yanked off the towel and dragged a comb through her hair.

She started to run from the room again.

She ran back and pumped smoothing elixir into her hand, rubbed it through her hair and ran the comb back through.

She started to run from the room yet again.

But she ran back, put on deodorant and spritzed on perfume and she began to run from the room.

Then, knowing she should ignore it (but she couldn't ignore it), she ran back, folded the towel on the rack, made the bed and grabbed her clothes that were strewn around the room during the sexual festivities last night.

She noted that Prentice's clothes were amongst hers and she grabbed those too thinking of him walking through the house in nothing but a towel, which caused her skin to start tingling.

Gathering their mingled clothes in itself was an act that caused her tingling skin to start to get warm as the memories of last night invaded.

With resolve, she ignored the tingling, the warmth *and* the memories.

Then she ran to the kitchen, stopping at the mudroom to toss their dirty clothes into the pile of unwashed laundry.

She'd flipped the switch on the coffeemaker when she heard Prentice calling her name.

She turned and looked to the top of the stairs.

He stood there barefoot, in jeans, his wet hair slicked back, his shirt unbuttoned all the way down, exposing his chest and stomach.

Her resolve to ignore the tingling and warmth slipped a hefty notch.

When she finally tore her gaze from his flat stomach and caught his eyes, he bizarrely asked in an exasperated tone, "A little help up here?"

Saying nothing more, he turned and disappeared down the hall.

She stared at the place where she last saw him, slightly concerned about the frustration in his tone. Mostly her mind was busy deliberating on the fact that Prentice had asked for her to help him with something upstairs.

Upstairs, she had made beds, gathered clothes, vacuumed, tidied and put Sally to bed.

But in the mornings she made coffee and breakfast in the kitchen, never part of the family pandemonium upstairs that usually centered (from what she heard), one way or another, around Sally.

Upstairs was *their* space. Cameron family space. And even making beds or reading to Sally, somehow Isabella always felt like she was intruding.

But now, Prentice seemed to be inviting her upstairs, asking for "a little help."

With only a moment's hesitation, she ran up the stairs.

She found Prentice in Sally's room, his shirt buttoned but not tucked in, his hands on his hips, his exasperated gaze on Sally.

Sally was dressed in the fancy, frilly flower girl dress she wore to Annie's wedding. The dress was on backward, its skirt askew mainly because part of it was tucked into her little girl pants.

She was glowering at her father, clearly digging her heels in about something and it didn't take an experienced parent to know it was the dress.

"Sally, I'm no' going to say it again, take off the dress," Prentice demanded, his voice firm, his patience obviously spent.

"I want to be a princess today!" Sally returned. Unwisely defiant in the face of her father's escalating frustration, she went on to cry in equal frustration, "And this is my only princess dress!"

"Princess." Isabella heard mumbled from beside her and she saw that Jason had joined them, dressed in his school uniform. His eyes were on his sister and he was shaking his head with disbelief. "Mental," he finished.

"Jace, your contribution isn't needed," Prentice said to his son.

Jason gave Isabella a hilariously disgusted look (at which Isabella did *not* laugh, even though she wanted to) and wandered out of the room.

Prentice's eyes cut back to his daughter and he said warningly, "Sally—"

"*I wanna be a princess!*" she shrieked, Prentice tensed and then he turned his gaze to *Isabella*, brows going up.

She stared at him.

He expected her to do something.

Her.

Isabella.

She had no idea what to do!

She looked at Sally.

Sally was still scowling stubbornly at her father.

It came to her.

"Hmm," Isabella murmured, putting her forefinger to her lips as her eyes traveled Sally, and Sally's gaze went to her. Isabella continued, "Of course, Cinderella *ended up* a princess but she didn't get that by demanding to wear her best dress during the day. In fact, that was something her evil stepsisters would do, seeing as they were spoilt rotten. The evil stepsisters likely wore their best princess party dresses *everyday* while Cinderella wore her normal clothes. That's probably why the fairy godmother came to visit Cinderella, because she needed to have a special occasion to wear her best princess party dress."

Sally's scowl had disappeared and she was watching Isabella in childlike horror at the very *thought* that she might be more of an evil stepsister than Cinderella.

Isabella felt Prentice's eyes on her but she didn't spare him a glance.

"So, I suppose, if you don't wait for a special occasion to wear your best princess party dress then, when you need her, your fairy godmother will never come to visit." Isabella shrugged with indifference then finished, "Oh well."

She turned to Prentice and saw he was watching her, biting back a smile. She didn't react to this. She just started to leave the room.

"I want a visit from my fairy godmother!" Sally cried, her voice desperate.

Isabella immediately switched directions, walked up to Sally and guided her to her wardrobe while muttering, "Then let's get you some normal clothes, sweetheart."

She was tugging Sally's flower girl dress over her head when she felt her wet hair swept over one shoulder and then she felt Prentice's hand at her waist at the same time she felt his lips at the nape of her neck.

She shivered, felt his presence depart and by the time she whirled, Sally free of the dress, all she saw was his back as he strode from the room.

When she and Sally descended the stairs, Prentice was sipping coffee in the kitchen, his shirt now tucked in and boots on his feet and Jason was making toast.

"Do we have to have porridge again today?" Sally asked, skipping to a stool.

Isabella entered the kitchen and started to get busy as she said, "No, honey, I'll make you some eggs."

"I don't want eggs. I want you to make some of your cookies," Sally replied, clearly determined never to give up on the idea that, one day, someone would relent and she'd get sweets for breakfast rather than just breakfast.

"No cookies. Eggs," Isabella returned, deciding today was not that day and *she* certainly wouldn't be the one who would relent.

"Pancakes," Sally pushed.

"Eggs," Isabella repeated.

"Pancakes!" Sally shouted.

Isabella turned to her and explained calmly, "Pancakes are weekend food. Tomorrow's Saturday. Saturday is the weekend. I'll make you pancakes tomorrow, with blueberries in and everything. But today you get eggs."

"Okay," Sally agreed happily.

Prentice burst out laughing.

So focused on Sally, Isabella's body jerked and her gaze snapped to him. Her mind blanked as she caught sight of his handsome, laughing face.

His handsome, *carefree*, laughing face.

No tightness around his mouth, no pain in his eyes, his face was relaxed and he was at ease in his kitchen with her and his children.

This so astonished Isabella, she didn't react when he snatched her in his arms, gave her a hug and a swift kiss on her neck even though he was still chuckling.

He released her and she stood swaying as he went to the cupboard, pulled down a mug, poured in some coffee, splashed in her milk and brought it to her.

Automatically, her finger hooked the handle as he murmured, "I'd like mine scrambled." She blinked up at him but he just grinned and turned to the fridge to get Sally some milk. He poured the milk in a glass while walking to Sally but he was speaking to his son, "Jace, get your rucksack ready, mate. We're running late. We'll need to leave right after eggs."

The words "late" and "eggs" made Isabella jolt out of her motionless, befuddled stance, preparing to sort breakfast.

Her body stilled again when she saw Jason, his eyes darting back and forth between Isabella and Prentice like he was viewing a fascinating tennis match. His gaze stuck on Isabella and she watched as he slowly smiled his father's smile.

Carefree, at ease, relaxed.

Joy shot through her as fear pierced her soul.

She jolted yet again when she felt Prentice's hand slide along the small of her back, stopping to give her waist a squeeze.

"Elle, baby, eggs," he prompted softly, let her go and said to Jason, "I'll finish the toast, Jace. Rucksack. Go."

Jason nodded to his father and raced upstairs.

Isabella made eggs.

Prentice made toast and, shockingly, didn't ruin it.

They ate while Isabella's thoughts descended into turmoil, happy, sad, elated, sated, content, but most prevalent of all, terrified.

After they finished breakfast, she trailed after Prentice as Jason ran ahead to the door.

She caught his wrist, starting, "Pren—"

He abruptly turned, twisted his wrist and grasped her hand, pulling her to him. Her body hit his at about the same time his lips hit hers.

The terror fled and all good things *Prentice* were the only things on her mind.

His head lifted and he murmured, "I should make today's deadline and be home in time for tea. Pick Jace up, will you?"

Without waiting for her to answer, he turned and walked out the door.

Long after it closed, Isabella stared at it.

Then she felt Sally's little hand slide into hers.

She looked down at the girl.

"We forgot to give Blackie breakfast," Sally told her, her face full of worry that a half an hour delay in Blackie getting breakfast would cause her new kitten to expire.

Alleviating Sally's worry obviously took precedence over the fear closing around Isabella's heart.

Therefore she set the fear aside to deal with later and she and Sally got Blackie some breakfast.

———————•◆•———————

AFTER THEY GOT Blackie breakfast, Isabella loaded Sally in the car and they went into town.

They did this partly because there were a few things for dinner that night that Isabella needed to pick up.

They did this mainly because Isabella decided that, although Sally couldn't have cookies for breakfast, that didn't mean Sally couldn't have cookies *at all* and they needed some ingredients for cookies too.

As she was driving and Sally was chattering, she made up her mind that, after the kids went to bed that night, she and Prentice were going to talk.

She was *not* going to get dazed and confused.

She was *not* going to let him touch her, kiss her, make love to her or sleep with her.

She *was* going to put her foot down and get things straight.

They were going through the market with a cart as Isabella decided exactly what they'd get straight.

She was going to leave Monday. They were going to tell the children tomorrow night. Maybe take them out to dinner or something. Then she'd have Sunday as a farewell day and she'd be gone.

That was as far as she got in her plan.

Isabella had to stop strategizing when she had to stop and explain to Sally that she could pick only *one* candy bar for her and *one* candy bar for Jason rather than Sally having *one* of *each* on the display.

Then she couldn't continue her mental planning session because practically everyone she passed in the aisles either smiled at her or said hello and this broke her concentration.

Then she couldn't continue her mental planning session because, on their way to checkout, Lucy Guthrie (who used to work at the pub where Dougal and Annie, Fiona and Scott and Prentice and Isabella hung out), stopped them. Isabella and Lucy chatted for ten minutes about how Sally was getting on, if they were going to have a mild winter and if Isabella and Prentice had sampled the new Indian place in town.

Somehow shaken by Lucy thinking Isabella and Prentice would sample anything together even though it seemed the entire village (including Prentice) were under the mistaken impression that they *were* together, Isabella didn't start her mental planning session again until much later.

It was after they went to the fruit and veg shop so she could get fresh fine greens for dinner and blueberries for pancakes the next morning.

And it was after they ran into Denise MacRae, Debs's best friend since childhood who spent as much time at Prentice's mum's house back in the day as Isabella did, which meant *a lot*, and her baby outside the fruit and veg shop.

And also after Denise's nearly one-year-old baby charmed Isabella with a smile and then began to flirt with her brazenly (as only one-year-old baby boys could do), rendering Isabella smitten.

This meant she stood outside giggling with baby Robbie while talking to Denise about all things baby, Sally, Jason, Prentice, school runs and football practices.

And the mental planning session also came after Gordon Taggart, who was walking his dog, stopped to chat with Denise, Sally, Robbie and Isabella. Sally and Isabella fell in love with Gordon's border collie instantly and they both took turns giving her hugs and cuddles (Sally) and scratches and body rubs (Isabella).

"Gon' ruin her for me, lasses," Gordon said on a smile, his eyes moved over Isabella's shoulder and then his smile turned sour.

Isabella's heart skipped a beat as the older man moved with a strange aggression around both Isabella and Sally.

She stared at him wondering if there was a magical spell over the village making the villagers be nice to her and the spell had suddenly been broken.

Or maybe villagers turned bad.

"Bella, luv, there's a photographer coming this way. Get Sally to your car," he warned.

Isabella looked around him and saw that there was, indeed, a photographer coming, already shooting pictures even though Gordon was doing his best to shield them.

That was when she realized that Gordon *was* doing his best to shield them and she wanted to kiss him.

Instead, she gave him a grateful look with an added, whispered, "Thanks, Gordon."

She grabbed Sally's good hand, touching Robbie's nose (to which he giggled at her), smiling at Denise and she and Sally walked as quickly as they could without appearing to be running away.

Isabella only resumed her mental planning session when Sally was painstakingly but happily stirring the thick cookie batter left-handed.

Her conversation with Sally that morning had given Isabella an idea.

What she was going to be to the children was like a fairy godmother but a modern, real kind.

She'd explain to Prentice that she'd like to stay in their lives, talk to them on the phone, send them things when the spirit moved her and maybe even come visit once in a while. And, when they got older, the children could come and visit her.

She'd also explain to Prentice that he and she couldn't carry on like they were. They were confusing the children and confusing themselves.

She'd explain that it felt lovely (more than lovely, so much more than lovely it wasn't funny, though she wasn't going to explain it like *that*) they'd had this time together to heal after what had happened between them. But he had to be lonely after losing his wife and she was always lonely (though Isabella wasn't certain she was going to share *that*) and they shouldn't mistake what they had for something more and they certainly shouldn't drag the children in it.

And she'd explain that all of it, the sex, the kisses, the touching, *everything*, had to stop.

Immediately.

Lastly, she decided, since this was all very rational and logical, Prentice would see her reasoning was sound and agree with her.

What Isabella *didn't* do was think how much this plan would hurt, not only to explain to Prentice but also to carry through.

Well, she *tried* not to think about it and failed.

So she decided she'd worry about that later, when she was at home in Chicago, back to her *existence*.

When the cookies were in the oven, she called Annie thinking it was high time to share all that had happened between her and Prentice, something she had been uncharacteristically keeping from her friend and then tell Annie what she intended to do.

When Annie answered, she sounded distracted and told Isabella she was busy with something and asked if she could call back in an hour.

Isabella agreed. She and Sally finished the cookies, she made Sally lunch and after lunch, read to her on the couch until Sally fell into a nap.

Then she decided to do some laundry.

While gathering towels in the bathrooms to put in the laundry, she decided to clean the bathrooms.

While cleaning Jason and Sally's bathroom, she decided to clean Prentice's which she hadn't touched yet.

After cleaning Prentice's bathroom, she saw four whisky glasses sitting on the railing of his balcony, three of which looked like they'd been out there for a while.

She thought this was strange but she gathered them, put them to soak in the sink, threw in another load of laundry and Sally woke.

It wasn't until after she'd picked up Jason that she realized Annie never returned her call.

Seeing as Jason mixed with Sally somehow created a vacuum that sucked time out of earth's vortex, she had taught Jason a few more chords on the guitar, settled a fight between them when Sally wanted to confiscate the guitar and learn herself, did another load of laundry, ironed all Prentice's work shirts and Jason's school shirts and put them away and was making hamburger patties when Prentice arrived home.

Annie never called.

Throughout her afternoon activities, she coached herself on how to be warm and friendly with Prentice while still keeping control of the situation.

Therefore she was certain by the time she heard the door opening, heralding the fact that Prentice was home, she was prepared and he wouldn't take her off-guard.

The minute he walked in that pleasant feeling that she'd had the night before when he had arrived home hit her again, all her coaching vanished and she went instantly off-guard.

He dropped his jacket on the armchair, walked behind the couch mussing Jason's hair as he did so and bent low to pick up Sally when she ran to him, screaming his name.

Holding his daughter in his arms, her little girl legs wrapped around his waist and her little girl arms wrapped around his neck, he gave Sally his devoted attention while he continued walking to the kitchen.

"We're having American cheeseburgers with homemade American fries for dinner!" Sally announced.

"Sounds good," Prentice murmured, smiling at his daughter.

"Today, we went into town and to the market. We got some candy bars and potatoes and we met a real live baby on the pavement. And I've decide I want a collie next," Sally kept the information flowing.

"Why don't we get used to Blackie first," Prentice suggested.

"Okay," Sally agreed unusually easily then again, she was likely sated by afternoon cookies, then she shouted, "Oh! And Elle and I made cookies today!"

There it was, the cookies.

Prentice's eyes went to Isabella, Isabella's guard slid into the vacuum that sucked time because his eyes were still smiling *and* they were filled with warmth when he inquired, "Why am I not surprised?"

"I don't know. Why aren't you?" Sally asked.

His gaze went back to his daughter, he chuckled and replied, "No reason, baby."

With that he kissed Sally's nose and put her down.

Then he got close to Isabella and with her hands filled with hamburger meat over a bowl she couldn't move away. Not in a warm and friendly (but controlled) way.

In fact, not in *any way*.

He leaned around to her front and kissed *her* nose.

If she'd managed to get back on guard (which she hadn't while watching Prentice come home and cuddle Sally), it would have slipped again.

Unfortunately, since she hadn't and her guard was whirling in the vacuum toward some black hole, instead of slipping her guard exploded in the vacuum, completely obliterated and irretrievable, and thus would need to be regenerated.

Thinking all of this meant she wasn't prepared for Prentice to go still at her side. Nor was she prepared for his eyes suddenly to slice to his son, brows drawn.

Isabella was watching Prentice and her thoughts of black holes flew away as worry invaded.

Prentice leaned a hand into the counter at her side and addressed Jason, "Jace, have you been studying Elle's book?"

Jason stopped strumming and answered, "No, Elle's taught me a few chords."

At these words, Isabella went still.

She couldn't imagine what Prentice would think of Isabella teaching his son guitar *on* his dead wife's guitar. A guitar Fiona had for decades and carried with her everywhere. A guitar she would probably have taught Jason on herself had she lived.

Although she couldn't imagine what he would think, she *could* imagine, whatever it was, it wouldn't be good.

Isabella concentrated on the hamburger patty in her hand as if it would be judged for form and presentation and, if found lacking, the sentence was death.

This was difficult to do considering she felt the heat of Prentice's eyes on her.

"You play?" he asked.

Without taking her eyes from the hamburger, she opened her mouth to speak but Jason got there before her, feeling in the mood to take over for Sally in keeping the information flowing.

"Aye, Dad. You should hear her. She's good. She says she learned to play because of Mum."

Prentice's voice grew quiet when he queried, "You learned because of Fee?"

He called Fiona "Fee."

That was sweet.

It was also sad.

Her throat blocked and she decided the best she could do was nod. Which she did.

At the hamburger patty.

Then she set it aside and grabbed more meat.

"The book's okay," Jason went on as he went back to strumming. "But Elle's better at teaching me. I looked at the book last night and—"

Strange vibes started emanating from Prentice and Isabella thought it unfortunate her hands were filled with meat because she *really* needed to fist them.

Prentice interrupted his son, "You had the guitar last night?"

"Aye," Jason answered distractedly, concentrating on his finger work. "We started last night. Elle showed me more when I got home from school."

Jason hadn't finished speaking when Isabella felt Prentice's hand at the small of her back and his lips at her ear.

"Put the mince down, Elle," he ordered in a whisper.

Oh dear.

She licked her lips and, screwing up her courage, she looked at him.

His face was carefully blank. She didn't think this was a good sign.

"Okay," she whispered back, dropped the meat, went to the sink, washed her hands and was still toweling them off (slowly) when Prentice closed in.

He pulled the towel from her hands, tossed it aside, and hands to her hips, he part guided, part shoved her into his study where he closed the doors behind them.

She turned and decided to do what she could to defuse the situation.

Which meant apologize and quick.

"Prentice, I—"

He cut her off. "You call me Pren."

She blinked, confused at what he said and also confused at his voice, which was thick to the point of being hoarse.

It hit her he was holding back emotion.

Her heart broke and she felt her eyes sting.

"Pren," she whispered.

"You're a fucking miracle worker."

Her body locked, all except her eyes which she blinked again.

"What?" she breathed.

"Jace hasn't touched that guitar, not once since his mum got sick, without him having one of his nightmares. Last night, you worked with him on it and he didn't have a nightmare," Prentice explained, Isabella stared at him in shock at his words and he walked to her, put his hands to her jaws and repeated, "You're a miracle worker."

"I—" Isabella started then stopped, not having any earthly clue what to say.

No one had ever called her a miracle worker.

Because, in her life, miracles didn't occur.

Except in this magical little village.

Something flashed in his eyes, his face dipped close and his fingers flexed at her jaw. "Has it occurred to you that if you'd been shown a little love and compassion, the nightmares *you've* had for thirty-two years would have gone away?"

No.

That had never occurred to her because in her life she hadn't been shown a great deal of love and compassion.

Except in this magical little village.

"No," she whispered.

He used his hands on her jaw to tip her face so her lips were against his and he muttered, "We'll have to work on that."

For a split second, her chest seized.

After that, his words made her mind, heart and soul unconsciously relax, as did her body, melting into his.

His arms stole around her and he kissed her softly.

It was one of the sweetest kisses she'd ever received (and all of the others had been from Prentice too).

When their mouths disengaged, she murmured, "Pren."

His voice was soft in that way that did funny things to her when he said, "Thank you, baby, for taking care of Jace."

"I . . . um . . ." she stammered and then said stupidly, "You're welcome."

He grinned right before he touched her mouth with his again and pulled away.

Sliding his arm around her shoulders, he led her to the door saying, "I'm fucking starved. I'll help with dinner."

Isabella was having difficulty keeping up.

Even so, she didn't think that was such a good thing. Evidence was suggesting that Prentice wasn't so hot in the kitchen. But she was too shaken by recent events to protest.

Prentice opened the doors and they walked out to Jason declaring loudly, "You know, you two can snog in the kitchen. It'll be sick but we'll get used to it."

Isabella's eyes jerked to Jason and she tripped over her own feet.

Sally giggled.

Prentice drawled in a voice filled with amused sarcasm, "Thanks for your permission, mate."

It was at that Isabella's eyes shifted to Prentice who didn't remonstrate his son *nor* did he explain that they weren't in the study *snogging* (well, not exactly).

"Just being real," Jason replied drolly.

"Oh my God, someone shoot me," Isabella muttered out loud before she could stop herself.

Jason threw her a playful grin.

Prentice gave her a squeeze when they hit the kitchen right before he let her go.

Then he asked, "I don't know. Can you still make cheeseburgers suffering from bullet wounds? Maybe we'll shoot you after you make dinner."

Jason burst out laughing.

Sally cried on a giggle, "Daddy! Stop being funny!"

It was too much. Isabella decided to ignore it all, cook dinner and then throw *herself* over a cliff.

She didn't get the chance.

She cooked dinner, Prentice manning the deep fat fryer with expertise (thankfully), they ate it and she and Prentice barely finished the dishes when the doorbell rang.

Jason went to get the door.

Isabella was wiping her hands on a tea towel when Dougal, Annie and Fergus walked in.

"Ready, mate?" Dougal asked before Isabella could call out a greeting at their surprise visit.

"Aye," Prentice answered, indicating from his ready response that for him this was not a surprise visit. With hands on Isabella's hips, he steered her toward the hallway. "Get your bag, baby."

Isabella glanced over her shoulder at him, confused.

Yes.

Confused.

Again!

"What's going on?" she asked, stopping Prentice's steering by halting while she looked around at the assemblage.

"We're going to the pub," Annie announced, scooping up Blackie and giving the kitty a cuddle. "Dad's going to watch the kids."

"Hurrah!" Sally shouted. "Fergus tells stories in funny voices!"

Isabella continued to look around realizing that her plans for the evening which she spent all day getting sorted, which included calmly, warmly, in a friendly, controlled manner, telling Prentice she was soon to be leaving and that their current (she couldn't even think in her head what to call it but she settled on the word "situation") *situation* could not continue, were being dashed.

"I didn't know we were going out," Isabella remarked.

"Forgot to mention it," Prentice said with a gentle shove at the small of her back then repeated, "Get your bag."

"But I—" she started.

Prentice interrupted her, "Bag, baby."

It occurred to Isabella that Annie hadn't returned her phone call. And Prentice "forgot to mention" he'd made plans for *them* to go to a pub, including arranging a babysitter who happened to be *Annie's* father.

Then it occurred to Isabella that she was being played.

She slowly turned and glared at Annie who was trying to look innocent but who never *was*. She looked at Fergus who smiled. Finally she looked at Dougal who didn't look back, instead he studied his boots.

Yes, she was so, *very* being *played*.

Her attention went to Prentice and she announced, "I don't feel like going to the pub tonight."

The hand Prentice had in the small of her back became an arm curved around her waist that he used to curl her into him, front to front.

"You will once you're out," he said. "Go and get your bag."

Now, she wasn't sure, but she was thinking she might be getting angry.

"No, I don't think I'll feel like it once I'm out," she said slowly, looking up at Prentice. "I think I'll stay in and listen to Fergus telling stories in funny voices."

"Hurrah! Elle's staying with us," Sally shouted.

Prentice grinned.

Now she was pretty sure she *was* getting angry.

"Elle, baby—" Prentice coaxed.

Isabella opened her mouth to say something but didn't get the chance.

"Come on Bella Bella," Dougal called, walking up to them using the sing-song way he used to say her name decades ago, telling her back then that what he was saying really was "Beautiful Bella" as both words meant the same. "You two need a Friday night out and a drink." He got close and his voice lowered so the children wouldn't hear. "It's been a tough couple of weeks, Bella. Prentice needs it, you need it. You know you do. Come out, down a few and relax."

He had her at "Bella Bella." She barely heard anything else he said.

He hadn't called her that in twenty years.

"I'll get my bag."

"Well, all right!" Dougal boomed.

Prentice gave her a squeeze.

She threw Prentice a glare.

This made him laugh out loud.

This made her glare turn to a scowl.

She pulled free from his arms, still scowling. She transferred her scowl to Annie who ignored it completely (as usual).

Isabella might be happy Dougal liked her again, liked her enough to sing-song her name and therefore felt the need for a celebratory drink at a pub but that didn't mean she forgot she'd been played.

Deciding to have her drink and bond with Dougal but completely ignore her soon-to-be shoved off a cliff best friend and her . . . whatever Prentice was . . . she turned on her boot and went to get her bag.

Chapter
FIFTEEN

That Path Led Home

Prentice

"Bye! Bye! Byeeeee!"

They were standing outside, Elle plastered to his front, her torso leaning to the side, and she was shouting and waving her arm fanatically at Fergus driving Dougal and Annie away.

Prentice had a grin on his lips, his hands on her hips and he was, with some difficulty, shuffling her backwards to the front door.

"Bye! Bye! Byeeee!" Prentice heard Annie call back in return.

He looked over his shoulder and saw Annie was leaning her entire upper body out the back window and waving fanatically at Elle.

Elle started jumping up and down, still waving, and now shouting, "*Hasta luego!*"

"*Hasta luego!*" Prentice heard the now distant Annie return.

Prentice chuckled.

He succeeded in getting Elle through the door, and once he did she abruptly turned and headed into the great room.

"That was *fun!*" Elle exclaimed, her back to him.

He watched her walk to the kitchen while he mentally agreed with her.

Their night at the pub *was* fun. More fun than he'd had in years.

Twenty of them to be precise.

Fiona was social, she enjoyed going out and his wife had a wicked sense of humor that she used often.

But Annie plus Elle, when they were in a mood (and twenty years ago, they always were), were wild and hilarious in an infectious way that was beyond anything he'd ever experienced before he met them and since.

He turned to secure the door and switch off the lights, the events of the evening flashed through his mind and a smile came to his lips.

At first, Elle was cross at both Prentice and Annie. She ignored them totally and seemed intent on dragging every minute of the history of Dougal's life for the last twenty years out of him.

She continued this through her first three vodka, lemon and limes, which she consumed in less than an hour.

Through this time, Prentice enjoyed the show.

Annie, however, on several occasions tried to get a word in edge-wise. When she did, Elle turned a cold shoulder to her or stared her down, and later, when she was drunker, she actually put her hand out, palm up, an inch from Annie's face.

At this (as with most everything Elle did in that hour), Prentice bit back laughter.

Annie's eyes stared at Elle's hand, her mouth dropped open, her face went red and she started to blow but Elle calmly turned, disregarding Annie completely and leaned into Dougal.

She stared at him as if he was the center of her universe and asked breathily as if his answer would be the key to the meaning of life something like, "And then, after you went to the chippie for the fifteenth time in the month of August in the year of our Lord two thousand and two, *what did you do next?*"

Eventually deciding her interrogation was over, Elle stood with her bag to go to the bar and buy her fourth drink.

As she did so, she pointedly continued to ignore Annie and Prentice, turned to Dougal and inquired, "Dougal, would you care for another beverage?"

Dougal, who had been keeping up with Elle drink for drink and had a few before they came out, replied, "Abso-fucking-lutely Bella Bella."

As amusing as this was, at that point Prentice was done.

Therefore, when Elle stepped over his legs to head to the bar, he leaned forward, caught her hips and pulled her off her feet and into his lap.

She let out a high-pitched shriek that brought the eyes of half the patrons of the pub their way, including, he noted distractedly, Hattie Fennick, who wore an expression that was the epitome of someone who'd sucked a lemon.

He ignored the patrons, and Hattie (who routinely wore that look), because Elle twisted in his lap, put her hands on his chest and demanded haughtily (and loudly), "Unhand me, Prentice Cameron!"

He also ignored her ridiculous demand.

"When you're out with me, you don't buy your drinks, I do," he declared.

"I think not!" she returned.

"Elle—" he warned.

"Pren—" she mocked his tone.

He grinned.

She stared at his mouth.

Then she blinked before she demanded, "Let me go, I'm thirsty."

"I'll get you a drink but only if you promise to drink this one slow-ly," he told her.

"I can't do that."

"Why no'?"

"Because they're yummy."

Something about Elle saying the word "yummy" was unbelievably cute.

But even more unbelievably sexy.

In response, his hands traveled from her hips, up her back and one twisted in her hair.

"Even so, baby, you're already pissed. You continue to drink like this, you'll be rat-arsed or passed out in another hour."

Her eyes slid away and she bit her lip considering this. Prentice watched with amusement as she struggled with her decision.

Her eyes came back to him and she replied, "All right. I'll drink it slowly. Passed out is not a good way to end an evening and I promised Sally pancakes tomorrow, and I'm not sure I can make pancakes hungover."

On that she did a pretend shiver at the thought of cooking pancakes hungover.

Prentice allowed himself a moment to appreciate her behavior and allowed his body a moment to savor hers shivering in his lap.

Then he used her hair to bring her face closer to his.

"You still cross with me?" he asked softly.

"Yes," she answered without hesitation.

"Are you having fun?" he went on.

"Yes," she answered, again without hesitation.

"Then why are you cross?"

"Because you and Annie played me."

"Aye, we did," he agreed with total honesty. "Regardless, the result is you having fun so why are you cross?"

Her face grew serious and it was such a departure from her adorable irritation that Prentice braced.

Her voice was as serious as her face when she answered, "Because I wanted to talk to you tonight."

He realized then that she had all day without him. Even with the children around, she had plenty of time to twist that head of hers into making ridiculous decisions. And, from the look on her face, she'd made some ridiculous decision she was going to impart on him that night.

He was fucking *thrilled* he'd come up with the idea of taking her to the pub with Annie and Dougal.

He made a mental note, until he'd bested his challenge, *not* to give Elle the time to twist that head of hers into making ridiculous decisions.

But, for the moment, he had to stall.

"We'll talk later," he lied.

"When?" she asked.

"Later," he repeated.

"Tomorrow?" she pressed.

No way in fucking hell.

"Maybe," he lied again.

She watched his face and suddenly she smiled a heartbreaking, sad smile.

His eyes dropped to her heartbreaking, sad smile and he determined that the answer was really no.

No way in *fucking* hell were they talking tomorrow.

Finally, she whispered, "Okay."

With some regret he transferred her sweet ass out of his lap into the booth beside him saying, "I'll get your drink."

And he bought her a drink.

When he did so, it was not lost on him that their intimate conversation had been watched by avid eyes, most especially Hattie who was still gazing at him openly, that sour expression on her face even though her husband Nigel was speaking to her.

By the time he returned from the bar, Elle had forgiven Annie and the night began.

As Elle promised, she drank this drink (and the ones following it) slower but the damage was already done. Elle was borderline smashed and Annie was in the room. Only one thing could happen and it did.

Madness ensued.

Therefore, the night included Annie challenging Prentice and Dougal to a team dart competition with Elle being Annie's partner.

And Elle was hopeless at darts.

In three games she barely hit the dart board no matter how much Annie coached her, which was a great deal, all of it misguided and most of it drunken but it was, nevertheless, coaching.

Annie and Elle found Elle's ineptitude screamingly funny and spent most of their time in fits of laughter, doubled over, their arms wrapped around their middles. Whilst they did this, Prentice and Dougal stood grinning at them, coaxing them to get on with the game or assuring other patrons that neither Elle nor Annie was under the influence of illegal substances.

After one throw where Elle took five minutes to line up her shot, the tip of her tongue at the side of her mouth, her eye squinting down the dart, her mouth eventually assuring Annie with mistaken confidence, "I think I've got it this time," (and then she embedded the dart in the wall beside the board) that Annie laughed so hard she fell into Elle who fell into Dougal who managed, miraculously (since he was also laughing), to keep them all standing.

After the dart game and another vodka, lemon and lime for Elle and some very animated but completely incomprehensible discussion between Annie and Elle about "recycling outfits," the night also included Elle suddenly and bizarrely shouting across the pub, "You are my new *favorite person!*" when Gordon Taggart walked in.

She then hurried across the pub (under the watchful, interested eyes of most of the patrons) and gave Gordon a huge hug.

When Prentice sauntered to them and extricated the astonished Gordon from Elle's tight embrace, she explained to Prentice, "Gordon tried to save Sally and me from the big, bad paparazzi today."

This was news to him and not good news.

Therefore, Prentice turned his now unamused gaze to Elle. "You didn't tell me you saw photographers today."

She took in his expression, bit her lip and then leaned into Gordon and whispered loudly, "Whoops."

In turn, Gordon leaned into Elle and advised, "Probably should tell him when the vultures are circling, lass."

Gazing at Gordon as if he was a renown sage, Elle nodded before she shared, "I got caught up in cookie baking, ironing and hamburger meat and I forgot."

Gordon smiled at Prentice but replied to Elle, "That happens."

"I just had an idea!" Elle cried suddenly and latched on to Gordon's arm. "You need to come over for hamburgers!"

Gordon chuckled before he replied, "I'd like that."

"Okay!" she agreed eagerly and put her hand to her ear, thumb and forefinger extended like a phone, the finger of her other hand pointing back and forth between her and Gordon as Prentice (now back to amused) pulled her away and she assured, "I'll call you."

Gordon smiled at Prentice but spoke to Elle, "Look forward to it, lass."

Elle turned and let Prentice guide her to their table as she said, "He has a cute dog."

"The collie Sally mentioned," Prentice guessed.

"You betcha," Elle replied, threw herself into the booth, grabbed her drink, sucked a healthy sip through her straw, slammed her glass back down and turned to Prentice who'd seated himself beside her. She slapped a hand on his chest and leaned close, declaring, "Sally needs a dog."

Prentice slid his arm along her waist and smiled before he replied, "Sally does *no'* need a dog."

"She *so* needs a dog," Elle returned.

"She's no' getting a dog," Prentice stated.

Elle turned her head to Annie but left her body leaned close to Prentice and called in reinforcements, "Annie! Does Sally need a dog?"

Immediately, head bobbing wildly, Annie concurred with her friend, "Sally *so* needs a dog."

Dougal grinned at Prentice.

Prentice sighed.

Then he repeated, "She's no' getting a dog."

Elle's head twisted back to face him. "But she *wants* a dog."

"She wants a horse, a trip to Harrods and to be a princess too."

He watched as Elle's eyes drifted over his shoulder and she whispered, "I could do that."

And she could.

Christ, he was fucked.

His arm gave her a squeeze as his voice gave her a warning, "Elle—"

Her eyes came back to his. "All except the princess part."

"You aren't buying her a horse."

"Okay," she relented. "Maybe not the horse. You live on a cliff. Horses don't do cliffs." Her eyes went unfocused and she finished on a mutter, "I don't think." Then she turned to Annie again and called, "Hey Annie, do horses do cliffs?"

Annie was cuddling against Dougal watching Prentice and Elle, but at Elle's question her eyes slid to the side as if contemplating this question.

She looked back at Elle and answered, "Nope."

Elle turned to Prentice and declared, "Okay. The horse idea is out."

Prentice wanted to laugh. He really did. However there were more pressing things to attend to.

"You aren't taking her to Harrods either," he stated.

"Why not?"

Prentice found he had no answer to that. He also found he liked the idea of Elle granting his daughter's wish.

He liked it a great deal.

His hand, curled at her waist, drifted up her side, bringing her closer.

"All right, baby, you can take Sally to Harrods," he said softly.

Her arms shot up in the air and she shouted, "Hurrah!"

Her exuberance was intoxicating, so much so he decided the night was over.

His other arm circled her and he brought her closer.

"Finish your drink, Elle," he ordered.

Her hands came to rest on his shoulders, her head tipped to the side and she asked, "Why?"

"Because it's time to go home."

She rested her body against his, her breasts pressed against his chest, her face close enough to kiss and she asked, "It is?"

God, she was cute.

"Definitely," he said firmly.

Her eyes moved over his face and they warmed as her body relaxed into his.

"Okay," she whispered.

She pulled away and turned, announcing to Annie and Dougal as she reached for her drink, "Prentice says it's time to go home."

"I bet he does," Annie mumbled through a chuckle.

"Dougal says it's time to go home, too," Dougal declared as he curled Annie closer.

Annie tilted her head back and looked at her new husband.

"Mm," she murmured.

Prentice watched his friend touch his mouth to his wife's.

Then he watched his friend's eyes turn to catch his.

That was when Prentice realized life's path took him and Dougal full circle, through a lot of beautiful landscape with a side trip to hell (for Prentice) and just a lot of wandering through hell (for Dougal).

But, in the end, that path led home.

Elle finished her drink, they climbed in Harry's taxi and Harry took them home.

He walked through the great room, turning off the lamp by the couch on his way, and went into the kitchen. He came up behind Elle who was raiding the cookie jar and circled her waist, his hand sliding across her belly as he pressed against her back, feeling her ass against his thighs and liking it.

"You want a cookie?" Elle asked, mouth full, her neck twisting so she could look at him.

"No," he replied.

He loved her cookies, he'd never tasted better.

But, at that moment, his mouth went someplace his tongue preferred to taste.

And as he ran it the length of her neck from the join of her shoulder to her ear, his body absorbed her tremble.

"We're not having sex tonight," she declared in a breathy voice.

There it was, the ridiculous decision.

"We're no'?" he asked her neck as his hand slid up her midriff.

"No. No more sex," she replied, her voice even breathier.

"Why no'?" he asked before he nipped her earlobe with his teeth.

Another tremble.

He grinned against her ear.

"It's confusing." Now her voice was a whisper.

"Confusing who?" he murmured in her ear as his hand reached her breast and his fingers curled around it.

"Confusing . . ." she started and then sucked in breath when his thumb slid across her nipple.

No tremble this time. Instead, he took her bodyweight and had to slide his other arm along her waist to keep her standing.

"Elle?" Prentice prompted in her ear, "Confusing who?"

His finger joined his thumb and he rolled her taut nipple between the two.

Her upper body reared into his.

God, he loved how responsive she was.

"Wh-what?" she stammered, *very* breathy this time.

He was enjoying this.

He braced her weight with his body and his other hand undid the belt of her jeans. He undid the button. Then he slid down the zip.

All the while he did this, he reminded her, "You said it's confusing. I'd like to know what's confusing."

His hand left her breast but went under her shirt.

"Um . . ." she replied, hesitated then her head fell back to his shoulder as his fingers pulled her bra down and he found her nipple again at the same time the fingers of his other hand found her wetness.

So wet.

So responsive.

Yes, he loved that about her.

"Baby?" he prompted her again for her answer.

Her hips ground down on his hand.

He smiled against her ear again.

"The children," she whispered.

"If they wake, I'll hear them."

"You're sure?"

"Relax," he coaxed.

The fingers of his hands moved.

She relaxed.

Completely.

Except her hips moved against his hand.

"Pren," she breathed, her neck and torso twisting toward him.

She wanted his mouth.

"Elle, baby, I'll no' kiss you."

Her hand encouragingly cupped his at her breast over the fabric of her T-shirt as her hips rocked against his fingers.

"I want you to kiss me," she whispered between breaths coming fast.

He liked that she wanted that.

And he'd give her what she wanted.

Just later.

"But I want to watch you come."

He listened to her quiet moan and ground his hard groin against her ass.

"Okay," she yielded softly.

In the catalogue of things he wanted to do to Elle, Prentice ticked off the selection of making (and watching) her come in the kitchen.

When he'd done this and her breathing had slowed, he cupped her sex but took his hand from her breast and put it to her jaw, twisting her beautiful face to his.

Then he kissed her.

After that he carried her to her bedroom.

He took off her clothes and smoothed one of her short, sexy, silky nightgowns over her body (another item in his catalogue).

Then he disrobed and took her to bed.

Feeling the satin against his chest, her ass tucked tight in his lap, their legs cocked together and their fingers linked, he realized belatedly that tonight at the pub, Elle had been Elle.

His Elle.

All night.

And the heavy warmth that always hit his gut when he was reminded of his Elle hadn't hit him.

It had already been there, all night.

And all day too.

His fingers tensed in hers.

"Pren?" she mumbled sleepily.

"Aye?"

"What about you?"

He liked it that she asked. And he liked it that, even sleepy and intoxicated, she asked it in a way that sounded like she cared.

"You can take care of me tomorrow."

She snuggled her ass deeper into his lap and he reconsidered that decision.

"Okay," she whispered.

And almost immediately he felt her body shift into sleep.

He pulled her close, listened to her steady breathing and decided to stick with his decision.

———◆———

PRENTICE WOKE WHEN the bed bounced.

He knew what that bounce meant.

Elle woke as well.

She likely had no idea.

He rolled to his back and went up on a hand, looking toward the foot of the bed.

He felt Elle get up on her elbow.

Then he heard her gasp.

"Morning!" Sally, who was on her knees at the end of the bed holding a struggling Blackie in her arms, shouted.

"Oh my God," Elle whispered, her body locking.

"When can we have pancakes?" Sally asked Elle, showing no reaction in the slightest that she was disturbed she'd found Prentice in Elle's bed.

Elle emitted a strangled noise.

Prentice bit back laughter.

Instead of laughing, to Sally he muttered, "Come here, baby."

Elle jerked in surprise at his words but Sally released Blackie without delay and crawled up Prentice's body.

Sally had been doing this nearly every Saturday and Sunday (and other days besides) for as long as she could climb on his bed.

As Sally moved, Prentice laid back at the same time he pushed an arm under Elle's body and curled her around so her front was pressed to his side. His arm locked and his fingers curved securely at her waist, holding her to him. His other arm went around his daughter as she collapsed on his chest.

"Are we going to have pancakes?" Sally asked him.

"In a while," Prentice answered.

Sally looked at Elle. "Can I have choco-chips in mine?"

Elle was up on an elbow, her other hand pushing against Prentice's chest, her hips unsuccessfully resisting his hold, her horrified eyes were on Sally.

"I . . . erm, I don't think so, sweetheart."

"Blueberries?" Sally inquired, tilting her head so she could rest her cheek on Prentice's chest but her eyes were still on Elle.

Suddenly, Elle's body ceased its resistance and her face grew soft. For a moment, she simply gazed at Sally.

After a moment she replied in a tone as soft as her face, "You can have blueberries."

It was then Sally reached out and stroked Elle's hair.

At his daughter's touch, Elle's eyes slowly closed and Prentice's heart clutched at the look of longing exposed on her beautiful face.

Isabella Evangelista was the woman that everyone thought had everything.

Seeing that look, Prentice realized she had a handful of good friends.

And, as far as he could tell, not one fucking thing else.

"You have pretty hair," Sally whispered, still stroking Elle's hair.

Elle's eyes opened. Her hand at Prentice's chest lifted, her fingers caught a lock of Sally's hair and started twisting it.

"So do you, Sally."

Prentice felt like he'd become invisible.

He didn't mind, not even a little.

He let them have their moment then Prentice gave his daughter a squeeze and said, "Go watch telly, baby. Let Daddy and Elle sleep in awhile."

Sally stopped stroking Elle's hair, her head darted up to look at him and Elle's body went solid again.

"Telly?" Sally breathed.

"Yes, telly," Prentice replied.

"But you don't like us watching telly," Sally reminded him.

He pulled her up his chest so her face was closer to his. "This morning, you get an hour of telly."

Sally lifted up with both her hands pressed in Prentice's chest and she shouted, "Hurrah!"

Then she scrambled out of the bed, not about to miss the unusual opportunity to waste time in front of the television.

"Close the door," Prentice called, rolling to Elle who had immediately begun struggling. Sally closed the door and Prentice shouted, "Close the other one too."

"Okay!" Sally shouted back before he heard the other door slam.

His full attention diverted to Elle because now she was full on struggling.

"Elle, relax."

Her body went still and she stared at him.

"Relax?" she breathed.

His face went into her neck, and with lips below her ear he replied, "Yes, relax."

"I can't relax!" she snapped and started struggling again. "Oh my God, I can't believe that just happened! Sally caught us *in bed.*"

He rolled on top of her to control her thrashing, caught her flailing wrists and pinned them to the bed beside her head. His face neared hers and he touched her lips with his.

"Baby, relax. It's okay," he assured her.

She glared up at him.

Eyes wide with horror and disbelief, she declared, "It is *not* okay!"

He grinned, "Why no'?"

"She's going to freak!"

Prentice started chuckling.

"This isn't funny!" Elle clipped.

Prentice was still smiling when he asked, "Did Sally look upset to you?"

He watched as Elle's horrified face became thoughtful before she replied, "Well . . . no."

"She's no' going to freak. She'll be fine." His head bent and his mouth went back to her neck. "She loves you," he said there.

And he meant it.

He figured Elle didn't hear him or didn't process what he said because her wrists pushed against his. He pressed her wrists deeper into the bed.

She stopped pushing but declared, "Prentice, I know how this works. Sure, she *seems* fine now. But in fifteen years when she's standing on top of a clock tower with an automatic rifle mowing down innocent bystanders, don't call *me* asking what went wrong."

At the thought of his effervescent Sally picking off innocent bystanders in a murderous rampage, Prentice burst into laughter as he rolled to his back taking Elle with him. Her hands released, Elle immediately pushed up on his chest. His arms locked around her waist, holding her captive.

She stopped pushing and glared down at him. "I need to get up. I need to make pancakes. I need to find out how to erase Sally's memory."

He grinned at her and said, "Sally doesn't need her memory erased."

She wasn't listening.

She was looking at the headboard muttering, "I'm sure the military has something. Who do I know in the military?"

He was back to laughing when his hand slid up her spine, into her hair and he bent her head to his, maneuvering it so his mouth was at her ear.

Softly, he ordered, "Forget about mind control drugs. You have more pressing things to see to this morning."

Her head twisted and she looked at him. "Yes? And those would be?"

His other hand caught hers and guided it between their bodies. Then he curled her fingers around his stiff cock.

Her eyes grew wide the moment before they went dazed.

There it was.

He had her.

"That," he whispered.

"We can't do that," she whispered back but her hand moved, forming a tight fist, her thumb sliding over the tip.

Christ.

Magnificent.

"We can," he groaned.

"What if the kids—?"

"They won't."

"You're sure?"

"Aye."

Her hand stroked then her thumb circled the tip.

Prentice gritted his teeth.

Her mouth went to his neck and she whispered, "We'll be fast."

"You go fast, baby, there'll be consequences."

Her head came up, her hand stroked and his body liked it so much his hips involuntarily bucked.

When her eyes met his he demanded on a rumble, "I want your mouth to work me and I want it to work me slow."

Her lips parted, her eyes glazed, her hand clutched his cock tightly, he growled and she breathed, "But . . . pancakes."

"We have an hour."

"But—"

His hand fisted in her hair and he forced her mouth to his.

Then he kissed her.

When he was done, his voice throaty, he ordered, "Slow."

"Okay," she agreed immediately.

Her face disappeared in his neck and she used her mouth on him, going to his collarbone then down his chest. He pushed himself up so his shoulders were against the headboard as she went further down.

Then further down.

And further.

His hands gathered her hair and pulled it back just in time to watch Elle slide his cock into her mouth.

Then he watched as Elle, in her sexy, satin and lace nightie worked him.

Slow.

It was magnificent.

———◆———

HE LOST HER.

And Prentice knew it was the fucking photographers.

He'd had her. She was back.

Entirely.

Then she slid away.

And, as the day progressed, she retreated more and more until he lost her.

They were late leaving the guest suite because, after Elle took care of Prentice with her mouth, Prentice took care of Elle in the shower with his fingers.

Considering she smelled like lilies of the valley, she looked so fucking sexy with her hair wet and he hadn't had his cock inside her for over twenty-four hours, he took care of both of them in the bed.

She'd been collapsed on top of him, her face in his neck, her breath had slowed, her bodyweight fully relaxed and heavy on him, his cock still hard and imbedded in her wetness, when she suddenly jerked up.

She stared at him in panic and shrieked, "Pancakes!"

In a flurry of movement, she exited the bed and ran around the room, pulling on underwear (which was, he noted rolling to his side and watching her, just as sexy as her nighties), spritzing with perfume, then yanking on a T-shirt.

She was hopping around trying to get in her jeans when her eyes hit him.

"Pren, what are you doing?" she demanded to know.

"I'm enjoying the show," he replied.

Her eyes narrowed as she pulled her jeans over her hips. "Get up."

"In a minute."

She zipped her jeans and buttoned them while saying, "We have to make pancakes and Jace has a soccer game we have to get to."

She called his son "Jace."

He liked that.

"We've got time."

She grabbed her deodorant and shoved it under her T-shirt, "No we don't. Look at the clock! Get up!"

She finished with the deodorant, slammed it onto the bureau and ran into the bathroom.

Prentice adjusted his position so he could watch her squirt something in her palm, rub it in her hair and then she yanked a comb through its length with agitated movements.

She exited the bathroom muttering, "I'm not going to have time for makeup."

Good, he thought.

She looked far more beautiful without that veneer.

She spied him still in bed.

"Pren—"

"Come here," he murmured.

Her face went dazed upon hearing his soft command.

Unfortunately, only for a moment.

Then her brows snapped together, she nabbed his jeans from the floor and snapped, "Get . . ." she threw his jeans at him and finished, "*up!*"

With that she ran from the room.

He rolled to his back, sat up and surveyed the room.

Her journals, jars and bottles were tidy on the nightstand.

However, the bed was unmade, their discarded towels from that morning and clothes from last night littered the floor and he could see from his place in the bed that she'd left the container of whatever she used on her hair uncapped and sitting on the sink beside her comb, which she also didn't put away.

He grinned to himself and got up.

She made pancakes whilst running back and forth to the guest suite. First, to put on makeup (much to Prentice's displeasure, however, it was light as that was, as she explained in mutterings to herself, all she had time for) then to do something with her hair (she left it long and loose but dried it) and then to add jewelry and a belt to her outfit of fitted, long sleeve T-shirt, jeans and high-heeled boots.

She tidied the kitchen whilst running up and down the stairs. First, to help Sally dress. Next to show Jason where his football kit was as he couldn't find it because Elle had actually put it away, something that hadn't occurred since Fiona died as Jason was responsible for putting away his clean clothes on the occasion that Prentice cleaned them, and

Jason never did. After that she had to calm Sally's fears because Blackie had taken a tumble whilst leaping from bed to bureau. Sally was convinced the cat had to go to the "Kitty Doctor" even though Blackie seemed no worse for her fall and was racing around the house like she was being chased by something very frightening and very *fast*.

As Prentice led them out to the Range Rover, Elle pulled on a thick knit, heavy, open front cardigan with a wide lapel and hood at the back that looked, even with Prentice's very limited knowledge of fashion, like it cost a fortune.

The cardigan had the annoying effect of instantly changing her from Elle to Isabella Evangelista and Prentice didn't like it.

That was until she buckled in beside him.

Even belted in, she fidgeted. If she wasn't fidgeting, she was twisting around to answer Sally's incessant questions and to ask Jason if he remembered this or that or half a dozen other things. After a while she scooped up her hair and twisted it in a messy knot at the top back of her head. She didn't do a stellar job with this, spikes shot out around the holder and tendrils fell down her neck.

She looked adorable.

And she looked like Elle.

Prentice relaxed.

Elle kept fidgeting.

They were standing by the field watching Jason's game when it happened.

He had his arm around her shoulders. Her arm had slid around his waist and she'd rested her weight against his body. Sally had stopped racing around with the other kids and was leaning against Prentice's leg, her arm wrapped around his thigh.

"You know, I have no idea what's happening," Elle whispered.

He looked down at her. She was gazing at the pitch, her eyes focused on something but moving and he knew she was watching Jason.

He smiled.

"Do you no'?" he asked.

She shook her head.

He squeezed her shoulder and her head tipped back to look at him.

"I've never been a sports person," she admitted.

He bent his head and touched his lips to hers before he murmured, "I'll teach you."

She smiled and it lit up her eyes.

No, it lit her entire face.

Prentice felt her smile hit him with the force of an oncoming lorry before her gaze drifted over his shoulder.

In an instant her smile died and her body stilled.

She started to pull away.

His arm tensed and he looked over his shoulder. There were two photographers on the other side of the pitch, the lenses of both of their cameras trained on Elle, Sally and him. You didn't have to be close to know they were snapping shots.

"Fuck," he muttered.

Sally's head shot back and she shouted, "Daddy!"

Elle pulled at his arm saying, "I should—"

"Don't move," Prentice ordered, reflexively placing a protective hand to the top of Sally's head at the same time halting Elle's retreat by locking his arm around her.

She looked at him. "Pren—"

"Don't move."

"But—"

He gave her shoulder a squeeze. "Ignore them."

"But—"

He dipped his head and rested his forehead against hers.

"Elle, baby, I said ignore them."

"But they're taking pictures of Sally," she whispered.

"Ignore them."

"And they're taking pictures of *you*."

Christ, she could be stubborn.

His hand went from her shoulder to the back of her neck, he gave her a squeeze there and he asked a question to which he did not expect a response, "Elle, what did I say?"

Her eyes searched his. Then they closed.

She nodded her head and opened her eyes and his Elle was gone.

Prentice saw it immediately and he wanted to walk across the pitch and do bodily damage.

He didn't.

Even though she'd retreated, still she agreed quietly, "Okay."

And she stood by his side in the curve of his arm (when she wasn't off doing something for Sally or chatting with one of the other mums) the rest of the match.

But she did most of this with her fists clenched.

When they went back to the house, she got the kids sorted and excused herself to her rooms, promising Sally she'd be back so they could make dinner together.

Prentice gave her some time before he followed her.

He stopped halfway up the second flight of steps.

The door to her rooms was open, the scent of lavender drifting out, Elle had changed into yoga gear and was in a yoga pose. She fluidly moved out of the position she was in to another one, and with fascination he watched her hold it, every inch of her body in her control, legs firm and strong, arms steady. She leaned forward and went into a pose where she was on one straight leg, her body balanced perfectly, her stance firm, she made it look effortless and graceful.

It was serene.

It was controlled.

It was beautiful.

It was extraordinary.

Although all of this was delightful, what it wasn't was Elle.

Silently, he turned and walked down the stairs.

She rejoined them in time to work with Jason on his guitar and for Sally to help her with dinner. She ate with them. She tidied the kitchen.

After, she disappeared.

Prentice gave her some time before he followed.

His feet in socks making no noise on the stairs, he stopped yet again halfway up the second flight.

He saw Elle through the door. She was curled into the chair, knees bent, feet up on its edge. The lavender scent was again permeating the air. Her head was bowed and he could see she was writing in one of her journals.

Peaceful.

Quiet.

Withdrawn.

Not Elle.

Again, he silently made his way back down the stairs.

She rejoined them again to get Sally to bed, walking her up the stairs, hand in hand. She stayed upstairs to read Sally a bedtime story.

"Do me a favor, mate, go to your room," Prentice said to Jason.

"But Dad—"

Prentice looked at his son.

Jason knew that look. He grabbed his guitar, said his goodnight and went up to his room.

Prentice watched his son until he was out of sight.

Then he made a decision.

It might be too soon but he didn't give a fuck.

They'd lost twenty years, he'd lost a wife, his children had lost their mother and, as far as he could tell, Elle had lived a life where she had very little that was meaningful to lose.

Life was too short.

There was no time to waste.

He went to the kitchen, found a bottle of red wine Elle had bought and put it on the counter with the corkscrew. He was taking down two glasses when she walked down the stairs.

"Where's Jason?" she asked, her eyes on the wine, her expression guarded.

"Early night," Prentice answered, grabbing the glasses by their stem and upending them then wrapping his hand around the neck of the bottle and nabbing the corkscrew.

"Prentice," Elle said as he walked up to her, "we need to talk."

Good, she didn't intend to delay in telling him what was on her mind.

That worked for him because neither did he.

Obviously, Prentice had changed his mind about talking that day.

It was just that he now also had something to say.

"Aye," he agreed.

"I . . ." she started but stopped when he threw an arm around her shoulders and guided her toward the stairs. She began again when they hit the stairs, "Where are we going?"

"We're going to talk," he said, resolutely moving her up the stairs.

"But where?"

"The best place in the house."

She fell silent.

At the top of the stairs, he directed her toward his rooms.

Her body jolted.

"Pren—"

His arm left her shoulders and the hand with the bottle went to the small of her back. He pushed her into his sitting room.

"I don't think this is a good idea," she whispered when he closed the door behind them.

"Why no'?" he asked, guiding her through the small sitting room into the bedroom, putting everything on his bureau and opening a drawer.

"Because . . ." she began, paused, and went on, "Can we talk in your study?"

He walked up to her with a pair of his thick socks.

"No," he held out the socks, gentled his voice and ordered "Put those on, baby."

She stared at the socks but didn't move. He lifted her hand, set the socks in her palm and walked away.

"Socks?" she asked his back as he opened another drawer.

"Put them on," he ordered.

"But—"

He turned to look at her.

She couldn't even see his face but she still bent and put on the socks.

When she straightened, he was close, and before she could say a word, he pulled one of his jumpers over her head.

"Um . . ." she muttered as she shoved her arms through and he tugged the tendrils of hair at her neck free of the collar, "I'm not getting it."

He looked at her shadowed form in his sweater. She swam in it.

Definitely better than the posh cardie.

He walked away, explaining, "We're going outside."

"We are?"

He pulled on a jumper. "Aye. Best place in the house."

He grabbed the wine and then guided her out the door to the balcony. He put the glasses on the railing and saw her give them a funny look while he uncorked the wine.

Her eyes went to his face. He couldn't see her clearly in the dark but he felt her gaze.

"Pren," she said softly.

He cut her off. "We need to talk about Fee."

Even though she was two feet away, Prentice felt her go still.

He ignored it and poured the wine. Handing a glass to her, he took a sip from his.

And Prentice decided it was fucking well time to get a few things straight. Straight enough so that head of hers couldn't twist them, no matter how hard she tried.

He got close and circled her with an arm around her chest, turning her so her back was to his front. He rested his weight against the railing and put pressure against her chest with his forearm as indication she should rest her weight against him.

She struggled with this for a moment. When he didn't release the pressure, with a sigh she relaxed against him.

His eyes went to the sea.

The night was chill, the moon mostly hidden, the sea only a midnight-blue blanket with caps of white.

As it always did, this vision settled him.

"I loved her," Prentice whispered, and Elle went solid against him for only a moment before her hands came up. Her fingers curling on his forearm, she left them where they were and she relaxed. Prentice went on, "I still do."

"You miss her," Elle said softly.

"Aye. Every day. Even after all this time, I can open the front door and forget she won't be on the other side."

Her hands squeezed his arm.

"We were happy," Prentice told her.

Elle nodded but he heard her breath hitch.

This time his arm squeezed her.

"I'll always love her, Elle."

"Of course," she whispered.

He took a sip from his wine and then rested his jaw against her head.

"I'm a man who's been blessed."

Her body jolted again and she stammered, "Wh-what?"

"I had Fee. She was no' long meant for this world but I knew her since she was wee and she was mine for a while. It was a blessing."

Elle relaxed and nodded again. "You're right, Pren."

"Then," he continued, "you came back." She went solid as a rock against him but he ignored it and carried on, "I've lived a good life in this village, with Fee, but you're still the best thing that's been in it."

"Oh my God," she breathed.

He ignored that too, put his wine glass on the railing and his mouth to her neck.

"To have Fee, who gave me her and then Jason and Sally and then to have you," he murmured. "I'm a man who's been blessed."

"Pren—" she started but her breath hitched again and she stopped.

"Come back to me, Elle," he coaxed softly.

She was pulling at his arm with her hands now but he held strong.

"I don't give a fuck about the photographers," he told her. "If they come with you, then Jason, Sally and I'll get used to it."

"You don't know how bad it can get."

"I don't care, either."

"You can't say that."

His mouth left her neck, his jaw went back to her head and his other arm stole around her belly.

"Aye, I can."

"You can't," she said firmly.

She was digging in.

He decided to switch topics.

"Tell me about your ex-husband."

Her body jerked again.

Off-guard.

Good.

"What? Why?" she asked, her voice higher pitched.

"Because I want to know."

"Why would you possibly want to know?"

"Because he was part of your life and I want to know about your life, which means I want to know about him."

"He isn't that interesting."

"Likely no'. You're still going to tell me."

"Pren—" she started, his arms tightened and she stopped.

His voice dipped lower when he demanded, "Tell me."

She was silent. This lasted awhile.

Finally, she said softly, "Actually, I think this is good."

"What?"

"Telling you about Laurent."

Laurent.

Christ, he even hated the man's name.

Over the years, he didn't think much of Laurent Evangelista because he didn't allow himself to think much of Elle.

When Prentice heard about their public split, he *did* think Laurent Evangelista was all kinds of fool for leaving Elle and going off with a shoddier version.

Now, he hated him.

No, actually, he detested him.

Because someone should have done something about that father of hers, those dreams of hers and how she fisted her hands in that alarming way.

And it was clear Laurent Evangelista did none of those things.

"I didn't love him," Elle announced, taking him from his thoughts.

"What?" Prentice asked, surprised.

"I didn't love him. I never loved him," she repeated. "Looking back, I'm not certain I ever even *liked* him."

At that, it was Prentice's body that grew solid. Feeling it, with a rough jerk she pulled away. He allowed this because he sensed she needed it.

He'd disallow it the minute she did not.

She walked two steps, put her glass to the railing and turned to him.

"You won't be surprised to hear that I married him because my father wanted me to. There wasn't much I did that my dad didn't want me to do." She waited for that to sink in and when she received no response, she went on, "Dad liked him. Thought he was a good catch. Said Laurent was *our people*. He'd known Laurent's parents for years."

"Elle—" he stopped speaking when she turned to face the sea and kept talking.

"I thought, though, that I'd get something from it. Finally get something *I* wanted," she told the sea and her voice dropped to a whisper when she continued, "I was wrong."

She was talking about children. A family.

It was time to disallow the space she no longer needed.

Prentice approached, Elle retreated but he didn't let her go. He caught her around the waist and pulled her to him, sliding his arms tight around her.

She stood stiff in his embrace.

"Why didn't you adopt?" he asked quietly.

"Laurent didn't want to adopt, so, we didn't adopt."

The way she spoke made it clear that in her desire to build a family she'd tried that too.

And she, again, failed.

In other words, what Laurent wanted or didn't want, Laurent got.

No matter what Elle wanted.

Yes, Prentice detested him.

"You know what's funny?" she asked the sea, her face turned away from him, her gaze thoughtful.

"No, baby. What's funny?"

"*He* divorced *me*." She looked at him and continued, "I never wanted him and, in the end, *he* divorced *me*. Isn't that funny?"

What it was, was ironic.

What it was not, was funny.

He didn't answer, he simply pulled her closer. Her head tipped back further to keep her eyes on him and her hands came to rest lightly on his waist.

Prentice liked the feel of Elle's hands on his waist. He'd like it better if it was her *arms* around his waist.

"Why do you think that?" she asked quietly.

He put a hand to her jaw and stroked her cheek with his thumb, asking, "Think what?"

"What you said about me. That I was the best thing to come in your life. With all the gifts you've been given, how can you think that?"

His mind flooded with all that was Elle.

Her pancakes. Her cookies. Her smile.

The way she cared for his home.

The way she cared for his family.

The way she handled Sally with infinite patience appearing to enjoy every second.

The way she understood what Jason needed and gave it to him after Prentice spent a year trying to figure it out.

The way she kept his children's mother's memory alive instead of trying to bury it deep.

The way she could make him laugh when she forgot to be Isabella and instead was Elle.

The way she responded to his hands, his mouth, his cock moving inside her.

The way she consistently gave of herself, second by second, to him, to his children, to her friends, the latter to whom she'd been giving for years without even noticing she was doing it or expecting that first thing in return.

Prentice was in love with her.

And he'd been in love with her for over twenty years.

But now, knowing what he knew about how she'd helped Annie with unfailing determination and seeing what he saw when she dropped everything and raced to his daughter's bedside at the hospital, he loved her even more.

He'd had a beautiful run with Fiona and he loved his wife deeply.

But he'd never been *in love* with Fee.

Not the way he'd always been in love with Elle from the first time he saw her with Annie, her beautiful face lit up with laughter, walking into the same pub they went to last night.

He studied that face in the dim light and slid his thumb along her lower lip.

"How can I no'?" he answered her question with a question.

She shook her head and tried to pull away.

His hand left her face so his arm could lock around her back.

She stilled and whispered, "I don't understand."

He pulled her even closer. "You don't have to understand. I do. Isn't that enough?"

She shook her head again, her body still tight. "I don't think—"

He cut her off, asking, "Do you like it here?"

He felt her frame jerk and she stammered, "P-pardon?"

"Do you like this house?" he inquired.

She slightly relaxed and her voice was soft when she replied, "It's a beautiful house, Pren."

"Do you like being with the children?"

Her voice was suddenly firm (and slightly loud) when she replied, "Of course I do!"

His fingers went to her hair, pulling out the holder so its weight tumbled into his hand.

He fisted it, dipped his face closer and asked, "Do you like being with me?"

"Pren—"

"Answer me, Elle."

She tried to turn her head away but he held her fast with his hand in her hair.

"Elle—" he prompted.

"What does it matter?" she whispered.

"Because if you like it and you want it, you can have it," he told her, pulling her head back so he could rest his forehead on hers. "I think it's about time you get what you want, baby. Don't you?"

He was getting somewhere. He knew this because her body relaxed into his and her hands at his waist slid around his back.

"I like it," she said softly and her body pressed closer. "And I want it."

Yes, thank Christ, he was finally getting somewhere.

He felt like roaring his triumph.

He didn't because she went on.

"But—" she began.

His hand in her hair tightened, his other arm giving her a squeeze, stopping her next words.

"No," he stated firmly.

"But, Pren—"

This time, he dropped his head and he kissed her silent.

That worked.

Just like it always did.

Her weight was resting fully against his body when he lifted his head.

"You want it," he said, touching her lips with his again. "I want it." He touched her lips again. "And the children want it. We've all lost enough. It's time to move on to something better."

"Okay," she whispered, suddenly acquiescent, dropping her head, putting her cheek to his chest and snuggling close.

He held her for a long time.

Then he kept her in his arm as he reached for her glass, handing it to her.

After he did that, Prentice reached for his own.

They drank their wine together and silently watched the sea.

———— ◆ ————

Fiona

YOU'RE GETTING SOMEWHERE, Fiona told her husband as she floated, arse to the railing, beside Prentice and Bella.

Her husband didn't answer.

You think you've cracked it, though, and you aren't even close, Fiona continued.

Prentice showed no signs of hearing her.

Fiona leaned forward and whispered fiercely, *Prentice, read her journals!*

Prentice swallowed the last sip of his wine and put his glass on the railing next to Bella's already empty one.

He turned Bella toward the door.

Brilliant, now *Bella* was leaving glasses outside. Fiona didn't particularly relish the fact that Prentice took Bella outside in the first place, seeing as he never did that with her. But, she *really* didn't relish both of them leaving the glassware to fend for their inanimate selves in the wild, Scottish elements.

Fiona put the glasses out of her mind and followed them.

She had bigger fish to fry.

Read her journals, read her journals, READ HER JOURNALS! Fiona shouted to Prentice.

They stepped over the threshold.

Fiona followed them.

When she did, she hit black.

Not her tent by the apple tree and the stream.

Black.

Pitch.

She floated to a stop, suddenly terrified out of her mind.

Where was she?

She wasn't real here, she was floating.

She looked down at herself.

See-through.

Oh no.

Was this hell?

Did she do something wrong?

In a panic, she floated forward, banged into an invisible barrier and was thrown back.

No! she shouted.

She didn't want to be alone for eternity with a silk tent, a guitar and some books, no matter how pretty the place was.

And she didn't want to be with her family for eternity, haunting them, watching them live their lives but never being a part of it.

But she really didn't want to be *here* (wherever *here* was). It was dark. It was frightening. And if she stayed there, she'd never know if Prentice breathed life back into Bella, just like the prince in a fairytale.

She flew forward again, faster, more determined.

She floated into the bedroom.

It was dark, Bella and Prentice in bed.

She looked behind her.

Nothing but windows, balcony and sea.

She was safe.

Fiona let out a ghostly sigh of relief.

She looked to the ceiling and said thanks. Then she asked never to be sent *there* again.

There was no answer.

Fiona shook off the residual fear and cautiously drifted to the bed.

Bella was asleep, dead to the world (as it were).

Prentice was wide awake.

Even though she was frightened that trying to communicate with the living was getting her into trouble (and sent to the pitch black), this was important, she had to risk it, so Fiona still reached out and touched her husband's hair.

Read her journals, she whispered.

She pulled her hand back instantly when his head turned at her ghostly touch. Then she braced, afraid she'd be sent to the pitch black.

She wasn't.

She watched as Prentice carefully extricated himself from Bella who, Fiona noticed, was wearing one of Prentice's T-shirts which was good since Sally would undoubtedly be in in the morning.

Prentice pulled the covers around Bella and she saw he was in sweats.

She had to hurry and float after him as he exited the room.

Navigating the house in the dark, he went straight to the guest suite.

He turned on the light beside Bella's bed, looked over his shoulder and out the two doors he'd left opened.

Then Fiona stared as he picked up and opened the journal that sat on the top of the stack and he read.

He'd heard her.

Hallelujah! He'd heard her!

Fiona saw that he was reading the latest journal, the one Bella just started.

She got close to him and advised, *That's not a good one to read, try one of the other ones.*

He obviously wasn't hearing her now because she saw his lips curve into a smile as he read what she wrote about the children.

Seriously, Prentice, try one of the other—

Fiona stopped when she saw the smile fade from his face when he read what Bella wrote that day.

He flipped the book shut and grabbed the next one.

He started at the back.

Fiona looked over his shoulder. Her ghostly body braced.

He'd flipped right to the page where Bella wrote about disposing of the pictures and his ring after carrying them with her for twenty years. Disposing of them because she thought he hated her. Disposing of them because he'd been cruel.

Disposing of them because she needed, for her own sake, to let him go, no matter how much it hurt her.

Fiona watched his face grow pale and his body get tight.

Then she watched him flip the book shut in his hand and he stared unseeing at the bed for long moments. He turned and sat on its side. Putting his elbows to his knees, he bent forward and placed his hands to the back of his head, even the one with the book.

He looked between his knees and clipped, *"Fuck!"*

Fiona got close and soothed, *You didn't know, even I didn't know. How could you know?*

He sat back and opened the journal again.

Randomly selecting pages, he read. Sometimes, just the page. Sometimes, he'd read for pages and pages.

He did this through all four journals.

Finally, he stood, his face set, jaw tight, a muscle jerking in his cheek.

Fiona knew how he felt.

She wished she could hug him, but unfortunately she couldn't.

He set the journal aside, turned out the light and started to walk away.

Fiona held back, worrying her ghostly lip, waiting for him to leave so she could rearrange Bella's journals like she liked them (Prentice had totally messed them up).

But he turned back, switched on the light and carefully arranged the journals, chronologically and stacked precisely.

Then he turned out the light again and retraced his steps to Bella.

As she crossed the threshold to her old bedroom, Fiona went back to the stream.

———◆———

Prentice

PRENTICE WASN'T THINKING.

Couldn't think.

Wouldn't allow himself to.

He put a knee to the bed and pulled the covers down Elle's body.

Then he joined her in bed and turned her to him.

He put his mouth to her neck and his hands went to her panties.

"Pren?" she whispered drowsily, her hands coming to rest lightly on his chest.

He pulled down her panties.

His mouth left her neck so he could yank them down her legs, over her feet and toss them away.

"Pren." Her voice was less sleepy, her hands more firm on him when he rolled into her.

He kissed her as he forced his hips between her legs.

At his kiss, she opened her legs and her arms wrapped around his back.

His mouth trailed down her cheek to her ear and he tasted the sweetness of her.

She sifted her fingers in his hair, lifted her head, now whispering in his ear, she repeated, "Pren."

His hands went up her shirt and he found her breasts.

His mouth found hers.

"I'll no' let you go," he vowed, his voice so rough, it was hoarse.

His thumbs slid over her nipples.

"Okay," she breathed.

"Never. I'll never let you go."

Her hand cupped the back of his head, the other trailing down his side, between their bodies, down his stomach.

"Okay," she repeated.

She pushed into his sweats and found him.

He groaned into her mouth.

Then he fucked her in a way that she could make no mistake he was claiming her as his. It was like their first time, hard, quick, out of control and pure magic.

Elle, being Elle, after it was over and their breath had slowed, mistook him.

She tried to exit the bed.

He caught her and pulled her back into his body.

"Where are you going?" he growled into the back of her head.

"I need to go to my bed. The children—"

His arm got tight and she stopped breathing. He even heard her breath going out of her lungs in a whoosh.

He didn't care.

He was not letting her go.

"You sleep here, with me."

She made a noise he couldn't decipher.

He didn't try.

Wishing to be certain she was clear and made no *further* mistake, he repeated, "From now on, you sleep here, with me. You sleep nowhere else, no' in this house. If you sleep somewhere else but this house, I'll be there too and you'll *still* fucking sleep with me."

She was silent, her body tense then she asked, "Has . . . um, has something happened?"

"Aye."

She was silent again then she asked with a tinge of incredulity, "Erm . . . how can something happen? It's the middle of the night."

He didn't answer, he just gave her a squeeze.

Elle, being Elle, didn't let it go.

"What happened?"

"I'm not fucking around anymore, that's what's happened."

"You . . . um," she paused then carried on, "you just woke up and decided you're not fucking around anymore?" This time there was more than a tinge of incredulity.

"Aye," he lied.

"Fucking around about what?" she asked.

He decided not to answer.

When she spoke again, she was whispering, "Pren, are you okay?"

There it was again.

She asked like she cared, like she was worried, like she wanted to take care of him.

Like she took care of fucking everyone.

But herself.

He gave her a gentle squeeze this time.

"No," he answered truthfully.

"Do you want to talk?"

"No," he answered, again truthfully.

"Can I . . . is there something I can do?"

He was right.

She wanted to take care of him.

"Aye."

"What?"

"You and Sally made chocolate chip cookies. They're delicious but I prefer the oatmeal ones. You want to do something, make those for me tomorrow."

Her body stilled before she breathed, "Are you serious?"

"Aye."

She was silent.

Then she said, "You wake me up in the middle of the night. We . . . erm, you know. Then you get all intense and say something's wrong but you won't tell me what. And now you're saying you want oatmeal cookies?"

He could see this would seem highly bizarre.

He didn't care about that either.

"Aye."

"Do you have a fever?"

Something relaxed inside him. He felt the fierce clutch of it let him go.

The warmth hit his gut and he smiled into her hair.

"I don't have a fever, Elle."

She pulled at his hold. "Maybe I should check."

His hold again grew tight. "Just go to sleep."

"Pren—"

"Sleep."

"But—"

His hand curled on her breast, her body stilled but eventually relaxed.

He nuzzled his face in her hair, his voice went low, soft and coaxing when he urged, "Sleep, baby."

She didn't answer.

She also didn't sleep, not for some time.

Finally, he felt her body get heavy and he let out a relieved sigh.

Before she drifted away, she murmured sleepily, "If you've caught something, you're quarantined to these rooms. I don't want the children getting it."

And there it was, yet again.

Elle taking care of somebody.

Since these somebodies were his children, Prentice smiled into her hair.

She fell asleep.

He listened to her breathing.

Against his will, the words she wrote in her journals slid into his mind.

His body pressed into hers.

Twenty years ago, Prentice walked out of a room.

A simple enough thing to do.

But in doing so, he'd left the woman he loved in hell.

He didn't know it then.

But he knew it now, from what he'd learned through her and

through Mikey.

He just didn't *understand* it.

Until he read her journals.

Now he understood it.

And it killed him.

Chapter
SIXTEEN

The Day Elle Austin Awoke

Fiona

T he next day, Elle Austin awoke.

Fiona watched it.

And, when it happened, Fiona smiled.

———◆———

Elle

ELLE WOKE TO the bed bouncing.

She had no time to think of the night before.

She had no time to think of one word of the life changing conversation she'd shared with Prentice.

She had no time to think even of the strange sense of disquiet she felt when Prentice led her from the balcony into his room, tenderly disrobed her, tugged one of his T-shirts over her head and put her to bed. It was a disquiet she couldn't put her finger on but it felt like someone she cared about was in pain.

She had no time to think of any of this because Sally, who was on her knees at the foot of the bed, shouted, "Good morning!"

Prentice's fingers unlaced from hers and they both got up on an elbow to look to the foot of the bed.

Prentice rolled to his back, his arm pushing under Elle as he did so, turning her so her front was to his side, his arm tight, fastening her there.

"Come here, baby," Prentice murmured to his daughter, his voice deeper with residual sleep and Elle decided she liked his just-woken-up voice.

She liked it a lot.

Sally didn't hesitate, she crawled up Prentice's body.

Elle decided she liked that too, watching Sally crawl up her father's long body.

She liked it a lot.

As Sally collapsed on Prentice's chest, her eyes never left Elle and she announced, "Me and Jace have made you muffins!"

Fear shot through Elle at the very *thought* of Sally and Jason operating the oven.

"You what?" she whispered.

Prentice's voice was a great deal more effective when he asked, low and vibrating, "I'm sorry?"

"We didn't cook them." They heard from across the room and all the inhabitants of the bed looked to the door.

Jason was standing there, his stance awkward, his expression showing, quite clearly, he didn't know what to make of the goings-on in the bed.

Elle's body went tight.

And when it did, so did Prentice's arm.

"We just made them and put the batter in the tin. We thought Elle could cook them," Jason gamely continued, still obviously uncomfortable.

It was then it hit her that Jason called her Elle. Not only then but he and Sally had been doing it for days. Even in front of Prentice, who never corrected them.

She felt something relax deep inside her, something that had been coiled tight for so long she didn't know it *could* relax.

But it did.

"I'll cook them," Prentice offered, completely unaware of the momentous event that happened someplace deep inside Elle. "How'd you make them, Jace?"

Jason looked to the floor, shuffled his feet and mumbled, "One of Mum's cookbooks." He took in a deep breath and looked at the wall. "Mum never made them though." His eyes skittered to the bed then to the opposite wall before he finished, "They're blueberry. We used the leftovers."

Elle's heart went out to him and she wanted to say something, she just had no clue what to say.

Sally, on the other hand, never had any problem knowing what to say.

"Jace decided that we should make Elle breakfast to pay her back, since she's always making us breakfast." Sally grinned at her father. "We had *fun*."

Elle wondered briefly what Sally's version of fun did to the kitchen.

She looked to Jason and said softly, "Thank you, honey."

Jason didn't reply. He looked like he was willing himself to spontaneously combust.

"I'll just go and—" he muttered.

Prentice cut him off by calling, "Hey mate, I've a question for you."

Jason's eyes hesitantly went to his father.

Prentice kept talking. "What do you think, is Elle ticklish or no'?"

Elle's body went tight again as Prentice's arm locked around her and Sally's head snapped to the side to look at her.

Elle tried to jerk away, saying warningly, "Pren—"

"Aye!" Sally squealed. "I think she is!"

On that, Sally pounced.

Prentice turned to Elle. As Sally wriggled and writhed, trying to get to Elle's ticklish spots with her fast-moving, little girl fingers, Prentice held her against him with one arm and tickled her with his free hand.

Relentlessly.

But then Prentice knew where her ticklish spots were already.

Giggling so helplessly she could barely move, she managed to turn her back to Prentice but he kept her close and continued tickling her. Finally getting control of Sally's squirming body and tickling hands, Elle pinned Sally's back to her front and returned the favor, giggling as she tickled Sally while the little girl laughed herself silly.

They all stopped when the bed bounced and they looked at its foot. Jason was sprawled on his side, his eyes were dancing and a smirk was on his lips.

"I'd say she's ticklish," Jason muttered dryly.

Elle heard Prentice chuckle.

Elle and Sally didn't laugh, they both just smiled at Jason.

"All right, everybody up. It's muffin time," Prentice ordered.

Sally scattered and Jason rolled off the bed.

Elle stayed where she was, mainly because she wasn't wearing any underwear.

Prentice also remained in bed and it was highly likely this was because he wasn't wearing *anything*.

"Jace, shut the door. We'll be down in a minute," Prentice called.

"Aye," Jason replied.

Sally turned at the door and asked, "Can we switch on the oven?"

"No," both Prentice and Elle replied.

Sally made a face, looked at her brother and trotted out the door.

Jason's eyes took in Prentice and Elle, he looked to the floor and left, shutting the door behind him.

Prentice instantly rolled into Elle, taking her in his arms.

Elle tried to push away.

She failed.

"We need to get downstairs," she informed him.

"Aye," he replied softly, his eyes roaming her face. "But I need to kiss you first."

"Pren—" she began but was cut off when he did what he said he needed to do.

She found, in short order, she needed it too.

Prentice was a good kisser. She hadn't had many kisses but she still felt she could say with some authority, he was *the best*.

She was dazed when his mouth broke from hers.

His hand went to her jaw, his thumb running along her cheekbone.

"I forgot how ticklish you were." He was still speaking in that soft voice, the voice that did funny things to her.

Concentrating on the funny things and how nice they made her feel, Elle didn't reply.

"I used to tickle you all the time." He grinned and continued, "When we weren't fighting." She watched as his grin faded but warmth hit his eyes when his thumb traced her lower lip while he watched. His gaze came back to hers and he murmured, "Do you remember?"

"I remember," Elle whispered.

She remembered everything about him and the time they spent together.

Everything.

Considering he was close, Elle got lost in his every-colored eyes, counting the colors again, comparing the occurrences, fascinated by this activity even though she'd memorized the results.

His forehead touched hers, his hand at her jaw tensed and he growled, "I love it when you look at me like that. Always did."

His growl slid through her like velvet.

Elle pressed into him.

His arm around her tightened but he sighed and lifted his head. "I need to cook muffins."

He didn't sound thrilled with this prospect.

"You do," she replied, trying not to smile. Prentice started to roll, taking her with him when Elle locked her body, catching his attention, and he stopped. "You also need to talk to Jace," she said quietly.

Both his arms went around her and he gave her a squeeze, murmuring, "Aye."

He pulled them from the bed, grabbed her panties from the floor, handed them to her and she slid them on while he put on his sweats. She was about to get her jeans when his hands came to her hips and he shuffled her to the door.

"I need to put on my jeans," she told him, resisting and attempting to turn back into the room.

She failed at this too.

He reached in front of her and grasped the door handle, informing her, "You're good."

She was . . . *good*?

Was he mad?

She was in a T-shirt!

With effort, she turned to face him but he slid an arm around her waist and pulled her out of the door's arc.

"I'm only wearing your T-shirt," she reminded him unnecessarily as he could *see* she was only in his T-shirt.

"Aye," he replied. "But you're covered."

She continued to resist as he forced her, hands again at her hips, through the door.

"Prentice! I'm in a T-shirt! I can't eat breakfast with your *children* in a *T-shirt!*" she hissed.

"Why no'?" he asked casually.

She stared at him in disbelief as he shuffled her down the hall.

He caught sight of her face, stopped before they turned to the stairs and said, "It comes down to your thighs, baby. You're far more covered than you were in your nightie when you made pancakes that first time."

"I wasn't just in a nightie. I was also wearing a robe," she replied impatiently.

He grinned and his face got close as his hands slid down over her behind and pulled her hips to him. "That robe didn't cover fuck all."

"It certainly did!" she snapped.

His grin turned devilish. "Trust me. It did *no'*."

She ignored how attractive his devilish grin was, and this was hard to do considering she hadn't seen it in twenty years and she remembered how she *particularly* liked it. "It most certainly *did*."

"Aye, I'll admit, on the face of it, it did. If you have a creative imagination, which I *do*," he said, his fingers tensing deliciously in the flesh of her backside. "It . . . did . . . *no'*."

She was staggered.

"Are you saying . . . ?"

"Aye."

"Back then . . . when you . . . ?"

"Aye."

"You thought of me . . . ?"

"*Aye.*"

He was growling again.

It felt like velvet again.

Regardless, Elle was stunned.

"But . . ." she whispered, "you hated me."

All playfulness swept instantly from his face, his hands went to her waist and curled around, holding her close.

"I've never hated you, Elle."

"But—"

"There were plenty of times I *wanted* to hate you, over the years and recently, but I could never do it."

"But—"

"No' ever."

"Pren—"

He kissed her quiet.

He took his time and did this thoroughly.

When he lifted his head he repeated fiercely, "Baby. No' *ever.*"

She felt tears hit her eyes and she whispered, "Really?"

He scanned her face, and for a second, she could swear, it looked like he was in pain.

He masked it before she could be sure and he whispered back, "Really."

Something else wound up tight in her released and relaxed.

So did her body, right into his and he took her weight.

"Can I get my jeans?" she asked softly.

"No."

Her body got tight again and she pulled slightly away, demanding, "Why not?"

Both his arms released her but only so both his hands could come to her jaw and tip her face up to his.

"Because last night you made a decision and now, today, you're at home. When you're at home you don't have to dress to eat breakfast. When you're at home you wear whatever the fuck you want to wear at breakfast."

Last night *she* hadn't made a decision.

He had.

And he hadn't let her protest.

He was watching her as these thoughts went through her head and then he interrupted them.

"I can see this may take time to sink in for you," he said then the devilish grin came back. "Luckily, I'm patient."

He was *not* patient.

Or, at least, twenty years ago he wasn't.

And evidence suggested he wasn't now either.

"Pren—"

"Muffins."

"Pren!"

He turned her around the corner that led to the stairs.

Sally saw them the minute they came into view and before Elle could form another protest, Sally shouted, "Hurrah! Now we can bake the muffins."

Stymied.

With no choice, Elle went to the kitchen and sat on a stool in nothing but Prentice's T-shirt, sipping coffee and surveying the chaos created by Jason and Sally making muffins.

They'd forgotten to grease the tins so they didn't have full muffins, just the muffin tops that Jason and Prentice were able to pry from the tin.

Still, they weren't half bad.

———— ✦ ————

Fiona

FIONA KNEW IT happened because Bella was tired.

She'd had a hectic day.

And Fiona had watched it all.

The tickling in bed (though she'd followed Jason when he left the room, worried about him after his reaction at seeing Bella and Prentice in his mother and father's bed).

The conversation on the landing when Prentice (not letting *any* grass grow) set about righting the wrongs he'd inadvertently done Bella.

The disastrous muffin baking.

She also watched Bella clean the kitchen with Sally's "help," which made the onerous task all the more onerous, while Prentice went after Jason. During this, Fiona watched Bella bite her lip and fist her hands.

Fiona wanted to be with Jason and Prentice, but Fiona knew her son. He was like his father. He felt deeply. But, in miraculously little time, he came to decisions and stuck by them, about people and events.

He knew his mind, Jason did, always had, even as a wee lad.

He might be confused but he'd sort it—with his father's help.

Fiona was more worried about Bella.

She whispered words to soothe her friend as the time slid by while Prentice was upstairs with Jason.

Then, when this didn't work, she shouted her soothing words.

Incredibly, this seemed to work and Bella began to focus more on Sally and making oatmeal cookies (and why they needed oatmeal cookies to add to the chocolate chip cookies in the cookie jar, Fiona had no idea) and less on tearing her palms with her nails.

When Prentice and Jason appeared again, Bella whirled to the stairs and watched them descend.

Jason had Fiona's guitar.

Bella went pale.

"Elle, will you show me more chords today?" Jason asked.

Bella's eyes flew to Prentice, and Prentice gave Bella a wink.

Bella (and Fiona, even though hers was unnecessary as she didn't breathe) let out a sigh.

"Sure, Jace. I just need to take a shower," Bella answered.

While Bella showered, Fiona watched (and giggled) as Prentice moved her clothes into her new room.

Therefore, when she came out of the shower, she halted and stared at the underwear, jeans and jumper lying on the bed. An outfit she didn't choose for herself.

She went to the wardrobe. She went to the drawers. She stared at the empty nightstand.

Finally she pulled on her clothes in a tizzy and ran from the room.

She found Prentice walking out of the closet in Bella's new room, her clothes from the drawers all over the still unmade bed.

She stood frozen.

Then she looked at him, eyes glassy, and mumbled, "Wha—?"

Prentice walked right up to her, cupped the back of her head in his hand and touched his lips to hers.

"Sort the drawers, will you, baby? I'm rubbish at that shit."

With that he walked out as Bella gazed after him mutely.

Fiona giggled again.

Bella stood there a long time, staring at the bed.

She was still standing there after Prentice returned (twice), hands full of her things from the guest bathroom, and he put them in her new bathroom.

His last trip, he got close, slid a hand along the small of her back and bent to her ear, "Baby. You need to sort it. Now. We're going to the beach."

She stared at him stupidly before she repeated, "The beach?"

"Aye," he looked at the bed, then at her, "or do you want to leave it until we get home?"

That woke her up and she shook her head wildly.

He grinned, gave her waist a squeeze and left the room.

Bella got busy and sorted the drawers. She made the bed. She went into the closet and sorted the mess Prentice had made of her hanging clothes.

Most of this time, Fiona giggled.

Bella and Sally packed a lunch and they went to the beach.

At the beach, Sally behaved like she always behaved even though Prentice took the children to the beach often both when Fiona was alive and after she'd died. In other words, like she'd been living in a cell her entire life and was only going to be let out for that one glorious day.

Bella kept up with her, as well as sat with Jason who'd brought along Fiona's guitar, and Fiona could say (with some pride) that she gave her son more than his hair. He was getting very good with the guitar, and the way he practiced (which was all the time just like Fiona had) he was going to be great, and Bella taught him some more chords.

At Jason's insistence, Bella also played while Prentice and the kids watched. She was nervous and it took her time to settle in but, once she did, it was good.

Prentice was impressed and didn't hide it.

Jason just smiled.

Bella, it was clear to see, was both pleased and embarrassed by the male Camerons' reactions.

Sally was adamant that she was getting her *own* guitar and Bella was going to teach her to play it when she got her cast off.

They had lunch. They horsed around. They walked the beach and its cliff path, Prentice and Bella hand in hand, Jason going ahead on his own, Sally running back and forth, tiring herself out (Fiona's daughter would sleep like a log that night, for certain).

They went home and it was all a go, sorting the spent picnic, making dinner, getting ready for school the next day as Sally was returning after her accident.

Bella had no time to think, she was kept busy all day.

Prentice, Fiona thought, was a genius.

Sally crashed within Bella reading two pages of her book.

Jason didn't long follow.

Prentice was walking down the stairs after checking on the children when it happened.

Fiona was floating by Bella as she tiredly made herself some nighttime herbal tea.

She had her hand curled around the mug, holding the teabag string against the side, when she missed the mug and poured boiling water over her hand. She cried out in pain and set the kettle down with a clatter.

Prentice was there in a trice.

He got close. "Jesus, baby, what'd you do?"

"I poured . . ." she stopped and cried, "*Ouch!*"

"Get to the sink," Prentice ordered.

Hustling her to the sink, he shoved her hand under and turned on the cold tap.

She held her hand under the tap as Prentice went to get ice. He returned and, front to her back, he reached his arms around her and held the ice to the angry red marks on Bella's hand under the tap.

Fiona hovered close.

With his head dipped so his cheek was close to hers, he moved the ice around her fingers and whispered, "The burn is still working through, baby, we need to stop it. The ice won't feel good but we need to keep it on there."

"Okay," Bella whispered back, her voice pinched with pain.

It took a while before he noticed. The angry red marks were taking his attention from the calloused white marks in her palms.

But he noticed.

And Fiona noticed when he noticed because she watched as his body grew completely still.

Bella, tired and mind fogged with the pain, didn't notice. He had actually uncurled her fingers with his thumb and tipped her palm up before Bella realized what he was about.

When he saw the marks, Prentice's inhalation was a sharp hiss.

Instantly, Bella curled her hand in a fist and her body jerked to the side, seeking escape.

She was in a disadvantageous position with his arms around her, his body close; she had no hope of getting away.

And she didn't.

He stepped in, pinning her against the sink, his arms locking at her sides, his thumb worked her fingers to open her fist.

Her body gave in but her hand resisted. The burn meant this caused undue pain. When she emitted a muted whimper, Prentice stopped.

Fiona would have held her breath if she had any.

Instead, she did the only thing she could do.

She hovered.

His voice was soft when he ordered, "Show me."

Bella's reply was immediate. "Step back."

"Show me, baby."

Her hand still a fist, she said in a tone that, though it was firm, fear threaded through it, "Prentice . . . step . . . *back!*"

His other hand circled her other wrist, he pulled both her fisted hands in front of them and his voice was an absolute, wretched ache when he demanded, "Show me."

Fiona watched the tears hit Bella's eyes and tremble at their edges.

"I don't want you to see," she whispered, her tone just as heartbreaking.

"Show me."

"You'll think—"

"Show me, Elle."

"But—"

His hands at her wrists gave hers a gentle shake and he whispered, "Show me, baby."

She closed her eyes and Fiona saw the tears drop silently down her cheeks.

Then she opened them *and* her fists and Fiona saw she held her breath.

Prentice stared at her hands.

Then his jaw got tight and *he* closed *his* eyes.

When he opened them, he ran his thumbs gently along the white marks and muttered tenderly, "Baby."

Bella's head dropped forward in a sad expression of humiliation and defeat.

Prentice's mouth went to her ear.

"You didn't have these before," he whispered but she didn't reply. "Elle, answer me. You didn't have these twenty years ago. Please, tell me I didn't fucking miss *this.*"

"I didn't have them," she replied to the sink. "I started to . . ." she stopped. "Later. After you." She drew in a breath and whispered, "It started when I lost you."

Fiona didn't know if that was what he wanted to hear or not and she couldn't tell because he shoved his face in her neck and, taking her hands with his still at her wrists, he wrapped his arms tightly around her middle.

Bella's head came up and Fiona could see she was still crying.

"They're mine," Prentice said to her neck.

Bella's body twitched and her face went blank.

"What?" she breathed.

His mouth went back to her ear and his voice was tortured when he said, "They're mine. My responsibility."

Fiona felt a heavy weight hit her ghostly chest.

Bella felt the same. Fiona could see it with a look.

"What do you mean?" Bella whispered.

"You'd no' have these marks, you'd no' carry this pain if I'd no' walked out of that *fucking* room."

"Prentice, you can't—"

She stopped speaking when he shook her with his hands at her wrists.

"You'd *no'*," he growled fiercely.

"Pren," she whispered softly.

"No."

"I can't have you thinking—"

"No."

"Pren, please."

"No. There would be no dreams, I'd have seen to that. Your father would no' be in our lives. And you'd have had your fucking family, I would see to that too. I don't give a fuck if we adopted or I had to buy you a family. I would have done it, whatever you wanted, to make you happy. Whatever you wanted, Elle. Anything. I'd have done whatever it took in order to give it to you. That's how much I loved you."

"Stop talking."

"But I didn't, I walked out of that room."

"Prentice, stop talking."

"I turned around and walked away. I didn't even fucking call you."

"Don't do this to yourself, it wasn't your fault."

"No?"

"I'm weak," she whispered.

Prentice was silent a moment before he laughed.

It was an ugly noise and it hurt Fiona's ghostly ears.

Bella felt the same.

Her pale face went ashen and, with a visible effort, she pulled free of his hands, turned off the tap, twisted in his arms and put her hands on his chest.

"It's true, Prentice, I'm weak. I always have been," she admitted this like it was a dirty little secret.

"He beat you to keep you from me," Prentice countered. "What's my excuse?"

Her head jerked and she asked, "Pardon?"

"You're father hit you to control you. Your behavior wasn't weak, it was survival. I had a good life, I'd never experienced that, no one ever treated me that way. What excuse do I have that I didn't go after you? Wounded ego?"

Bella lifted her hands to either side of his neck and held on tight.

"Stop doing this. There's no purpose."

"No purpose?" he clipped. "If you stay, in a week, a month, ten years, it will eventually sink in that I left you to that. I didn't protect you. I didn't believe in you. What do I do when the bitterness creeps in, Elle, and you can't bear to be with me anymore? What do I do?"

Her fingers curled into his neck but he didn't give her the opportunity to reply.

"You needed me to protect you and I didn't. I left you to that," he continued, his hands came to hers at his neck and he pulled them away. His thumbs sliding along her palms, he went on, "And it was so bad, you harmed yourself because of it."

She winced but recovered quickly and assured him, "I survived."

He gave a short, unamused laugh. "Aye. You survived. But life isn't survival, Elle, life is beautiful."

She shook her head and said softly, "Not for everyone. Not for a lot of people, Pren, just for those fortunate few."

Fiona watched as Prentice's mouth got tight at her words, but he replied, "True enough. But *you* deserve a beautiful life and *I* would have given it to you if I hadn't given up, believed you'd played me, stopped believing in you, stopped believing in *us*."

Fiona saw Bella was no longer listening.

Her eyes had grown unfocused.

Prentice saw it too.

He was losing her.

Do something! Fiona shouted.

"Elle," he called but she didn't reply. His hands curled into hers and gave them a gentle jerk as he repeated, "Elle."

She shook her head as if clearing it and her eyes refocused.

"You said in ten years—" Bella whispered.

"Aye," Prentice interrupted, his tone harsh. "Ten years, twenty years, fifty years. Who gives a fuck if, in the end, it might mean I lose you again."

"Fifty years?" she breathed.

Fiona knew with a look that Prentice wanted to stick with the matter at hand and was losing patience at her shift. "Elle, we—"

Bella interrupted him, asking incredulously, "You want me here for fifty years?"

Now Fiona knew that Prentice was getting annoyed. "Aye, we established that last night."

"Why?" Bella asked suddenly, her voice somehow both breathy and sharp.

Prentice's brows drew together. "Why what?"

"Why do you want me here?"

"Elle . . ." Yes, definitely impatient. Fiona knew this because he released her but leaned into her, resting a hand on the edge of the sink, he tore the other through his hair.

"Tell me." Her voice was getting sharper, colder. "Tell me why you want me here. I want to know."

"Elle—"

"*Why?*" Bella's voice was a lash and her body had grown solid.

Prentice stared at her, his impatience vanishing, understanding dawning.

Fiona knew they were in trouble.

Prentice was *not* a man prone to flowery words. In fact, the words she'd heard him say about her the night before on the balcony (they still made her ghostly belly melt) were the most flowery she'd ever had from him.

No, Prentice was more a man who spoke through actions.

This wasn't a time for action; it was a time for words and Fiona doubted that Prentice could give Bella what she obviously needed.

Fiona was wrong.

His face gentled, his hand came to rest on her jaw and he answered her question in that soft voice filled with love.

"Your pancakes, your cookies, your smile."

Uh-oh.

Even said in his beautiful, soft voice, Fiona didn't think that was a great start.

Bella, staring up at him with fear and doubt barely masked behind the coldness in her eyes, didn't either.

Prentice wasn't done.

"The way you care for my home, the way you care for my family."

Fiona decided this wasn't going too well. No woman wanted a man to want her because she was a good housekeeper and babysitter and made good pancakes.

"The way you are with Sally, enjoying every second of her, never making her feel silly or getting impatient with her liveliness."

All right, that was a *wee* bit better. Fiona watched Bella's face shift slightly, still guarded but Prentice had struck a chord.

"The way you are with Jason, how you handle him with such care. Showing him that Fiona's guitar, something she loved, wasn't an instrument of mourning, which she'd hate, but an instrument to celebrate her and keep her memory alive."

Bella started to shake her head but his hand at her jaw tightened.

"The way you make me laugh when you forget to be what your father wanted you to be and you're just you."

Her head jerked.

"Prentice—" Bella broke in.

Prentice wasn't done.

His face dipped closer to hers. "The way you respond to me, no inhibitions, so quick, so wild, my kiss, my touch, my tongue," his voice dropped deep, "my cock. I love kissing you, baby, touching you, fucking you. And I love knowing you love it too."

Fiona could have done without hearing *that* but she saw he was getting to Bella because her eyes had grown glazed.

"Pren," she whispered.

"The way you give of yourself, every second, to *everyone* without knowing you're doing it or expecting that first thing in return. You're the most generous person I've ever met in my life." He got even closer, his arm sliding around her waist, his hand at her jaw gliding into her hair. "And I want you in my life until I'm no longer breathing."

Bella was struggling with this, Fiona could see it. She wanted to believe but she couldn't.

Or she wouldn't.

"I—" Bella started to protest.

Prentice cut her off. "And I want you in my children's lives."

Bella bit her lip which had begun to tremble.

Suddenly she said something bizarre.

"I think you're confused."

Prentice's brows drew together, indicating to Fiona he thought what she said was bizarre as well.

"Confused how?"

"With who I am and who you *think* I am."

"What?"

His voice was no longer soft and loving. Prentice wasn't happy he'd laid it out for her and, apparently, it had no effect.

Fiona didn't think this was a good sign.

"You think I'm that girl you met twenty years ago," Bella explained. "I'm *not* that girl. I never was. And you're confused."

"So, who are you?" Prentice asked, his voice now edging towards impatience.

Bella heard it and decided not to respond.

Fiona watched as his hand fisted in her hair. "You're telling me that all this is *a game*?"

Bella's body jerked yet again and her face went pale.

"A game?" she whispered.

"Aye, a game," Prentice clipped. "You're saying you dropped everything in order to come to Sally . . . that was a game."

"No!" Bella replied sharply.

"The laundry, the ironing, making the beds, hoovering the floors, baking the cookies, that wasn't you? That was what your father said you were doing? That was you playing house?"

It was a low blow and Bella flinched like she'd been physically struck.

Fiona wished she could kick Prentice.

Where was he *going* with this?

"Of course not," Bella whispered.

Prentice was relentless. "It wasn't *you* that played darts with Annie, Dougal and me? It wasn't *you* who asked Gordon over for hamburgers?"

Bella shook her head.

Prentice kept after her.

"It isn't *you* who's teaching Jace how to play guitar? It isn't you who stares into my eyes like you do, like you're lost in what you see and you don't want to be found. And it isn't *you* who wraps your hand around my cock like you never want to let it go and moans in my mouth when my tongue slides into yours?"

Okay, Fiona thought, *overshare.*

Bella's face was confused and her reply was hesitant, "Yes, um . . . well, that all *is* me but—"

"So, tell me, Elle, if that's all you then how the fuck am *I* confused?"

Bella didn't have an answer for that, evidently, because she didn't speak.

She just stared at him.

He let her go but didn't move away. His hands slid down her forearms and caught her wrists. Bringing them up between them, his thumbs slid into her fists, pushing back her fingers. Then he stroked her palms.

Bella closed her eyes.

Prentice spoke and his tone was now gentle. "I'm not confused, baby, *you* are."

Bella opened her eyes.

"I'm not that girl you knew," she whispered.

God, Fiona thought, *Bella's stubborn.*

"You are," Prentice, Fiona knew, could be stubborn too.

"I'm not."

"Baby, you *are*, then and now. But, now, with time and maturity, you're even *better*."

Her eyes filled with tears and Fiona worried her lip. She watched as Bella curled open her fingers and lifted her hands, showing him her palms.

"*This* is me, Prentice," she said, her voice harsh. "*This* is who I am. *This* is who you'd have in your house. *This* is who I've always been, weak, trapped, useless. I *saved* you when I left you years ago. Don't you understand? That girl didn't exist, *you* made her. She was only alive for *you*. *This*," she jerked her hands still in his wrists, "is who I am."

"You can't believe that."

"I *know* it."

They stared at each other.

Fiona hovered anxiously.

Then Prentice broke through.

His eyes went soft and he lifted one of her hands to his mouth. Touching her palm to his lips, Bella (and Fiona) watched him kiss the scars tenderly. He repeated this gesture with her other hand.

He dropped it and placed it against his stomach, holding her hand flat over it with his.

"Then it's good you're with me so she can be alive again because I'm in love with her. I always have been," he whispered. "And it's good you're with me so *I* can feel alive again." He pressed her hand into his gut and his face moved closer. "Nothing," he stated, "I felt nothing here." He pressed her hand into his gut again. "Nothing, since Fiona died. And I didn't think I *could* feel again after I lost Fee. Now it feels warm. Even when you first returned, you made it that way, when I saw you smile, when you made the children laugh, anytime I caught sight of your sweet, sexy ass—"

Bella wasn't ready to give in, the daft cow (now Fiona wanted to kick *her*), "Prentice, stop—"

Prentice, fortunately, wasn't ready to give in either.

"Life, for me, luckily has been a beautiful journey. It put me in this village. It brought me Fee who walked at my side and then Jason and

Sally who continue to share that journey with me." His voice dipped low and his hand took hers from his belly to press it against his heart when he finished, "But, baby, through that long journey, I've only ever been home twice. Once, twenty years ago and now I'm home again, with you. *You.* I know exactly who you are. I just have to introduce *you* to her."

Bella was staring at him, lips parted.

Prentice held her gaze.

Fiona hovered.

The tears welled up in Bella's eyes and slid silently down her cheeks.

Prentice tensed as he watched them fall.

Finally Bella spoke so softly, Fiona (even with super-ghostly senses) could barely hear her.

Even so, it hurt to listen to the hesitant but hopeful ache in her words.

"You're saying . . . I can be free?"

Prentice closed his eyes slowly but briefly.

Then he put both his hands on her jaw and tipped her face up to his, getting close, his body against hers. "Baby, with me, you can be whatever the fuck you want to be. But most especially, you can be free."

"I want to be free," she whispered and you could tell she wanted that, you could tell she'd wanted that *forever.*

"Then I'll help you to be free," Prentice whispered back.

She closed her eyes and fresh tears slid down her cheeks.

"You always did," she replied.

Prentice made a low noise, like a groan, and bent his forehead to hers.

Fiona didn't close her eyes but she felt her own ghostly tears falling.

Bella opened her eyes and Fiona waited.

Prentice broke the silence. "I can't promise you heaven, but I'll no' let anything harm you." He paused and smiled. "And Jason will no'."

"Jason likes me," she whispered, as if this was an impossibility.

"No, baby, Jason and Sally don't like you. They both fell in love the first time they laid eyes on you." He touched his lips to hers and finished, "Just like their dad."

More tears slid down her cheeks.

These were a different kind.

And when they did, Fiona knew immediately that Isabella Austin Evangahlala was gone for good.

Prentice's "Elle" had finally awoken and come back to life.

Therefore, Fiona smiled.

Bella threw her arms around his neck, shoving her face there, holding him tight.

Prentice's arms slid around her waist, bending and twisting his head so his lips were resting on her hair nearly at her nape, holding her back.

"Can I tell you something?" she whispered her question into his ear.

"Aye, Elle, anything," he replied.

She sucked in a breath and whispered, "There will be no bitterness. Ever. It took you a long time but it had to so you could give me everything I've ever wanted. And, Prentice, the only things in my whole, *entire* life I ever wanted were *you* . . ." She pulled back, he lifted his head, she pushed a finger in his chest and then pointed upstairs. "And them. Even though I didn't know it would be them, in the end it is."

His voice had grown hoarse with emotion when he started, "Elle—"

Her hands went to the sides of his head, her fingers gliding in his hair and she cut him off by saying, "If you want me then I'm here. And I hope we have fifty years but if we don't, if we have five weeks or five days, I'll never be bitter." She came up on her toes and put her mouth to his, finishing on a whisper, "I'll only be happy because finally, finally, *finally* I have everything I've ever wanted and you must know that it was *you* who gave it to me."

Prentice stared into her tear-stained face but he hesitated only for a moment before he slanted his handsome head and kissed her.

Fiona popped back to the stream.

She stared at her tent.

Then she giggled.

It took Prentice *a day*.

It took him *a day* to breathe life into Bella.

He was a genius!

Then again, Bella had been fiercely in love with him for twenty years so, really, it wasn't that much of a challenge.

Still.

Fiona wandered into the tent, picked up the guitar, sat on the chair, threw her legs over the arm and she played.

Chapter
SEVENTEEN

Fairy Godmother

Elle

Elle was nervous.

Therefore, when the door opened heralding Prentice's arrival home, she didn't give it a thought when she felt that special feeling that slid through her when he came home.

Instead, she jumped right before her body froze.

Sally jumped too.

Then she screamed, "Daddy!" and ran headlong toward Prentice as he made his way to the great room, throwing herself in his arms as if she hadn't seen him in one hundred years.

Prentice scooped his daughter up and held her in front of him but his eyes never left Elle.

"We all ready?" he asked.

At his words, Elle's heart skipped a beat.

No, it was safe to say she wasn't ready.

That morning, after Prentice woke Elle early and made love to her, he shared with her his fabulous idea that they would all go out to dinner that very evening. At dinner, he would make the announcement to the children that Elle was going to be a permanent fixture in their lives.

It should be noted that *Prentice* thought this was a fabulous idea.

Elle, on the other hand, thought it was a disastrous idea.

Prentice had kissed her protestations away, changing the subject by reminding her that the kids needed to get to school, but before that they needed breakfast.

Obviously, although Elle was terrified at the prospect of dinner that evening as Prentice described it, she had to focus on priorities.

Elle helped get the kids ready for school and made them breakfast. Not wasting any time, at breakfast, ignoring Elle's baleful glare, Prentice informed the children they were all going out for dinner that night.

This was met with loud hurrahs (Sally) and knowing smirks (Jason, but only before he stated, "I hope it's curry.").

Later, while she was standing by the door of her rental car in preparation to take the kids to school, Prentice gave her a hard, fast (but effective) kiss. After his kiss, and everything that had happened the last six weeks (especially the last two days), she'd been in such a daze. He'd already climbed into his Range Rover and Jason and Sally were both calling to her before she snapped out of it, got into her car and Prentice followed her down the long, winding drive.

She went directly from the school to Annie's. There, she banged on the door until her late-sleeping friend stumbled to it, hair mad, face like thunder.

Until she caught sight of Elle.

Immediately Annie's expression cleared and she bustled Elle into her and Dougal's cozy cottage. Elle made coffee while Annie got presentable.

Then they sat in the sitting room and Elle started to confide to Annie every second of every moment since she'd come back to the village for Annie's wedding.

She related about three sentences before Annie interrupted her, called Mikey in America (even though it was super early in the morning) and put him on speakerphone.

Both Annie and Mikey were crying by the time Elle was done.

"I'm so happy for you, girlie-girl," Mikey said over the phone, tears clogging his voice.

Annie was sitting next to Elle on the couch, holding Elle while sobbing (loudly).

Elle was happy too.

Or, she wanted to be.

She just didn't trust it.

When her friends got control, Elle told them, "Prentice wants to take the kids out to dinner tonight to announce we're together and I'm moving in."

"That's lovely," Annie replied, wiping her eyes on the hem of her T-shirt.

Elle looked at her friend. "It isn't, Annie. It's nuts. It's too early. They aren't used to me yet."

"Not used to you?" Mikey's voice sounded with disbelief. "Darling, they seemed pretty used to you when you were making them tuna casserola, as darling Sally called it, and you'd only been there, like, a day."

"It was two," Elle corrected.

"Whatever," Mikey muttered but Elle could hear the grin in his voice.

"Mikey's point is valid, Bella," Annie put in. "Kids are pretty adaptable and I'd say they've adapted to you extremely well. Especially since, you know, you're kind of *already* moved in and even a two-year-old with learning difficulties would sense you two are together."

This was true.

Heck, Jason even freaked out at the idea that Elle would stay somewhere else when she was in the village.

Nevertheless, Elle continued doggedly, "But I think Prentice should tell them at home, where they feel safe to have whatever reaction they want to have. And I shouldn't be there so, again, they'll feel safe to have whatever reaction they want to have."

"Precious, they're kids. Kids pretty much feel safe having whatever reaction they want to have *wherever* they are and *whoever* they're with," Mikey's voice came through the speakerphone.

This was true too. Sally, at least, didn't seem to filter her responses to anything no matter where she was.

"Then we shouldn't court an emotional scene at the new Indian restaurant," Elle declared.

"I hardly think you're going to have an emotional scene. Or, at least, not a bad one. Those kids love you," Annie put in.

This *appeared* true. Then again, Jason had always seemed totally okay with the idea of Prentice and Elle until he saw Elle in his mother's bed. Then he seemed unsure and uncomfortable.

Therefore, Elle didn't trust that the kids loved her either. Maybe they were getting there but she didn't want anything to derail that.

"I don't know—" Elle started.

"Well, I do. I've known those kids for over two years, Bella. They've been through the mill. Now, even Jason seems to have come to terms with what life has dished out and you've played a large part in that," Annie stated.

Elle shook her head. "He would eventually have come around. Prentice would have seen to it."

Annie shook her head right back. "Prentice had no clue." When Elle started to defend, Annie leaned closer. "He didn't, Bella. I'm sorry to say it but it's true. For over a year Jason showed no signs of healing . . . until you showed up that is."

This was, although it was difficult to admit, true too.

"Okay, then I've worn everything I've brought," Elle stated somewhat desperately. "I don't have an outfit to go out to the new Indian restaurant and tell two children that their mother has been replaced with a virtual stranger."

Mikey's laughter could be heard over the speakerphone.

Annie's could be heard in person.

"Virtual stranger," Mikey mumbled, still laughing. "That's funny."

"I know, she's a hoot, isn't she?" Annie asked Mikey, also still laughing.

Elle glared at Annie.

"I'm not being funny. I need a decent outfit," Elle snapped. "Everyone knows that you have to have a good outfit when you face some life trauma."

"This isn't a trauma, Bella, this is a celebration," Annie returned.

"Okay, you need a decent outfit for that too," Elle retorted.

"I hate to say it, Annie darling, but Bella is *so* right. She needs a decent outfit," Mikey threw out.

"Then we'll go shopping," Annie replied casually. "Yeesh, this isn't rocket science."

Elle didn't want to go shopping.

Elle wanted to look into buying islands so she could sweep Prentice, Jason and Sally away to one. Prentice could build them a house. Elle could home school Sally and Jason. And the world could stay at bay, no photographers, no Carver Austin, no nothing that would threaten their happiness.

"I know the *perfect* place!" Annie announced and Elle's body jolted. "It's in the next village. They have posh shops for tourists. Fabulous clothes. Gorgeous. We'll go there!"

Witnessing her friend's excitement and knowing how much Annie loved to shop, Elle's heart sank.

It stopped beating when Mikey declared, "When you and Prentice get married, Bella, there better be log throwing."

Elle stared at the phone with wide eyes and parted lips.

Then she whispered, "Married?"

"Yes, married. You can't live in sin forever even if it is with a broody-hot guy who, from the sounds of it, is very good at sin," Mikey noted.

Elle immediately regretted the depth of her sharing.

"Yes, you can, Mikey," Annie objected.

"No, you can't, Annie," Mikey retorted.

"Don't be so traditional," Annie replied. "It doesn't become you."

Elle wasn't listening to them.

She was thinking about Prentice and being married.

Having his ring on her finger (again). Belonging in his house. Belonging in his life. Belonging to his children.

Belonging to him.

For always.

She remembered the first time he'd asked and how happy she'd been.

No, not happy, ecstatic, thrilled, overjoyed, over the *moon*.

This time, older, wiser (both of them) and sensing the beauty of their lives, rather than youthfully expecting it, she wasn't over the moon.

She was . . .

There were no words to describe it.

"Married," she repeated, still whispering.

"Bella?" Annie called but Bella's eyes remained on the speakerphone.

"Mikey?" she called softly. "Do you think I'll have my fairytale?"

There was silence for a moment before Mikey replied, "Girlie-girl, of anyone I've ever known, except Annie who already got hers, you're *due*."

She *was* due.

Boy, was she due.

Elle grinned at Annie.

Annie grinned back.

"Hello! What's happening?" Mikey shouted.

Annie and Elle giggled and shortly after they let Mikey go back to sleep and they went shopping.

Prentice called while Elle was in the changing room of the posh clothing shop, about to step into the fourth dress she'd tried on but having a stack of sweaters, jeans and blouses that were in her "to buy" pile.

When she saw his name on the phone, she panicked.

How did she answer? "Hello, Prentice," or "Hey there," or "What's up, Pren?"

She went with, "Hi," and felt like an idiot.

Proof positive that it was too soon to tell the children she was moving in. She didn't even know how to answer the phone when Prentice called!

"Baby," he replied in his soft voice that did sweet, funny things to her system, and she immediately stopped feeling like an idiot.

Elle shook off those sweet, funny things and asked, "Is everything okay?"

"Aye. We've a booking for six. I'll be home at quarter to. Can you have the children ready?"

Instantly, Elle was unsure.

She knew what *her* ready meant but what did *his* ready mean?

What if she did something wrong?

"By ready, what do you mean?" she asked hesitantly.

"Out of their uniforms, in something presentable and not at each other's throats."

Elle sighed in relief. She could probably do that.

Depending, of course, on Sally's mood.

"Yes, I can have them ready," Elle replied.

His voice went back to soft when he murmured, "Thanks, baby." Then he asked, "What are you doing?"

She looked at herself in the changing room mirror and froze.

He was going to think she was a pampered, spoiled rich girl, loads of cash in the bank, no job, nothing to do but shop.

She should be at his house, mopping the floors, making homemade bread, handwashing delicates, inventing wholesome family recipes, not out gallivanting with her best friend and spending hundreds of pounds.

She began hyperventilating.

"Elle, are you there?" he asked.

"Yes," she wheezed.

"Are you okay?"

No, she was not.

Elle forced herself to sound (somewhat) normal, "Yes."

"You sounded strange."

"I'm fine."

There was a pause and then he asked again, "What are you doing?"

Elle wondered if honesty was the best policy.

Apparently, she wondered too long.

For when Prentice's voice came at her, he sounded borderline unhappy, "Elle, are you with Annie?"

"Um . . . yes?" she asked as if he could confirm that she was indeed with Annie.

"What are you doing?"

"Um . . ." she muttered but didn't answer.

"Elle." His voice held a warning.

"We're shopping," she blurted then closed her eyes tight.

"For what?" he pressed.

Elle opened her eyes and explained on a rush, "Clothes. See, I didn't think I'd be staying this long, definitely not *staying* staying, as in, *moving* here. I've run out of clothes. I'm recycling outfits. I need clothes."

She held her breath waiting for his answer which came at her in a voice filled with relief.

"Thank God."

Elle blinked before she inquired, "Thank God?"

"Aye, baby," he replied softly. "Thank God you and Annie aren't perusing a litter of border collie puppies for Sally. Or buying her princess dresses. Or arranging five-star accommodation for your trip to London to take Sally to Harrods. Or something equally mad."

In all that had happened, Elle forgot about the trip to Harrods.

Therefore she breathed, "Oh," and went on stupidly, "I'll have to look into that. Can I use your computer in the study?"

He was chuckling when he replied, "It's your house now, Elle, you can use anything you want. But don't you think we should take you back to Chicago to get you packed up before you take Sally to Harrods?"

Elle blinked again before saying, "Chicago?"

"Aye, it's half-term next week. I reckon we all can go."

Elle felt her heart contract. Chicago meant Carver Austin. Elle couldn't imagine her father's fury when he saw her in photos with Prentice and the children.

No, that wasn't right, she could. She could *easily* imagine it and it wouldn't be pretty.

It would be worse if he saw them in Chicago, worse because he could get to them swiftly.

And he would.

And Elle didn't want her father anywhere near them.

She quickly offered, "I'll pay someone to deal with it."

There was silence before Prentice asked, "You want to pay someone to do it?"

Oh no.

She'd sounded like a pampered, spoiled rich girl!

"Um . . ." she muttered.

Prentice's voice was low when he said, "He'll no' harm you, Elle."

That thing that had relaxed deep inside her but coiled up tight during their conversation, relaxed again when Prentice read her mind and made his vow.

"Pren."

"I hope he finds out we're there."

Elle saw her own eyes get wide in the mirror. "You do?"

"The *only* good part of those fucking photographers is that there are so many of them, he can't escape the way it is between you and me. I want that bastard's nose rubbed in it. I want him to see you happy. And I want him to know I made you that way."

That thing relaxed further.

But not completely.

"But Pren, what if he confronts you or me and the children are there?"

"Then you and I'll have a deal. The children are present, you take them away and I'll handle Carver."

"He's not easy to handle," Elle warned.

Prentice's voice was gentle when he replied, "No' for you, baby. For me, it won't be a problem. Fuck, I'm looking forward to it."

That didn't sound good.

"Pren—" Elle started.

"Trust me, Elle."

"But—"

"Trust me."

She took in a breath and nodded to herself in the mirror. "Okay."

"I'll take care of you, Elle."

That thing relaxed further and she whispered again, "Okay."

But he wasn't done. "That time in your life is over. *Over.* It ended last night. You may burn your hand and Jace may lose a football match and Sally may get the flu and other shit might happen, but it'll be ours and we'll handle it. You're no' taking shit from anyone, no' ever again. I'll see to that."

After his promise that thing inside her was so relaxed Elle had to lean against the mirror to keep standing.

"Pren—" she started but she didn't know what she was going to say.

She didn't have the opportunity to say it, Prentice interrupted her, "I've got to go."

"All right," Elle whispered.

"I'll see you quarter to."

"Okay."

"Love you, baby," he murmured.

Her breath hitched on his words, words she adored, words she hadn't heard in a long time, words that settled warmly deep inside her delaying her reply, but he didn't give her that opportunity either, he rang off.

Two seconds later, Annie threw back the curtain to her changing room.

Elle threw her arms over her body which was clad only in underwear.

Annie ignored Elle's state of dishabille and demanded to know, "Are you going to become one of those sickly ooey, gooey, lovestruck heroines from a fairytale? Because if you are, Dougal and I are going on vacation until you snap out of it."

Elle stared at her friend then hissed, "Annie, close the curtain!"

Annie looked to her left then to her right then to Elle. "There's no one out here."

"I don't care, close the curtain."

"Bella, sickly? Ooey? Gooey? Hello?" Annie replied.

Elle took a step forward, pulled Annie into the changing room with her and snapped the curtain shut.

That done, she faced off with her friend. "If I remember when you finally got through to Dougal, you were sickly, ooey, gooey, lovestruck *and* enthusiastically detailed."

Annie grinned. "It wasn't me who described my first time doing it with Dougal *against a wall.*"

Elle just *knew* she'd shared too much.

"That's because you did it in the front seat of his truck, *twenty years ago,*" Elle retorted.

Annie's face grew dreamy. "Oh yeah. That was nice."

Elle rolled her eyes and informed her friend, "Pren and I were just talking on the phone."

Annie's dreamy expression faded and a happy one took its place. "I know. I listened." She came forward and framed Elle's face with her hands before she whispered, "Isn't it fun?"

"What?" Elle whispered back, entranced by her friend's carefree, happy face, something she saw a lot lately but she hadn't seen for many a year and she wasn't quite used to it.

"To talk to them on the phone," Annie answered.

Elle closed her eyes.

Yes, it was fun.

It wasn't being whisked away on a jet only to be put in a limousine and taken to a yacht to cruise the Mediterranean in order to eat a cordon bleu dinner (something Laurent had done).

It was just normal stuff like Pren coming home after work, Pren eating sponge in the kitchen after a long day, Pren tickling her in bed while she tickled Sally and Jason grinned on.

And it was the *best*.

When Elle opened her eyes, they sparkled with tears.

She didn't have to answer, Annie knew.

In the end, Elle didn't buy a dress as she was in the wilds of Scotland and wearing a dress to the local Indian restaurant was probably not the thing.

She bought a pair of tailored, tweed trousers with a wide, cuffed hem and a ribbed, blond, slim-fitting turtleneck (not to mention, she bought a bunch of other stuff). She paired these with black, spike-heeled sandal pumps with a notch opened at the toe and a thin, saucy ankle strap. She'd got the kids ready and then did her hair and makeup while Sally sat on the bathroom's long counter, watched and babbled.

Now Prentice was home, asking if she was ready.

Which she was *not*.

"Can I talk to you a second?" she blurted.

"We don't want to be late for the booking," Prentice replied, his eyes guarded.

"A second," Elle repeated and didn't wait for his response. She turned and walked straight to the study.

She was staring at the drinks cabinet wondering if she should belt back some whisky when Prentice arrived and closed the doors behind him.

He didn't delay in approaching her and before she knew it, he had her in his arms and his head was descending.

Elle jerked hers back, exclaiming, "No!" When Prentice froze, Elle went on, "No kissing. We need to talk, not kiss."

He grinned and asked, "Why no'?"

She couldn't exactly tell him he was such a good kisser, anytime he did it, she lost track of pretty much everything.

Heck, just standing in his arms, his warmth beating into her, their bodies brushing was running interference with her thoughts.

"We just . . . can't," she answered lamely.

His eyes grew warm (or, more accurately, *warmer*). "All right, baby, what did you want to say?"

She didn't waste any time and launched right in, "I think you should tell the kids here, at the house, where it's safe and I think that I shouldn't—"

She didn't finish, he agreed instantly, "All right."

She stared at him in shock. She didn't think he'd agree!

Her mind was telling her there was more to say, like the fact that he should do it without her present, but Prentice also instantly let her go, turned and, taking her hand, strode from the room, dragging her behind them.

"Pren—" she started but it was too late.

They were in the great room, Prentice had wrapped an arm strong around her waist and he glued her to his side.

Without further ado, he announced, "Jace, Sally. Elle and I have something to say."

"Pren—" Elle began again but it was Jason who interrupted her this time.

"Is Elle staying?" Jason asked and Elle looked at him.

He was studying his father, and Elle peered closer not sure she believed her eyes but she could swear he looked *hopeful*.

"Aye, Jace," Prentice answered.

"For good?" Jason asked.

"Aye," Prentice replied.

Elle watched in fascination as Jason's ten-year-old boy's body visibly relaxed and those beautiful eyes, his father's eyes, warmed with something Elle couldn't decipher, but was striking nonetheless (in a good way) and they came to her.

She had no time to process this.

"Hurrah!" Sally shouted and ran to them, throwing her arms around both Prentice and Elle's legs but even attached to them, she was jumping up and down.

Elle thought that outside of Prentice's kisses, his lovemaking, waking up in his arms (even when he was grumpy), seeing his devilish grin, watching him come home and talking to him on the phone, Sally's hugs were the best thing she'd ever experienced in her life.

But she'd been wrong.

Sally hugging *both* her and Prentice while jumping up and down excitedly at the thought that Elle was moving in while Jason gazed at her with that look in his eyes was the best thing she'd ever experienced in her life.

And it was so much the best thing, the feeling overwhelmed her and she burst into tears.

She was moved fully into Prentice's arms. She wrapped her own around him and held on while shoving her face in his neck.

She heard Sally ask worriedly, "Why is Elle crying?"

Sally's worry made Elle cry harder.

"She's happy, baby," Prentice answered, his hand running soothingly up and down Elle's back.

"Happy?" Sally asked, now sounding confused.

"More like mental," Jason muttered, sounding amused.

At Jason's mutter, Elle giggled through her sobs.

"Is Elle laughing too?" Sally asked, now sounding *really* confused.

"Yes, baby," Prentice answered, sounding like his son.

"Girls," Jason mumbled, "totally mental."

Elle's tears subsided but her laughter didn't and she held on to

Prentice but twisted her neck to look at the children.

She wished she was the kind of person who knew how to say the right thing, something strong, something momentous, something that would mark this occasion in a happy way for them all forever.

But Elle wasn't that kind of person.

So she just smiled.

Jason smiled back.

Sally rushed forward again and hugged Elle's legs.

The little girl tipped her head back and asked, "Can you make a chocolate cake so we can celebrate?"

"No, lass, we're going to dinner to celebrate," Prentice replied as he shifted Elle to his side.

Jason was now smirking. "Elle might want to do something with her face."

Elle's hands flew to her cheeks, exclaiming in feminine horror, "My mascara!"

Prentice tipped his head down to look at her and Elle saw he was grinning.

"Just wipe it all off, baby, we're going to be late," he ordered.

"I'll do a touch up. It won't take a second," Elle replied, swiping at her cheeks, hoping she wasn't making it worse.

"Just wipe it off," Prentice repeated.

"It won't take a second," Elle repeated too.

"Elle—" Prentice started.

"Pren, it won't take a second."

"Can I come?" Sally asked excitedly.

Elle extricated herself from Prentice's arm and caught Sally's hand, answering, "Of course, sweetheart."

They walked to the stairs as Prentice called, "Do it in a hurry."

Elle looked down from her ascent of the stairs and repeated, yet again, "Pren, it won't take a second."

As she and Sally turned out of sight, she heard Jason say, "I don't get it. She looks prettier without all that gunk."

Elle slowed their gait so she could hear Prentice reply, "I know, mate."

"So why?" Jason asked.

"She's a woman," Prentice sighed.

"Seriously," Jason said, "totally mental."

Elle giggled as she entered her rooms, Sally's hand in hers, and she led Sally to the bathroom so she could do a touch up.

———————— ◆ ————————

DINNER RAN LONG, mainly because Prentice felt the need (and acted on that need) to tell everyone they encountered that Elle was moving, permanently, to the village.

And at this news, everyone they encountered behaved like it was Christmas *and* their birthday all rolled into one, and they all decided to sit down and chat for a while and some of them sat down and chatted for a *long* while.

By the time they got home, it was well past Sally's bedtime and the little girl was drooping. Elle didn't even take off her shoes before she saw to getting Sally to bed.

Sally was so tired she didn't want to be read a book. After Elle got her to brush her teeth and change into her nightgown, Sally just curled up with a somehow equally exhausted Blackie in her arms (though, Elle figured Blackie's exhaustion had something to do with the decimated toilet roll in Jason and Sally's bathroom) and snuggled into her pillows while Elle tucked her in.

"Elle?" Sally whispered after Elle turned out the bedside lamp, leaving only the glow of the nightlight.

Elle sat down on the bed and pulled Sally's heavy hair away from her neck, answering, "Yes, honey."

"Will you teach me to make chocolate cake?" Sally asked.

Elle's breath caught in her throat.

There were women who wanted to own seven hundred dollar shoes.

And there were women who wanted to run nations.

At that moment, there was nothing more that Elle wanted in the world than to teach Sally how to make chocolate cake.

Somehow, Elle managed to reply, "Sure, Sally."

"And how to walk in high heels?" Sally went on.

Her throat threatening to close, Elle forced out, "Of course."

"Hurrah," Sally cheered sleepily.

Elle leaned down and kissed the girl's temple before she got up and made her way to the door, thinking that Cinderella and Sleeping Beauty got it wrong. They should have bypassed the handsome prince and went direct to the broody-hot architect who designed the castle and also happened to have two beautiful children.

"Elle?" Sally called when Elle hit the door to her bedroom.

Elle turned to face the room. "Yes, Sally."

"Thank you for making Jace happy again," Sally whispered, and Elle felt her breath escape in a rush as her heart stopped beating.

She didn't answer, couldn't, she could only hold on to the door-frame and hope she didn't pass out.

"And Daddy too," Sally went on quietly.

Elle's heart squeezed.

Maybe Sally Cameron didn't slide through life shielded by her indefatigable good cheer.

Maybe Sally Cameron felt just as deeply as her father and her brother but, in her six-year-old's way, she did what she could to take care of her family.

Summoning a strength she didn't know she had, Elle pushed away from the door, walked to Sally's bed and again sat on its side, sliding her fingers through Sally's hair.

"You don't have to thank me, sweetie," Elle whispered.

"Yes, I do," Sally whispered back.

Elle leaned forward and got close to Sally's ear. "No you don't, Sally, because we're even. I was sad when I came here. So very sad. But you and Jason and your daddy made me happy too."

"I'm glad," Sally replied softly.

"So, I should thank you," Elle told her.

Sally twisted her neck, Elle's head came up and Sally grinned at her before saying, "You're welcome."

Elle stifled a giggle and grinned back.

"Now, go to sleep," Elle ordered.

"Okay, Elly Belly," Sally said cheekily through her grin.

With a light kiss on Sally's smooth cheek, Elle left the girl and wandered to Prentice's rooms in a daze, Sally's words and what they meant tumbling through her mind. She didn't know it but she entered the bedroom with a small smile playing at her lips.

Prentice was taking off his shirt but his hands stilled when his eyes came to her.

"Sally's in bed," Elle announced. Not noticing Prentice's posture, she walked to the bed, sat on the side and pulled up her pant leg to get to her shoe. "Jason too?" she asked.

"Aye," Prentice answered, and Elle's head came up in surprise for he was closer than she expected him to be.

In fact, he was standing, now shirtless, right in front of her.

Her hands still on the strap of her shoe, Prentice got closer.

"Is something—?" Elle started.

"Don't take off your shoes."

Elle blinked and sat up straight. "What?"

Prentice didn't answer. His hands went under her armpits and he lifted her to her feet. He turned so his back was to the bed, she was facing him and, before she knew what he was about, he'd swept the turtleneck clean off her body.

She watched him throw it across the room before her eyes came back to him and she began, "Pren—"

But she didn't say more because her trousers were sliding over her hips.

Her hands went to his wrists but he ignored them, grasped her at the waist, lifted her free of the trousers that had pooled at her feet and he kicked them aside.

Then she stared, dumbfounded, as he sat on the side of the bed and, hands at her hips, pulled her between his opened legs.

She was trying to come to terms with standing, wearing nothing but her bra, panties and saucy shoes in front of a seated Prentice, his hands sliding to her waist then back and down, to cup her bottom, his eyes roaming her body, a body that seemed to heat under his gaze.

"Got a call from Dougal today," he announced bizarrely before he leaned forward and ran his tongue along the top edge of her panties.

"Yes?" she breathed, forgetting her near nudity and Prentice's strange announcement as her mind focused with pinpoint accuracy on what his tongue was doing.

"Aye," Prentice said softly against the skin of her belly. One of his hands stayed cupped at her behind, the other one slid forward, the tips of his fingers trailing the lower edge of her panties, around and in and her breath caught as Prentice went on, "He asked me for pointers."

"Pointers?" Elle parroted, losing concentration on what he was saying as her mind preferred to focus on the heat that was building *everywhere*.

"Aye, Elle," Prentice whispered against her then he rubbed the stubble of his chin on her skin, his head tilted back to look at her. "He wanted pointers on how to fuck Annie against a wall."

Elle's body froze but her eyes went wide and her stomach plummeted.

"Oh my God," she breathed.

"Apparently Annie told him, because you told her *and* Mikey, that I had a particular talent in that area."

"Oh my God," Elle breathed again.

Visions of Prentice throwing her out of his beautiful home because she had *such* a big mouth filled her head but visions of Prentice's devilish grin filled her eyes as his strong hands suddenly yanked her forward so she was straddling his lap.

His arms went around her, one tight at her waist, the other hand sliding up and fisting in her hair.

Elle put both hands to his neck and tried to remember how to breathe.

When she accomplished this feat, she whispered, "I'm sorry. So, so sorry. I got carried away and—"

"I'm no' sorry," Prentice cut in, his grin still wicked. "Dougal said I'm practically a legend."

His heart-stopping grin finally penetrated her panicked mind and her eyes narrowed.

"A legend?" she asked dubiously.

His hand in her hair maneuvered her mouth to his. "Aye, *practically* a legend."

"Pren—" Elle started but he kissed her quiet.

Later, much later, when he stopped kissing her because she couldn't bear it any longer but his hand was in her panties, his finger was in *her* and Elle was rocking against it and breathing heavily into his mouth, Prentice finished.

"Let's see if we can take away the practically part."

Elle nodded dazedly, thinking, equally dazedly, that he'd already managed that. Then she sucked in breath when his thumb found her, put on delicious pressure and swirled.

"Come for me so I can watch, baby," he growled his order against her mouth.

Her hips ground into his hand, her fingers clutched his shoulders and Elle did as she was told.

------ • ------

Prentice

EVEN LATER (*MUCH* later), Prentice slid out of Elle's silken wetness.

Then he gave himself a moment to gaze down at her in his bed, her head to the side, her cheek to the pillow, her hair spread against it, her breath heavy, eyes closed, fingers still clenching the pillowcase.

He was kneeling between her legs, her sweet ass was in the air and, as his hand drifted over one smooth, curved cheek, he looked beside him.

She was still wearing those sexy, black, spike heels.

Jesus, he couldn't believe it but the fucking sight of her ass, her shapely leg and her foot still wearing that sexy shoe made his still hard cock jerk almost ready again.

His hands guiding her gently, he shifted her to her side then, one by one, he unbuckled and took off her shoes, kissing her ankles as he did so, tossing the shoes aside, after which he joined her in bed.

Yanking the covers from under their bodies to over them, he pulled her in his arms.

She snuggled close.

He dipped his chin, and into her hair, he murmured, "You're a legend too."

Her head came up and she looked into his eyes.

"I am?" she asked with what appeared to be genuine shock.

Even though he didn't want the thoughts to intrude, not now, not after just having her, making her come twice and holding her in his arms, Prentice couldn't help but feel the jealous anger, knowing, if it wasn't for her fucking father and his own ego, he could have been her only lover.

Instead, she'd clearly had plenty of experience.

His voice was gruff when he replied, "You are."

Her eyes drifted away as did her thoughts before she settled into him again and whispered sleepily, "That's funny."

His hand stroked her hair when he asked, "What?"

"What what?" Her voice was quieter. She was sliding into dreamland.

"What's funny?" Prentice pressed, his hand halting its stroking, his arms going around her to give her a gentle squeeze to stop her from falling asleep.

"That you think I'm a legend." She nestled closer. "Laurent thought I was frigid. I didn't enjoy sex with him." Her voice dropped lower when she finished, "*At all.*"

Prentice's arms squeezed again, this time reflexively.

This made him inexplicably glad.

In fact, it fucking thrilled him.

Laurent Evangelista, renowned international playboy, apparently was shit in bed.

He'd have to be if Elle, who was the most responsive woman Prentice had ever had, didn't respond to him.

That only meant one thing.

And Prentice knew he shouldn't ask.

He knew it.

But he asked.

"And your other lovers?"

"My other lovers?" She, again, sounded drowsy.

"Did they think you were legend?"

She laughed and it too sounded sleepy.

"What's funny?" Prentice inquired.

She cuddled closer, her arm sliding along his stomach to curl around his waist and she settled in, her weight getting heavy as she said, right before she fell asleep, her words stunning him solid, "There weren't any. Just Laurent. And now . . . you."

Prentice's eyes stared unseeing at the ceiling.

He understood it was selfish, hearing this additional evidence of Elle's loneliness, but he couldn't deny what registered deep in his soul.

And he knew exactly what it was because he'd felt it many times before.

He felt it when he first met Elle.

He felt it when they were reunited after their first separation, when he saw her adorable, nervous stutter step while she was approaching him in Fergus's driveway the second summer she came to Scotland.

He felt it again, only moments later, when she was in his arms and she said to him with such deep feeling, "Not as much as I missed you."

He felt it when she agreed to marry him.

He felt it when he watched Fiona walk toward him down the aisle.

He felt it both times Fee told him she was pregnant and after both times she safely delivered a healthy child.

He felt it when he moved his family into the house he'd designed and built for them.

He felt it when he read the ridiculous goodbye note Elle left after the first night they shared together, a note that included a PS that there was coffee made and Danish at the ready.

He felt it when Sally woke up from her coma and recognized him instantly.

He felt it when Elle forgave him for his betrayal.

And he felt it now.

And that feeling was blessed.

Careful not to disturb her, Prentice rolled and turned off the light.

And, within seconds of pulling Elle close, Prentice joined her in a deep, dreamless, peaceful, sated, blessed sleep.

———— ◦ ————

Fiona

FIONA WOKE UP in her tent wondering when she'd get to go wherever she was going.

Her work was done.

And she was pretty damned satisfied with it if she did say so herself.

Therefore, she was kind of surprised she went back to her tent.

This couldn't be it.

If Fiona existed, both her Nans and her Granda' were somewhere out there and Fiona couldn't imagine why she'd be kept from them. She couldn't imagine eternity was alone.

Then again, it could be that horrible black place, so she probably shouldn't complain.

She wandered out of her tent and stopped dead.

A man stood at the stream. He was wearing a white suit. He had thick white hair, a white goatee and a white string tie.

He looked like a thinner, younger Colonel Sanders of chicken fame, except his string tie wasn't black and he wasn't wearing glasses.

"Are you God?" she whispered, thinking it was kind of funny that God looked like Colonel Sanders.

Then again, the Colonel's chicken was nothing to sneeze at, it couldn't be described as divine but it certainly tasted good.

The man smiled and shook his head.

"An angel?" she breathed as he walked to her.

"I'm not an angel, Fiona. I'm a messenger."

"An angelic messenger?" Fiona asked.

"Um . . ." he hesitated, "something like that."

"Are you here to take me to heaven?" she inquired, certain she knew the answer, certain that he was definitely there to take her to heaven but suddenly uncertain she wanted to go.

She hadn't had a chance to say goodbye to Sally and Jason.

Or Prentice.

Or, even, Bella.

"No, Fiona, your work is not yet done."

Fiona stared at him not getting a good feeling about this.

Then she asked, "My work?"

He nodded.

"What work?" Fiona went on.

"Before you . . ." he paused a moment then continued, "move on, you have to commit one selfless act."

There it was.

She got it.

And she just *knew* it.

She had to give up Prentice and her family to Bella before she could *move on.*

"Tick that one off, Messenger Man," Fiona stated proudly, straightening her shoulders. "Last night—"

"You don't think it would be that easy," Messenger Man interrupted her and Fiona was back to staring.

Easy?

He thought that was *easy*?

That wasn't easy!

It was, at first, frustrating. Then annoying. Then heartbreaking (okay, so all of the time it was heartbreaking).

And a lot of other things besides.

What it wasn't was easy.

"I don't get it," Fiona told him and she went statue still when his hand came up and rested on her arm.

She stared at his hand.

No one had touched her in fifteen months.

She didn't know this man but his touch felt good.

She swallowed and looked back at him.

"There isn't much time and there isn't much I can say. You're learning your way but you have to be faster, Fiona. If you don't, they'll win," he told her.

"Who'll win what?" Fiona inquired, confused.

"*They'll* win . . ." he hesitated again before he said, "*you.*"

Instantly, she understood.

And it frightened the life out of her (figuratively, of course).

"The black," she whispered and he nodded sadly.

"We can hold it at bay for only so long," he explained.

"I don't want to go there again," Fiona told him in a horror filled voice.

"And you don't belong there but you have to succeed and you have to do it soon."

"But, Bella—"

"Has experienced a lifetime of pain," he interrupted her. "One night of understanding is not going to erase that, Fiona."

What he said made sense.

And it was also irritating.

"I've been doing everything I can," Fiona informed him. "And it hasn't been easy."

"It isn't supposed to be."

"Well, then, you gave me a good task because it's not," Fiona shot back.

"There are dangers," he warned, his voice was dire and Fiona felt her stomach twist.

"Dangers?" she whispered.

"To Isabella. There are dangers lurking," he replied.

Oh no.

"What dangers?" Fiona asked. "Her father?"

He shook his head, clearly not going to answer.

Fiona's irritation grew. "You have to help especially if Bella's in danger! I wouldn't know what to do!"

"Use your magic," he advised.

Fiona, again, stared. What was he on about?

"Magic?"

"Yes, your magic." When she continued to stare, he explained, sounding impatient, "You *are* her fairy godmother."

Fiona broke her stare to blink.

Then she asked, "Fairy godmother?"

His brows drew together. "You didn't know?"

"No," she snapped. "I didn't know. I'm Prentice's wife. Sally and Jason's mother. I thought I was a ghost. A fairy godmother is fat and jolly and has a magic wand and didn't used to be *in love with* and *married to* the heroine's handsome hero, for goodness sake!"

Messenger Man got closer and squeezed her arm. "There are those, not many, who slide straight to black. There are those, not many, who lived lives so filled with good deeds, they move directly on. But all the rest, Fiona, are put to one final test. *Especially* if they've lived lives, no matter how short, filled with bounty. You," he squeezed her arm again, "had a life cut short but it was a life filled with bounty. You have to share your bounty before you move on. It might be difficult, my dear, but it is the way, the only way, for you to move on."

Fiona sucked in the breath she did, indeed, breathe in this strange world.

"It's hard," she admitted quietly. "And it hurts."

"Selfless acts normally do," he replied, dropped his hand and, even though what he was saying was upsetting (and also kind of pissed her off), she missed his touch when it was gone. "But you want them to be happy, all of them, I know you do."

Fiona nodded. "I do."

"Then find your magic, Fiona, and do your deed so you can go home."

"How do I find my magic?" she asked.

He shook his head but answered, "I misspoke, you don't have to *find* it, you have to *recognize* it."

She blinked and said, "What?"

But she asked nothing and no one.

Because he was gone.

Disappeared.

Vanished.

She stared at where his white-suited body used to be.

Then she looked to the blue sky with its fluffy white clouds and she shouted, "This moving on business better be worth it!"

She received no reply.

Chapter
EIGHTEEN

Carver

Prentice

The doorbell buzzed to Elle's apartment and Prentice woke instantly.

This was unusual, Prentice was a deep sleeper.

But from the moment they arrived in Chicago, he'd been waiting for this.

And he was looking forward to it.

Therefore he rolled into Elle who had woken too and looked into her shadowed face.

"Don't move," he ordered.

"But—" she whispered, her voice sleepy but full of fear, and Prentice felt his temper flare.

And he was glad for it.

He wanted to be angry. He did not intend to keep a very tight hold on his control. If it snapped, he'd welcome it.

"Don't move," Prentice repeated.

"The children," she said.

"It'll be okay."

"I don't—"

His mouth found hers and he kissed her quiet before murmuring, "Elle, baby, trust me."

He heard her pull in a soft breath and watched her shadowed head nod.

He threw the bedclothes aside and the bell buzzed again.

Jesus, the bastard was impatient.

Prentice wanted to make him wait. However Carver could wake the children, both also deep sleepers like their father, and Prentice courted this if he delayed.

So he didn't delay.

He also didn't put on a shirt but walked to the front door only in a pair of pajama bottoms.

He did this on purpose.

He wanted Carver Austin to be confronted with Prentice and Elle's intimacy. He wanted that man's imagination to run wild. He wanted him to know that he'd pulled Prentice from Elle's arms, from her bed. He wanted him to wonder what they might be doing there.

It didn't say much about him but he didn't care.

After what that man did to Elle and took from the both of them, Prentice wanted Carver Austin to be tortured by every conceivable way Prentice could make Elle happy.

Prentice weaved his way around the many obstacles to the front door.

They'd been in Chicago three days and there were boxes everywhere. They spent the mornings packing or, Elle, Prentice and Jason did. Sally spent it mostly digging through stuff, showing treasures she found to Elle and asking, "What's this?" and alternately chattering. They spent the afternoons seeing the city.

Sightseeing was strange, not unpleasant but not as pleasant as it could be and this was mainly because people recognized them everywhere they went. They gawked, they whispered behind their hands and more than once they lifted their phones and took photos.

Sally seemed not to notice a thing.

Jason found it funny and once made a face at one of their impromptu photographers.

Prentice found it startlingly easy to ignore.

It would be easier to ignore if it didn't make Elle visibly anxious.

All of this partly had to do with Elle already being famous, partly the photographers who'd already sold their pictures, but mostly it had to do with fucking Hattie Fennick.

Hattie Fennick had sold Prentice and Elle's story to a rag and it was printed the day before Prentice, Elle and the kids flew to Chicago.

Hattie had fortunately painted Prentice and Elle as star-crossed lovers, torn apart by a wicked, evil man and thrown back together by fate.

Knowing Hattie, who could be vicious but who wasn't stupid, Prentice reckoned this wasn't the picture she'd *wanted* to paint but the only one she could if she didn't want to be stoned by the villagers.

At his office where Dougal had arrived unexpectedly to show him the spread in the magazine, Prentice had been surprised to see two photos of Elle and Prentice taken twenty years ago mingled with the others.

Which meant Hattie had also given them photos, photos Prentice didn't know she had, intimate photos of Elle and Prentice that made Prentice feel unsettled that Hattie had at all.

One was at a party at the beach. He remembered that night though he couldn't recall Hattie being there. The night was, as always with Elle, a good night. The photo was obviously shot without Prentice or Elle knowing it was being taken. They were standing by the bonfire, her arms were around his neck, his hands were resting at her waist. She was pressed against him, gazing lovingly up at his face. They were both smiling.

The other was on the pavement in the village. He remembered that day as a good one too but again couldn't imagine why on earth Hattie had a photo of it.

The photo was also shot without Prentice or Elle knowing it was being taken. Elle had been horsing around and had jumped on his back. She had her thighs tight to his hips, her arms were around his chest. He had his arms behind him, his hands on her ass. She was leaning into his back and his neck was twisted to look at her as she peered around his shoulder. They were both laughing.

Seeing the photos he realized with disbelief that he'd forgotten exactly how beautiful Elle used to be when she was younger.

He thought he'd remembered but he had not.

Also seeing them he was stunned at how much more beautiful she had become. Especially now, when she slept deep and peacefully every night and had gained back some weight.

He would have thought that was an impossibility but it was not.

Those photos were mingled with others he hadn't seen but he knew they likely existed, these taken recently. One, shot the day Sally left the hospital, showed Prentice lifting his daughter to put her in the Rover. Elle was close to them, Jason close to Elle. There was also a photo of Elle and Sally standing on the pavement talking animatedly to Denise and Gordon. Another was at Jason's football match showing Elle standing in the curve of Prentice's arm, her head tilted back, her face smiling as they spoke to each other. Sally was gazing into the distance but her arms were wrapped around Prentice's leg.

And finally, there was another photo of Prentice and Elle that Prentice wasn't aware it was being taken, shot only days before the article ran. They were alone at the beach, Debs had taken the kids for the day.

The final photo was almost an exact replica of the first one, except it was day rather than night and there was no bonfire. They were in each other's arms, looking in each other's eyes and they were smiling.

The magazine the article ran in (and the article got it *mostly* right, though it dramatized some of it and made Carver seem even *more* of a monster than he already was which was quite a feat) was popular and had a huge circulation.

The bad news about this article was that there was a possibility that Jason and Sally could see it or hear friends talking about it. They didn't know Elle and Prentice had a history and Prentice didn't want them to know, not now. He would find a way to tell them later, when things were settled, when Elle was settled, which she gave too many indications that she was currently *not*.

The good news about the article was the possibility that Carver had seen it.

But even if he hadn't, it was now obvious Carver *had* seen the photo of Elle holding Sally's hand, her other arm around Prentice's waist, Prentice holding her close with his arm around her shoulders and Jason walking in front of them but looking back. All of them were laughing as they came out of a restaurant the first night they were in Chicago.

A photo that was printed that day in a Chicago newspaper.

A photo with the caption, Reunited lovers Isabella Austin and Prentice Cameron, out on the town with Cameron's children.

Prentice would have paid them to print it.

Prentice would have paid them double for dropping Laurent Evangelista's name from Elle's.

Luckily, he didn't have to do either.

He turned on the light in the foyer and pressed the button for the speaker on the security panel by the front door.

"Yes?" he asked and listened to the static that seemed satisfyingly heavy.

Finally, Carver Austin demanded to know, "Is my daughter there?"

Prentice grinned before saying, "Carver, it's late. If you want to see Elle while she's in town, call her. We'll meet you for lunch."

"Let me up," Carver commanded.

"No. It's late. Elle's sleeping."

"Cameron, I'll stand here all night pressing this infernal button, damn it, let me up."

"Suit yourself," Prentice replied casually and hit the button to buzz him up.

He looked back into the apartment filled now with boxes.

Although Elle's apartment was large, roomy and had an amazing view of Chicago, it was pristinely clean and decorated in a beautiful but cold way that was vaguely unwelcoming. It was as if it was a show apartment, meant to be viewed not to be lived in.

Upon entering it, he'd felt a not vague at all sense of alarm at the thought of his Elle inhabiting this impersonal space until he'd seen Elle nervously surveying her own home likely looking at it through

Prentice's eyes.

So he'd kissed her, open-mouthed and long, even in front of the children.

"All right," Jason said, cutting their long kiss shorter than Prentice meant it to be, "I said you could snog but I'm thinking I didn't mean it."

Sally giggled.

So did Elle.

And her nervousness, something that Prentice noted was always at the surface, sometimes minutely, sometimes acutely, slid away.

At least, Prentice thought, he hadn't seen her clench her fists, not since the night she burned her hand.

That, he hoped, was something.

There was a knock on the door and Prentice opened it.

At the sight of Prentice, Carver's face paled before it flushed with anger.

Prentice watched Carver's jaw tense as he pushed in asking, "Where's Isabella?"

He closed the door behind Carver but Prentice didn't guide them out of the foyer. "As I said, she's sleeping. Is there something you'd like me to tell her?"

Carver started to move to the hall. "I'll speak to her directly."

Prentice was stunned that this man thought he could stride into Elle's home in the middle of the night, wake her up and have an unpleasant chat.

Hell, he was stunned Carver seemed to think it was his due that he'd woken Prentice and treated him like an unwelcome butler so he could have his fucking chat with his daughter.

However, he didn't allow either reaction to delay him from curling his fingers around Carver's upper arm, stopping his advancement.

Carver's eyes went to Prentice's hand and then to Prentice's face. "Take your hand off me."

Prentice didn't do as he asked. "You'll no' be waking her. If you have something to say, say it to me. Then leave."

"I said, take your hand off me," Carver repeated.

"As it's the middle of the night, my guess is you have something on your mind. Share it so I can get back to Elle."

"I will repeat," Carver said softly, angrily, "take your hand off me. I'll talk to Isabella myself."

Carver yanked at his arm as his body leaned toward the hall but Prentice's fingers flexed and he got close to the older man.

"And I'll repeat, you're no' waking her. You have two choices, you leave your message for Elle with me or I eject you from this apartment physically."

"You wouldn't dare," Carver straightened and hissed back.

Prentice didn't reply.

Carver read his non-answer correctly and threatened, "If you man-handle me, I'll call the police."

"I hope you do. I'm sure the gossip magazines will enjoy relating this latest story in all its glory."

Prentice was pleased to see Carver go pale again.

Yes, he'd seen the article that painted him as a monster.

Prentice felt like laughing.

He didn't.

Carver jerked his arm out of Prentice's hand and he stalked to the living room. He'd turned on a lamp before Prentice arrived and was surveying the chaos of boxes and filled rubbish bags which was far more welcoming, even given its sense of departure, than the room was normally.

Carver's eyes cut to him and then dropped to his chest before he ordered, "For God's sake, put on a shirt."

"I'll just have to take it off in five minutes so I'll no' waste my time," Prentice returned. "Say your piece and then go."

Carver glared at him, anger etched in every line of his expression.

Prentice held his glare, finding himself completely at ease as he studied Elle's father.

He was old and, if not frail, he was no longer strong. His power was gone, what he emanated was false, conjured, believed in only by him.

He was a joke.

Carver didn't think so. Prentice knew this when his eyes lit with something vile.

And he didn't hesitate with spilling his malevolence into the room.

"A million dollars," he said.

"Pardon?" Prentice asked, taken off-guard by his bizarre words.

"No, make that three," Carver amended. "One for you and one for each of your children."

Prentice realized what he was saying and he didn't feel at ease anymore.

The anger had returned.

"Get out," Prentice said between clenched teeth.

"All right. Six," Carver responded instantly. "I'll give you six million dollars and you'll leave Isabella and never see her again."

Prentice could not fucking *believe* this bloke.

"Get out," he repeated.

"Twelve," Carver countered.

Prentice leaned in at the waist and clipped, "Out."

Carver crossed his arms on his chest and said condescendingly, "Cameron, let me do the math for you. That's four million for you, four for your son, four for your daughter. Invest it wisely and those children will live a very happy life."

"They already live a very happy life without four million dollars," Prentice retorted.

Carver grinned. "All right, son, then it'll be *happier*."

No, Prentice could not *fucking* believe this *fucking* bloke.

"As happy as the life Elle has lived with her millions?" Prentice asked.

He scored his point, he saw it and it fucking *thrilled* him.

Carver recovered quickly and stated, "Isabella's not well. She never has been, just like her mother."

It was safe to say Prentice was no longer angry.

He was enraged.

However, letting anger loose was one thing.

Fury quite another.

Therefore, against his wishes but for Elle, he controlled it.

Only barely.

"Elle's not well?" Prentice asked in a deceptively calm voice.

"Mentally," Carver confirmed with a nod of his head. "You should know that, considering she's spending time with your children."

"You're telling me Elle is mentally ill," Prentice stated.

"Yes, son, just like her mother. If you haven't noticed it, I'm sorry to be the one to inform you."

"Oh, I've noticed," Prentice replied and Carver's eyes widened slightly before he hid his response.

"Then you should protect your children. She's—"

Prentice cut him off. "I've noticed, regardless of her beauty and intelligence, she lacks confidence. I've noticed that despite her friendly manner and innate kindness which instills loyalty in those around her, she doesn't trust others' reactions to her. I've noticed she has dreadful nightmares that frighten her senseless even though she long since should have moved on from them. I've noticed she was unhappy, nearly pathologically so, because she'd lived under the thumb of an unfeeling bastard who cowed and humiliated her regularly, and when he wasn't doing that he was abusing her physically. Like her mother." When Carver's face got red, Prentice finished, "So, I don't know for certain but I reckon what you say is correct, she's just like her mother."

"Are you implying—?"

Prentice leaned in again and interrupted harshly, "No, Carver, I'm no' implying fuck all. I'm saying it straight out, you sadistic, condescending bastard."

Carver leaned in as well. "How *dare* you?"

"I dare pretty fucking easily now that I know what you did to her, what you did to the mother she loved. Your reign of terror is over, old man. You're done. Now get, the fuck, out."

Carver's eyes went to the door. "I'll be speaking to Isabella."

"No, you bloody well won't," Prentice shot back.

"Yes, he will," Elle said from behind Prentice and he turned.

Elle was standing in the doorframe wearing a dove-gray satin dressing gown over a matching satin nightie edged in intricate black lace that was visible at her chest through the drape of the dressing gown. Her hair was loose and tousled and her face was makeup free.

She looked glorious although her face was pale and her eyes were stunned and resting on him.

"How do you know about my mother?" she asked quietly.

Bloody, fucking hell.

"Elle, baby, let me handle this," he coaxed. "Go back to bed."

"How did you know?"

Christ.

"Elle—"

"Was it Annie?" she inquired, and Prentice felt his jaw grow tight. Elle saw it, her eyes widened as she somehow immediately jumped to the right conclusion and she whispered, "You read my journals."

"Elle—"

She threw her hand out. "That's what all of this is." She looked away and he saw her lips tremble before she said softly, "I knew it."

"Elle," Prentice walked toward her, stopping close and putting a hand to her neck, "we'll talk in a minute. Go back to bed."

Her eyes came to his and they were shining with unshed tears. "You read my journals and feel sorry for me."

Prentice glared at her.

Better to do that then turn to Carver Austin and strangle him in front of his daughter. She might not like her father but Prentice figured she'd frown on that.

"No," she went on before Prentice could form a reply, "you feel *guilty* and you feel sorry for me."

"Don't be daft," Prentice said softly.

"I'm not being daft!" she all of a sudden snapped.

Prentice was surprised at her quick, sharp defense.

Then he was pleased.

Because this wasn't Isabella who meekly gave in. The woman standing in front of him with tousled hair, wearing silk was *his* Elle who *never* gave in.

She'd handed him his opening so he went with it.

"You are Elle, what you're saying is absurd."

"It is *not*."

"Right, so, instead of wanting you in my life, in my home, in my *children's* lives because you're fucking gorgeous, you bake exquisite chocolate cake for my daughter, you make my son laugh and you get wet the minute I fucking kiss you is *not* why we're together, it's because I read your journals and I feel sorry for you. Is that what you're saying?"

"Yes!" she flashed.

"And that's not absurd?" he returned.

"You don't know your own mind," she retorted. "You're blinded by guilt."

Prentice burst out laughing.

Through his laughter, he saw her scowling at him and she snapped, "This isn't funny!"

His hand at her neck pulled her to his body as he talked through his dying laughter, "It's hilarious, baby."

"It. Is. *Not*."

He dipped his head and nuzzled her ear with his nose before he said there, "It is."

"You're impossible," she clipped.

"I'm in love with you," he replied and lifted his head when he felt her body grow still and he saw her eyes had gone soft and the tears had disappeared. "No' because I'm blinded by guilt which is ludicrous. I knew I loved you *before* I read your journals. I'm in love with you because I just am."

"Excuse me," Carver bit out from behind them and Prentice turned.

He did so while sliding his arm around Elle's shoulders and pulling her close to his side, saying, "Fuck, I forgot you were here."

"I'll ask you to mind your mouth when you're around me and my daughter."

Prentice grinned. "Elle likes it when I talk dirty." He looked down at her and asked softly, "Don't you, baby?"

Elle's eyes rounded in horror then they grew warm and she looked like she was trying hard not to laugh.

Yes, he hadn't lost her. Standing at his side was *his* Elle.

Prentice nearly laughed.

Again, he did not.

"Isabella—" Carver started, but Elle's humor faded and her eyes turned to her father.

"I thought we'd said what we had to say."

"We did but that was *before* you decided *again* to throw away your life on *this man*," Carver replied.

"Finally, something *I'd* like to talk about," Prentice announced, and he felt Elle's body twitch at his side while Carver's angry eyes slid to him. "Twenty years ago, for no reason other than to be an asshole, you took away the woman I loved. I'll expect an apology before you leave."

"I . . . you—" Carver spluttered.

"And one for Elle too," Prentice went on.

"I can't . . ." Carver started then finished on a hiss, "You must be joking."

"Don't feel like apologizing?" Prentice asked then concluded, "That's fine, then. You can just leave."

"Isabella—" Carver started yet again but it was Elle who cut him off.

"Prentice asked you to leave, Dad."

"You can't tell me—" Carver began.

Prentice looked down at Elle and interrupted him by asking her, "Does he have keys?"

"I changed the locks after our last conversation and asked security to change the code for the front door," she replied.

Prentice smiled and gave her shoulder a squeeze. "Excellent."

Carver butted into their discussion, "Cameron, I'll remind you about my offer. I'm willing to negotiate."

Prentice looked to the man. "You're saying you're willing to pay me *more* than twelve million dollars to get out of Elle's life?"

He knew Elle had heard that part because she showed no reaction to his words.

"Yes," Carver bit out.

"How much more?" Prentice asked, Elle went tight at his side and he gave her shoulder another squeeze.

"Name it," Carver snapped.

"All right, Carver, since this doesn't seem to be sinking in, I'll explain it to you. I love your daughter. I've loved her for decades. My children love her. We're happy, finally, fucking happy. You don't have enough money to make me walk away from that. There *isn't* enough money to make me walk away from that."

"You're only saying that because Elle has more than four times that amount in her trust," Carver shot back.

At his words, it was Prentice's body that went tight.

Then he looked down at Elle and asked, his voice sounding stunned because he fucking well *was*. "You have over forty-eight million dollars?"

She licked her lips, the nerves acute and visible and she nodded. "At my last meeting with my accountants, it was around fifty-three."

Prentice couldn't wrap his mind around fifty-three million dollars.

Carver cut into this endeavor and declared, "I'll give you fifty-four."

Elle sucked in breath.

Prentice's surprised eyes sliced to the man and he muttered the first thing that came to his mind.

"You're mad."

"Fifty-four million dollars, you'll have it tomorrow. No strings," Carver confirmed. "We'll find a way around red tape, taxes, everything. You'll have it mid-morning. Tomorrow afternoon, you walk away."

"Mad," Prentice repeated.

"I'm not mad, I'm deadly serious," Carver returned.

"You're mad," Prentice stated again.

"I have it and Isabella knows it," Carver's eyes moved to his daughter. "Don't you?" he demanded, and when she didn't answer he leaned forward. "Look at her, Cameron. She knows it and she knows you're going to take it."

"Definitely mad," Prentice muttered yet again.

"Stop saying that!" Carver snapped.

"Carver, if you think I'm going to take that money, you are *definitely* mad."

Elle's body jolted violently at his side but Prentice ignored it and ignored Carver's mouth dropping open. He didn't, however, ignore just how fucking satisfied witnessing the bastard's angry astonishment made him feel.

"Now, I'll say it one last time before we call the police. It's late. We've got less than a week to pack Elle's things before we go home. We need to get back to bed. Please leave."

Carver's eyes shot daggers at him. Prentice simply returned his furious stare.

Carver broke contact and his gaze took in his daughter, top to toe, before he returned it to Prentice.

"You'll regret it," Carver warned in a low voice.

"That's doubtful," Prentice returned.

"I regretted it, marrying her mother," Carver went on, Elle gasped and Prentice pulled her more tightly against his side.

"The feeling, Carver, was obviously, and sadly, mutual," Prentice replied softly and then, his voice firm, his intent unmistakable, he finished, "Now, we're done."

The bastard gave them both a scathing look before he stalked, back ramrod straight, out of the room.

Prentice followed him and locked the door behind him.

When he turned, Elle was standing in the foyer.

"You just turned down fifty-four million dollars," she whispered, her eyes wide, and when she finished speaking, her lips stayed parted.

"Aye," Prentice agreed, moved forward the two steps that separated them, kissed her forehead then walked around her to the living room.

He switched out the light and when he turned to the door, Elle was standing in its frame.

"You should know," she said quietly, "I can't get to that trust unless it's to make an investment that's agreed by a small board made up of executives at my mother's family's bank or if it's an emergency. I live off the interest."

He walked to her, sliding an arm around her waist and leading her into the foyer so he could switch off the light.

"When you sell this apartment, the money will go back into the trust?" Prentice asked.

"Yes."

"And if you don't use the interest, it reverts to the trust?" Prentice went on.

Having turned off the light, he was guiding her through the boxes. "Yes."

"Then you better start looking into charities you want to patronize, baby. I don't think you'll have a lot of use for your millions in the wilds of Scotland," Prentice advised.

He heard her pull in a soft breath but she didn't respond.

He stopped her by the bed and found the tie on her robe.

"Where's Evangelista's money?" he asked softly, yanking on the tie before he lifted his hands and slid the robe from her shoulders.

"I used all of it to build and endow two orphanages, one in Vietnam and the other in Ethiopia," she whispered.

His hands had stilled in the act of closing around her waist to pull her with him into bed.

His voice was gruff when he stated, "I don't think I heard about that."

"You wouldn't," she said softly. "No one knows but Dad. I did it anonymously."

Christ, but he loved her.

One arm slid around her waist, the other hand went to her neck and he fell back to the bed, taking her with him.

Her weight landed on him and he rolled instantly, covering her soft body with his.

"I'm no' sure what you expect, Elle," he said against her neck. "But we should get something straight."

Her hands were gliding around to his back but her touch was tentative.

"What?" she asked, her tone just as tentative.

His head came up, he looked at her in the dark and answered, "When I told you I would take care of you, that's what I meant." His hand drifted up to her jaw, his thumb moving across her cheekbone and his voice went soft when he continued, "You live in my house. I pay for the food that goes in your belly. I buy your drinks at the pub. I fill your car with petrol. I put clothes on your back—"

"Pren—" she whispered.

"I'm no' telling you what to do," he informed her. "You want to work, make your own money, contribute something to the household, do it. You don't want to work and you want something, it's your money, get it. You want to do something special for the kids, though, we talk about it first. I don't want them spoiled." His hand tensed on her jaw and he asked, "Are we agreed?"

"What if I want to do something special for you?" she whispered, her arms were wrapped around him now and they weren't tentative, they were holding on tight.

His mouth found hers in the dark and he kissed her softly before his lips glided to her jaw then to her ear.

"In about five minutes, baby, you're going to do something special for me," he murmured there.

"What's that?" she breathed, her hands had started roaming whisper-soft against the skin of his back and he felt his cock start to grow hard at her touch.

He didn't answer her question.

Instead, he slid his lips and his tongue down her neck and along her collarbone.

At the base of her throat, he stated, "Outside of you baking your oatmeal cookies every once in a while, anything special I want from you will have the same theme."

Her fingers slid into his hair, her other hand moved around his waist, across his stomach and down.

When she pressed her hand into his pajamas and wrapped her fingers tight around his cock, his mouth found hers and he muttered, "You guessed it."

"You're impossible," she whispered as she stroked.

He didn't answer, he was too busy growling into her mouth.

Her thumb found the tip, circled, and it felt so fucking good Prentice bucked his hips into her hand.

Her soft words took his mind off her hand when she said, "You took care of me."

As good as her hand felt, he wanted to stop and hold her. He wanted to do whatever it took to assure her.

But he decided not to make a big deal about it and hope she got the point.

"Aye," he replied, his lips moving against hers. "Always, Elle."

She stroked again, his mouth took hers in a kiss, his tongue sliding inside, tasting her then dueling with hers as she started to move agitatedly under him, his kiss, as usual, getting her excited, her hand automatically stroking faster.

Her mouth broke from his and her head lifted, her tongue sliding down his neck.

"You know that, don't you, baby?" he asked at her ear when her lips hit his shoulder.

"I didn't," she answered against his skin. Pushing him back, she rolled into his side, her hand never ceasing its beautiful work, her head coming up and he felt her eyes on his face before she finished quietly, "I do now."

His arms crushed around her, holding her tight.

"Can we stop talking now?" she whispered in his ear as her hand kept at its sweet torture. "I want you in my mouth. I can't talk when you're in my mouth and I wouldn't be able to concentrate if you were talking."

He tried to hold back laughter but this effort shook his entire body.

Her head came back up and he felt her eyes on his face again.

He also felt their heat.

"Are you laughing?" she asked, her voice sounding irate, her hand ceasing its stroking but holding on tight.

"Aye, baby, I'm laughing. What I'm *no'* going to be doing is *talking.*"

It wasn't in his catalogue of things he wanted to do with Elle (or, in this instance, what he wanted Elle to do to him), and he could only describe it as "interesting" when her mouth took him inside while she was giggling.

But he also wasn't complaining.

————— ◆ —————

Elle

"PREN?" ELLE CALLED quietly.

They'd made love and he was holding her, her back to his front, their legs tangled, their fingers laced and lying on the pillow in front of her.

"Aye, baby," Prentice answered, his words stirring her hair.

"Why did you read my journals?"

His fingers tightened in hers a moment before they relaxed and he sighed.

"I needed to find a way to get through," he replied.

"Those thoughts are private," she whispered. "Or they were."

She didn't know what to feel about him invading her privacy. It didn't feel good, it didn't exactly feel bad. She wasn't angry, considering the fact that he'd just turned down fifty-four million dollars to be with her, but she was something.

"Aye, they are," he agreed. "But you were keeping yourself from me and I didn't understand why. I can't say I'm proud of doing it but I can say I would do it again." He pressed closer and went on, "I'd have done anything, Elle, to make you mine again."

Okay, now it *definitely* didn't feel bad.

Still.

"Did you read them all?" she asked.

"Parts of them, yes," he answered honestly.

She closed her eyes and his fingers tightened in hers again.

"You wore my ring," he murmured, his voice suddenly hoarse.

Her stomach clutched and her heart skipped.

"Pren—"

His voice was still thick when he continued, "Twenty years and you kept it with you."

Elle was silent, partly because she didn't know what to say, vaguely embarrassed that he knew she'd pined for him for twenty years. And partly because she was holding her breath and wasn't physically able to speak.

Prentice didn't have the same problem.

"I can't say I'm proud of the way I treated you when you came back. What I can say is that I wouldn't have behaved that way if you didn't mean anything to me."

Elle had to admit this made sense.

And even though it felt good, really good, to know she still meant something to him, especially as she'd held him so close to her heart all those years, it didn't help her breathing in any way.

Prentice kept on sharing. "I tried to forget you, Elle, but I never did. I told myself I'd moved on but I didn't."

She felt the tears sting her eyes, the wetness sliding out the sides.

He shifted their laced fingers so they were tight against her chest and she felt his face burrow in her hair.

"I still have your things," he confessed, she felt herself go still and her eyes go dry.

"My things?" she whispered.

"Everything you ever gave me, every gift, every letter. Fee never knew I kept them. I didn't want her to know. I felt guilty that I kept it from her but I couldn't let them go." He pulled in breath again and sighed into her hair before continuing, "I didn't understand at the time, didn't let myself think of it. But now I realize it's because her knowing would hurt her and I didn't want to do that. But also, they were mine. I didn't want to let them go and I didn't want to share with anyone, even Fee, that I couldn't." When Elle laid still and silent, Prentice finished, "They're in a box in Mum's loft."

After he finished, Elle breathed, "Oh my God."

He had, in his way, been pining for her too.

Prentice carried on, "Mum's asked me twice in the last twenty years when she was clearing the loft if she could get rid of them, but I wouldn't allow it."

"Oh my God," Elle repeated, comprehending how huge this admission was but not quite able to process it.

"She thought I was daft." The throatiness had gone from his voice and a touch of humor was there. "When we get back, we'll move that box home."

She felt her breath escalate at his words as his chin moved her hair from her neck and he kissed her there before going on, "I'm not upset you got rid of that ring, baby. I never liked it. I always thought you deserved something more, and even the day I gave it to you I intended to replace it with something better."

Oh . . .

Wow.

"Pren—"

"I *am* upset about the reason why."

"Pren—"

"And I'm sorry for that reason. More sorry than I can say that I said those things to you."

Her voice was aching when she tried again to get through, "Pren—"

He continued to resist her efforts and asked, "Did you wear it when you were with Evangelista?"

She swallowed, worried about what her answer would say about her and then, considering Prentice was being so *very* honest, she felt she had no choice but to nod.

Prentice's voice sounded with disbelief when he asked, "Did he know what it was?"

Elle nodded again.

She felt Prentice's body start shaking with gentle laughter.

His voice sounded highly satisfied when he remarked, "I bet he loved that."

"We argued about it," Elle whispered, and Prentice's gentle laughter became not so gentle. "A lot," she added and Prentice's not so gentle laughter became vocal.

Elle let his hand go, rolled in the circle of his arm and she looked up at his shadowed face.

"Laurent used to tell me Dad should have let you have me, considering the fact I wasn't much of a wife."

Prentice's voice was still tinged with amusement but it was also firm when he replied, "I think the better way to put that, baby, is he wasn't much of a husband."

Elle remembered how hurtful Laurent's words had been back then, believing that he was right. She couldn't have children. She couldn't respond to Laurent in bed. She hated to travel with him even though she tried to enjoy it as much as he did.

Now that hurt slid away.

Because Laurent was wrong and Prentice was right.

She might not have been the greatest wife but then again, she'd never loved him.

But Laurent had, in the beginning, declared his undying love and devotion to her and he could have at least *tried* to make her feel the same back.

And if he did, indeed, care for her so deeply, he wouldn't have treated her so cruelly when he found out she couldn't conceive. He would have taken more care of her when she didn't respond in bed. And he wouldn't have forced her into the globe-trotting life she found so tedious.

And he wouldn't have cheated on her repeatedly nor would he have been so hideously obvious about it.

Elle found herself getting angry, thus she declared, "He was a toad."

Prentice's body shook with laughter at the same time that laughter rose huskily from his throat. "No, baby, he was a *fool*." She felt his hand glide down her back to cup her bottom and he continued, "He gave up this?" He gave her behind a squeeze and murmured, "Mad."

Without her mind commanding her body to do so, she nuzzled closer and she found her mouth saying teasingly, "I'm getting the impression, Prentice Cameron, that you like my behind."

"Aye," he growled and his fingers flexed again, "though I wouldn't put it that way."

"And what way would you put it?"

His hand not at her bottom drifted into her hair and he used it to pull her head back so his mouth could descend to hers.

"I don't like it, I love it," he muttered against her mouth. "You have the sweetest ass I've ever seen."

His words poured over her and they felt like warm, clean, fragrant water.

"Pren—"

"Especially when you're on your knees, your ass is in the air and my cock is inside you."

She felt her body heat and her legs started shifting restlessly as she repeated, "Pren—"

"And when it's snug in my crotch," he growled, "baby, the . . . *fucking* . . . best."

She snuggled closer and brushed her lips against his, her hands moving, somewhat urgently, along his skin as her leg lifted and hooked around his hip.

His hand slid between her legs, he touched her wetness and her hips jerked before they swayed into his palm.

"There it is," he muttered, his voice filled with masculine satisfaction, something else that sent heat through her system. "Proof you like it when I talk dirty."

"You're impossible," she retorted, hearing her voice filled with feminine satisfaction mingled with laughter.

"No," he whispered, his finger slid inside, she stopped laughing and gasped with pleasure against his mouth, "I'm greedy."

Then he kissed her, his tongue sliding in her mouth, his finger moving in tandem with his tongue.

And he kissed her until Elle's mind was in a fog and her hips rode his hand.

His mouth tore from hers and his lips slid to her ear as his finger stroked her. "I know I just had you, baby, but I want you again, this time, on your knees."

She didn't hesitate before saying, "Okay."

His finger pressed deep as his voice rumbled, "Christ, I fucking love you."

Elle wanted to respond but Prentice didn't give her the chance.

His mouth took hers in another kiss then he took her on her knees, and after, when he had her cuddled close to his warmth, she fell asleep before she remembered to tell him that she loved him too.

Chapter
NINETEEN

Spooked

Fiona

Fiona floated, her arse close to the stool next to Jason's, her ghostly eyes were pointed toward the kitchen.

She was avidly watching Prentice and Bella whilst Jason was avidly concentrating on what was on his breakfast plate and trying not to grin.

Sally was forking hash browns into her mouth, swinging her legs and humming to herself through a full mouth, completely oblivious.

Prentice had his hips to the counter, his jaw was tight and his hand was wrapped around a mug of hot coffee in a way that looked like his hand would rather be strangling someone.

The someone he'd rather be strangling was Bella, who was scrubbing a skillet like she wanted it to disappear under her ministrations.

They were having a tiff.

And it was hilarious as it always was and, lately, it had been happening *a lot*.

It had been over a month since they'd returned from Chicago. Fiona hadn't been able to go but something happened there, something that had to do with Bella's odious father and whatever that something was it flicked a switch on in Bella.

In the time after "The Kettle Incident" (as Fiona was calling it in her mind) and before they went to Chicago, Bella had been anxious. It was obvious and it was worrying not only because Fiona's eternity hinged on Bella's happiness but just because it was difficult to see Bella in that state.

Bella didn't trust that her life could turn on a dime and, after all she'd endured, why would she?

After they came back from Chicago, Bella was changed. She seemed slightly more settled, more assured but still she was somewhat uncertain, nervous and hesitant.

With Prentice's unwavering devotion (and it was indeed devotion, even if it was sometimes irritated devotion) and Sally and Jason's too, Fiona watched Bella's confidence grow then blossom and finally bloom.

But it bloomed out of control.

Bella of old was back with a vengeance.

And Fiona loved it.

Prentice, on the other hand, found it frustrating on occasion and on other occasions annoying and sometimes downright infuriating.

Fiona thought watching her family with Bella would be hard.

It wasn't.

Seeing them happy and whole again was a gift. It was a *weird* gift but after watching more than a year of Prentice struggling and Jason grieving, it was definitely a gift and a treasured one too.

Now Fiona just had to practice on her "magic," whatever the bloody hell that was, and after a month with Fiona intensely aware that time was sliding by, she had no more clue.

She also had no clue as to what danger threatened Bella. Her father, from what tidbits she heard Prentice and Bella murmuring about, was obviously out of the picture. And the entire family had become old news, there weren't even photographers around the village anymore.

Apparently Isabella Austin Evangelista shacking up with an

architect (an award-winning one at that) wasn't a hot news item worthy of continued exploration.

It was, the photographers found, mostly Bella looking fantastic as always but not stepping out on the town. Instead, she was going grocery shopping, picking the kids up at school, chatting with villagers on the pavements and the like.

Boring.

To them.

But Bella was clearly having the time of her life.

"Kids, books," Prentice ordered when he saw their plates clean.

Jason scurried off his stool, happy to get away from the heavy air in the kitchen so he could grin his father's wicked grin somewhere where he wouldn't be hit by the heat of Prentice's irritated gaze which had happened before.

Jason, like his mother, thought Prentice and Bella's fiery relationship was amusing. Likely because Fiona's son wasn't stupid and he sensed that there couldn't be anger without love. If you didn't care about someone, you wouldn't care enough to fight with them.

Fortunately for Jason, (unfortunately for Fiona but she was working through it), he didn't realize their volatility had a whole hell of a lot to do with passion too.

Which Prentice and Bella also obviously had, in abundance.

Sally didn't move so quickly.

"Elly Belly?" she called. "Can you give me a manicure after school?"

"I gave you one yesterday, sweetie," Bella answered, still scrubbing the skillet, which was, Fiona thought it important to note, thoroughly clean and had been for the last five minutes.

"Can you teach me guitar?" Sally went on.

"The guitar's too big for you still, Sally. Like I said before, give it a year or so and we'll start."

"Can we have your apple caramel-umble for pudding tonight?" Sally pressed. Apple caramel-umble was the name Sally had given the pudding Bella had made the week before. It was supposed to be a crumble but she'd been distracted by her boxes arriving and she was unpacking at the same time she was getting the Christmas decorations out therefore she accidentally doubled the brown sugar and the butter so it ended up a gooey, caramelized mess, which the children had adored.

"We had that last week, Sally, now go upstairs and get your books," Bella said as Prentice delivered the children's plates to the side of the sink.

"Daddy," Sally, finding her efforts with Bella unsatisfactory, switched targets. "Now that we're used to Blackie, can I have a puppy?"

Prentice leaned his hips against the counter next to the sink and leveled his eyes on his daughter. His method for dealing with his children was far more time-economical than Bella's.

"Books," he commanded firmly in a voice that didn't invite argument or discussion.

Sally was also not stupid, she knew that voice. She made a pouty face but slid off the stool and hurried up the stairs.

Prentice watched her progress, and the minute Sally disappeared, his head turned to Bella.

"Elle—"

"Save it!" she hissed under her breath.

Prentice looked to the ceiling.

Then he looked back at Bella and asked with impatient disbelief, "Honest to God?"

Bella went still as a statue, dropped the skillet, turned to him and put her soapy hands on her hips.

Her reply was also said with impatient disbelief, "Seriously?"

Fiona didn't know what they were arguing about.

She had, in the past month, *not* managed to recognize her "magic" but she *had* managed to figure out how to pop herself back and forth between her ghostly haunting of her old home and her serene tent by the stream. She usually went back there at night when she was exhausted from trying to make pixie dust fly from her fingertip or shouting soundless "abracadabras" and then throwing the force of her emotions at one of Prentice's whisky glasses on the balcony, trying to make it explode. She'd return in the morning to haunt her family, search for clues as to what danger plagued Bella and try to discover her magic.

Thus, this morning, she'd missed their fight.

Which, in a way, made their incomprehensible verbal tussle all the more amusing.

Prentice was losing patience, Fiona could tell this when he leaned toward Bella and his voice got lower and far more irritated.

"This is your home now, Elle."

"I'm aware of that, Pren."

"You need to make it yours," he demanded.

"It already is," she snapped.

"You need to put your mark on it."

She threw her hand out to indicate the abundant Christmas decorations that she, Prentice and the kids put out, most of which were old but some of which Bella had bought, not to mention some framed pictures of her, Annie and Mikey that she'd dotted around the place and replied, "I already have!"

He got even closer and said even lower, "You fucking well know what I mean."

She leaned closer too and returned, "Redecorating isn't putting my mark on a house, Prentice Cameron."

Fiona emitted a useless, ghostly gasp and floated back several feet.

Prentice wanted Bella to redecorate?

Fiona had spent months choosing furniture, spent years buying and even paying off paintings that she'd found, deliberated greatly over the frames she'd buy to put her family's photos in.

The blinds . . .

The crockery . . .

The . . . the . . .

The *nerve*!

Fiona tried not to take sides when they were fighting but she was firmly on Bella's side in this one.

Prentice dragged his fingers through his hair, indicating that his patience was spent before he muttered, "Fucking hell, Elle."

Elle grabbed the children's dishes and started to rinse them mumbling, "It never *ceases* to *piss me off* all the times you *say it* that *my name* rhymes with *fucking hell*."

Prentice ignored her rant and threatened which meant promised,

"If you don't do it, I will."

"Be my guest," she shot back.

He glared at her bent body as she slammed the children's plates and cutlery into the dishwasher.

Then he pulled in a deep breath, and when she straightened, kicking the door closed to the dishwasher and starting to walk away, he leaned forward and caught her at the waist.

Pulling her back to his front, she struggled for a minute before his mouth went to her ear.

"All right, Elle, I didn't want to say it but here it is. That bedroom is now yours and mine but it *was* Fiona's and mine." Fiona's spectral body grew still at the same time Bella's corporeal one did. "I thought I'd be okay with it, sleeping with you there, fucking you there, but as time goes by, I find I'm no'. So I need you to make it *ours* so I can fucking move past this. I'm asking you to help me with that. Now do you fucking *get me*?"

Fiona watched as Bella's face paled and then her body relaxed, her anger fled and she turned in the curve of his arm.

Her hands went up to curl on his neck, she leaned into him and asked softly, "Why didn't you tell me?"

"I just did," he clipped, still angry, probably because he had to share something difficult or, since he was a man, because he had to share *at all*.

"Yes, but before you said," her voice dipped low and she assumed a (very bad) Scottish accent to indicate she was mimicking Prentice, "'You need to redecorate this fucking room, Elle.'" She pressed closer and went back to her own voice. "You didn't tell me *why*."

"Now you know."

Her expression for the first time in weeks grew uncertain. "I'm not good at decorating."

"Ask Sally, I'm sure she'll be more than happy to give you some ideas," he bit out, obviously not noting her expression, and he was also not being humorous but flippant.

Bella decided (wisely) to ignore his flippancy and teased, "I'm not sure we want a room decorated in pink and purple with plentiful amounts of glued-on glitter."

"I don't give a fuck what it looks like, just as long as it's something that's ours."

Fiona glared at her husband as he obviously didn't feel like letting go his anger even though Bella had given in.

Prentice always could hold a mean grudge.

Bella was more patient with it than Fiona ever was and she leaned in further and whispered in his ear, "I'll see to it Pren."

She kissed his jaw and tried to move away but Prentice's arm tightened.

"What I said doesn't mean—" he started but Bella cut him off.

"I know."

"You know I love it when we—" he began again only for Bella to interrupt him again.

"I know."

Fiona started dematerializing as Bella kept whispering something about having to do something about Prentice being grumpy in the morning.

This was difficult for him, she knew, and he didn't need an additional witness, even her, who he didn't know was there.

Luckily, Bella knew it was difficult too and she was doing a fine job in making it easier.

Fiona stopped dematerializing when the doorbell rang. She fully materialized and watched both Prentice and Bella's heads swing to the door.

"I'll get it!" Sally shrieked from upstairs and Fiona's body turned to watch her daughter run headlong down the stairs.

No, strike that.

Fiona's body turned to watch with unadulterated fear as her daughter ran headlong down the stairs.

Fiona's lass had been knocked over by a car, she was fully healed now, the cast off and she seemed no worse for the wear. It would be an even bigger tragedy if, after surviving that, Sally broke her neck falling down the stairs.

"Sally, be careful," Bella called, unadulterated fear heavy in her tone, and Fiona let out her nonexistent breath (whilst Bella did the same audibly) when Sally made it to the bottom, turned on one foot, nearly toppling over, and dashed to the front door.

Bella and Prentice both made their way toward the great room but they didn't have to approach the door because the caller announced himself, and when he did this, he did it *loudly*.

"Mikey's home!"

"Hurrah!" Sally screeched, beside herself with glee. "Mister Mikey's here!"

Prentice turned his eyes to Bella.

Bella did the same to Prentice and shrieked, "This is brilliant! Mikey's great at decorating!"

Then she too ran forward, throwing her arms around Mikey while Sally jumped up and down and clapped.

Fiona's eyes moved to Prentice and she saw he was standing frozen, staring at Bella swinging around in Mikey's arms. He looked arrested in time, his eyes glued to the two friends, his face filled with awe as if he was watching a miracle occur.

At first, Fiona thought this was strange.

Then, slowly, her eyes slid to the friends and she too stared.

This scene couldn't be any more different than the one that happened in Fergus's entryway three months before.

Bella, in jeans and jumper, her feet bare, her face makeup free, her hair in a messy bunch on top of her head, her arms around her friend, her mouth laughing, her face aglow.

She was not detached, quiet, remote and cold, wearing a fancy suit, posh shoes with her hair all twisted in an elegant bun.

She looked not only like she belonged in a family home in the wilds of Scotland but like she was created to live this existence.

Bella pulled away from Mikey but kept her hands curled on his shoulders. He still had his hands at her waist and he too was looking down at his friend's face with wonder etched in his features.

"I can't believe you're here!" she cried. "What a tremendous surprise and *perfect* timing. Prentice wants me to redecorate the bedroom and I have *no clue*."

Mikey blinked and for a moment Fiona thought he might very well cry.

He pulled himself together just as he pulled Bella close again and drawled to Prentice, "Then I'm here in the nick of time, as usual. Decorating is *not* Bella's forte."

Prentice had moved forward and was offering his hand, now smiling warmly at Bella's friend while he greeted, "Mikey, good to see you, mate."

Mikey shook his hand and leaned back, proclaiming dramatically, "Good to see *you* too." He gazed down at Bella and asked, "Girlie-girl, what's in the water here? Because I want some of it. You look ten years younger and he's hotter than hot, and since he was hotter than hot before, he's off-the-scales hotter than hot now."

Bella snuggled into Mikey's body, wrapping her arms around his waist and resting her head on his shoulder as she looked at Prentice. At her cuddle, Mikey looked like Fiona reckoned anyone would look before they dropped dead of a heart attack. Then his face grew soft.

Bella didn't notice.

"I think he either made a deal with the devil or he's the bastard love child of Father Time," Bella remarked with a radiant grin thrown in for good measure.

Mikey burst out laughing but Fiona looked at Prentice and saw him gazing at Bella with that expression he got before Fiona was popped back to her tent by the stream.

"Mister Mikey!" Jason shouted as he also ran down the stairs.

"Jason, be careful on the stairs," Bella cautioned as she moved out of Mikey's embrace.

Jason ignored Bella, ran up to Mikey and then her son gave him a quick hug.

Jason stepped back and asked, "What are you doing here?"

"Surprise inspection," Mikey muttered, his eyes on Bella.

"What?" Jason asked, his voice filled with humor.

"Nothing, bucko," Mikey answered. "I just was sitting around, thinking, 'What am I going to do for Christmas?' and it came to me that Bella said the guest suite in your house was magnificent so I figured I just *had* to spend time there and, therefore, invite myself to Christmas with all of you. So here I am!"

Jason grinned and declared, "You're mental."

"Yes, indeed I am," Mikey replied, sounding proud of Jason's assessment.

"Oh my God! School!" Bella shouted. "Kids, car! Mikey, I'll be back in twenty minutes, tops."

"Elle, I'll take them this morning," Prentice offered.

"No, it's out of your way and you have that meeting. I'm good, Mikey's good." She was hustling the kids to the door then she suddenly changed directions, dashed forward, threw herself in Prentice's arms, pressed a quick kiss on his mouth and dashed back, going back to her babbling. "Mikey, coffee, toast, get your stuff settled in the guest suite, twenty minutes."

"Bye, Mister Mikey! Bye, bye, bye!" Sally jumped up and down as Bella hustled her forward at the same time shoving on a pair of shoes.

Jason waved behind him and they all hurried out the door.

The minute it closed, Mikey turned to Prentice.

"I'd give you a hug if I didn't think you'd punch me. Or I'd offer you a million dollars if I didn't know you'd turned down fifty-four or if I actually had a million dollars." His voice lowered and his eyes grew bright when he finished, "So, Prentice Cameron, the only thing I can do is say thank you."

Prentice tilted his chin up slightly and gave Mikey a moment to compose himself before he commented, "I'm guessing we passed inspection."

"You all get gold stars," Mikey replied and Prentice grinned.

Then Prentice's eyes went to the door and he asked, "Have you ever seen her like that?"

Mikey looked behind him toward the door and answered, "Yes, often, at school." He turned back around. "After she lost you, when she was vulnerable and he could beat her down, rarely."

Prentice's jaw grew tight.

"Prentice," Mikey said softly, "that was then, this is now. Let it go."

Prentice tilted his chin again but this time it was more of a jerk.

Mikey's voice was still gentle when he stated, "Annie tells me she's not self-harming anymore."

Prentice's eyes narrowed. "You knew about that?"

Mikey nodded. "Both Annie and I talked to her. She was seeing a doctor."

The color went out of Prentice's face. "She's not seeing a doctor now."

"She's also living thousands of miles away from her abusive father with whom she used to live in the same city and, regardless of her age, he was unrelenting in his attention. And she doesn't have photographers breathing down her neck because she's not attending all the soirees and high-brow events her detestable ex-husband and then her despicable father demanded she appear at, which by the way, she *loathed*. Instead, she's living in a beautiful house with the only man she's ever loved, helping him raise his children. So," Mikey threw out his hand absently, "I'm no psychologist, but I'm guessing she doesn't need a doctor anymore."

Prentice wasn't convinced. "Life has a way of twisting and turning."

"Yes," Mikey agreed. "It does. And usually one can go with the flow. But when one finds they can't, they need a strong, solid anchor." He nodded to Prentice. "You aren't made of iron but I think you'll do."

Prentice didn't reply then again, he didn't need to. He was Bella's anchor and they both knew it.

That was why Mikey smiled before he clapped and exclaimed, "All right! I need coffee and you need to get to a meeting."

"I'll bring in your bags," Prentice offered.

"I'm gay, not disabled." Mikey smiled through his refusal. "Go to your meeting." When Prentice didn't move, Mikey started waving at the door, saying, "Shoo, shoo."

Prentice shook his head but slapped Mikey on the shoulder.

"Good to have you back, mate," he mumbled before he strode to the door, grabbed his coat off a hook, gave Mikey a departing nod and left.

Mikey stared at the door, the tears he wouldn't allow himself to shed earlier pooled in his eyes and he whispered, "Have a good day at work, Superman."

Then Fiona watched as he turned to the coffee.

———— • ————

"BELLA, NO. WHAT you're saying is you want *four* different colors of *cream*," Mikey declared in a disgusted tone and Fiona agreed with him.

You need blue, Prentice LOVES blue, Fiona screamed.

Bella hesitated, looking mystified and maybe a little scared.

She glanced at Fern and asked, "Can we see that blue swatch again?"

Bella, Mikey, Annie and, of course, Fiona were in Fern Goodacre's little shop. Fern sold candles, candleholders, pretty, unusual jewelry made by locals, frames, artsy knickknacks and other gift items. Fern also had a small side business in interior design that she ran from the back room of her shop.

A lot of local folk said Fern was really good but Fiona was not the type of lass who would hire an interior decorator so she didn't know. But Janice MacHolm used Fern to decorate her sitting room and Fiona always thought it was really lovely.

They were all crammed in the back room of the shop and Annie and Mikey (and of course, Fiona) were also cramming their ideas into Bella's head.

Which might have been a wee bit out of line but, good God, the woman had picked four different colors of cream!

"Can I just say," Fern started, glancing at Mikey and Annie, "I actually like the cream on cream."

"What?" Mikey cried, openly aghast.

"See, this has a little salmon," Fern said, separating swatches on the table they were sitting around, "this a little blue, this a little more blue and that one, well, that one's just cream."

Annie tilted her head to the side and pointed. "Well, that one is blue and that one is kind of blue but the rest just look like cream to me."

Fern was gazing at the swatches and her eyes went funny. "Actually, I'm thinking it would be kind of brilliant, subtle, fresh, clean, bright, but with hints of color making it warm and interesting." She looked at Bella and grinned. "I really like it."

"You do?" Bella asked quietly.

"Aye. I could work with this, definitely," Fern replied.

"Really?" Bella breathed.

"Let me put some ideas together," Fern offered. "I'll work on it tonight, come over to see the space tomorrow and we'll talk more."

"I'd like that," Bella smiled.

"But it's all *cream!*" Mikey exclaimed.

Bella bit her lip and her eyes slid away, clearly tentative and worried.

Fiona watched Bella. She hadn't seen that look from Bella in a while.

This decorating business was for some reason causing her anxiety, so Fiona decided to lay off and she also decided to get Mikey, who was the naysaying ringleader, to do the same.

Shut it, mate, she shouted at Bella's friend.

"Seriously, girlie-girl, those rooms are *huge* filled with *windows*, you can *so* go bold," Mikey, clearly not like his friend and unable to hear voices from beyond the grave, declared.

"Bold," Bella whispered and looked at Mikey. "Fiona was good with bold, the rest of the house—"

Mikey paled at her words, having been informed of why they were on their errand, and he turned to Fern instantly. "Cream. Cream is good. Work with the cream."

"No," Bella said, her gaze had slid beyond Fern and she got up, scooted around the small space and pulled out a roll of peacock-blue fabric. She turned to her audience and said, "This is gorgeous."

"I love that," Fern said, getting up to join her and touching the fabric. "No one's ever used it and I've always wondered why because I think it's lush."

"It's *bold*," Mikey announced.

"It would be great for toss pillows or something. Just a splash of color," Bella replied and then looked at Fern and asked, "Don't you think?"

"Oh I do!" Fern said excitedly. "All that cream framing these bright flashes of blue. Only toss pillows or maybe a bedroll. Perfect!"

"I like it too," Annie declared.

"Is someone going to wait on me?" They heard asked peevishly from the door and everyone turned to see Hattie Fennick standing there.

Fiona turned too and when she did, her ghostly body went completely still.

Hattie Fennick was glaring at Bella with such hate, if Fiona had breath, that look of frank, open hostility would surely have stolen it.

Danger, Fiona thought.

Then Hattie scowled at Fern with such ill-will that Fiona thought she was being silly about the way Hattie glared at Bella.

Hattie hated everyone. She was a notorious cow.

And Hattie was also incapable of being dangerous. She was just a bitter, little nobody who no one liked because she took out her bad temper on anyone who was unlucky enough to cross her path.

"Hattie, we're getting some ideas down for Prentice and Bella's bedroom. Can you wait just a tick?" Fern inquired.

Hattie's eyes went back to Bella and her lip curled.

"You're using *Fern* to decorate Prentice's *bedroom?*" she asked as if she wouldn't ask Fern to paint the house number on her recycling box.

"Prentice and *Bella's* bedroom, darling," Mikey corrected, and Hattie sliced a derisive glance at him before she looked back at Bella.

"So, if you're redecorating *Fiona's* house, can we assume you're going to stay longer than a few months before you run away again?" she queried, and Fiona watched Bella brace as both Annie and Mikey shifted into defense mode.

Really, Fiona thought, Hattie was *such* a cow.

"Hattie," Fern said in a low voice.

"Well, everyone's thinking it," Hattie snapped.

"No, everyone *isn't*," Fern snapped back. "In fact, you're the only one who *is*."

"This is the one who sold Prentice and Bella's story to that magazine," Annie talked over the byplay, informing Mikey of Hattie's duplicity.

"*Really?*" Mikey asked then raked Hattie top to toe with his eyes. "You obviously didn't negotiate a good enough fee or, perhaps, you *like* that handbag?"

"Mikey," Bella said softly.

"Americans," Hattie muttered in xenophobic abhorrence.

"Poorly-accessorized, small-minded Scottish people," Mikey muttered back, using nearly Hattie's same tone.

Fiona giggled.

So did Annie.

"I'll just take care of you now, Hattie," Fern offered but Hattie walked in, slammed the candle she was holding on the wee table and glared at Fern.

"Don't bother. I've decided I don't want it," she declared, cast a venomous gaze about the room and stormed out.

Mikey snatched up the candle and smelled it, exclaiming loudly enough for the departing Hattie to hear, "Oo, *meadow*, my favorite scent! I'll take it!"

Annie and Fiona were still giggling but Fern was looking at Bella.

"Are you okay?" she asked.

Bella shook her head but said, "Yes, fine. It's not unusual from her, Hattie's never liked me."

"Hattie doesn't like anyone," Annie proclaimed.

"I don't know," Fern whispered and her eyes were on the door.

"You don't know what?" Mikey asked.

"It's just . . ." Fern started then she glanced again at Bella. "I grew up with her. We were in the same year as Prentice at school. She really liked him."

"What's not to like?" Mikey inquired then declared, "The man is hot."

Fern grinned at Mikey. "Aye, well, he always was a fine-looking lad. It's just the *way* Hattie liked him." She looked at Bella. "It always spooked me."

Annie and Mikey (and Fiona) leaned forward as Annie asked, "How so?"

Fern shook her head. "I can't say, can't put my finger on it. But it was just . . ." she paused and shivered, "strange."

"You. Are. Creeping. Me. *Out*," Mikey stated flatly.

"Sorry," Fern whispered on a grin to Bella.

"You know, Dougal said something once," Annie put in softly and everyone turned to her. "Something about how he heard Hattie say something about Fiona. Something very Hattie, just mean. But Dougal said something like, 'Reckon it's Prentice. Hattie always hated anyone who caught Prentice's eye.' I didn't think anything of it but it's true." Annie looked at Bella. "She barely knows I exist except to be passably nasty but she's always been actively spiteful to you, and I saw her look at Fiona once and it was downright chilling."

Fiona's ghostly body shivered just listening to Annie and thinking that Hattie looked at her like she'd caught Hattie looking at Bella just now which, evidently, she had.

"She made a play for him once," Fern threw in, everyone looked at her and then instantly moved closer. "I only know about it because I overheard Old Lady Kilbride talking about it." Fern tilted her head to the side and looked at Bella. "Sorry Bella, but it was just after you left."

Bella gave her a small smile and Fern carried on.

"I, personally, saw the first part but I didn't know she took it further. See, Prentice was getting pissed at the pub and everyone saw her sidling up to him, even me. It was kind of sad, really, because everyone knew Prentice was upset, sorry Bella," she said again, and when Bella shrugged and gave her a small, encouraging smile, Fern forged ahead. "And everyone knows when he's upset he gets kind of moody and they should leave him alone."

"You can say that again," Mikey put in and Fern gave him a grin.

"Apparently," Fern continued, "she made her play when he was walking home. I don't know what happened but Mrs. Kilbride said Hattie was in fits. Mrs. Kilbride heard her from the pavement, shouting the house down over at her mum's. Her friend was there, what was her name?" Fern paused. "The one who moved to Dundee?" When no one answered, Fern carried on, "Anyway, she was saying something about Prentice being good enough for toffee-nosed Americans, sorry Bella," she repeated on an embarrassed grimace and went on, "But not good enough for the local lasses and demanding to know what was wrong with her."

"I'd need a whole week, twenty-four seven, to detail what's wrong with her," Mikey muttered.

"I hardly think Hattie Fennick is worth this kind of intense conversation," Bella remarked.

"You've got to admit, it's weird," Annie replied.

"Okay, so she had a crush on Prentice back in the day, and because of her unrequited love she doesn't like me and didn't like Fiona. That's understandable. We have or had what she wants or wanted. And this is Hattie. It can't be a surprise that she'd be poor loser," Bella explained.

"This is true," Annie said.

It *was* true, Fiona thought, but it still was spooky.

And Fiona was on the lookout for spooky.

Because spooky could become dangerous.

Watch out for Hattie Fennick! Fiona shouted at Bella.

"But, I'll watch out for Hattie Fennick," Bella announced, and at this dramatic statement everyone looked at her funny so she grinned. "I mean, I wouldn't want the likes of Hattie Fennick messing up my Scottish fairytale come alive, now would I?"

Mikey slid an arm along her shoulders and tucked her into his side. "Nothing's going to mess up your Scottish fairytale come alive, *especially* not the likes of Hattie Fennick," he assured and gave Bella a squeeze.

"All right," Bella said decisively. "Now, I've got a bedroom to decorate. We need new furniture. And bed linens." She turned to Fern. "Do you deal with that too?"

Fern smiled and replied, "Absolutely."

Fifteen minutes later, Bella had warmed to her theme and was standing in the store discussing ideas with Fern on how to redecorate the sitting room whilst Annie and Mikey were perusing her wares when the bell over the door rang and Prentice's sister Debs stormed in.

She was breathing so heavily she was wheezing, her hand held to her throat.

"Debs, what on earth?" Bella asked, hurrying to Debs while Fiona floated along.

"The . . . you . . . Mrs. Kilbride . . ." Debs panted, "said you were here. I ran here the minute I saw it."

"Saw what?" Bella asked, and without another word Debs opened her big bag and pulled out a magazine.

"Oh crap," Annie breathed as everyone got close.

"I thought they'd gone," Bella whispered as she looked at the magazine as if it might grow teeth and bite her.

"Apparently, they had, into hiding!" Debs declared and showed Bella the cover.

On the front was a photo of Laurent and his strumpet, a bright yellow jagged line separating them, an announcement above them stating, It's over!

In the bottom corner there was a photo of Bella and Prentice snogging.

Actually *snogging*.

Not a peck on the lips but a full-on *snog*.

The small title by their photo said, While Isabella Lives Happily Ever After.

Fiona stared as Bella groaned, "Oh no."

"Girlie-girl!" Mikey hooted. "They got a picture of you and Mr. Broody-Hot *making out*! Look at that! It's gorgeous! I love it!"

Bella glared at Mikey while Annie asked, "How on earth did they get that?"

Bella took the magazine from Debs's hand and started flipping through it.

"Remember a week ago, you, Dougal, Pren and I were at the pub?" Bella asked Annie, still flipping. "Well, Pren kissed me by the car." Her head came up. "We thought the photographers had all gone."

"Well they hadn't," Mikey commented.

"Yes, Mikey, I can see that," Bella snapped.

"Oh, wow, hey, Mikey. You're here," Debs smiled at him in belated greeting and Mikey returned her smile.

"Why are *you* so happy about this?" Annie asked Mikey with narrowed eyes.

"Because Bella's making out with a handsome man, living the life of her dreams and that ass is alone, as he should be. And there isn't any way he can escape this, he'll see it and I love it. I think it's brilliant!"

Mikey answered.

"Well, Pren isn't going to think it's brilliant. Look!" Bella exclaimed and turned the magazine around for everyone to look.

They closed in and Fiona floated above them to have a look.

There was a spread, mostly Laurent and his floozy but also photos of Bella and Prentice. Photos taken recently, more shots of them snogging by Prentice's Rover and the inside shots were far more intimate. They were really going at it, Prentice even had a hand cupped tight on Bella's ass. And there were also pictures of Bella dropping the kids off at school.

"Yeesh, did you two do it in the Rover or what?" Annie asked.

"No! We didn't do it in the Rover! Still, this is, it's . . ." Bella paused and finished with, "Oh. My. *God!*"

Annie got close and slid an arm around Bella's waist. "Prentice doesn't care about this stuff, sweetie."

"Yes, well he's never had pictures of him making out published yet," Bella returned. "Look at it Annie!" She shook the magazine at her friend. "He's got his hand on my ass!"

"Mm, that's my favorite part," Mikey murmured.

Debs took the magazine out of Bella's hands and examined it while muttering, "He's my brother and I still think he looks fit."

"Sick," Fern giggled and Debs giggled with her.

"This isn't funny!" Bella shouted as her handbag rang. She dug into it, pulled out her mobile and stared at the display in horror. Then she looked at her audience with an expression that could only be described as dire, hit a button, put it to her ear and said, "Hey, Pren."

There were collective giggles (including Fiona's) and Bella glared daggers at them as she wandered away. Fiona wandered with her and got close to listen in.

"Are you at Fern's?" Prentice asked.

"Yes," Bella answered.

"While you're with her, talk about the sitting room," Prentice ordered, sounding distracted.

"We already did." She hesitated. "Listen, Pren—"

"Sorry, baby, I've got a staff meeting in five minutes and we're breaking ground in the New Year on that job. There's loads of shit to sort."

Bella sucked in breath. Prentice heard it.

"Elle?"

"Um . . ." she began.

"Elle," he cut in, "are you with Annie?"

Bella's shoulders went straight and she snapped, "Yes, and would you *stop* asking if I'm with Annie when you think we're misbehaving?"

"Oh crap," Annie mumbled in the background.

Prentice obviously didn't appreciate her tone of voice and Fiona knew this by *his* tone of voice when he answered.

"Were you with Annie two weeks ago when the police pulled you over for drag racing?" he countered.

Fiona giggled to herself because she thought that Bella drag racing was funny, especially Prentice's reaction to it when Fergus called and told him it happened. Bella didn't get in trouble, only a warning, but the whole village had heard about it and thought it was a scream.

"We weren't *drag racing*," Bella replied. "I just got my new car and we were testing it out."

"By racing each other in the streets?"

"Well—"

Prentice interrupted her, "And last week at the pub when you two challenged the rugby team to a game of quarters."

"Quarters is like riding a bike, you never forget how to do it, and Annie and I are good at quarters. The rugby team was smashed and we were only a little tipsy," Bella defended.

"You play quarters when you're in uni," Prentice returned.

"And when your forty and having fun!" Bella snapped.

"I don't have time for this," he ground out, sounding like his patience was at an end.

"All right, fine. Just so you know, that night at the pub with the rugby team?" she informed him. "Later, when we were necking in the parking lot, there was a photographer. There's, like, five pictures in a gossip rag of us going at it. Have a good staff meeting." Then Bella pressed a button on her phone, turned to the group and announced, "Honestly, it's like he's an old man."

"Actually, it seems to me it's like twenty years haven't passed," Debs whispered, Annie, Fern and Mikey grinned at her and Bella's phone rang again.

She answered without greeting, simply reminding him, "Pren. Staff meeting?"

Prentice didn't greet Bella either.

Instead, he demanded, "Don't put the phone down on me."

"I . . . what?"

"Don't *ever* put the phone down on me."

Bella went still at the tone of his voice. So did Fiona's spectral body.

He sounded serious and he sounded *angry*. Not Bella-and-Prentice-having-a-tiff angry.

Something else entirely.

Bella turned her back to her spectators and started, "Prentice, I—"

Prentice interrupted her.

"You could get in a car wreck, I could get in a car wreck, and the last thing you did was put the phone down on me." Fiona saw Bella's face pale as Prentice continued, "When you're done speaking, no matter how frustrated you are, you fucking tell me goodbye."

"I'm not going to get in a car wreck," Bella assured quietly.

He ignored her. "We fight, it's what we do and as fucking daft as it makes me, I love that about us. But when you're separated from me and I'm talking to you on the fucking phone, no matter if we're talking or fighting, you say goodbye."

"Pren—"

"Twenty years ago, I walked out of a room and neither of us said goodbye."

Bella pulled in breath and her eyes squeezed tight.

"People who care about each other always say goodbye," Prentice finished.

She opened her eyes and replied softly, "All right, Pren, I'll say goodbye."

"Always, Elle," he demanded.

"Always," she whispered.

"Now, I'm late. Don't, for the love of Christ, get into trouble with Annie."

"I won't. I promise."

He expelled an audible breath, his voice got soft and he said, "Love you, baby."

Bella's face got soft when she heard it. She started to say something and then her body jerked.

"Pren?"

"Aye."

"Are you mad about the magazine?"

"I don't give a fuck about the magazine."

"Really?"

"Really, baby," he replied, still using that soft voice. "Now, I have to go."

"Bye, Pren."

"See you soon, baby."

He rang off and Bella turned back to her friends.

"Pren didn't like me hanging up on him," she announced.

"Broody," Mikey declared and then finished, "*Hot.*"

Bella giggled.

So did Fiona.

And Fern.

And Debs.

"I need coffee and one of Bella's Christmas cookies," Annie declared.

"You made Christmas cookies?" Debs asked, eyes wide, clearly having had Bella's Christmas cookies (Fiona hadn't, but she'd heard about them and she'd seen the ones Bella made with Sally at the weekend and they looked *delicious*).

"She's Bella. It's Christmas. That means Christmas cookies," Mikey confirmed.

"Fern, can you come over for coffee and cookies?" Bella asked.

"I'll have cookies tomorrow," Fern replied. "My girl is in to help then. I'll be at your place at eleven o'clock?"

"Works for me," Bella smiled.

They said their goodbyes and Fiona floated after them as they walked down the pavement toward Bella's new Land Rover.

While Fiona drifted after them, she thought of her husband, who was good at brooding normally but had honed it to a fine art when Fiona died.

Fiona also thought about it being Christmas.

They'd always had great Christmases except last year which was a disaster, although Prentice tried everything he could and had help from both their families.

And although he was definitely happy to have Bella back and Fiona's family was whole again, Fiona reckoned Prentice was apprehensive about Christmas.

And maybe, even though he had the love of his life *back* in his life, it seemed he was still missing his wife a little.

This made Fiona both happy and sad.

She forgot about danger and magic and got close to Bella as Bella hit the button on her keyfob to open her Rover.

Take care with Prentice! she shouted. *He's worried about Christmas.*

Bella moved to the driver's side door and whispered, "I know. I will."

Fiona wished she could hug her.

As they all piled in, Fiona felt a shiver go through her body.

She turned and looked down the street and then stared, her ghostly eyes narrowing, not believing what she thought she'd just seen.

She wasn't sure because she'd disappeared around the corner but Fiona could have *sworn* she saw Hattie Fennick standing there.

With a camera.

———— ◆ ————

ANNIE DIDN'T HAVE one of Bella's cookies.

She had five. Fiona counted.

Bella, Annie, Debs and Mikey (and Fiona) were all at the kitchen bar, sitting on stools, Bella and Mikey on one side, Annie and Debs on the other, and they'd made their way through a serious amount of cookies as well as righted most of the wrongs in the world.

But mostly they chewed over the idea that Hattie was in a perpetual foul mood because of her unreciprocated love for Prentice.

It was nearing time that Bella had to go pick up the kids and Fiona saw her glance at the microwave clock.

This was one of the many reasons why Fiona found Bella being there a gift, knowing her kids would be picked up from school by someone they looked forward to seeing. And knowing that Prentice didn't have to arrange it and could go about his business knowing his children were looked after by someone they cared about.

On Fiona's thoughts, Bella's purse, sitting on the counter beside her, rang. She put down her mug, dug through her purse, and her brows knit as she looked at the display.

"What'd I do now?" she muttered, Annie, Mikey and Debs grinned at each other and Bella put her phone to her ear as Fiona drifted close, "Hey, Pren."

"Elle, don't go to the school. I'm picking up the kids today."

Bella's head tilted to the side and she said, "That's sweet of you, Pren, but I'm good. It only takes a few minutes and Annie and Debs are here to keep Mikey company."

"No, baby, I have to go. The Headmaster called. Jace has been in a fight."

Fiona's spectral body got stiff just as corporeal Bella's did.

Fiona's son was not a fighter.

Okay, that was a lie, he'd stick up for himself and, if he believed in something, he'd defend it. But he'd normally do this verbally not get in a *fight*.

"Jace got in a fight?" Bella whispered and Mikey, Annie and Debs's grins died.

"Aye. I'll pick up Sally then talk to the Headmaster. We'll be home soon."

"Do you want me to—?"

"No, baby, I'll take care of it."

"All right, see you soon."

"Aye, see you."

Fiona was about to transport herself to the school as Bella stared at her phone after Prentice disengaged.

Then Bella looked at Debs and asked, "Has Jason ever fought at school?"

Fiona stopped herself and looked at Debs as she shook her head. "No, never. He's like his dad, he's got a temper but he's a smart lad, knows how to keep his cool. I haven't seen him lose it since he was wee. It would have to be something really bad for him to fight."

Bella pulled in a deep breath and whispered on her exhale, "I think it's Christmas. Prentice is on edge too. Holidays can be bad if you've lost a loved one."

"Yes, darling," Mikey replied softly, "but now they have you."

Bella smiled a small smile at her friend and said in the sad tone of someone who knew, "No one plugs the hole left by a dead parent, Mikey."

Mikey, always quick with a retort, had none for that. He simply pressed his lips together and looked at Annie.

They dropped the discussion but Bella got quiet and started fidgeting, and although Fiona wanted to go to the school, instinct told her to stay with Bella.

And her instinct was right.

In half an hour, Fiona watched Bella clench her hands into fists.

Mikey caught it too.

He reached out, forced Bella's hand open and held it on the counter, murmuring, "It's going to be fine."

Bella turned to him and said quietly, "You know, I've never been happier, not even the first time I was with Pren." Mikey squeezed her hand and she continued, "But even knowing what it would mean, that I would lose them, if I had magic, I would use it to breathe life back into Fiona so I could give them all back what they lost."

Fiona's ghostly heart clenched.

Debs made a noise that sounded like a swallowed sob.

Annie whispered, "Oh, sweetie."

Mikey shook Bella's hand then gripped it tighter. "Well, girlie-girl, you *don't* have magic and you've taken on this job so now the only thing you can do for those kids is be the next best thing." He leaned in closer to his friend and went on, "And you know better than anyone that the next best thing is a whole lot better than nothing."

Bella pulled in breath through her nose and on the exhale she nodded.

It was then the front door opened and Prentice, Jason and Sally walked in.

Fiona stared, her ghostly heart hammering in her chest when she caught the look on Prentice's face.

She'd never seen it before but the only way to describe it was *enraged*.

The coffee klatch all tensed as Jason ran up the stairs not looking at anyone, his face mottled red and Fiona, his very own mother, couldn't read if he was angry or upset.

Everyone (and Fiona) watched as he disappeared from sight and then their eyes turned to Prentice when he said, "Sally, upstairs."

Even Sally look subdued but she still opened her mouth to protest.

"*Upstairs*," Prentice ordered in a tone that sent Sally scurrying upstairs.

"Prentice, what on earth?" Bella asked and Fiona turned to see Bella was standing.

Prentice made it to the kitchen, and with an irate flick of his wrist, he flung a bunch of magazines on the counter, magazines Fiona had been too surprised to notice he was carrying. They skidded through the cookies and coffee mugs and Debs, Annie and Mikey's hands flew out to limit the damage.

Bella didn't notice. Her eyes were on Prentice.

Prentice didn't notice either. He was stalking to the phone. He yanked it from its receiver and punched in a number while Bella walked to him and Fiona floated close.

"Pren—" she started, his eyes sliced to her and he lifted an angry hand to stop her from talking.

Bella froze and stared at him.

"Alice," Prentice said into the phone, "get me Hattie Fennick's number." He paused and clipped, "I don't give a fuck, home, mobile, whatever. Just find a way for me to call that bitch."

With that he slammed the phone into the receiver.

Fiona couldn't believe her ears.

Alice was the administrator at his offices. She was a sweet young thing, efficient and organized and had been with Prentice since he started his firm. Fiona had never heard Prentice speak to her like that.

And Hattie was in the picture.

What had that cow done *now*?

Bella edged closer and asked, "Prentice, why are you calling Hattie?"

Prentice tore his hand through his hair as his gaze cut to the magazines Debs, Annie and Mikey were all flicking through, their faces tight and angry.

Then his gaze came back to Bella. "Davey Fennick came into school today with half a dozen gossip rags, all of them with stories and pictures of us which he shared, apparently gleefully, with Jason."

"But," Bella replied, "he's seen us and even himself in magazines."

"No' the ones which talk about how we were together twenty years ago," Prentice returned, light dawned and Bella grew pale.

Fiona wished she had figured out her magic so she could go zap Hattie Fennick a good one.

"Oh my God," Bella whispered and her hands clenched into fists.

Prentice noticed it instantly and in an effort to control his rage his jaw tightened so much a muscle ticked there.

But his hands came to hers, he forced them open and laced their fingers. "Elle, he's upset but he isn't upset about that."

Bella stared up at him. "What's he upset about?"

"Davey didn't only bring the magazines, he also brought stories, likely heard at home, about you and me and Fiona."

Bella's brows drew together and Fiona glided so much closer she nearly drifted into Bella.

"What stories about you and me and Fiona?" Bella asked.

"You don't want to know," Prentice replied.

"I *do* want to know," Bella returned.

I want to know too! Fiona shouted.

"Elle—" Prentice began.

Her fingers tightened in his and she gave his hands a gentle jerk.

"Tell me, Pren."

Prentice sighed, dropped one of her hands and pulled his fingers through his hair again as he brought Bella closer.

"Davey told Jason I never loved Fiona. Davey told Jason I only ever loved you. Davey also told Jason that if I had to choose between you and Jason and Sally, I'd choose you because I love you more than I love them. And lastly, Davey told Jason that Fiona knew this and it's what made her sick, it was why she died."

Bella gasped.

Fiona did too.

They both stared at Prentice in horror.

Bella's face got red.

Then she opened her mouth.

And then she shouted, very, very loudly, "I'm going to fucking *wring Hattie Fennick's neck!*"

Prentice's body jerked and his face went blank before he realized he wasn't dealing with Isabella Austin Evangahlala.

He was dealing with Elle Austin, and Elle was a whole lot less predictable than Isabella.

"Elle—" Prentice tried to pull her even closer but she snatched her hand away and paced into the kitchen while everyone watched her.

She halted in a jerky way and whirled to Prentice.

And she shouted (again) and (again) it was very loud, "That insufferable *bitch*! I'm going to conk her on the head and shove her over a *cliff!*"

Prentice moved toward her saying, "Elle, calm down."

"Calm!" she yelled, scooting away from him and pacing, her hands moving around angrily. "Calm! I can't be calm! Hattie Fennick is a malicious bitch and," she stopped, twirled and glared at Prentice, "apparently, her *son* is a little *snot!*"

"Baby—" Prentice came at her again. She tried to avoid him but he caught her with an arm around her waist and pulled them together front to front then he repeated, "Calm down."

"I will *not* be calm!" Bella was still shouting. "Anyone who had a *brain* in their *head* knew you loved Fiona! What is Hattie thinking, filling her son's mind with that *garbage?*"

"Elle—" he started but Bella kept right on ranting.

"I was gone, you didn't know I would ever come back. You went on with your life. Of course you loved her. She was *Fiona!* Everyone loved her! You thought you were going to spend the rest of your life with her. And you can't get a brain tumor from thinking bad thoughts! Hattie Fennick! What a *bitch!* And her son, repeating it, even if he *is* ten years old! What a little *snot!*" Her body jerked and her eyebrows snapped together. "What did the headmaster say?"

"Due to the circumstances, he's being lenient with Jason," Prentice answered.

"He better be." Then she snapped, "Is he being lenient with the Fennick boy?"

"They think both boys learned their lesson and—"

Bella cut him off by announcing firmly, "Davey Fennick should be expelled."

"Elle, Jason hit Davey. What Davey did was wrong but Jason knows better."

"That may be so," Bella clipped, "but I don't care. I'm glad he hit him. I only hope he hit him *hard!*" Bella yelled.

Annie giggled.

Mikey chuckled.

Debs was grinning, huge.

Fiona was with Annie, she was giggling herself silly.

Even Prentice's mouth was twitching.

Gone was the anger, he looked like he was trying hard not to laugh.

It was then Fiona felt it and her eyes went to the top of the stairs.

Both Sally and Jason were sitting on the top step watching the show. Sally looked confused and maybe a little worried. Jason's face was red but this was not anger or upset, he was nearly choking himself from holding back laughter.

Bella swung her gaze around the lot of them and snapped, "I see nothing funny about this."

It was at that Jason lost his battle with his hilarity and snorted.

Everyone's eyes moved to the stairs.

Prentice won *his* battle and with a firm voice, he ordered, "Rooms."
Jason and Sally scampered.

Bella pulled back in Prentice's arms and jerked her extended hand
across her neck, declaring, "I've had it up to here with Hattie Fennick."

Prentice's eyes cut to her and they narrowed just as his body grew
tense.

"What else has she done?"

"Oh, I don't know," she replied dryly. "She came into Fern's today,
said a few choice things and they were *vile*. And Annie told me she gave
Fiona dirty looks. And I'll remind you, she *sold* our *story* to a *magazine*
for *money*." Bella threw her arm out. "Now she's got her son causing
trouble for Jason at school!"

"I'll talk to her," Prentice replied.

"No, when you get her number, *I'll* talk to her," Bella shot back.

"Elle—"

"No, Pren. I don't like the idea of her talking to you. Now she's
creeping *me* out with all this venom. This is all because she has a screaming crush on you. She has since you were in school," Bella announced.
"Fern said so."

Prentice blinked before he asked, "I'm sorry?"

"Fern told us she's liked you since forever," Annie chimed in.

"And, looking back, she totally has," Debs added.

"Which, I don't blame her," Mikey declared. "But there's a fine line
between being forlorn at unrequited love and being, well, *her*."

Prentice released Bella and turned to his audience, announcing,
"Hattie Fennick doesn't have a crush on me."

Bella crossed her arms on her chest and demanded, "Did she or did
she not make a play for you when you were walking home from the
pub after I left twenty years ago?"

Prentice's head turned to Bella and he opened his mouth to speak.
Then he closed it.

Then he muttered, "Fuck."

Bella looked at Mikey, Debs and Annie and nodded sharply, stating,
"She did." She looked back at Prentice and declared, "I'm talking to her.
Hattie Fennick and I are getting a few things straight."

Prentice turned to face Bella fully. "Elle, you aren't saying a word to that woman. Neither am I. I'll talk to Nigel."

"Nigel can't control her, never could," Debs put in.

Prentice turned to his sister and leveled his very, *very* serious gaze on her, replying, "He's going to have to learn."

Annie made a face at Mikey, her eyes rounding and her bottom lip curving down in a non-verbal, "Eek!"

Bella still had her arms crossed on her chest and she was glaring at Prentice.

Prentice turned to Bella and asked, "Are we agreed?"

Bella nodded her head jerkily but said, "She messes with Jason again or her son does or if Sally enters this mix, she and I are going to have words. No!" Her hand came up, index finger extended to the ceiling. "*I'm* going to have words. She's said quite enough."

Prentice gazed at her a moment then he grinned, his arm shot out and hooked her around the waist, pulling her to his body right before his mouth came down on hers hard.

"They do this a lot," Annie whispered to Mikey, her face tender.

"Aye, it's relentless," Debs muttered, her face smiling.

Mikey just watched the couple, his face soft and he didn't say a thing.

Prentice's head came up and he looked at the group, completely unembarrassed about semi-snogging Bella in front of them but he didn't let Bella go.

Bella curled into him, putting her head on his shoulder as she looked at the crowd.

Bella's face was happy.

"Who's staying for dinner?" Prentice asked.

Chapter
TWENTY

Princess Castle

Elle

It was ten thirty Christmas Eve, the kids were upstairs in bed (hopefully sleeping) and Prentice and Mikey were in the television room assembling Santa's present for Sally, a four-story, mini-princess castle.

Elle was rushing around in the great room stuffing stockings, unearthing presents from Santa she'd hidden that she'd bought and wrapped while the kids were at school, arranging them under the tree and pulling together her potato, cheese, sausage casserole that she would pour the scrambled egg over and toss in the oven first thing in the morning for breakfast.

Fergus, Annie and Dougal had been over for dinner that night and tomorrow they were to have Christmas morning at the house but head to Fiona's parents' for Christmas dinner before leaving there and going to Prentice's parents' house to spend the evening with them.

This was Elle's idea and she'd been hesitant in suggesting it to

Prentice, not wanting to mention Fiona and her family in his mood but feeling the need to do so, at least for the kids (as well as Fiona's family). But she wasn't hesitant after she'd actually suggested it.

The minute it came out of her mouth, he stared at her a moment then both his hands shot out, grasped her at the hips and he pulled her so forcefully into his arms that her breath left her on a wheeze. He shoved his face in her neck and held on tight.

Her arms slid around him too and she whispered in his ear, "Pren."

"I want them to have their grandchildren, I want my children to have their grandparents and, on Christmas especially, I want them to have something of their mother," he whispered into the skin of her neck. "What I didn't want to do was upset you your first Christmas with us by asking that of you."

Well, there it was, the reason Prentice was on edge.

Elle had closed her eyes and she held on tighter too.

Then she said softly, "Honey, Fiona *is* our family."

Her words made his arms get tighter, Elle pulled in breath and felt him kiss her neck, his arms loosened and his head came up so he could say in his sweet voice, "Fuck, but I love you."

Before she could return the sentiment, he'd kissed her and after he was done kissing her she was too dazed to remember to return it.

After their short conversation, Prentice had relaxed and so did Elle and they finally started enjoying the holiday full force without his tenseness invading.

Now she was covering the casserole with foil before she slid it in the fridge, which would herald the end of her chores so she could go in and help Prentice and Mikey then, finally, go to bed and tomorrow . . . Christmas.

Christmas.

She couldn't wait.

Prentice had warned her not to spoil the kids, he didn't want to raise their expectations which could get out of control with her efforts to top herself year to year considering they had a woman in their lives who had the means to make even their wildest dreams come true.

But that didn't mean Santa didn't bring Sally her princess castle *and* a princess dress with shoes *and* a fairy outfit with wings so she could have a choice if she wanted to be a princess or a fairy and use all the fairy things Elle had sent her from Chicago.

Jason, who still practiced on Fiona's guitar daily, sometimes for hours, was getting an electric guitar with amplifier just in case he wanted to branch out. He also was getting a PlayStation.

Prentice had okayed these purchases mostly because he'd also paid for them, not allowing Elle to do it. So Elle was going to add her own gift, a trip to Disneyworld their next holiday and she'd informed Prentice of her intent the day before.

Prentice had, at first, not okayed that. Words were exchanged, they got heated but Elle didn't give in and eventually, after a fair amount of (annoying, Elle thought) effort, she talked him around.

So Sally and Jason were going to be a *wee bit* spoiled, it wasn't the end of the world. And this was how she'd convinced Prentice.

Or she told herself that.

What she had a strong idea was the real reason he gave in was because he saw how excited she was to give his children a special Christmas. Some days before, in bed in the dark, Prentice had shared with her that the last one was, for understandable reasons, really not that great. Princess castles, electric guitars and the promise of Disneyworld was not going to bring back their mother, but it would bring smiles to their faces and happy expectation for months of what was to come and that was something, something good and something good was always better than nothing.

So Elle was looking forward to seeing their faces when they opened their gifts and learned of the upcoming holiday.

She couldn't wait.

And she couldn't remember one single Christmas—not in her life— that she couldn't wait for the morning to come. Even when she was young, before her mother died, the atmosphere in the Austin household was too heavy to be conducive to Christmas cheer.

But the last several days, with Mikey there, Prentice relaxed, Christmas cookies, Christmas music, Christmas decorations, Christmas wrapping, friends and family all around, it had been a blast and Elle could not *wait* for the big day.

And, incidentally, having shared all this with Prentice, she didn't know that was the real reason why he gave in on a *wee bit* of spoiling.

She slid the casserole in the fridge, a smile playing at her mouth, and was closing the fridge when she heard a knock at the front door.

Her eyes went to it as the smile left her face.

Who could that be at ten thirty at night on Christmas Eve?

Deciding it was likely Annie left something behind, but wondering why she didn't just call, Elle moved to the door. The outside light wasn't on therefore, as Elle made it to the door, she switched on the light and then stopped dead when, through the window at the side of the door, she saw who was on her doorstep.

She blinked slowly, hoping he'd go away, so focused on making this happen she didn't hear Prentice's boots on the floorboards behind her.

When her eyes opened again, he was still there.

He was looking at the door, probably thinking it would open considering the light had gone on, but when it didn't, he looked to the side and caught her eyes the instant Prentice asked from behind her, "Who is it, baby?"

Elle didn't answer. She just held the familiar blue eyes holding hers.

"Elle?" Prentice called and he was closer, she knew it, she heard it. She also knew instantly when Prentice saw him because he bit out, "Fucking hell, you have to be fucking joking."

Then she was moved aside, Prentice twisted the locks, opened the door and immediately lifted a hand and planted it in Laurent Evangelista's chest, shoving him back.

Laurent's eyes never left Elle until he suddenly found himself flying back and he snapped, "What on—?"

"Get off my land," Prentice growled, up came the hand again and he shoved Laurent back another step but this time the shove was angrier, more forceful and Laurent didn't fly back two steps, he flew back six, arms reeling. He controlled his forced retreat, his body tightened and grew alert.

"Do not put your hand on me again," he warned, straightening, his eyes now glued to Prentice.

"Won't say it again, mate, get off my fucking land," Prentice clipped.

"What's happ . . . oh my *Lord*," Mikey breathed from behind Elle who was standing, silent and stunned to immobility, in the door.

Laurent didn't tear his eyes from Prentice who'd stopped, blocking the front walk and planting his fists on his hips.

"I wish to speak to Isabella," he announced.

Elle stared at her ex-husband who she hadn't seen in person in ages.

Tall, though not as tall as Prentice, very lean to the point of almost being too thin, he carried it off and made it attractively lanky due to broad shoulders and consistent workouts through playing tennis and polo that did not bulk out his body but nevertheless kept it fit and athletic. Dark-blond hair. Deep-blue eyes. Chiseled features that were almost feminine but not quite, the constant sardonic expression he wore coupled with the world-weary sophistication he emanated adding to his allure.

Women the world over thought he was unbelievably handsome.

Elle, knowing him all too well, absolutely did not.

"I'm afraid that's no' a Christmas wish that'll come true, Evangelista," Prentice returned, his voice low, vibrating and rough with anger. "Now, again, get *the fuck* off my land."

Laurent glared at Prentice then his eyes shifted to Elle and she watched with surprise as he shifted his features to go soft, coaxing, a look she'd seen often, however, it was one she hadn't seen in a very long time.

It was the look he'd assume in the early days of their marriage when he'd approach her about moving on from Paris to Gstaad, from Gstaad to Rome, from Rome to Istanbul, from Istanbul to wherever.

He knew she didn't want to go to the next party, the next villa, the next yacht, and in the beginning he'd take the time to cajole her, to try and convince her it would be fun, to remind her of all their fabulous friends who weren't *her* friends but *his* and they were so vain and superior and surprisingly, with all their money, expensive education and travel, uninteresting, that she didn't miss even one of them when they were gone. And when he tried to coax her, he would assume that look.

In the end, he didn't bother. He'd simply drop the tickets in her lap and tell her to get packed.

And seeing that look on his face, she knew. She knew everything.

She knew he knew she was with Prentice (he couldn't *not* know with all the magazines they'd been featured in). She knew he knew who Prentice was. She knew he knew she was happy. She knew he thought she couldn't ever be happy in the wilds of Scotland with an award-winning architect and his two beautiful children, not when she could have the world laid at her feet. She knew she spent years trying to convince him she didn't want the world laid at her feet and he'd never, not once, listened. She knew he was competitive and it was eating at him that he was bested by a man like Prentice, so much more of a man than Laurent it wasn't funny but that was also something Laurent would never understand.

And lastly, she knew that he'd asked her father how to find her and her father had told him. In fact, it was highly likely Carver Austin *sent* Laurent here.

And instead of feeling beaten, tired or defeated at another indication that life just would *not* give her her happily ever after, she felt something else.

She felt fury.

"Isabella, darling, *please*, allow me to—" Laurent started, Prentice's body shifted as if to advance but Elle spoke.

"He told you, didn't he?" she asked, her voice so cold, icicles formed on each word and Prentice's body shifted a different way to look back at her while Elle felt Mikey's hand settle on the small of her back.

But Elle's eyes didn't move from Laurent.

"I don't know what you—" Laurent began but Elle let him say no more.

"My father, he told you where I was," she declared, watched Laurent suck in a breath to deny through a lie but she went on before he could speak. "It's Christmas Eve, tomorrow is a big day, a joyful day, there are children in this house, I'm with my family, it's late and you show up on the doorstep knowing I hate you, knowing that seeing your face could conceivably ruin my day or even my whole Christmas and thinking that's a perfectly all right thing to do." Losing her composure, she leaned in and asked on a hiss, "What's the matter with you?"

"I needed to be certain you were here. I needed—" Laurent launched into his explanation but Elle interrupted him again.

"*You* needed? Who cares what *you* needed, Laurent?" she asked then didn't wait for him to answer. She crossed her arms on her chest and announced, "I'll tell you who *doesn't* care." She jerked her thumb to her chest, "*Me.*"

Laurent winced before he tried, "Isabella, my love—"

She cut him off yet again, "Go away."

He made to take a step forward, Prentice's body swung toward him, he stopped and said, "Isabella, I'm asking you *please.*"

But Elle was done.

Because in that instant, seeing Prentice blocking his way not about to let him get to her, feeling Mikey's hand warm on the small of her back, his body close and staring at Laurent's face, knowing he could be even *more* of a jerk when he was already a world-class jerk, it came to her.

She *was* living her happily ever after.

It just came with some trolls along the way.

Therefore, impatiently, as if he was simply an annoying nuisance (which he was), she ordered on a sigh, "Go away and stay away." She shook her head and went on, "Honestly, I never want to see you again. Not ever." She began to turn to walk into the house but thought of something else so she turned back. "And, if you speak to my father, tell him the same thing. He does not exist in my world, not anymore and not ever again."

After delivering that line, she turned and started into the house but turned back when Laurent called after her, speaking swiftly, urgently and almost desperately, "I only ever loved you."

"Oh my *God*," Mikey snapped, his words so heated it was a wonder Elle didn't get singed by their fire. "Is he *insane?*"

But Elle's brows had simply lifted with mild curiosity and she asked, "You only ever loved me?"

He nodded, glanced quickly at Prentice, took a tentative step forward but stopped on a sway as Prentice moved aggressively to block him and growled, "I don't think so."

Laurent ignored Prentice, though he made no further advance but lifted a hand toward Elle, saying softly but in a voice that carried, "All of them, all the others, they meant nothing to me, darling. I need to speak to you. To explain. This separation between us, this distance, it's out of hand. I've been living a nightmare these last years, lost without you. Something must be done. I loved you in the beginning. You know that, I know you do. But I also loved you in the end and I need to explain why I did what I did, behaved the way I behaved. You need to know it's only ever been you. I've always only ever loved you."

"No you haven't," Elle retorted so instantly to his ludicrous, heart-felt declaration that Laurent's body twitched and he blinked.

"What?" he asked, sounding and looking ridiculously confused.

"You haven't," Elle repeated. "You see, Laurent, I know what love is. I have love, a lot of different kinds of it and you *never* gave that to me. Not in the beginning and definitely not in the end. So don't stand there telling me you only ever loved me. I'm not entirely certain you know what love means and if what you feel for me, considering how you treated me, is twisted somehow in that head of yours to mean love then I'll give you one more thing. I'll give you the knowledge that you . . . are . . . *wrong*. You don't treat someone you love the way you treated me. Never. You'd rather die than do something like that. Trust me. I love the man standing in front of you, I would tie myself in knots not to hurt him, I'd throw myself in front of a bus for him, I'm not kidding, and I know he'd do the same for me. That's love." She threw her hand out toward Laurent. "You have no idea and that makes me sad for you because, honestly, if you think what you feel for me is love then you'll never get it and that's not only sad, at your age, it's pathetic."

She again turned, this time with determination, skirted Mikey and walked into the house without looking back.

She walked right to the television room and saw the princess castle was mostly complete. There were some decals left to stick on and the furniture was still in plastic wrap in a pile on the floor but it was assembled and it looked fantastic.

Elle smiled. Sally was going to be in fits of delight.

"Baby?" Prentice called and Elle turned to see him and Mikey coming through the door, both of their eyes on her, both of their faces carrying a mixture of concern and residual anger.

"This looks *great!*" she cried, throwing her hand out to the castle.

Mikey rocked to a halt and blinked. Prentice stopped too and stared closely at her.

"Sally is going to *love* that!" Elle kept exclaiming. "It's even better than the pictures on the box. I cannot *wait* for the morning."

Both Prentice and Mikey stared at her. Then they looked at each other. Their gazes came back to her.

That was when Mikey asked, "Uh . . . girlie-girl, are you okay?"

"Yes," Elle answered. "Tired but it's late and it's been a hectic day. But I'll help you with the furniture once we get this out to the great room and then we can go to bed and tomorrow . . ." she smiled, "*Christmas!*" She clapped, her face wreathed in smiles.

Prentice and Mikey again stared at her before looking to each other then Prentice looked back at Elle and walked to her.

Once he arrived, he pulled her loosely in his arms and informed her cautiously, "He's gone."

"Good," Elle replied and asked, "Should we take this in the other room now? I can unwrap the furniture while you and Mikey finish the decals."

Prentice's arms gave her a little squeeze and both his head and voice dipped low when he said, "Elle, baby, what happened outside—"

"Is over," Elle interrupted him. "It's Christmas Eve and he's had five minutes of it, he doesn't get anymore."

"So you're okay with what happened out there?" Prentice asked.

"No," Elle answered. "But *I* didn't show up on my ex-husband who hates me's doorstep to act like a selfish jerk then be sent packing, *he* did. He has to deal with that. I don't. And you said he's gone so it's over, I'm moving on to princess castles then to bed then Christmas."

After making her declaration, she held Prentice's beautiful every-colored eyes as they held hers. Doing so, he watched his eyes smile. But she lost sight of them when his head dropped and her eyes closed when he touched his mouth to hers.

When his head came up, he muttered, "Right, let's get this done."

"Yes," she smiled and gave him her own squeeze, "let's get this done."

"We've got a plan," Mikey cut in, moving toward the sheet of sticker decals that would adorn the princess castle with printed stone and abundant flowers. "Sally's castle then bed. I'm *beat*. And sleep means waking up to Bella's breakfast casserole and the moment I taste that high-calorie extravaganza *cannot* come soon enough. So, chop chop!"

Elle transferred her smile to Mikey, Mikey returned it, she gave Prentice another squeeze, he returned it then he let her go and they chop chopped.

"BABY," PRENTICE SAID softly as Elle wandered out of the bathroom and into their room, ready for bed.

"Yes?" she answered, her eyes going to him then her brows drawing together because he was in his pajama bottoms but he was also wearing a sweatshirt and a thick pair of socks.

She was in a short, silky, lacy nightie and she felt comfortable. The heat was turned down at night. Prentice set the automatic timer on the thermostat to do it so the house could get chill, although she wouldn't really know because by that time Prentice was using a variety of ways to warm her up. But, considering he knew they'd have a late night, he'd turned off the automatic timer and only turned it back on when they'd finished the castle, said their goodnights to Mikey and headed to bed.

The air hadn't even gone cool yet.

"Are you cold?" she asked right before he tossed a pair of his thick socks to her.

She bobbled them then caught them.

"On," he ordered, strode to the closet and disappeared.

Elle stared at the socks in her hand. Slowly, her head turned so she could look out the windows to the moonlit sea.

Her heart started racing.

Prentice took her out there on occasion, not often but it happened. Sometimes he'd take a bottle of wine for her and his whisky. They'd sip and stare at the sea, each in their own thoughts, doing this mostly silently.

She loved it when he did that, she loved the quiet togetherness, the sea their view, comfortable in each other's company without words.

But something told her tonight, knowing she was tired, Christmas less than an hour away, he wasn't in the mood to sip whisky and stare at the sea with her back tucked to his front, his arms around her, her head resting on his shoulder.

It was something else.

And tomorrow was Christmas so that something else could be *something else*.

Prentice exited the closet with one of his thick, wooly sweaters.

"Pren—" she started.

"Socks on, Elle," he interrupted her.

She stared at him for another moment. Then she bent over and pulled on his socks. When she was done, he was close and he pulled the sweater over her head. It was huge and covered her from neck to thigh, well past her nightgown, but it left her legs bare. Even with her legs bare, the minute she shoved her arms through the sleeves, Prentice grabbed her hand and led her out to the balcony.

Heart still racing, Elle didn't argue or resist.

She followed.

He closed the door behind them and guided her to the railing before he stopped them and guided her into his arms.

She tipped her head back to look at his face in the moonlight and the illumination from the soft lamps lit on either side of the bed that were coming through the windows of their room. When she did, she saw he was already looking down at her and she noted he looked serious.

She opened her mouth to speak, knowing he had to feel her heart beating against his chest where it was pressed close but she didn't utter a peep.

Because he spoke first.

And when he did, it was to ask, "You'd throw yourself in front of a bus for me?"

She bit her lip as she tried to control the beating of her heart.

This was an impossibility so she answered, "Well—"

That was all she got out before Prentice spoke again.

And when he did, this time it was a thick, hoarse whisper, "You'd throw yourself in front of a bus for me."

She would and he knew it. He knew it and she knew that he felt that knowledge burrow deep and he liked it.

Elle felt tears stinging the backs of her eyes, her body melted into his, her arms tightened around him and she whispered back, "Yes, Pren, though I hope I never get the chance."

A short, sharp laugh escaped his throat but that was it before his head dropped and his forehead came to rest on hers.

Then he said in his soft, low, sweet, beautiful voice, "You know I love you."

"I know," she replied just as soft but probably not as sweet and beautiful.

"You love me," he declared.

"With everything I am," Elle confirmed, his eyes closed slowly and his arms squeezed her tight.

They loosened, his eyes opened to look into hers and that voice kept coming at her. "And you know I want you in my life until my last breath."

Her heart tripped over itself.

"Pren." That was all she could get out, she could say no more and Prentice didn't give her a chance.

He pulled slightly away at the same time he reached behind him to wrap a hand around her left wrist. He shifted it between them as his other hand went to the pocket of his pajama bottoms. The next second he was sliding a large diamond ring on her finger, the diamond brilliant, gorgeous and *huge* but the setting was simple, unadorned, the luster, brilliance and size of the diamond the only thing it needed.

"I'm making that official," Prentice told her, his voice still sweet but it was again thick as Elle stared at the ring and couldn't speak at all because her heart was still beating a mile a minute, but now it was doing it in her throat. "*That* is the ring I wanted to give you twenty years ago. *That* is the ring my Elle deserves to wear on her finger, the ring that lays my claim to her, shows the world she's mine and shows her how much she means to me. So *that* is what she'll have."

Elle's eyes, filling with wet as her lips trembled, lifted to his and when they did his hand, warm and strong, curled around hers tight and pressed it to his chest.

"Merry Christmas, baby," he whispered.

Elle stared at the man she'd loved for forever, the man who breathed life into her, the man who set her free, the man who, again, slid the perfect ring on her finger making all her dreams come true and she knew she was right earlier.

She had her happily ever after.

And it was *happy.*

So she stuffed her face in Prentice's sweatshirt, yanked her hand free from his so she could wrap her arm around him again, both her arms spasmed and she burst into tears.

Prentice gathered her closer, pulling her deeper to his warmth and he held on tight as she wept tears of joy into his chest.

When this went on for a good long while, he whispered into her hair, "Baby, we need to get you inside. It's cold and your legs are exposed."

Her head jerked back then it jerked side to side.

She pulled her arms from around him, lifted her hands and placed them on either side of his head. With wet on her face, tears still spilling over, she got on her tiptoes to get closer.

And in a fierce voice, Elle told him, "When Cinderella is on her balcony with her handsome Prince, Sleeping Beauty, Snow White, they don't feel cold, Pren, they don't feel anything. They just feel happy."

She watched his face shift, go soft, his eyes warm and his arms convulsed around her as he murmured, "Elle."

"I love you," she whispered, got higher on her toes and touched her mouth to his then moved back half an inch. "I love you." Her fingers slid into his thick, fantastic hair and she repeated, "I love you."

"Elle—"

Her fingers clenched in his hair and she pressed her body deep into his.

"I love you, Prentice Cameron."

Elle stopped talking and stared into his beautiful eyes, eyes she'd look into every day for the rest of her life and for the first time in that life she felt blessed.

Prentice allowed her a moment to experience that added gift then his neck bent and his mouth crushed down on hers.

Sometime later, his body bent so he could lift her in his arms and carry her to their bed.

In their bed he gave her another gift and as often as she got it (which was often), it was always special.

But this time, after, sliding to sleep with Prentice's warm, strong, big body curved into hers, his arm around her, his fingers laced in hers, keeping her safe, holding her close and doing it with his ring on her finger, it was beyond special.

It was *magical*.

Chapter
TWENTY-ONE

Then they were gone.
And he knew she was too.

Elle

Elle was sitting in her Land Rover outside the school waiting for Jace and Sally to get out.

It was three weeks after Christmas, there was a dusting of snow on the ground and the weather had hit a chill so cold the snow was going nowhere, not for a while.

Elle's gaze was on the kids pouring out of the school but she didn't see them. She had a dozen things on her mind.

First, she had to get Jason to his guitar lesson, something he requested after he got the electric guitar and, about five minutes after the last present was unwrapped on Christmas morning, he worked with his father to set it up. He strummed once, the sound blasted back from the amplifier and he instantly fell in ten-year-old boy love. Considering the amount of time he practiced, Prentice had agreed to the lessons. It was clear Jason was committed to the guitar and, further, Prentice liked the idea that it linked him to his mother in an unusual but beautiful way.

When Jason got his guitar lessons, Sally, not to be left out, declared she wanted dance lessons *and* gymnastics lessons. Surprisingly to this too, Prentice agreed. He decided at her age she couldn't know which she had more of an interest in, he was just pleased she had any interest at all. So he told Elle that Sally might as well try them both and later, if she was still committed, follow through with the one she preferred.

Therefore Elle had to get Jason to his lesson, Sally home to change into her leotard then off to her lesson, then, after dropping Sally off, head to Fern's to make final decisions on furniture and bedding (their rooms were, at that very moment, completely bare and being painted, they were sleeping in the guest suite). After all that, it was back through town to pick up Jason then Sally, get home and start dinner.

She'd spent the morning booking their Disneyworld holiday online, the rest of the day cleaning the house and doing laundry all the while intermittently making tea for the painters, and she hadn't thought once about what they were going to have for dinner.

So as she sat in her Land Rover contemplating the mad dashes through town she would soon be making, hoping she could do what she needed to do at Fern's in time to pick up the kids as well as thinking about what she had in the fridge for dinner and not concentrating much on her surroundings.

Until she saw something that caught her eye and she focused on the figure that appeared to be trying to hide, and poorly, around the corner of the school.

Hattie Fennick.

Hattie Fennick with a camera around her neck.

Elle pulled in a shocked breath as she watched Hattie scanning the kids streaming out of the school and Elle knew, she *knew* Hattie was waiting to take Jason and Sally's picture. Just like she sold her and Prentice's story to the gossip magazine, she'd been selling the recent photos too.

It was *Hattie* who was their source, keeping the photos and stories coming and thus the interest alive.

In fact, just last week they'd printed a photo of Prentice and Elle wandering down the sidewalk two villages over, having a date night, the kids at Fiona's sister, Morag's house. They were illuminated by a streetlamp, Prentice's arm was wrapped around Elle's shoulders and both hers were wrapped around his stomach. Her front was pressed to his side, he had his head tipped down to look at her, she had hers tipped back to look at him, she'd said something to make him chuckle and she was laughing with him.

The caption read, *It's Wedding Bells for Isabella and Prentice!* And in a little square at the bottom right corner of the photo was a blown up shot of her hand wearing Prentice's ring and that had its own caption of, *And her hunky architect is not messing around!*

As annoying as it was, she had to admit she loved that photo. They looked happy mainly because they were.

But that was two villages over. The shot had been taken after they had dinner and were walking back to Prentice's SUV so it was after nine at night. There was practically no way Hattie would just happen to be in that village (with a camera), which was smaller by half than Prentice's, which meant it was tiny. They had a takeaway Chinese, the Italian restaurant she and Pren went to and a news agent. There was no reason for Hattie to be there.

This meant Hattie Fennick was stalking Elle, Prentice and the kids!

Hattie Fennick was stalking them and getting paid to expose snippets of their lives and steal photos of their memories and sell their privacy to the world.

As this knowledge burned into her brain, Elle lifted her hands and curled her fingers on the steering wheel in an effort to stop herself from opening her door and marching straight to Hattie, yanking that camera from her neck, smashing it on the ground and giving Hattie a piece of her mind.

It would not do to throw a temper tantrum in front of all the kids at Sally and Jace's school with the parents there to pick them up.

No, she thought as her narrowed, angry eyes stayed focused on Hattie, she'd pick her time and it would be the right time.

The bed in the guest suite was smaller than the one in their room and the one they would be purchasing.

But it was cozy and comfortable.

They were good. The furniture could wait another day to be ordered, Elle decided as Hattie lifted the camera to her eye and Elle knew that Sally and/or Jason was headed her way.

Yes, she thought, glaring at Hattie taking photos of her children, the furniture could wait.

———— ◆ ————

Fiona

"IS EVERYTHING OKAY, Elly Belly?" Fiona heard her daughter ask, her small hand held by Bella's as Bella walked her into the dance studio.

Fiona thought her wee lass looked adorable in her baby-pink tights and leotard, even with that big coat over it, scarf wrapped around her neck, wooly hat pulled over her ears, feet encased in warm boots (she would put on her ballet slippers in the studio).

Bella didn't take any chances with the cold, Fiona was pleased to see.

But Fiona, for once, wasn't thinking about her sweet Sally.

Her focus was Bella, who Sally couldn't help but notice was angry, walking stiffly, face set. Hell, *anyone* would notice it that was how angry Bella was, she wasn't even shielding Sally from it.

Bella's thoughts were elsewhere, it was plain to see and Fiona knew where they were.

Fiona had seen Bella notice Hattie Fennick and she'd seen Bella's reaction.

And Fiona wasn't ready.

She had not realized her magic. She'd spent hours practicing, hours at her tent calling to the Colonel Sanders Messenger Man in hopes he'd materialize and give her some clue.

He hadn't and she was no closer to finding her magic so she could use it when the time came.

And Fiona feared the time was coming now.

Christmas had come and gone and all was well, joyful, happy— even including a visit from Laurent Evangelista (who was an even bigger tosser than Fiona reckoned he was and she reckoned he was a pretty big tosser). Bella had barely reacted to his appearance. She dealt with it and moved on, no clenching of the fists, no nothing.

Fiona was proud of her.

Prentice, Fiona noted, was prouder.

But there was no word from Bella's father. No mishaps roasting the turkey. The television didn't explode when Prentice and Mikey installed the PlayStation.

The only danger, Fiona reckoned, was Hattie Fennick.

And Fiona knew, just looking at Bella's face, that Bella intended to do something about it.

And now.

Wait! Fiona shouted at her as she floated by Bella and her daughter's side. *Wait until later! Talk to Prentice! Tell him about it tonight! Don't go on your own!*

Bella gave no indication that she'd heard Fiona as she walked toward the doors, pushing them open and lying to Sally, "I'm fine, sweetie. Just have something on my mind."

"Okay," Sally said softly, disbelief and worry clear in her tone.

Bella! Don't! Fiona didn't give up and kept shouting. *She's dangerous! Just wait, wait and talk to Prentice. He's your knight in shining armor. He's made to keep you safe. Don't do something stupid!*

Again, Bella gave no indication she heard her ghostly friend as she forced a smile at the instructor then helped Sally take off her winter things and put on her slippers.

She bent and kissed the top of Sally's head, her hand lifting slightly to curl around Sally's soft cheek and Sally tipped her head back to look at Bella.

"I'll be back in an hour, honey," Bella said softly.

Sally nodded. "Okay, Elly Belly."

Hearing her nickname, Bella didn't have to force her farewell smile for Sally.

She dropped her hand, nodded at the instructor and a couple of the parents as she headed back out to her 4x4, Fiona so close to her side Bella shivered at the cold caused by Fiona's spectral body and not the deep chill in the air.

Bella, listen to me, Fiona begged, wrapping her ghostly hands around Bella's arm causing her to shiver again. *Please, please, at least call Prentice.*

Bella bleeped the locks to her Rover, yanked open the door angrily and climbed inside.

Then she whispered, "No. I'm going to take care of this once and for all."

Bella! Fiona shouted but Bella shook her head.

"No," she kept whispering, "no one interferes with my happily ever after, but they *really* don't interfere with Prentice's or the kids'."

Fiona closed her eyes.

Bella switched on the ignition.

Bloody hell! Fiona yelled, glaring at Bella's stubborn profile.

Then she made a mistake.

She dematerialized and materialized at Prentice's office to try her hand at yelling at him in order to get through.

Leaving Bella alone.

She should never have left Bella alone.

———— ✦ ————

Prentice

PRENTICE WAS AT his drafting board at the office, sifting through phone messages Alice had left for him, thinking he'd need to have a look at the building where his offices were housed because, that afternoon, a chill had slid through them so arctic, it was uncomfortable. He'd never felt it before and they were experiencing a severe cold snap so he reckoned the heating wasn't up to the task.

However, strangely, the chill subsided as suddenly as it came. Prentice still made a mental note to look into it.

These thoughts were in his head when his mobile rang.

He looked down at it, seeing a number come up on the display rather than a name. His head tilted to the side, he picked it up, engaged and put it to his ear.

"Cameron," he greeted.

"Prentice?" a female's voice asked.

"Aye," he answered.

"Hello, this is Lydia, Jason's guitar teacher."

Prentice's body started to tighten as his mind went alert, wondering why she'd be calling him considering Elle dealt with the children's instructors. Elle found them, she checked their references and she hired them. Except for telling Prentice about them and him meeting them briefly, since their lessons happened while he was at the office he had little to do with them.

"Yes?" he prompted.

"Well, I've been calling Bella but she isn't answering and she hasn't picked up Jason from his lesson. She's over a half an hour late and she's never late. I've got another student coming in soon and I was wondering if wires were crossed? Perhaps you were supposed to pick up Jason?"

Prentice gut tightened along with his body but it did it harder, sharper, making him feel instantly sick.

"No, I—" he started to say but his phone vibrated in his hand. He took it from his ear quickly, glanced at it, saw he had an incoming call and he put it back to his ear and said, "Just a minute, another call is coming through. Maybe that's Elle. I'll be right back." He took the phone from his ear again, hit the button to engage and put it back. "Cameron."

"Hi, Prentice, this is Gemma, Sally's ballet instructor. Listen, the lesson just ended but all the other kids are gone and Bella isn't here as usual to pick up—"

Prentice was no longer listening. He was out of his chair and moving to the hook and his coat.

"Someone will be there soon," he told Gemma then didn't wait for a response. He went back to Lydia, told her the same thing and disconnected from her too.

He grabbed his coat and shrugged it on at the same time calling his mother to ask her to pick up the kids and he swiftly walked out of his offices without a word to Alice or anyone.

He got in his Rover and drove just as swiftly home.

———— • ————

Elle

"THAT'S WHAT I get," Nigel Fennick muttered. "That's all I get, day and night, day and bloody, *fucking* night."

Elle's head lolled on the back seat of Nigel Fennick's car, blinking away the fuzzy feeling in her head as she felt cold sting, sharp and piercing, at her wrists.

Something, or it felt like *someone*, an invisible someone, was picking at the ropes binding her wrists.

That was bizarre, impossible, but she couldn't think of that. She had to focus on clearing her head after she'd knocked boldly and imperiously on Nigel and Hattie Fennick's front door, Nigel opened it and she'd furiously demanded a word with Hattie.

Nigel had stared at her a moment, sighed deeply, invited her in and she walked into the living room only to stop, watch Nigel turn to her and then watch his face studying her.

As she watched, it twisted with something ugly and unbelievably frightening. She tensed in preparation for flight but before she could react, he'd picked up a vase and conked her on the side of the head with it.

Yes, conked her on the side of the head!

She'd blacked out instantly and woke up in the back seat of his car, wrists and ankles bound and a gag tied around her mouth, something or *someone* working at her bounds and Nigel ranting from behind the wheel as he was driving.

"Prentice this. Bella that. Sally and Jason this, that and the other. My God! She has a husband! She has a son! Does she pay a mind to us? *No!*" he ended on a shout and Elle closed her eyes, her heart beating wildly, fear saturating her entire body.

He'd gone mad.

Or Hattie had driven him to it.

This wasn't how it was supposed to happen. At the end of the fairy-tale, the heroine gets to live in her castle and enjoy her happily ever after.

Okay, so Elle could put up with trolls making an appearance every now and then. And the handsome hero could be annoying but he was always beautiful and loving even when he was being annoying.

The heroine wasn't supposed to end up in the back seat of a car, bound, her head pounding, terrified, and the wicked witch actually be-ing a wicked construction worker at the end of his rope with his catty, awful, miserable wife and taking it out on the heroine!

Elle had enough wicked in her life. It was now her happily ever after.

Didn't he know?

"She makes money from those photos and we need a new boiler," Nigel raged on. "Does she buy a boiler? No . . . she . . . does . . . *not*. She goes to Edinburgh and gets her hair done and it cost two hundred *bloody pounds!* She buys a membership to the gym, pays some bloke to work with her and she goes there every evening. She doesn't make dinner for her family, she gets in her car and goes to the *bloody gym!*"

Elle hadn't noticed Hattie got her hair done or that she'd lost any weight.

Then again, she tried not to notice Hattie at all.

"And I know why," Nigel seethed, bringing Elle's attention back to him. "She thinks she can catch *his* eye. She lies in bed beside me and pretends *he's* there lying beside her. Do you know? Do you know how it feels to lie beside your wife every night for over a decade and know she doesn't want you at her side? Do you know how that feels? *Do you know?*" he ended on a screech and Elle winced.

Elle didn't know and she didn't think that would feel very good but it wasn't worth conking someone on the head, binding them and throwing them in the back seat to drive around while ranting.

"Well, I'm done," he raved. "I am bloody, fucking *done*. She wants Prentice Cameron, I'll give her a clear shot."

The cold at her wrists vanished but Elle barely noticed as her body went rock solid with terror at his words.

"But for Prentice Cameron, he'll experience *again* what it's like no' to have the woman he loves at his side," Nigel maniacally vowed and Elle started panting behind her gag just as the icy feeling came back to her wrists. "The body's there for me but it isn't. He'll know that feeling, I'll bloody well make it so, he'll know. He'll bloody fucking *know* what it's like to be alone."

The ties binding her wrists came undone and almost immediately the cold could be felt at her ankles.

"They'll never find you," Nigel muttered. "They'll never, ever find you. They'll think you ran away again. They'll all think you left him again. They'll never know."

Elle circled her hands to work out the pins and needles and tried to steady her breathing, letting the cold she knew was her ally work her ankles without moving and making it more difficult. As the cold worked her ankles, she concentrated on getting her thoughts in order. She tried not to think about how stupid she'd been, not telling anyone where she was going. She'd called Fern to reschedule but she hadn't explained why.

And now the kids were surely done with their lessons and waiting for her to pick them up.

Waiting and worried.

And Prentice . . .

She closed her eyes tight, the car came to a halt and her eyes shot open.

It was late, dark. So dark she knew they were well out of town. They had nothing but the moonlight. She had dark, she still had bound ankles, she didn't know where she was.

The only thing she knew was she had to get away. She had to get back to her happily ever after.

She had to.

She heard Nigel exit the car and she rolled to her back. Lifting her hands to pull the gag from her mouth, the wintry workings at her ankles seemed to get more frantic and the ropes were loosened but not undone when Nigel pulled open the door at her head.

She could delay no further.

Before he could lean in, Elle lifted up, scooted on her behind toward the other door then turned on the seat and did her best to kick out with her bound feet.

It worked. Nigel wasn't prepared, she hit him in the chest and he went back, slamming his head on the doorframe with a pained grunt as he went.

Elle twisted her torso and fumbled with the door handle.

It's locked! She heard the disembodied shout in a feminine voice with a Scottish accent, a voice that was vaguely familiar but that famil-iarity was deep in her memory banks.

She couldn't focus on hearing voices, even familiar ones, because she had to get out.

Then she heard the door lock disengage but it wasn't her that pressed the button.

What was happening?

She didn't ask. She just went back to the handle and opened the door, pushing herself out and, without full use of her lower extremities, falling to a hip. She rolled to her bottom and scooted quickly away from the car, stopped and both the frosty touch as well as her hands went to the bounds at her feet.

"You stupid bitch!" She heard Nigel shout as she kicked her feet free of the ropes, rolled and got to her hands and knees. "*Stupid bitch!*" he shrieked as she lifted up on the fly, already running. "Don't you run away from me!" he yelled.

Elle ran faster.

No! No' that way! That's the cliff! Go to the road! The voice came back, urgent, scared, and Elle switched directions instantly. *Good! The road!*

Elle ran and as she did she wondered why she still wore high-heeled boots when she lived in the wilds of the Scottish Highlands with a job as a happy homemaker. Happy homemakers didn't wear high-heeled boots.

Or, at least, if she made it through this night, *she* was never going to do wear them again.

She heard him pounding after her and she ran faster, as fast as she could, but in those heels she couldn't run fast enough.

He grasped the back of her jacket and she cried out as her limbs kept moving forward but her torso jerked back. He pulled her to him then clamped his arms around her and jerked her around, marching her back where they came.

"No!" she cried, struggling violently, tearing at his hands with her fingernails, dragging her feet, bucking her body, slamming her head backwards in hopes of connecting. "*Help me!*" Elle screamed. "*Somebody help me!*"

"No help out here for you, lass. And when I'm done, I'll no' hear Hattie raving about Isabella Austin Evangelista. No more. No more," Nigel whispered crazily in her ear as he forced her through the darkness, and that was all she could see, a vast sea of darkness, and she knew where he was taking her. She couldn't see it but she knew it.

There was nothing beyond that darkness.

Nothing but cliff at the bottom of which was to be Elle's watery grave of sea.

Knowing that, she kicked back, arched her body and shrieked, *"Somebody help me!"*

And at her words, she and Nigel Fennick came to an abrupt halt and she heard his grunt of surprise.

But Elle didn't process this.

She was staring in front of her, no longer struggling.

Because floating before them in the darkness was a see-through Fiona Cameron.

———— ✦ ————

Prentice

"PRENTICE, I HARDLY think—" Hattie, standing in her front door, began but Prentice leaned into her, getting into her face and she clamped her mouth shut.

"Bring me your boy," he growled.

"She wasn't here," Hattie snapped back. "She *isn't* here."

"Her Rover is at your curb, woman," Prentice returned.

"So? Maybe she's visiting Mrs. Kilbride. She lives just across the street," Hattie shot back.

"You think I haven't already knocked on her door?" Prentice retorted.

"Why on earth would she—?" Hattie started but Prentice interrupted her again.

"Your boy has been home since school," he stated.

"Of course," Hattie replied shortly.

"And you told me you just got home but if Elle was here, he'd know and I need to know. She's disappeared, she's no' answering her mobile, no one has seen her, no one has heard from her except Fern who only knows she canceled their appointment at the last minute, no' why. I need to retrace her steps and her Rover is at your curb, Hattie, so if you haven't seen her and Nigel isn't here then I need to speak to Davey to see if he has."

"I have." A young boy's hesitant voice came from behind Hattie, and Prentice's gaze jerked around the woman to see her son standing behind her in their hall.

"Davey, upstairs to your room," Hattie ordered on a turn, and Prentice beat back the desire to wrap his fingers around the silly, bitter cow's throat.

"You've seen her?" Prentice asked and his gut, already tied in a tight knot, clenched even further when he took in the boy's pale face and frightened eyes.

When Davey didn't answer, Prentice pushed by Hattie and strode swiftly to the boy who backed up at his advance but slammed to a halt against the banister of the stairs.

"Prentice Cameron! You are no' welcome in my home!" Hattie shouted from close behind him, but Prentice ignored her and bent his face to the boy's.

"Why are you afraid, Davey?" he asked, his voice low, his meager reserves of control slipping, his focus on trying not to terrify him further because he needed to know, and now, what the boy knew that was making him look so fucking scared.

"Davey, up to your room!" Hattie snapped and only Prentice's neck twisted so he could lock eyes with the bitch.

"Why won't you let him speak to me?" he clipped.

Hattie tossed her hair and crossed her arms on her chest. "I already told you, I don't know why you're here or Bella's Rover is in front of my house, Prentice. The never-ending drama of your life doesn't intrude in ours. We have no' one thing to do with you and jet-set Isabella Evangelista."

He straightened and turned to her. "You do. You know you do. You live and breathe Elle and me. It's coiled in you like a rotting vine."

"Hardly," she hissed with another toss of her hair but Prentice was done, he didn't have time for Hattie Fennick, he never had, and he turned back to Davey.

"Talk to me, boy," he demanded.

"Go to your room," Hattie ordered.

"Talk to me, damn it!" Prentice shouted and Davy got tense but he spoke.

"She came, earlier, Dad let her in then I saw Dad carrying her out to his car."

Prentice's body shot straight as he heard Hattie breathe, *"What?"*

"She was bleedin' from her head," Davey whispered.

Fear cut through his body leaving nothing but raw in its wake because he suddenly knew, he knew what life was like at the Fennick household when someone as controlling, twisted, bitter and malicious as Hattie lived in it, obsessed with another man and his family.

"Where would he take her?" Prentice bit out quickly. Davey's mouth opened and shut and then again before he swallowed. Prentice gave up on him, turned to his mother and repeated, "Where would he take her?"

"I don't—" she started, her face pale.

She was shocked, completely unable to comprehend what her warped obsession with another man wrought on her husband.

Prentice didn't have time for her to think so he turned and advanced, fast, Hattie retreating. She slammed against the wall by the door and stared up at him with deeper shock as his body pressed close and he got nose to nose with the bitch.

"Where would he *fucking* take her?" Prentice gritted through his teeth.

"I-I—" she stammered.

"Where?" Prentice roared.

"The cliffs," she whispered. "The cliffs at Kenkames."

Prentice said not a word nor spared a glance.

He sprinted out of the house to his Rover.

———— ✦ ————

Elle

"BLOODY HELL," NIGEL Fennick breathed, and even though Elle was staring at Fiona floating and shimmering in front of her, her beautiful dark hair drifting like it was caught in a stiff but delicate breeze, the ends of the attractive tunic she wore doing the same, Elle knew Nigel was stunned and this was her chance.

And it could be her only one.

So, at the same time, she kicked back with her boot, hitting him sharply in the shin as she scratched at his hand, her nails digging in. He yelped, his leg went back automatically to avoid her foot, his arms loosened, she pulled free, rounded him and ran.

Head for the road! Fiona shouted, zooming eerily beside her.

"You said that already!" Elle shouted back but did it anyway.

I know! I have super-ghostly sight, you don't, so you have to listen to me! Fiona shouted back.

Super-ghostly sight.

Insane! Elle thought.

Seriously, you need to rethink your footwear, Fiona advised and Elle kept running even as she rolled her eyes.

"You don't think I know that?" she returned.

Faster! Fiona yelled. *He's gaining!*

Elle tried to run faster, her breath coming in deep pants, her boots and Nigel's boots hitting the road sounding jarringly in the quiet, dark, deserted night.

"Where are we?" Elle asked through her pants, deciding to zig and zag to see if she could put him off, so she did at that same time hoping whatever Fiona's answer was would give her the information she needed to get out of this bloody mess and back home.

Kenkames. No' populated and nobody will be up here this late at night, Fiona answered.

"Marvelous," Elle muttered right before she heard Fiona's ghostly scream and Elle was tackled, going down hard, first to her knees then her hand slammed into the asphalt of the road. The pain in her wrist shot up her arm then she hit the road at her chest, her breath going clean out of her.

Let her go, you fool! Fiona shouted as Elle sucked in air but still she immediately started struggling, twisting, turning and kicking out. *Let her go!* Fiona repeated. *Let her go! Let her go, go, GO!*

Suddenly Nigel's weight was off Elle, she rolled several times to the side, got to a knee and looked back to see Nigel struggling with the supernatural body of Fiona.

RUN! Fiona screeched as, with parted lips, Elle watched Fiona lifting Nigel clean in the air and darting away, both of them several feet off the ground.

Now! Fiona yelled.

Elle found her feet, turned away from her surprising attacker and by far and away more surprising rescuer.

And she *ran.*

———◆———

Prentice

"PRENTICE—" DOUGAL STARTED, his voice coming from Prentice's speakerphone on his mobile.

"Just do it, Dougal. Call the police and head up to Kenkames," Prentice ordered.

"You should leave this to the cops, Prentice. You should—"

"I'm no' discussing it, I'm telling you. Call the fucking police, get in your fucking car and head up to fucking *Kenkames,*" Prentice ground out, hit the button on his phone to end the call and tossed it in the passenger seat.

Then he focused on the road. He needed to focus on the road. He was in a 4x4 going twice the speed limit. He needed to get to Elle, get her safe and beat Nigel fucking Fennick bloody and not die in a fiery crash before he could do it.

And that was what he was bloody well going to do.

———◆———

Fiona

FIONA FORCED NIGEL in his car, locking it and keeping it locked with her newly realized powers.

Once she accomplished that, she floated outside it, hands on hips, glaring at Nigel.

It wasn't anger that brought on her powers.

It also wasn't effort.

Or concentration.

It was love.

Magic came from love.

Who knew?

All she knew was, faced with the possibility that, if she didn't do something there would be no Isabella Austin soon-to-be Cameron in this world, Fiona couldn't abide that.

Her children needed Bella.

Her husband needed her.

Annie, Fergus, Mikey, they needed her.

And Bella needed her happy ending.

And Fiona loved her enough to make it so.

So she did.

You're mad, Nigel Fennick, and you need help, she informed him through the car window as she floated at its side and he struggled with the handle to a door she kept locked.

He stopped struggling and scowled up at her.

"You don't exist," he declared.

No, you're right but then again, I also do, she replied. *When Prentice finds Bella they'll send someone up here to get you and then you need to get help.*

"Go to hell!" he shouted.

No bloody way, she shot back, gave him one long, last glare then she dematerialized and materialized at Bella's side.

A Bella who was walking, holding her side. She was walking quickly, very quickly, but she was still bloody *walking.*

Why are you walking? Fiona snapped.

Bella's body jolted and her head jerked to the side.

"You're back," she noted unnecessarily.

Aye, I'm back and there's a bad man no' too far away who's lost his mind and wants you dead so why are you walking?

"I can't run anymore, I have a stitch in my side," Bella explained. "And anyway, you *carried* him away. A grown man . . ." Bella shook her head, disbelief stark on her features. "A grown man."

Fiona drew in a needless, frustrated breath then advised, *Bella, run.*

"Have you taken care of him?" Bella asked.

I hope so. My powers are new, so let's no' take a chance, agreed?

Bella studied her. Then, thankfully, she started jogging.

Faced forward, she whispered as her breath started to get heavy, "You've been with us."

Fiona didn't answer.

"You've been with us for a while," Bella went on.

Fiona kept silent.

Bella waited before she continued, "You gave him to me."

Just run, Fiona whispered back, zooming beside her.

"You gave him to me," Bella panted as she kept running. "You gave them all to me."

Of course, I'm your fairy godmother, Fiona replied and Bella came to a rocking halt and turned sharply to her.

"What?" she gasped.

Oh for goodness sakes!

Bella, run! Fiona yelled.

"You're my fairy godmother?" Bella asked, still panting.

Bella—

"Who would do that to you? God?" Bella queried, her expression, Fiona thought, in normal circumstances, would be hilarious—incomprehension mixed with a liberal dose of anger.

But it wasn't hilarious considering they were in the middle of nowhere on a roadside cliff in the freezing cold (though Fiona couldn't feel it, she saw the chapped red in Bella's cheeks so she knew it to be true), running from a madman.

Colonel Sanders, Fiona answered, watched Bella blink and couldn't bite back her smile.

"Colonel Sanders made you my fairy godmother?" Bella demanded to know, her hands going to her hips. Then she declared, "Well, that's crazy. And it's . . . it's . . . it's *mean.* Why would he do that?" she asked but didn't wait for Fiona to answer before she declared. "I'm never eating his chicken again."

Yes, she was hilarious. Even in the middle of a trauma.

Fiona floated close, and surprisingly Bella held her eyes and her ground, not frightened of her, not at all.

Love, please run, Fiona whispered.

Bella continued to hold her eyes. Then she turned again and ran. She kept doing this quietly, her breath beginning to heave as Fiona zoomed at her side.

After a while, Fiona informed her, *Once you're safe, it's likely I'll move on.*

"Okay," Bella forced out then, carefully, "That's good, right?"

Right, Fiona answered and hoped she wasn't lying.

"Okay," Bella breathed.

I don't want them to know, Fiona said softly and watched Bella close her eyes tight even as she continued running.

She opened her eyes again.

"Okay," Bella repeated, it was breathy, again forced, but it was also sad.

Thank you for taking care of them, Fiona went on and heard Bella's breath hitch and not with the effort of running.

"It's my pleasure, honey," she pushed out.

I know, Fiona whispered then they saw them, headlights.

"Thank God," Bella breathed, her pace quickening.

Fiona saw the 4x4. She recognized it. She reached a hand out and slid it along Bella's neck.

Bella's head turned, her eyes caught Fiona's and Fiona smiled.

That was when she disappeared.

———— ♦ ————

Prentice

THE INSTANT HE saw Elle running, Prentice stood on the brakes, pulled on the parking brake and was out the door. He barely cleared it when Elle hit him full on.

His arms closed around her trembling body, trembling even as she pulled in deep breaths, wrapped her arms around him and held on tight.

"Baby," he whispered into the top of her hair, seeing the blood at her temple that had run down her cheek, but other than that she seemed unharmed and he sent thanks to God quickly but he meant every silent word.

"Nigel—" she struggled to get out between pants and Prentice's arms squeezed.

"I know," he told her.

"He's . . . he's . . ." she pulled in breath, "he's lost his mind."

"I know," Prentice repeated.

"He's—" Elle began but she stopped when they both heard the car and saw the headlights.

Their heads shot around and they saw Nigel Fennick's car racing their way.

"Oh my God!" Elle cried, and Prentice caught her hand.

Pulling her with him he dragged her to the back of the Rover.

The cliffs were to their right, the hills to their left. At Nigel's speed, it wasn't a good choice but he only had one and that was to round the boot of the Rover and head for the hills.

So he did, his head turned, watching Nigel's fast approach, praying he could get them off the road to the safety of the hill where Nigel in his car couldn't follow, running while pulling Elle behind him.

Suddenly he saw something form, floating over the road.

Nigel saw it too and cut the wheel to the right, too hard.

Way too hard.

He lost control of the car.

Prentice abruptly stopped, his chest freezing as the realization of what was about to happen hit him, Elle slamming into his back, and they watched in horror as Nigel and his car flew over the cliff.

There was silence except a distant, disembodied male scream of terror then the loud, crushing crash of car slamming into rock.

"Oh my God," Elle breathed, pressing close. "Oh my God, did he just . . . ?"

Elle spoke more but Prentice didn't hear her.

And he didn't hear her because the floating form had turned and her sweetly familiar eyes across the distance landed on him.

"Fee," he whispered.

Her head tilted to the side and he remembered that. Christ, he remembered that. She did it when she was about to smile and say something beautiful to him or to their children.

Or when she was about to say something self-mocking or teasing.

And he watched as she said something self-mocking.

That's unfortunate. It appears I should have taken away his keys.

A jolt tore through his body.

Christ, her voice. *Christ.* He never thought he'd hear it again. Never allowed himself to even dream. Not like that, not husky with humor.

Not at all.

Head still tipped, his dead wife smiled and said something beautiful.

Stay happy, my darling, you worked for it and so did Bella. You both deserve it.

He heard her aching voice was now filled with love right before she started glimmering slightly.

And he heard her whispered, *I love you,* right before she disappeared.

Prentice stared into the darkness, Elle pressed to his back, and he didn't move.

He couldn't believe he'd seen what he'd just seen.

But he'd seen it.

Elle pulled her hand gently from his and her arms slid around his stomach. She moved in closer, pressing deeper, her arms going tight.

"She saved me," Elle whispered.

But Prentice didn't move, he didn't speak, he just stared where he'd last seen his wife, her words echoing in his head.

"She told me, when we're safe, she'll move on," Elle said on a squeeze.

Prentice stayed silent and motionless.

"She doesn't want the children knowing she's been here," Elle finished, and Prentice closed his eyes and dropped his head, the knowledge that his wife, his beloved Fee, had been with them, and he knew then, he knew she'd been with them awhile, and this knowledge burned through him like acid.

How had she endured it? Any of it? All of it?

Christ. His Fee.

Elle held him close and also didn't move or speak.

Then she whispered, "Pren, you know, think about it, you know she helped us find each other again."

Prentice kept his eyes shut and his head bent but he murmured, "Aye."

"I feel she's gone, Pren, she's going home. Do you feel it?"

He did and it was like losing her again.

There was a strange beauty in Fiona keeping Elle safe for him.

But losing her once was bloody well enough.

"Aye," he repeated and that one syllable was so rough, Elle pressed even closer and he felt her rest her forehead to his back.

Prentice took in a deep breath, lifted his head, opened his eyes and looked where he last saw Fiona.

I love you too, Fee, he said in his head, hoping his words reached her.

He only knew they did when she came back and he felt an icy touch glide along his jaw. Fiona's touch. Her fingers trailing there like they did time and again when she was alive.

Then they were gone.

And he knew she was too.

This time for good.

He pulled in another breath, long and deep, and when he released it, with some effort and not a small amount of pain, he let his wife go.

He turned in Elle's arms.

She tipped her head back to look at him through the darkness.

When her searching eyes caught his, he murmured, "Let's get you home to the kids, baby."

He watched her close her eyes and he watched her head fall forward and hit his chest.

Then he watched as well as felt her nodding but she did it through a sob.

———◆———

Fiona

"ARE THEY OKAY?" Fiona asked Colonel Sanders Messenger Man as, her hand wrapped around his elbow, they whooshed through the streaking stars.

"They're okay," he answered.

Fiona bit her lip and then noted, "Prentice seemed—"

"He'll be fine," Messenger Man told her. "You've done your job well, Fiona. You leave them healthy, happy and *safe*."

"That was hard on him," Fiona whispered and she knew this to be true by the look on his face, the line of his body, and because it was hard on her too.

Bloody hard.

Nearly unbearable.

"No one tells the handsome prince's story but sometimes," Messenger Man stated, patting her hand in the crook of his elbow, his touch warm and welcome, "it also isn't so fun."

"Nigel—" Fiona started.

"He'll work harder not to go to black," Messenger Man said firmly, giving her the knowledge that Nigel was very dead.

Fiona really should have taken his keys.

And she had no doubt his mission would be more difficult than hers, and considering hers was bloody hard and he was a lunatic driven to attempt murder by his cow of a wife (still, he could have chosen a different path that didn't include mayhem), she felt that was fair.

"Hattie—" she continued.

"The police and Dougal made it to Prentice and Isabella within five minutes of you leaving. Hattie Fennick will shortly know she's lost her husband due to her fixation. How she copes with that, I've no idea. Beings have free will. I have no way of knowing how she'll react. I do know that if she makes the foolhardy decision to remain in that village, her life will be an even less happy one."

Fiona had no doubt of that either.

She decided to change the subject. "Where are we going?"

He didn't answer at first and she turned her gaze from the streaking stars to look at him and see he was grinning.

"You said it, you know it . . ." he paused and his grin turned into a smile. "We're going home," he whispered on another squeeze of her fingers but she felt it, the warmth, and she saw it, the brightness, and she looked forward as they whooshed through it and her first instinct was to laugh which she did, loud and long.

Because Messenger Man was right.

She wasn't home.

She was *home*.

Finally.

EPILOGUE

Dance with Me

Elle/Fiona

Twenty-three years later . . .

E lle moved out of the room heaving with smiling, laughing, drinking people, most of their eyes on the handsome man with the beautiful woman in his arms swaying on the dance floor like they weren't surrounded by hundreds of people who loved them but instead they were very, very alone, not just in the room, but in the universe.

She moved gracefully but quickly down the hall in her high heels, stopping only to test the doors, finding most of them locked.

Near the end, knowing time was of the essence and getting desperate, she turned the knob to an unlocked door, sighed a grateful, relieved sigh and opened it to find a broom closet. Without delay, she located the light switch, flipped it on and slid inside, closing the door behind her.

She put her back to it, peered into the empty room and whispered,

"I know you're there."

The room had no reply.

"Please," she kept whispering. "For him. Tonight, especially. Please."

Her eyes shifted around the closet, the shelves filled with cleaning products, piles of dust rags, the corners having brooms and mops resting upright, mop buckets on the floor but that was it.

Nothing else.

"Please," she repeated, still in a whisper. "We haven't much time."

She waited and counted. One second. Two. Three. Four. She got to seven when the air started shimmering and her heart started beating faster.

Then she was there.

And Elle Cameron looked into Fiona Cameron's ghostly eyes.

"Hurry," she urged softly.

Fiona shook her head. "It won't be pleasant. It might even be painful."

Elle held Fiona's eyes and repeated urgently, *"Hurry."*

Fiona bit her ghostly lip.

"Fiona," Elle begged. *"Hurry."*

With a deep breath she didn't need to take in, Fiona nodded then she surged forward, her ethereal body penetrating Elle's corporeal one. Elle felt the shafts of ice cold slicing through every inch of her flesh, muscle and bone, the pain excruciating but she clenched her teeth and held on.

Then she closed her eyes.

When she opened them, it was Fiona who could see through Elle's eyes.

Hurry, Elle said into Fiona's head. *It's the next song.*

"I know," Fiona replied, turning, her fingers closing on the knob, feeling it in her hand, so solid, so real, so surprising when she was in this world, she hesitated.

Hurry! Elle cried into her head.

"All right, all right, don't get your knickers in a twist," Fiona muttered, turning the knob, opening the door and sliding out of the room whereupon her ankle instantly twisted in the impossibly high heels Elle had on her feet. "Crikey, I see you never learned. How do you walk on these things?"

Just go, Elle retorted then added, *But try not to break my ankle while you do it.*

Fiona rolled her eyes but she went.

She was far more keen to get back to the ballroom than Elle was keen for her to do it.

Far, *far* more.

She made it just in time to hear the DJ announce, "And now it's time for the father daughter, mother son dance. If the bride and her father and the groom and his mother could please take the dance floor . . ."

His invitation trailed off and Fiona moved toward the dance floor.

Her human eyes saw Jason striding toward her, tall, handsome, his shoulders broad, his gait wide and confident, his muscled body looking very good in his tuxedo, and her eyes filled with tears.

Not Elle's tears.

Hers.

He looks so like Prentice when we were married, Fiona told Elle in her head.

I'll bet he was beautiful, Elle replied.

You wouldn't believe, Fiona told her.

Yes, Elle said softly, *I would.*

At Elle's soft words, Fiona's smile hit Elle's lips.

It broadened when Jason arrived and he smiled down at her as he reached in and took her hand then lifted it and touched his lips to her knuckles before guiding her to the dance floor.

Her son was a gentleman and he was openly affectionate.

This did not surprise Fiona.

His arm closed around her as his hand brought hers up to press against his chest, his jaw dipped to press against the side of her head and the music started playing.

Held close to Jason, Fiona's breath in Elle's body hitched.

Jason heard it, his arm got tighter and his fingers around hers squeezed.

He tipped his head so his mouth was close to her ear.

"You okay, Elle?"

Fiona didn't reply. She just nodded.

His fingers squeezed hers.

"I remember your wedding to Dad," he whispered, moving her around the dance floor with strength, confidence and male grace. So like his father. *Just* like his dad. "You danced with Dad to 'Someday My Prince Will Come.'"

Fiona nodded even though she hadn't been there for Prentice and Elle's wedding. She hadn't been back since she'd finally gone home.

Not until this special day.

But it seemed Elle had picked the perfect song.

"And Annie and Sally conspired so Sally could drop so many rose petals in the church that the pastor said they were still finding them a year later. Her flower girl basket was bigger than a breadbox and stuffed so full she could barely carry it," Jason went on, pulling her closer, swirling her around. "Do you remember?"

Fiona nodded again though she didn't remember. Still, she thought it was sweet Sally and Annie did that. A little weird, but sweet.

"Sally had decreed that every heroine at the end of a fairytale deserves to walk on a bed of rose petals to meet her hero," Jason continued before he chuckled and Fiona didn't think it was weird anymore.

Just sweet.

Oh, her Sally. She was sweeter.

"Annie and Sally definitely gave you yours," he finished softly.

Fiona pulled in breath through her nose.

Then she turned her head slightly and whispered in her son's ear, "And every handsome prince deserves a special gift too, when he finds his princess."

"Still talking fairytales, Elle," he muttered, his deep voice filled with humor. "I'm thirty-three, I know Sally grew out of them only about a month ago," he teased. "But I'm also a man and I hate to break this to you, love, but I never grew *into* them."

At that, Fiona felt it was time.

So she tilted her head back, Jason's came up, she saw his devilish grin, her heart skipped and his eyes caught hers.

Then he came to a dead halt and his arm convulsed so tight she couldn't breathe and his hand tightened in hers so hard she felt pain for the first time in over two decades.

He saw. He remembered.

She knew it.

He never forgot.

Never.

"Mum?" he whispered, his voice abrasive, thick, his beautiful eyes given to him by his father were shocked.

"Hello, love," Fiona's voice, not Elle's, whispered back. "Congratulations, my darling."

Jason stared into his mother's eyes. He swallowed before his jaw got so tight, a muscle ticked there.

"How—?" he started, his voice still rough but Fiona couldn't explain and there wasn't time anyway.

She needed to use the little time she had wisely and make it perfect.

"I like her," Fiona interrupted him, her eyes shifting to the pretty brunette twirling around the dance floor with her father all the while smiling happily up at him. Fiona looked back at her son. "We get news. She's perfect for you."

"Mum," he whispered again.

Fiona nodded.

"*Mum*," he groaned, let her hand go, that arm curved around her and both pulled her deep, holding her tight and unmoving on the dance floor as he buried his face in her neck.

Fiona held her son tight right back.

"She's like you," he murmured into her neck.

"I know," Fiona replied in her own murmur.

And she did.

Jason's bride was a lot like Fiona.

"*Just* like you," Jason stated fiercely, his words accompanied by a tight squeeze of his strong arms.

Fiona sighed and it felt really, *really* good because it was a happy one.

Then she turned her head and whispered in his ear, "I've not much time, my beautiful boy." His head came up and his bright gaze caught hers. She lifted her hand to his strong jaw and prompted gently, "Dance with me."

Jason Cameron stared into his mother's eyes a moment before he nodded.

He took her hand, held it tight, pressed it deep into his chest, and he danced with his mother at his wedding, his beautiful, every-colored eyes never leaving hers.

——— ♦ ———

FAIRYTALES COME WITH many different happy endings, for their heroines *and* their heroes.

And, that night, Jason Cameron got his.

——— ♦ ———

Sally

THREE YEARS LATER, her eyes floating open, her head turning, her vision filled with Elly Belly sitting next to her hospital bed holding Sally's newborn child.

Elle's head came up from gazing lovingly at Sally's beautiful baby's face and Sally's breath caught when she stared into her mother's eyes.

And that was when Sally Cameron Ferguson got hers.

THE END

The next tale in the Ghosts and Reincarnation Series, Lucky Stars, is available now.

Connect with
KRISTEN *Online:*

Official Website: *www.kristeashley.net*

Kristen's Facebook Page: *www.facebook.com/kristenashleybooks*

Follow Kristen on Twitter: @KristenAshley68

Discover Kristen's Pins on Pinterest: *www.pinterest.com/kashley0155*

Follow Kristen on Instagram: KristenAshleyBooks

Need support for your Kit Crack Addiction?

Join the *Kristen Ashley Addict's Support Group on Goodreads*

Made in United States
Troutdale, OR
08/13/2023